Praise for

Heidi Swain

'Sweet and lovely. I guarantee you will fall in love with Heidi's wonderful world' **Milly Johnson**

'Wise, warm and wonderful – a real summer treat!' *Heat*

'Sparkling and romantic' *My Weekly*

'The most delicious slice of festive fiction: a true comfort read and the perfect treat to alleviate all the stress!' **Veronica Henry**

'A fabulous feel good read – a ray of reading sunshine!' **Laura Kemp**

'Sprinkled with Christmas sparkle' **Trisha Ashley**

'A story that captures your heart' **Chrissie Barlow**

'Fans of Carole Matthews will enjoy this heartfelt novel' **Katie Oliver**

Heidi Swain lives in Norfolk with her family and a mischievous black cat called Storm. She is passionate about gardening, the countryside and collects vintage paraphernalia. *The Secret Seaside Escape* is her tenth novel. You can follow Heidi on Twitter @Heidi_Swain or visit her website: heidiswain.co.uk

Also by Heidi Swain

The Cherry Tree Café

Summer at Skylark Farm

Mince Pies and Mistletoe at the Christmas Market

Coming Home to Cuckoo Cottage

Sleigh Rides and Silver Bells at the Christmas Fair

Sunshine and Sweet Peas in Nightingale Square

Snowflakes and Cinnamon Swirls
at the Winter Wonderland

Poppy's Recipe for Life

The Christmas Wish List

Heidi Swain

The Secret Seaside Escape

**SIMON &
SCHUSTER**

London · New York · Sydney · Toronto · New Delhi

A CBS COMPANY

First published in Great Britain by Simon & Schuster UK Ltd, 2020

Copyright © Heidi-Jo Swain, 2020

The right of Heidi-Jo Swain to be identified as author
of this work has been asserted in accordance with the
Copyright, Designs and Patents Act, 1988.

5 7 9 10 8 6 4

Simon & Schuster UK Ltd
1st Floor
222 Gray's Inn Road
London WC1X 8HB

Simon & Schuster Australia,
Sydney

Simon & Schuster India,
New Delhi

www.simonandschuster.co.uk
www.simonandschuster.com.au
www.simonandschuster.co.in

A CIP catalogue record for this book
is available from the British Library

Paperback ISBN: 978-1-4711-8570-0
eBook ISBN: 978-1-4711-8571-7
Audio ISBN: 978-1-4711-9151-0

This book is a work of fiction. Names, characters, places
and incidents are either a product of the author's imagination or
are used fictitiously. Any resemblance to actual people living
or dead, events or locales is entirely coincidental.

Typeset in the UK by M Rules

Printed and bound by CPI Group (UK) Ltd, Croydon, CR0 4YY

MIX
Paper from
responsible sources
FSC® C020471

*To Michael, my dad,
who I don't see nearly often enough,
but who is forever in my thoughts
and always in my heart*

Chapter 1

If I closed my eyes and concentrated, I could see the sea stretching ahead of me, all the way to the distant horizon. I could breathe in the fresh salty air and almost taste the tang of it on my lips. If I stood in that exact spot, I could see the sun rising, quickly reaching the glistening rockpools, tempting me to explore their secret depths. And if I concentrated even harder, I could hear the waves lapping the shore, gulls wheeling overhead and feel the warm, soft sand, pushing up between my bare toes . . .

'Tess?'

I concentrated that little bit harder.

'Are you all right?'

I screwed my eyes up tighter still, hoping to catch sight of my mother. She would be sitting in a deckchair, wearing her favourite yellow sundress and waving with one hand, a well-thumbed paperback clasped firmly in the other.

'Earth to Tess. Do you read me?'

1

It was no good. The spell was broken. No amount of focused concentration could block out the noise of the office and my colleagues who, I discovered when I finally opened my eyes, had crowded around my desk, concern etched across their brows.

Apparently, it wasn't possible to close your eyes and stick your fingers in your ears without drawing a certain amount of attention, but I had been deeply immersed in my moment of mindful meditation and would have been happier if they'd just left me to it. That said, I supposed I should have been grateful that my team had even noticed my 'absence'. Considering the week we'd had, I was surprised any of them actually cared for my wellbeing at all.

'Oh, you are still with us then?' Chris snapped.

Not that Chris's tone was particularly caring, but given the fact that it was now seven forty-five on a Friday evening, and we still had work to do, it was hardly surprising that tempers were frayed.

'Where else would I be?' I told him, as I smoothed my hair, sat up straighter and tried my level best to look, at least, present.

It wasn't easy when I could still hear the call of the sea in the distance and imagine the warmth of the sun on the back of my neck. My body might have been behind my desk in the offices of Tyler PR but my mind was very much elsewhere. Every atom of me was craving the freedom of a holiday, a three-day minibreak even, but as senior project manager in my father's firm the chances of that happening were pure fantasy.

Judging by the enormity of my current workload, it was looking more and more likely that I would end up sacrificing the larger chunk of my holiday entitlement again this year. I couldn't deny that my role came with what looked like, on paper at least, an extremely generous holiday quota, but I had never managed to take it all. In fact, the higher up the pay scale I had worked so tirelessly to climb, the less opportunity I'd had to recharge my batteries.

And if I was being honest, that had been exactly how I liked it, especially during the last year and a half since my mother's unexpected death. Powering through whatever life threw at me had felt like the right way to go then, but not now. Now I was in danger of a meltdown because I had the wherewithal to recognize that I was heading towards burn out and that marching on had brought me no closer to accepting my loss at all.

Conversely, my father had no idea about my fragile mental state. He just noticed the parts of my life he wanted to and had always derived great pleasure in telling his contemporaries that he was incredibly proud of my commitment to the business. He abhorred nepotism, had consequently made me work twice as hard as everyone else to prove myself and loved the fact that my work ethic matched his own. He was completely clueless that this latest project had brought me to the brink and had me dreaming of an escape even during my waking hours.

'We thought you were going to pass out,' frowned Lucy, my assistant, as she handed me a glass of water and fanned me with a file.

'*You* thought she was going to pass out,' tutted Sonya, another colleague.

3

Relatively new to the role, efficient and eager, Lucy had a tendency to flap when the stress ramped up but I was working on ways to calm her. A cool and collected head was needed in this business, even if only on the outside.

'I'm fine,' I said, taking a sip of the water and waving the file away. 'I was just gathering my thoughts.'

'Come up with anything useful?' Chris asked.

He didn't sound very hopeful and I knew he was desperate to get home. We all were, but we needed to have a damage limitation strategy firmly in place before we thought about our plans for the weekend. Not that I was particularly looking forward to mine.

'Possibly,' I nodded. 'Meet me in conference room one in twenty minutes.'

As usual, I was the last to leave and it was almost midnight before I let myself into my apartment, kicked off my heels and poured a glass of restorative wine. Had anyone believed that being the boss's daughter came with perks I could have quashed their assumptions with any one of my time sheets from the last few months.

I couldn't remember the drive home. My mind had been miles away from the road – not at the seaside this time – but trawling through the atrocious pics in the red-tops which had sent my week into a tailspin. What had the guy been thinking? I ignored the sharp knotted-up pain in my stomach and flopped down on the sofa.

When I had interviewed for the job in Dad's public

relations firm, after graduating with a first in marketing seven years ago, I could never have foreseen that I would be trying to untangle anything like the mess which had descended during the last few days.

When I had been tasked with nothing more taxing than the morning coffee round and the daily sandwich order (Dad was a firm believer in learning the business from the bottom up), I had dreamt of working with prestigious clients on million-pound projects and taking on the unusual role of matching their specifications to the perfect 'celebrities' to endorse their brands, but had I known that my biggest project to date was destined to go belly-up just weeks before it was due to launch, I would have stuck to ordering the egg and cress.

'Shit,' I muttered, spilling some of the wine as my mobile began to trill, dragging me back to the present and making me jump.

I picked up my bag with my free hand and shook it out on the sofa, scattering the contents and at the same time praying it wasn't more bad news. I shuddered as I recalled the graphic images of my high-profile footballer with his tongue down the throat of some scantily clad girl, splashed across the front pages.

The clever journalist had put them alongside the studio image of him with his wife and daughters which I'd ensured was released just days before to further bolster his 'reformed character' image ahead of the family values advertising campaign my client had employed him for. It had been the ultimate humiliation, and not just for his wife and girls.

'Dad,' I said, when I eventually located my phone. 'Hi.'

'All sorted?'

As ever, he was straight down to business. Sometimes I found it hard to believe that the father he had turned into was the same, formerly so laid-back one who carried me about on his shoulders when I was little.

'I think so.'

'You think so?'

I felt myself bristle.

'We've done all we can for now,' I added a little tartly. 'We have a plan in place and I'll pick it up again on Monday.'

'Oh right,' he said. 'There was no way of wrapping it up tonight?'

'No,' I said firmly. 'I couldn't reach any of the advertising team after ten, so we thought we'd call it a day.'

Truth be told, for the sake of my team's sanity, I hadn't tried to ring out again after our last in-house meeting of the evening.

'And you're sure you don't want me to step in?'

'Absolutely not.'

Of course, I didn't want him to step in. How ridiculous would that make me look? He was quiet for a second and I held my breath. For an awful moment I thought he was going to say he was going to anyway.

'I'll see you tomorrow then,' he eventually said.

I slowly breathed out and closed my eyes. Now I was the quiet one.

'You still there, Tess?'

'Yes,' I answered, clearing my throat, 'yes, I'm still here.'

It was me who had broached the subject of sorting through Mum's things. It was me who had insisted we had to make time in our packed schedules to start properly going through everything. I had read somewhere that the process could be cathartic, offer some level of closure and I could definitely do with a dose of that, even just a small one.

Initially, Dad had kept saying that it wasn't a good time, but I had quickly countered his argument by pointing out that it never would be and he had reluctantly agreed to setting the date for this weekend. It was ironic that after all my reading up on the subject, I was now the one who wasn't ready.

It was now heading towards two years since Mum had died of a heart attack that no one had seen coming, but she was still everywhere. Her clothes still hung in the wardrobes, her jewellery was all laid out and sometimes, in her bathroom, I could still smell Chanel. It was utterly impossible to believe that she was gone for ever when her possessions appeared poised to welcome her back. It was impossible to believe that she was gone for ever when I hadn't spent anywhere near enough time with her in recent years. Had I known the sand in her hourglass had all but run out I would have ensured things had been different.

In my heart, she would always be the woman from my childhood. The smiling mum on the beach in her yellow sundress with her hair in a ponytail and a book in her hand, but in my head, I knew she hadn't been that woman for years.

As the business had grown, she, like Dad, had turned into a completely different person. A person it was too late for me to get to know now.

'You'd better come early,' said Dad, 'there's a hell of a lot to do.'

I didn't stop to pick up a paper the next morning and I didn't turn my phone back on again either. If there was more bad news to come about my failing footballer, then I wanted to delay hearing about it for as long as possible.

I pulled off the road, onto the gravelled drive and buzzed the intercom. The iron gates swung slowly inwards and I drove through. The impressive house, set among towering oaks, hadn't been our original family home. Up until my late teens, we lived in a three-bed detached, but my parents then felt this prestigious corner of Essex was more befitting the stylish new Tyler image when the business began to thrive.

It was beautiful, but far too big. Dad had no need for the five en suite bedrooms but Joan (the housekeeper) and her husband, Jim (the gardener and handyman) were happily ensconced in the staff flat and I knew Dad would never leave. As far as he was concerned, the house was the icing that crowned his success, even if he could only occupy a fraction of it at a time.

'Tess,' he said, striding out to meet me as I cut the engine, 'here you are at last.'

It was barely eight, hardly the latest of starts for a weekend which followed an extremely stressful week.

'Any more news?' I stole myself to ask.

'Nothing in the papers this morning,' he said.

'Thank god,' I exhaled, my shoulders dropping a good three inches.

'Breakfast!' Joan called from the kitchen.

'Have you eaten?' Dad asked, guiding me towards the house.

'Not since yesterday morning.'

He nodded but didn't say anything. He had never understood how stressful work situations curbed my appetite, because they fuelled his. The smell of bacon wafting through the house made my very empty stomach grumble and the knot of pain tightened in response. It was a vicious circle – my anxiety stopped me eating and the resulting cramps made it too painful to eat.

'To be honest, Dad,' I blurted out, before I had a chance to check myself, 'it might be longer than that. I'm really not sure I can carry on working like this.'

Given how quickly he had sent me to have my heart checked after we lost Mum, surely he would get the gist of what I was trying to say. It had been an intense few months – long working days and almost impossible deadlines – and I feared that if I didn't slacken the pace soon, I would end up doing myself some irreparable harm. After this current campaign was in the bag, I really was going to have to take a break. Surely, he would understand that?

'Of course you can,' he said stoically, drawing himself up to his full height as we stepped into the palatial kitchen.

'You're a Tyler, Tess. We don't give up, remember? We thrive on stress. Our ability to power through is what keeps us one step ahead of the competition.'

I wanted to point out that I *used* to thrive on stress. Channelling my grief into my work was the very thing that had given me the strength to put in the increased hours, but now my mental as well as my physical energy was spent. I'd had enough and if I was being honest (to myself at least), it wasn't just my grief that I was struggling with.

More and more often I was having to justify, cover up and even lie about certain so-called celebrities' lifestyles and behaviours in order to make them an attractive enough proposition to match with our clients, and I didn't like doing it. The pay cheque my position in the firm afforded me might have given me a fabulous car and an admirable apartment, but what did any of that matter if I couldn't sleep at night?

'Look,' he said, when I didn't defer to his tough Tyler ethos, 'maybe you shouldn't be so hard on yourself. You dropped the ball this time, but—'

'Dropped the ball?' I interrupted.

I knew I sounded indignant but, surely, he wasn't going to try and pin the footballer's fall from grace on me?

'It was his agent who gave him leave to go out and celebrate those goals,' I said defensively. 'I had no idea—'

'But you should have,' Dad interrupted, 'and you know it. You should have known his schedule better than your own.'

I bit my lip to stop myself announcing that I was sick of

babysitting adults who should know how to behave. This was clearly not the time to try and get my point across. The day was going to be tough enough and I didn't need to fall out with 'the boss' on top of everything else.

'Well, he's on a tight leash now,' I said instead, swallowing down my annoyance. 'He won't be straying again.'

'But you can't use him for the campaign, Tess,' Dad countered. 'The public won't have an ounce of faith in him now.'

I thought of the elaborate damage limitation plan my team had been working on late the night before.

'But—'

'No buts,' said Dad, holding up his hand before I could explain. 'We have the Tyler reputation to think of and I know you said not to, but I did make a couple of calls last night. I think Vicky Price might be a possibility.'

'Vicky . . .'

'Price. She plays football for England and is available to step in.'

I knew who she was, I just couldn't believe Dad had 'stepped in' when I'd specifically asked him not to.

'She's just had her second baby and I thought it would be an interesting twist to have a woman spearheading the project. Her agent was very keen.'

'Have you approached the advertiser?' I asked.

'No, I thought I'd leave that to you,' he said bluntly, piling the eggs Joan had scrambled on to a plate. 'Now come on, eat up.'

I couldn't believe he had gone ahead and done that.

Bringing Vicky Price in *was* an inspired idea, but in doing it he had made me look completely inept.

After some cajoling from Joan, I did manage to eat a modest breakfast which was just as well, given the amount of work involved in sorting through Mum's things. Had my belly stayed empty I would have probably ended up keeling over.

'Half of this hasn't even been worn,' Dad grumbled, as he shifted outfit after outfit into the hanging boxes sent by the charity taking the clothes. 'These have all still got the labels on.'

He was right and flicking through them I could see the amounts Mum had spent was breathtaking. The charity would make a fortune at the fashion show they were holding later in the year to auction off their very best donated stock.

'No wonder her credit cards were always stretched to the limit,' Dad moaned on. 'Your mother had transformed into a professional shopper.'

I wanted to point out that her retail habit was most likely born out of boredom and all the hours she spent alone, but I didn't. I had been hoping Dad might have felt able to express his grief once we started going through everything, but watching him move perfunctorily from one packing box to another, I wasn't sure he felt any. Watching him move swiftly along the rails without a single lingering look made me feel incredibly sad.

'No sign of the yellow sundress,' I sighed in the hope that harking further back might evoke an emotional response.

'The what?'

'The dress Mum always used to wear to the beach when we holidayed in Wynmouth, remember?'

Dad straightened up. He looked wistful for a moment but then frowned.

'Your mother was a different woman back then,' he said stiffly.

'And you were a different man,' I muttered under my breath.

I knew my parents' marriage hadn't always been as perfect as the one they projected to the outside world but Dad's apparent indifference was hard to take.

'She probably parted with that dress the day she charged her first designer handbag, Tess.'

I nodded, but didn't say anything further.

Looking at the packed rails of clothes brought a lump to my throat and made me realize I hadn't spent anywhere near the amount of time with Mum as I had in the office with Dad. I hoped she hadn't thought I had in some way 'sided with him' because I worked for him. I had always assumed that there would be plenty of time for us to catch up, but her fragile heart had other plans.

'Well, I have to say,' sighed Joan, as she appeared with a tray bearing cups of tea and a plate of biscuits just in time to stop me getting too maudlin, 'it doesn't look as if you've made much headway.'

'We haven't,' I said, looking around. 'I thought we'd be finished in here today, but we've barely scratched the surface.'

'This is going to take far longer than just one day,' said Dad, piling jewellery boxes and a small trunk next to the door. 'Surely you realized that?'

I shrugged. It was beginning to feel like he'd done nothing but find fault with everything I'd said since the moment I'd arrived.

'You look all in,' he went on. 'Why don't you take this lot and go through it at yours?'

The lure of a long hot bath and a bedtime before midnight was very appealing and I was grateful that he had noticed I was flagging, even if he did make it sound like yet another flaw.

'Are you sure?'

'Yes,' he insisted. 'You'll need to be rested and raring to go Monday morning, won't you?'

I tossed and turned that night and ended up dozing in bed for the larger part of Sunday morning. When I did eventually get up, I flicked through the TV channels to drown out the persistent buzzing in my head, finally settling on a show about couples looking to escape the rat race and settle in the country.

After coffee, I turned my attention to the small trunk Dad had packed into my car along with Mum's jewellery collection. I was surprised to discover it was full of what looked like mementos – notebooks, letters, paintings I had presented her with as a child – not the sentimental sort of things I had associated with her at all in recent years and I felt the hot prickle of tears begin to gather behind my eyes. A photograph album caught my attention and I pulled it out and settled back on the sofa.

'Oh, for pity's sake,' I sniffed, as I scanned through the snaps.

There were dozens of Mum, Dad and me on holiday in the very place I had been dreaming of escaping to ever since my stress levels had started to get the better of me. Wynmouth on the Norfolk coast might not have been the dream holiday destination for most, but to me when I was growing up, it was utter perfection. Not just the little place itself, but the feeling of heady happiness it always instilled within me.

It had been a very long time since I had felt that kind of uncomplicated contentment. These days my pleasure levels were derived from beating someone else to the punch or muscling in on a project a rival firm had been hoping for. There was nothing straightforward or wholesome about my happiness now.

I had been a teenager the last time we visited Wynmouth and Mum and Dad were amazed that I could still be amused with a stroll along the beach and a forage among the alien rockpool worlds. There were no arcades, no fast food outlets, no noisy fairground rides, but there had been something, the sudden fluttering in my chest reminded me, to hold my teenage attention. I carried on flicking through the pages until I found one photo in particular.

'I wonder,' I mused, setting the album aside and reaching for my laptop.

It didn't take long to find what I was searching for. Crow's Nest Cottage in the heart of the sleepy village had always looked like the perfect holiday rental to me, hence my insistence that I was photographed standing in front of it.

Built next to the pub and just a stone's throw from the dip down to the beach, it was a higgledy-piggledy little place, but full of charm. We had never stayed there. The limited holiday fund my parents had then was just enough to secure us one of the few static caravans on the clifftops outside the village, but I had always promised myself that I would stay at the cottage one day and here it was, still listed as holiday accommodation.

My fingers lingered over opening the availability enquiry form. Was there even a slim chance that I would be able to convince my father that now was a sensible time for me to take a break, and if I somehow did, would Wynmouth be the same? Would it be capable of filling me with that same sense of calm? Because that was what I was desperate for. That was what I was craving every bit as much as the invigorating sea air. Throwing myself into my work hadn't helped me get over losing Mum, but perhaps Wynmouth would.

Then I remembered the hasty departure surrounding our last holiday. Dad had insisted on packing up and leaving early, saying an unmissable work opportunity had come up and it was imperative that we left straightaway.

'It's the opening of a lifetime,' he had said, urging us to pack. 'A chance to *really* put Tyler PR on the map.'

Whatever the opportunity was – I was too heartbroken

to care – it must have succeeded because by the following year the business was flying and we had spread our holiday wings far further than Norfolk. We had never returned to Wynmouth and yet it was still the place I dreamed of, the very spot my moments of mindful meditation always led me back to.

My phone began to ring and I reached for it.

'Have you seen the Sunday papers?' Dad barked, the second I answered.

'No,' I swallowed. 'What is it?'

'Your man's been on another bender and his wife's thrown him out.'

I took a moment to take a deep breath. It was in no way soothing.

'I've got my laptop right here,' I said with an urgency I didn't feel as I opened a new tab next to the Crow's Nest Cottage page, 'if you send me the address, I'll email Vicky Price's agent and the advertiser straightaway.'

Chapter 2

Even before I ended the call from Dad, I knew that it would be impossible to take off anytime soon, but I still submitted the cottage availability form. It was my misguided attempt to fool myself into thinking that I was putting some sort of self-care practice into action.

Vicky Price, her agent and the advertiser were thrilled with the prospect of us all working together, but the other guy, now back in rehab, and his increasingly belligerent agent, were less than impressed by the turn of events. It was beyond belief that either of them could really think that he was still right for the job, but they did, and their grumbling had rapidly turned into threats of legal action. We had a watertight contract in place to ensure that couldn't possibly happen, but the mere mention of bad press for Tyler PR had sent my father marching along the warpath and given me a migraine to end all others.

'Are you going home?' Lucy asked me, late on Tuesday

afternoon. 'I really think you should, you look absolutely dreadful.'

Not only was I battling a sledgehammer attacking my fragile skull, but I was feeling increasingly nauseous too and the office lights were hurting my eyes. My brain felt far too swollen to fit my head and no number of painkiller combinations had helped.

'Lucy's right,' said Sonya, eyeing me with a frown. 'You should go, Tess. We can manage until tomorrow.'

If Sonya was telling me to go home, then I must have looked really bad. The last thing I wanted was to desert my post, but I had no choice. I had exhausted every avenue of trying to cope with the pain and nothing had helped.

'All right,' I caved. 'I'll go, but if anything happens, you ring me, okay? I'll keep my phone turned on and I'll be in even earlier tomorrow.'

When I arrived home, I checked my emails. There was one from someone called Sam about the cottage.

> Thank you for your enquiry regarding the
> possibility of staying in Crow's Nest Cottage.
> The cottage has already been booked for the
> two weeks you specified. Apologies for any
> disappointment this may cause.

Given everything else I had to worry about, I felt far more disappointed than I probably should have and even though I knew it was pointless I sent a reply anyway.

Hi Sam. Thank you for letting me know. Is it
available any time during June or July?

I had hoped to find myself back on top form the following
morning, but what I discovered when I opened my eyes
was that the world had shifted on its axis and my head
was spinning.

'Don't you think you should call the doctor?' asked Lucy,
when I eventually managed to find a position that stopped
the dizziness long enough for me to dial her home number.

'No,' I said firmly. 'It's just a bit of vertigo. I've had
it before.'

'I can drive you to the surgery,' she carried on regardless.
'It's no bother.'

'Honestly, Lucy, there's no need.'

'But you had a migraine yesterday,' she pointed out,
as if I needed reminding. 'I really think you should get
checked out.'

'I promise you, it's not a problem,' I said soothingly. 'It's
an inconvenience more than anything,' I added, thinking
of the rotten timing, 'and purely stress-related. It'll pass the
second we're back to business as normal.'

'Well, if you're sure—'

'I am,' I interrupted, 'but there is one thing you could do
for me, Luce.'

'Name it.'

'Come and pick me up and drive me in.'

'What?'

'Drive me into work,' I pleaded. 'I can't get behind the wheel. I wouldn't be safe, but if you could get me to my desk and I sit relatively still I'll be fine to carry on. I *need* to carry on.'

There followed a sentence containing more than a few words that I would never have had down as being in mild-mannered Lucy's vocabulary.

'So that's a definite no then?' I sighed, when she eventually ran out of steam.

Neither Chris or Sonya were up for it either so I spent a miserable morning trying not to move or worry too much about what was happening in my absence. I couldn't help thinking that Chris was going to be in his element. As second in command he would no doubt be savouring the chance to make an impression.

Early afternoon I heard a key turn in the lock.

'It's only me,' Joan called out. 'Stay where you are.'

'What are you doing here, Joan?' I asked, from my propped-up position on the sofa. 'Not that it isn't lovely to see you.'

'Chris phoned and told your dad you were sick,' she explained as she bustled in carrying a basket. 'I know you're like your father and you don't do ill, so I wanted to check you were being sensible. I nabbed your dad's key. I hope that's okay?'

'Of course,' I said, remembering not to nod just in time. 'But I'm annoyed with Chris for dobbing me in.'

I'd had no intention of telling Dad I wasn't well. I knew he was working from home, so my absence from the office for a few hours could have gone completely unnoticed, had it not been for my deputy's meddling.

'I don't think he rang to cause trouble,' said Joan, who always strove to see the best in everyone. 'Apparently, he had some query about an urgent contract that needs signing off and didn't want to disturb you. Ring any bells?'

'Oh yes,' I groaned. 'A whole belfry full.'

Chris was behaving exactly as I suspected he would. He was using my loss of balance to his advantage and had grabbed the opportunity to write himself into Dad's good books. As the person who had taken him on and trained him up, I supposed I should have been proud of his ambition. Had I been in his position, I would have done exactly the same thing.

'I thought I'd bring you some lunch,' Joan kindly carried on. 'Are you well enough to eat it?'

'I'll try,' I said, knowing it would be pointless to say no.

Still reeling from the second bout of vertigo I'd had in the last three months I really didn't fancy the chicken soup she had taken the trouble to make; however, after the first few sips my stomach began to unclench and it was gone in minutes.

'Thank you,' I said gratefully, as she cleared up after me. 'That was delicious.'

'I thought it would be just the thing,' she smiled, 'and that it would be easier in a cup.'

She was right, as usual.

'So, what did Dad say about me being off work?' I bravely asked.

'Not much. When I told him I'd come here and check up on you, he said he'd call in at the office.'

I wasn't sure I liked the sound of that.

'He was muttering something about letting Chris oversee the contract as it needs to be dealt with quickly. The lad sounds like a very willing member of the team to me.'

'Oh, yes, he's that all right,' I agreed, my mood deflating further.

'Well, don't you worry about it,' said Joan.

'I'm not worried,' I shrugged. 'Why would I be worried?'

'There's more to life than work you know,' she carried on, squeezing my hand. 'Not that I would ever let your father hear me say that of course.'

We exchanged a conspiratorial smile and she began to gather her things together.

'I'll pop back again tomorrow,' she said, heading for the door. 'You make you sure you get plenty of rest. It sounds to me like everything's under control.'

Worryingly, it sounded like that to me too.

Having finally slept, after managing some more of the wonderful soup Joan had left, I was feeling much better the next morning. Not quite well enough to drive myself to work, but certainly less inclined to fall over whenever I stood up. However, rather than push my luck and book a taxi and risk a relapse I uncharacteristically decided to have another day at home. Joan's words, coupled with my stirred-up memories of what my life used to be like, along with what had happened to Mum, had got me thinking, and I had surprised myself by coming to the hasty conclusion that, no matter what anyone said, I was definitely going to take a proper break.

I didn't want to let Dad or the business down, but this latest dose of dizziness had forced my hand somewhat and I had finally realized that if I didn't want either my mental or physical health to suffer further then I was going to have to properly rethink my priorities and strike a better work/life balance. I couldn't just keep thinking about it, conning myself into believing that would be enough, I needed to get on and make it happen. But not in Crow's Nest Cottage ...

Thank you for your further enquiry. Crow's Nest Cottage will not be available from the end of May as it is being withdrawn from the holiday rental market. Should you still wish to stay in the area, do let me know and I will recommend other accommodation, further along the coast.

As sad as it was, that was the end of that, because if I couldn't stay in the cottage, I would rather not revisit Wynmouth at all. Determined not to have my resolve to take a break thwarted, however, I decided I would jet off to somewhere far-flung and exotic instead.

'How are you feeling?' asked Joan, when she arrived with yet more edible treats and a bunch of yellow roses cut fresh from the garden.

'Better,' I said, 'almost one hundred per cent.'

She didn't look convinced, but I meant it, even if I did still look a bit peaky. Even just making the decision to get away had done me no end of good.

'There now,' she said, once she had finished stocking the fridge. 'That looks more like it.'

I had to admit the shelves had been a bit Old Mother Hubbard prior to her arrival. Wilting watercress and almost-out-of-date skimmed milk weren't exactly set to contribute much to aiding my recovery.

'Any news from the frontline?' I asked, while she artfully arranged the roses in a vase before lifting Mum's trunk on to the sofa so I could properly sort through it without having to bend down.

'Your dad seems very taken with Chris,' she told me.

This came as no surprise and, if I played my cards right, might now end up working in my favour.

'He says he's a credit to you, Tess,' she smiled. 'That you've done an excellent job training him up.'

That *was* a surprise and I was delighted to hear it, although it would have been even better coming from Dad.

'Well,' I smiled back. 'At least I've done something right.'

'You do everything right,' Joan said firmly. 'The way this chap has stepped up is proof enough of that.'

And how fortuitous had that turned out to be? Chris had

wasted no time in nailing his colours to the mast and, given my decision to pull my feet out of the 'live to work' mire and plant them in the 'work to live' meadow, that was to be applauded rather than resented. My accomplished deputy had presented his ambitious streak at just the right time.

Later that afternoon, I delved deeper into Mum's trunk. Right at the very bottom and hidden under what looked like a sheet of lining paper, I discovered some A4 envelopes containing pages and pages of what looked like diary entries printed from a computer.

Each sheet had a date at the top and as I flicked through, I could see that they were all in chronological order. A part of me was saying that whatever was printed on the pages I held in my slightly shaking hands was absolutely no business of mine at all and that I should put them back where I'd found them.

However, there was another part, a stronger part as it turned out, which was whispering that this was most likely the last possible link I had with my mother and that I might discover something which would help me finally begin to come to terms with losing her. I sat and began to read the top sheet from the envelope which was dated the furthest back.

I didn't have to read too far down the page to realize that what I had discovered was far from comforting. Tears quickly blurred my vision and my breath caught in my throat.

I saw them together last night and it tore my heart in two. I can't talk to anyone about it, so I'm going to write about it instead. I need to express what I'm feeling somewhere and this feels like the safest place . . .

They were in a restaurant on the other side of town. It was a different woman this time. She looked beautiful, so much younger than me . . .

I dropped the page as if the words had burned my fingers. I had always known that women found Dad attractive. You only had to see how they reacted around him to realize that, but I hadn't known that he had been tempted to stray beyond the marital bed. But that's what these words Mum had written were suggesting, weren't they? And looking at the number of pages spread out around me, this clearly wasn't a one-off she was recording.

For a while I sat in stunned silence and then my anger began to grow.

I was floored by my father's blatant hypocrisy. How could a man who championed family loyalty above everything else, treat his wife with such little respect? What gave him the right to keep banging on about family values and family first, when he had been seen out in a restaurant, wining and dining another woman who was evidently nothing to do with our family at all?

I wanted to read more, but my head was beginning to spin again. I thought of Mum's packed wardrobes. How she had put a brave face on things and presented a pristine façade to the world when the truth behind the mask was one of sadness and heartbreak. Up until now I had never really understood why Dad was incapable of grieving for her, but now I realized he hadn't loved her at all.

Suddenly I didn't much care whether I was letting Dad down or if Chris was capable of running the office or not. I had to get away as soon as I could and I was going to take Mum's diary with me.

I was back at work early the next morning and, following my mother's example, I was immaculately made up, dressed to impress and ensconced behind my desk long before any of the others arrived.

I had been hard pushed not to drive over to the house and confront Dad, but common sense won out. I wouldn't be talking to him until I had read everything Mum had written and I had my emotions firmly back under control. All I wanted from this early appearance at the office was to maintain my composure and take off with my dignity intact.

'Tess,' said Chris, his confident stride across the floor faltering when he spotted me. 'We weren't expecting you in. Are you sure you're all right to be here?'

'Yes,' I said as I briskly grouped together the papers on my desk. 'Thank you. I'm fine now.'

'What have you got there?' he frowned, beadily eyeing the file.

'The Vicky Price contract and paperwork.'

'Oh.'

'I wanted to make sure nothing had been overlooked.'

'Now, about that,' he swallowed, nervously running a finger around the inside of his collar.

'It looks like you've thought of everything,' I said, raising my eyebrows. 'There's nothing left for me to do at all.'

'Well, your father thought it was best to act as quickly as possible, what with the advertiser clamouring to start filming the ads, and I—'

'You,' I said, cutting him off, 'thought you would take advantage of the fact that I wasn't around and claim a rather substantial victory for yourself.'

His face began to turn an interesting shade of red.

'Well, I wouldn't put it quite like that,' he objected.

'How would you put it then?'

I had spotted Lucy loitering in the doorway. Hearing my question, she backtracked and quietly closed the door. Chris opened and closed his mouth a couple of times like a fairground goldfish gasping for air in its plastic bag.

'Come on, Chris, you'll have to do better than that if you're going to survive at Tyler PR,' I said robustly. 'You have to have an instant answer for everything, and the right one at that, if you want to continue impressing my father.'

'I'm so sorry, Tess.'

'Don't apologize,' I told him. 'Never apologize. Mr Tyler would hate that.'

'What?'

The poor chap looked as though he didn't have a clue what was going on.

'Oh, it's all right,' I said, deciding he had squirmed for

long enough. 'I'm congratulating you, Chris. On a job well done.'

'What?' he said again, looking more like a fish out of water than ever.

'Hats off to you,' I said, putting the paperwork back into its folder and holding it out for him to take. 'You saw an opportunity and you took it.'

He didn't say anything.

'Had I been in your position, I would have done exactly the same. To tell you the truth, I probably would have been disappointed in you if you hadn't.'

He still didn't look as though he believed me.

'Dad is going be promoting you in no time,' I told him. 'Just make sure the digital contract matches the paper one exactly. You know the system glitches occasionally and that's the last thing we want, wouldn't you agree?'

'Yes,' he finally said, his voice cracking before he cleared his throat. 'I was planning to cross reference everything this morning. It's the reason why I've come in so early.'

'You're not that early,' I said pointing at the office clock. 'You need to set your alarm a bit earlier if you really want to get the jump on me.'

The rest of the morning passed without incident. Lucy told me that Dad had left word the day before saying that he was going to work from home, which was a huge relief, and with the contract clutched tight in Chris's competent hands I took some time that afternoon to trawl the internet in search of the perfect getaway, but it was easier said than done.

The whole world was literally just a flight away but I couldn't make up my mind where to go. I had all but given up on my search and was about to log out of my computer, when an email pinged into my personal inbox . . .

Dear Miss Tyler, I'm mailing to inform you that Crow's Nest Cottage has become available for the next two weeks due to an unexpected cancellation. I appreciate that it is extremely short notice, but if you could let me know if you are still interested in renting the cottage from this Monday – the 18th – I will be happy to renegotiate the price. Looking forward to hearing from you. Sam

Chapter 3

Needless to say, given my acknowledgement that I needed to look after myself and my recent discovery about Dad's behaviour, I didn't feel even a hint of guilt as I typed that I was indeed interested in taking the cottage for the next two weeks. My vertigo, coupled with Joan's timely words about work and Mum's heart-wrenching diary entries, were all the proof I needed that I was taking the right course of action and just in the nick of time.

I was going to Wynmouth without a backwards glance, although not a clear conscience. I wasn't sure I would ever be able to forgive myself for not spotting the signs of Dad's philandering. I should have been there to support Mum but instead, I had been so obsessed with work, I'd been oblivious, but not anymore. I was going to spend the next two weeks re-evaluating my life and my relationships and get myself back on the right track. It was too late to make a difference with Mum, but learning the lesson would be the best way to respect her memory.

I held my breath as I dialled the home number to make my excuses for not being able to carry on clearing Mum's things as we'd planned when I left the weekend before and prayed that Dad wouldn't be the one to answer.

'The Tyler residence.'

It was a relief to hear Joan's voice. Explaining to her that I still wasn't up to scratch would be a doddle and, if she relayed my message, then I wouldn't have to speak to Dad at all. I could send him a text on Monday saying that Chris was in charge and that I would be back at work in a fortnight. Simple.

'Hi Joan,' I said, 'it's me.'

'Tess, love,' she said, quickly dropping the formal tone. 'How are you feeling? Did you go to work today?'

'Yes,' I swallowed, 'yes I did, and I think I overdid it a bit.'

It was only a little bit of a lie. I was pretty tired.

'There,' Joan tutted. 'I told you not to rush back, didn't I?'

'I know.'

'I take it you won't be coming tomorrow then,' she stated, rather than asked. 'I'll tell your father not to expect you.'

'Thanks, Joan.' I smiled. She was certainly making it easy for me. 'I appreciate that. I'll see you soon.'

'Not that soon, I suspect,' she said shrewdly. 'You take care, Tess, love and don't worry about your father. Or work.'

'I won't,' I whispered and hung up.

With the scene set, and my booking confirmed, all I had to do when I got up Saturday morning was prepare for my secret getaway. Having not taken a holiday for so long, my causal wardrobe was somewhat depleted, but a whirlwind shopping trip soon rectified that.

My appetite had made an unexpected comeback thanks to Joan's coaxing and I ate my way through most of what she had loaded into the fridge as I packed my bags and then settled down on Sunday to prepare emails for Chris and Lucy. I explained what to expect in my absence and apologized for not letting them in on the finer details of my short-notice departure. The less they knew, the less my father would be able to get out of them.

By the time I had scheduled the emails to be sent the next morning – when I would be winging my way to Wynmouth – I was feeling a little nervous. Or was I excited? It had been so long since I had done anything so self-centred, anything that didn't revolve around work, that I really couldn't be sure. My current mental state was hard to pin down, especially as Mum's diary had added its own unique layer of turmoil to it, but Wynmouth would soon set me straight. I hoped.

The journey to my personal paradise should have taken no more than three hours, but I was behind the wheel for nearer five. Not one, not two, but three crash clear-ups had hampered my stretch of motorway journey and I was well into Cambridgeshire before I started to notice the change in the scenery. It felt like an age since I had slowed down enough to look at green things growing.

A little further on I crossed the final county line and drove deep into Norfolk. Eventually, the first signpost directing me towards Wynmouth came into view and I swallowed down a lump in my throat as I tried to quell my mixed emotions.

'Home sweet home,' I whispered as I slowly pulled into the village and the sun, which had been positively shining down all morning, disappeared from view. 'Well, for a couple of weeks anyway.'

The bank of grey cloud blowing in from where I knew the sea was waiting for me to spot it could have dampened my spirits, but I didn't let it. After all the waiting and remembering, I was finally here. I had finally found my way back to the one place in the world where I had always felt happy and the sun always shone, in my mind at least.

I let down my window and breathed in a lungful of the longed-for salt-laden air as I drove around the large expanse of grass known predictably as The Green and smiled at the wooden sign featuring an image of a tall ship in full sail. The paint wasn't quite as bright and pristine as I remembered and there was a definite lean to the stake which secured it, but I knew a sailor featured too and that there was a legend told about him on stormy nights. I couldn't recall the details but hoped to be reacquainted with them soon.

The picturesque row of traditionally built brick and flint shops caught my eye next and looked comfortingly familiar, although perhaps a little smaller and certainly quieter. I scanned around but there wasn't a soul in sight. It was quite deserted, but then given the gathering clouds perhaps the locals had headed home in case it rained, and of course it wasn't the school holidays yet which would no doubt make a difference to numbers too.

I carefully swung the car around the tight bend which would lead me to the Smuggler's Inn pub, my long-coveted Crow's Nest Cottage and then a view of the beach.

'I can see the sea!' I shouted in the timeless tradition, even though there was no one to hear me.

The road dipped gently down – and the stretch of beach I had been dreaming about finally came into view. It was only the narrowest of glimpses between the two rows of houses lining the lane, but it made my heart skip nonetheless.

With no one behind me I slowed the car to a stop, pulled on the handbrake and took it out of gear. The little lane was single track, one way only and, in my opinion, offered the prettiest slice of coastal view in the whole of Norfolk. I could see the pub on the left and knew my cottage was just beyond it but set back a little with the tiniest garden and picket fence in front.

On the other side there was a row of what would have once been fishermen's terraced cottages. There were half a dozen or so, also built in the traditional style and from local materials, and I hoped they weren't all given over to the holidaying masses. Hypocritical I know as I was a holiday-maker myself, and I also knew that a village like Wynmouth needed to make ends meet. But I hated the thought of the place being devoid of local families, and bursting at the seams with tourists during the summer and then abandoned and boarded up in the winter.

It was all about striking the right balance, but aware of the soaring real estate prices on such picturesque properties in other places along the coast, I knew that most definitely hadn't been achieved. The scales were weighted firmly in the holidaymaker's favour there.

A sharp toot behind me brought me back to my senses and I waved a hand in apology to the impatient-looking chap on a tractor. At least there was one fisherman still in the village then. The old tractors, rust-riddled affairs thanks to the salt-laden sea air, were used to pull the little boats up and down the beach and in and out of the sea.

'Sorry,' I called as I pulled away and indicated left, but I don't think he heard me.

He had inched so close to my bumper that I didn't think he could see my indicator either, but he must have known where I was going. There really wasn't anywhere else, unless I wanted to take the car beachcombing. Focused on making the tight turn without scraping my paintwork, I hadn't been able to look at the cottage as I squeezed by but it didn't matter. I would be turning the key in the lock soon enough.

Fat raindrops had started to fall as I pulled into the pub car park and unloaded my bags and by the time I had walked back around to the lane and negotiated the incline up to the cottage it was falling faster, but it didn't stop me taking a moment to admire the riot of colourful flowers in the front garden or the brick and flint façade.

The cottage was every bit as beautiful as I remembered. As I wrestled with the gate, which was a little twisted on its hinges, and scrabbled about in the leaking porch, searching for the pot with the door key hidden under it, I felt extremely happy to be back in Wynmouth, even if it was raining and some of my memories were already being subjected to a little fine-tuning.

'It's under the one on the other side,' said a woman's voice close behind me.

'Shit,' I swore as I dropped the pot in my hand, and it landed on the step with a sharp crack.

I picked it up and turned around.

'Sorry,' said the woman, who was loaded down with bags, 'I didn't mean to make you jump.'

'And I didn't mean to break this,' I said, showing her the damage and feeling my face flush as I bit my lip. 'It's cracked all the way down one side.'

'It doesn't matter,' she said kindly, shaking her head. 'I'm sure we'll be able to glue it back together.'

I set the pot aside, located the key and finally stepped into the cottage. The door opened straight into the bijou sitting room I had seen online. It was even cosier than I had imagined with a squishy sofa and chair, an old pine desk under the sash window and a well-stocked bookcase next to the brick fireplace which housed a log-burning stove. It was definitely tighter for space than I had imagined when I posed for my holiday snap.

You would have been stretched to make it a comfortable holiday spot for two, unless you were in the first flush of romance and happy to live on top of each other. Not an emotion I had felt for a very long time. Relationships were another thing I had sacrificed in my quest to keep focused on my career. Anything beyond half a dozen or so dates – or sooner if things felt even remotely as though they were heading towards serious – were ruled out. I had disappointed a good share of men in recent years and my heart had taken a bit of a battering too. As a result, I was sworn off romance (although not uncomplicated sex with no strings attached), for good.

I baulked at the thought that, if my interpretation of what Mum had written was correct, then I was like my father in that sense. I was certain that he and his lover could have managed to feel right at home with the compromised space in Crow's Nest Cottage, but then quickly kicked the thought away. I would get around to the further details of Mum's diaries at some point, but now was not the time. Now I wanted to enjoy getting to know the cottage which, given its dimensions, probably wouldn't take long.

I heard the woman with the bags follow me inside and breathe a sigh of relief as she put them down. For a moment I had a horrible feeling the cottage had been double-booked but then it dawned on me who she was.

'You must be Sam,' I said, confident that I had made the right assumption.

'No,' she smiled, quickly closing the door on the rain. 'Sam's the cottage owner and landlord of the Smuggler's next door. I'm Sophie. I'm a friend of his.'

'Oh,' I said, glancing around the room again and this time

noticing that things weren't perhaps looking quite as perfect as they should. The sofa cushions definitely needed plumping and the shade on the table lamp was a little askew, 'I see.'

Sophie followed my gaze.

'Sam had an unexpected appointment this afternoon,' she explained, 'so he asked me to welcome you. It's just the finishing touches to see to now, but I'm sorry it's not been done yet. It's been a bit of a rush for me to get around. Usually Sam would see to everything himself and in plenty of time.'

'Well, it doesn't matter,' I told her. Slightly flat cushions and a wonky lampshade aside, it was still lovely. 'It looks great to me, even prettier than I imagined it would be.'

Sophie looked relieved.

'I'm Tess, by the way,' I added. My excitement to have finally made it over the cottage threshold had momentarily robbed me of my manners and I had failed to introduce myself. 'Tess Tyler. Though I'm guessing you know that already.'

Just for a moment Sophie's smile faltered.

'Tyler?' She frowned.

'That's right.'

'Well, it's very nice to meet you, Tess,' she said. 'Welcome to Crow's Nest Cottage.'

'Thank you. I can't tell you how pleased I am to be here.'

I was just about to go into how I had dreamed of coming back to Wynmouth for years, but a sudden rumble of thunder made us both jump and Sophie carried on the conversation before I did.

'Sam was so pleased you could come at such short notice,' she said as she quickly straightened the shade and flicked on the lamp and then turned on another next to the fire.

The room looked even cosier bathed in a peachy warm glow, but it was chilly. Certainly chilly for May, I realized as I gave an involuntary shudder. I'd only packed a couple of jumpers and one pair of jeans. Everything else I'd treated myself to on my speedy shopping trip was geared up for much warmer weather.

'These old walls take a while to heat up in the summer,' said Sophie, noticing my goosebumps. 'And we haven't had the sunniest of starts this year.'

I hoped there would be at least a few hot days to come. I didn't much fancy getting to know the beach again under the protection of an umbrella. Not that I would be using one in a thunderstorm. Right on cue the lights flickered and another boom, closer this time, rolled overhead.

'Thor is in a grump this afternoon,' Sophie mused, looking out at the sky. 'Why don't I get these bags unpacked and the kettle on while you explore and then I'll light the log burner. It will heat the hot water and radiators and warm the place up in no time.'

'That would be great,' I said appreciatively, 'but can't I give you a hand? What is it that you've got there?'

'It's your welcome pack,' she explained. 'Lots of lovely local produce and a few essentials so you don't have to venture to the shops for a couple of days, unless you want to of course.'

'That's such a kind thought.'

'It should have all been ready for your arrival so I wouldn't have to interrupt you at all,' she confided, 'but I had a last-minute influx of customers and couldn't close up early today. Not that I'm complaining, but I am sorry to intrude before you've had a chance to even boil the kettle.'

'It's really no bother,' I told her, because I didn't mind at all. Sophie's warm welcome was exactly what I would have expected from a Wynmouth resident. 'Do you work in the pub with Sam?'

'Occasionally,' she told me, 'but I have my own business too. It's a café.'

'A café?'

'Yes, right next to the beach.'

I wondered if she had taken on the boarded-up building I could remember, which was near where the tractors pulled the boats in and out of the sea. That was right next to the beach but had been long abandoned when I knew it. I had always thought it was spooky but the local kids I sometimes hung out with used to dare each other to break in and graffiti the walls. If that was the place Sophie was referring to, it must have taken a miracle to transform it.

'Because of the weather, it's not particularly busy at the moment,' she continued, 'so I can't very well turn folk away when they find me, even if they do come a little outside the regular opening hours.'

'Of course not,' I agreed, 'and as I said, it's no problem at all.'

While Sophie unpacked, I went off to explore and found

the rest of the cottage was every bit as pretty as the sitting room. There was just the one bedroom upstairs with a large welcoming brass-framed bed complete with lavender-scented fresh linen and a bathroom with a roll-top bath which I couldn't wait to relax into.

The view from the bedroom was of the lane in front but on tiptoe from the bathroom at the back I could just see the curve of the coast and the cliffs where the static vans Mum, Dad and I stayed in were pitched. I wondered if the beach huts were still there too. I would have to take a walk to find out, once the weather had improved.

'Do you take sugar?' Sophie called, just as I was remembering my last trip to the huts. 'I've made a pot of tea.'

The doors of the wood burner were open when I went back down and warm tendrils of heat were already making their way into the room.

'No thank you,' I said. 'Just a splash of milk would be great.'

Sophie handed me a mug and explained how to stoke the fire as I'd never been in charge of one before and then she closed the doors so the radiators would heat up faster. It all sounded simple enough and looking at the contents of the fridge and cupboards I knew I probably wouldn't have to buy another morsel to eat during my entire visit. Joan would have been delighted.

'What's that lovely smell?' I asked as my stomach caught a heavenly scent and hastily reminded me that I hadn't eaten since breakfast.

'Your dinner,' Sophie smiled, 'assuming you aren't allergic to seafood?'

'I'm not,' I quickly reassured her. 'I'm not allergic to anything.'

As I took in the delicious aroma, I was rather relieved about that.

'It was on the pub menu today,' she explained. 'I supply some of the heartier dishes you see, and I saved a serving for you from earlier. You'll just have to heat it up when you want it later. I've put it on the side for now.'

'Thank you,' I said, inhaling again. 'Is it a curry?'

'Sort of,' she nodded. 'It's a bit of a foodie fusion really. My aunt's Caribbean curried crab with coconut recipe, but made with fresh Norfolk crab.'

'Wow,' I laughed. 'What a fantastic combination. I have to admit it's not what I would have expected to find on a pub menu in Wynmouth, but I can't wait to try it.'

Sophie looked delighted by my enthusiasm and my stomach gave another embarrassingly loud rumble. It almost matched Thor's efforts.

'You don't have to wait for dinner time of course,' she nudged. 'You can eat whenever you like on holiday.'

'I didn't have any lunch,' I told her. 'The journey took longer than I expected and I didn't want to stop.'

Sophie eyed me astutely.

'You sound like my daughter,' she nodded. 'She's about the same age as you and she never used to make mealtimes much of a priority either. That's all changed now,' she added, flashing me another smile before checking her watch. 'But look at the time!' she exclaimed. 'I have to go. If there's anything you need just pop next door and ask. Although,' she added as she reached the front door, 'I'd wait until this storm has passed, if I were you.'

She ducked out into the rain and headed back towards the pub, banging the wonky gate behind her in her haste. I picked up the cracked flower pot, carried it inside and set it down on the hearthstone before checking the fire. I could hear the radiators were gurgling into life and didn't think it would be long before I was able to run myself a bath.

Once I was happy with the fire I sat on the sofa, reached for my bag and automatically pulled out my phone.

'Don't even go there,' I sternly told myself as I toyed with the idea of turning it back on.

It really would be better if I didn't see Dad's reaction to my defection. My text had been brief, but clear enough.

> Hi Dad. In view of the fact that I haven't been feeling all that well recently, and that Chris has proved himself more than capable of handling things in the office, I've decided to take a break. As you may recall, it's been quite some time since I took a holiday so I'm sure you'll understand. I'll keep you posted as to when I plan to come back. Please, don't worry about me. See you soon. Tess x

I was pretty certain he would be raging like a bear with a sore head by now. I had added the 'don't worry' to remind him to look beyond his temper and try to think of me as his daughter for once instead of his employee. I was rather proud that I hadn't said sorry for taking off. I had recently found myself all too often apologizing for things I had no reason to be sorry for.

Before I gave in to temptation, I took the phone and my charger and deposited it into one of the drawers under the old pine table which stood in the window.

'Out of sight,' I muttered to myself, 'out of mind.'

Or at least that was what I hoped.

Chapter 4

I went to bed early that night completely blissed out after my delicious dinner (courtesy of Sophie's clever culinary skills), and the longest soak in the tub. I could have stayed in the bath all night, had it not been for fear of turning into a prune. The bed was extremely comfortable and as the storm headed off, I cracked the window open a little so I could fall asleep listening to the sound of the waves as they rolled in and broke on the shore.

Considering the jumbled-up state of my emotions, I slept more soundly than I could have hoped and dreamt of my last adventure down at the beach huts. Waking to the sound of gulls and feeling refreshed and revived as opposed to slightly panicked as my phone alarm blared out was a wonderful feeling. It was still an early start, but then I'd already fathomed that some old habits were going to be hard to break.

I took a moment to stretch out in the bed, tried to dismiss how alien it felt not to already be scanning through my inbox, and wondered if any of the local kids I used to hang around with still lived in the village. We had only ever been on first-name terms and I probably wouldn't be able to recognize them now, but I would keep my eyes peeled for familiar faces, nonetheless. Surely, there was one I would recognize should I happen to bump into him.

When I eventually opened the curtains, I was delighted to see that there wasn't a cloud in the sky and in stark contrast to when I arrived the air felt warm. I wouldn't be needing an umbrella today or an extra layer. While waiting for the kettle to boil I opened the back door which led out into a tiny walled courtyard. It was too damp to sit out, but I would certainly be making use of the bistro set as soon as the sun had dried everything enough.

'Good morning!' called a smartly dressed elderly gentleman with a Jack Russell terrier on a lead when I set off to explore a short while later.

I hadn't been planning to head out quite so soon, but after my first caffeine hit of the day, my brain had been determined to lead my body to the drawer where I'd stashed my phone and so I was sensibly putting temptation firmly out of reach. I'd also added Mum's diary to the drawer and even though I wanted to read more, I thought I would benefit from winding down a bit before I picked it up again.

It was a novelty to be heading out so soon after I had decided to go though. With no work to go to, I had realized there was no need to straighten my hair into submission, or waste time on flawless make-up. It was all very liberating, although I had still mascaraed my lashes and applied a slick of lip gloss.

'Morning,' I smiled back, before jumping out of the way to let the beach tractor by.

The driver stared down at me and carried on, and then nodded to the old man as the machine trundled slowly and noisily by.

'Are you heading down to the beach, my dear?' the man asked as I looked up and down the lane, checking for more vehicles.

'If I don't get run over first,' I told him.

'Are you here on holiday?'

'Yes,' I said, 'I'm staying in Wynmouth for a couple of weeks.' The words made my heart race. 'You?'

'Visiting my sister. She moved here a few years ago after she lost her husband.'

'She's a local then.'

'Oh, dear me, no,' the man laughed before turning up the road which led to the pub car park. 'You have to have lived here for seven generations to be considered a local. At least!'

He brandished the walking stick he was carrying and pottered on.

'Bye!' I called after him. 'Nice to meet you.'

My breath caught in my chest as I stepped out of the lane and on to the seawall and I allowed myself time to absorb the beautiful view I had been craving in recent weeks.

'You're here, Tess,' I whispered, a smile slowly spreading across my face. 'You're actually here.'

The tide was out so far the sea was hardly in sight and the beach seemed to stretch into the distance forever. I rushed down the steps, on to the pristine sand and pulled off my sandals. I didn't care about the chill beneath my feet, I wanted to let my toes sink into the silky sand. The heady cocktail of pure and wholly natural sensations surrounding me and the plethora of emotions rushing through me, brought a lump to my throat. Standing there, taking it all in, I felt proud that I had put myself first for once, taken the plunge and run away to the seaside, rather than resolutely powering on at work.

I instinctively turned left, shielding my eyes from the welcome glare of the sun and spotted the rockpools not too far away and the tops of the beach huts in the distance beyond them. It was all still here then and, at first glance, exactly as I remembered it. I pictured Mum, wearing her sundress and reading in a deckchair as I explored the pools, and Dad poring over the newspapers beneath the shade of a striped beach umbrella.

Everything had seemed so simple then; we were a happy family with uncomplicated lives and we might not have had much money to throw about, but it never mattered, not to me anyway. As I imagined my pre-teen self skipping about and yelping as I darted in and out of the chilly sea, I knew these happy memories were made long before Mum had written her heart-wrenching diary. How I would have loved to turn back the clock and warn her of what was to come. I would have given anything to keep things as they had been before the business, among other things, became the focus of my father's ambitious attention.

I gave myself a little shake and turned away, striding out towards where I knew the sea was waiting, picking up the odd bit of litter and stuffing it in my pockets as I went. I would explore the pools when I had purchased a bucket and net. With two weeks at my disposal, there was absolutely no need to rush to discover every delight Wynmouth had to offer on my very first day.

With no phone glued to my hand, I had absolutely no idea what the time was. It felt strange, deviating from my self-imposed strict schedule and, if I was being completely honest, a little unsettling not having that uninterrupted connection to the wider world, but I pushed the feeling away and carried on.

Sometime later, with my pockets pleasingly weighed down with pebbles and smooth fragments of soft green sea glass, I left the beach and made for the pub, purposefully ignoring the call of my mobile as I walked by the cottage door. It thought it wouldn't hurt to introduce myself to Sam, the landlord, and I wanted to leave thanks for Sophie for both the welcome pack and the delicious dinner.

I found the pub door open, but it looked so shaded inside after the brightness on the beach, that I couldn't make out if I could go in or not.

'Are you open?' I called through the door and into the darkness within.

'If the door's open,' came a man's deep voice in quick reply, 'we're open.'

'Great,' I said, taking a step inside but finding my way blocked by the owner of the voice who was carrying a large chalkboard sign in his arms.

'I was just about to put the board out,' he elaborated, squeezing tightly past and treating me to a delicious breath of woody aftershave before I had a chance to step out of the way. 'I'm doing breakfasts today, if you fancy a bite?'

What I fancied, I quickly discovered, when I saw him in the light of day, was him. His sun-streaked blonde hair, ready smile and sparkling green eyes caught me off guard and I suddenly felt far hotter than I had from the brisk walk back from the beach.

'I really just wanted a coffee,' I swallowed, pressing myself back into the wall so he could get by again. 'If that's okay?'

'Of course,' he nodded, stepping up behind the bar and turning to look at me properly.

Was it my imagination, or did he, just for a second or two, seem to be caught off guard too? His eyes certainly seemed to widen as they lingered on my face and the flush spreading across his tanned features almost matched my own. He opened his mouth to say something, but then seemed to change his mind and cleared his throat instead.

'Personally, this sea air makes me want to eat for England,' he finally said, his composure apparently recovered, 'but one coffee coming right up. Americano?'

'Please,' I said, looking about me while he had his back turned. 'That would be great.'

Even though my eyes had adjusted to the change in light

level, the inside of the pub was still shadowy and completely unknown to me as I had never been inside before. The interior featured a lot of dark furniture, an immense fireplace, tall ship paraphernalia, tarnished tankards hanging above the bar and deep windowsills piled with artful arrangements of old books and stoneware beer bottles. Nothing looked as if it had been touched in years, but that all seemed to be part of the place's traditional charm. Without the distraction of a screen in front of me, I was able to take in all of the tinier details and they were lovely.

'One coffee,' the guy smiled, putting a cup and saucer down in front of me. 'And are you sure I can't get you anything to eat?'

Now I thought about it, my time out in the sea air and on the beach had given me a bit of an appetite.

'I'm doing sausage sandwiches and baguettes today,' he added temptingly.

'Oh, go on then,' I caved. 'I'll have a sandwich, please. On wholemeal, if you have it.'

'Of course,' he said approvingly, 'and you won't regret it. Wynmouth has the best butcher for miles around.'

He was certainly right. The sandwich was delicious, and I felt pleased that I had spotted a couple of packets bearing the butcher's logo in the fridge after Sophie had stocked it. Which reminded me of my original reason for popping into the pub. I wasn't in the habit of letting a good-looking guy throw me off course, but then I was on holiday, so anything was possible, wasn't it?

'I meant to say before,' I explained as I swallowed down the last delectable mouthful. 'I'm Tess Tyler. I'm renting the cottage next door.'

'Yeah,' said the guy, shaking his head and sounding every bit as remiss as I felt. 'Sorry, I guessed as much. My head's a bit all over the place this morning.'

I wondered if that was as a result of the look he had given me when I arrived or, assuming that he was Sam the land-lord, if it was because of the last-minute appointment Sophie had mentioned which had thrown this schedule.

I would have liked to flatter myself by thinking that it was the sight of me which had elicited his muddle-headedness, but realistically I knew if he was the man in charge, then it was more likely to be the appointment. Any deviation from my weekly work pattern could play havoc with me for days. There was no telling how I was going to cope now I had thrown my regimented hour-by-hour routine by the wayside.

'I'm Sam,' he then said, confirming my assumption. 'The landlord here and the guy you were emailing about the cottage.'

'Pleased to meet you, Sam,' I smiled.

The brisk tone of his emails in no way matched his laid-back, casual look. I would never have put him and his writing style together.

'Pleased to meet you too, Tess,' he smiled back, this time meeting my eye without his cheeks colouring.

He really was a good-looking guy and I couldn't help

thinking that there was something familiar about him, but it was probably more to do with the fact that he seemed gifted with a knack of putting folk at ease – a perfect trait for a landlord to have – rather than us having met before.

I had felt something similar when I was with Sophie, although not the same spark of attraction, so perhaps it was just the Wynmouth charm which provoked the sensation. I certainly didn't remember Sam from my previous holidays, so it wasn't the familiarity of recognition I found in his hypnotic gaze, but then those days were long passed now.

'How are you finding the cottage?' he asked. 'Have you got everything you need?'

'Yes,' I told him, 'everything's wonderful, and I wanted to thank Sophie for making it so welcoming. Her curried crab was delicious.'

'I'll be sure to tell her,' Sam said as, unasked, he made me another coffee. 'I'm sorry I couldn't be there to set things up for you myself, but I had an appointment I couldn't miss.'

I didn't say that Sophie had told me as much because I didn't want him to think she had been indiscreet. Which she hadn't.

'It wasn't a problem,' I said instead.

'I've been waiting for ages, you see,' he carried on. 'I'm having a new leg and there was an appointment cancellation, so I took it.'

'You really don't have to explain,' I shrugged, then realization struck. 'Hang on . . .' I bit back the words and Sam started to laugh.

'It's all right,' he said, 'you did hear that right. I'm treating myself to an upgrade.'

He walked back around the bar again and it was only then that I realized that the part of his lower left leg revealed beneath his khaki cargo shorts was prosthetic.

'It's costing me a fortune,' he explained, his open expression clouding a little, 'but the last one I had from the hospital has never really fit right and it's been giving me grief for ages.'

'Right,' I said, 'I see.'

'I'm investing in myself instead of this place,' he sighed, looking around the pub. 'I just hope it's not a mistake. It feels a bit self-indulgent, to be honest.'

It didn't sound like a decadent purchase to me.

'Personally,' I told him, trying to imagine how painful an ill-fitting prosthetic must be, 'I think it sounds more essential than self-indulgent.'

He smiled again, making my stomach flip, and I took another look around the pub as he welcomed a couple more customers and took their orders. The place looked absolutely spot on: exactly what you would expect to find in a quaint Norfolk seaside village.

'I don't think you need to worry about this place,' I told him when he came back and then, thinking of my own sudden understanding of self-care, added, 'sometimes you just have to put yourself first.'

I was hardly the greatest at practising what I preached just yet, but at least I'd made a start. That I had finally made it back to Wynmouth, as opposed to just daydreaming about the place, was proof enough of that.

'You're absolutely right,' he said, fixing me again with his gorgeous green eyes and leaning further over the bar. 'Now tell me, what wind blew you to Wynmouth, Tess? A regular holiday in the Norfolk seaside or something more complicated? Are *you* putting yourself first by any chance?'

They were all questions I really didn't feel up to answering, especially as my thoughts were still in such a muddle. I could have said that I was simply on holiday or that I was taking a break from work, but the complication of Mum's diary swam in front of my eyes, and I didn't trust myself to open my mouth again for fear of blurting the whole sorry story out. Thankfully I was saved from having to formulate a response.

'I see you've found your way to the best pub in town, my dear.'

I looked over my shoulder and saw the man I had spoken to earlier, and his dog, framed in the doorway.

'What you mean, George,' said Sam, winking at me as the man came further in, 'is that she's found her way to the *only* pub in the village.'

I felt my temperature rising again in response to the friendly gesture. He was still giving off a very familiar vibe, but he definitely hadn't been around during my former holidays. I was certain I would have remembered a lad with a prosthetic limb. Unless of course, he didn't have it then. It didn't feel like the sort of question I could very well ask on a first meeting, even though Sam's demeanour suggested he would have happily told me.

'Well, yes,' said the man I now knew as George. 'I suppose you're right there, landlord, but it is a fine pub nonetheless.'

'Thank you very much,' said Sam with a little bow. 'I take it you and Tess have already met.'

'We have,' I said, 'we exchanged pleasantries at what I now realize must have been an ungodly hour earlier this morning.'

'Everyone starts early around here,' said George, doffing his well-worn panama hat in my direction. 'Lovely to meet you properly though, Tess. What a pretty name.'

'Thank you.'

'Oh, and this little bundle of mischief is Skipper,' said Sam, peering over the bar at the dog who stared keenly back. 'He has a fondness for chewing my leg if he gets half a chance.'

'Is that why you're staying behind the bar?' I laughed.

'That's *exactly* why I'm staying behind the bar,' Sam laughed back.

'Now, that was just the one time,' said George, springing to Skipper's defence.

'Once was enough!' cut in Sam, making George laugh too.

'I take it he's already told you that he's the one and only real pirate in these parts?' George said to me.

'He might have mentioned something,' I nodded, 'but it didn't look like wood when I took a look at it.'

Sam looked at me and raised his eyebrows.

'His leg, I mean,' I hastily added, feeling my face flush again. 'His leg didn't look wooden.'

Sam bit his lip.

'I'll get your coffee, George,' he grinned. 'And Skipper will find his usual bowl next to the fireplace full of water.'

'Thank you, dear boy,' said George, oblivious of my embarrassment as he wandered further into the darker recesses of the pub.

Once my cheeks had stopped flaming, I settled my bill and thought about what I would do with the rest of my day. The pub was a little busier now, but not much. Perhaps there would be an influx of customers in the evening.

'So,' said Sam, handing me my change and making my skin tingle as his fingers brushed my palm. 'What are your plans for this afternoon, Tess?'

'I'm not sure yet.'

It felt extremely indulgent as well as unnerving, not having every minute of my day mapped out for me. Of course, I had plenty to deal with, that was my whole reason for heading back to Wynmouth, but I still didn't think it would hurt to take a little bit longer before settling down to do it.

'I might head back to the cottage for a nap,' I said, feeling every bit as lazy as I no doubt sounded, 'or I might have a wander further along the coast. I'm not sure yet.'

'Depending on the tide, you might enjoy a spot of rock pooling while the sun's still out,' Sam suggested.

I was very much looking forward to revisiting the pools, not that Sam knew I had explored them before, but I wanted to save them until the moment felt right. They had always been such a highlight and that was exactly how I wanted to keep them.

'And further along, just over the nearest groyne, there are some beach huts,' he continued.

'I noticed those this morning,' I swallowed, 'when I was walking on the beach.'

'They're always a popular spot,' he went on, lowering his voice a little, 'for one reason or another.'

I looked up and our eyes met for the briefest of seconds. I felt my breath catch in my throat as his gaze flicked to my lips and back up again. Was it possible that he knew? No, it was just my imagination. It had to be.

'Occasionally, there'll be one available to rent,' he carried on sounding perfectly normal again. He reached for a cloth and began wiping down the already flawless bar. 'So, keep an eye out for any signs hung on the doors, if you fancy it, that is.'

'I will,' I said huskily.

'And then of course there's Sophie's café back the other way,' he reminded me. 'Visitors are always welcome there.'

'It seems to me that visitors are welcome everywhere in Wynmouth,' I pointed out.

'More or less,' Sam laughed but then his brow creased, 'although unfortunately, there never seems to be quite enough of them these days.'

I looked around again, there were still only a very few customers.

'But surely it will be busier next week,' I pointed out,

'what with the bank holiday weekend at the end of it.' Sam didn't look convinced. 'And aren't the schools on half-term too? I bet you and the other local businesses have loads planned to keep the tills ringing then.'

If they hadn't, then they should have. In a village like Wynmouth, May bank holiday weekend should have marked the start of the summer season, but that was my marketing head talking and I wasn't supposed to be using that.

'What have you got planned for the pub?' I couldn't resist asking nonetheless.

Sam bit his lip but didn't answer.

'Don't tell me, you haven't organized anything at all, not even for the weekend?'

'Not yet,' he said, avoiding eye contact by focusing on folding the cloth into a neat square, 'but it's all in hand.' He added, nodding at a notebook which looked as though it had a few scribbles in it.

It didn't look much like a properly thought out promotional strategy to me, but I did have one suggestion that could swell his coffers a little.

'Well, as we're on the topic of increasing revenue,' I carried on, trying to smile winningly, 'I was wondering—'

'Were we talking about that?' he cut in.

'Yes,' I said, 'sort of.'

'Go on then.'

'I was wondering,' I said again, 'if there might be a possibility of you letting me stay on in the cottage for longer than two weeks, should I decide I want to.'

It was a reckless suggestion, given that I'd only stayed for one night so far, but I wanted to know if it might be a possibility. I was the most organized, disciplined and scheduled person I knew (if you discounted my father and at that moment I did), and it was going to take me some time to shake off the shackles and chill out.

I had some potentially life-changing decisions to make, as well as Mum's diary to read and come to terms with, and the two-week timebomb ticking in my ears wasn't the sort of pressure I needed on this occasion. As a rule, it would have been ideal, but this trip to Wynmouth was all about breaking the rules.

'Well,' said Sam, as he rubbed his hand around the back of his neck, 'I'm really not sure about that.'

'In your email,' I hastily reminded him, 'you told me that you were taking the place off the holiday market, didn't you? Madness really, as you're heading into the summer season . . .'

'Yes,' he conceded, 'I did, but that was because—'

'So, it's just going to be sitting there empty anyway.'

'I suppose,' he shrugged. 'Although I am planning to—'

'I'm talking about a month at least,' I interrupted, throwing caution to the wind and imagining four whole stress-free weeks stretching ahead of me, 'and I'm prepared to pay the going rental rate. More than that, if necessary.'

Sam looked a little taken aback.

'Don't make a decision now,' I said, hopping down from the bar stool I had been perched on and making for the door.

'Have a think about it, and I'll come back and pay you in a few days.'

'That rather sounds like you're assuming I'll say yes,' he called after me.

'I have a feeling,' I responded, as I stepped outside and breathed in the fresh sea air, 'that you won't be able to resist.'

Chapter 5

The euphoric thrill of being back in Wynmouth, along with excitement derived from making the rash request to lengthen my visit, stayed with me all of that day and part of the way into the next. Had I not then been confined to barracks because of the relentless rain and biting wind, I daresay the feeling might have stayed with me even longer, but by the end of Thursday, having struggled to keep my hands off my phone and having read the rest of Mum's first couple of diary entries, I was feeling pretty low.

There was a level of acceptance and resignation as Mum described her feelings about seeing Dad out with another woman and I found that more depressing than anything. She had obviously been so in love with him that she was prepared to put up with the humiliation and I hated the fact that not only had her life had been cut so cruelly short, but that the last few years of it had been so miserable. If only she had confided in me . . .

Without the benefit of my regular work routine or the sunny beach to walk on and now more of Mum's sad words ringing in my ears, my mood had become as dark as the inside of the cottage and I was tempted to retract my request of a month's rental, but I didn't.

'You're just going through a period of readjustment,' I told myself, as I returned the diary to the drawer and stoked the fire. 'You aren't used to such a dramatic drop in your activity levels and you're bound to feel overwhelmed by these shocking revelations.'

I lay, curled up on the sofa under a blanket and gave the weather beyond the window a hard stare. This was not what I had signed up for. I toyed with the idea of going back to the pub for a few hours. I could take a book and pretend I was reading as I watched the world go by. At least there were other folk there, even if they were few and far between, but then, given everything else I had to deal with, I reckoned I didn't need the distraction of the beguiling green eyes which belonged to the lovely landlord on top of everything else.

A spark of attraction had been the last thing I had expected to feel when I rushed to confirm my cottage reservation, but the touchpaper had been lit and the sensible thing now was to stand well back because even my no-strings fun ethos had occasionally been known to tie itself up into unwelcome knots.

By mid-morning on Friday there was the tiniest hint of a break in the cloud and when I spotted it, I wasted no time in setting out to chase it. I pulled on the raincoat which hung on a hook just inside the door, grabbed the umbrella beneath it and rushed out. I didn't care if I was in for a soaking; if I stayed cooped up for much longer, I would go completely stir crazy.

'Tess!' called Sophie when she spotted me on the lane which led down to the beach.

I waited for her to catch me up.

'Hello, Sophie,' I smiled.

'Oh, my goodness,' she tutted, swapping the basket she was carrying from one hand to the other so she could link her arm through mine before I had a chance to take a step away, 'don't you look down in the dumps?'

'Do I?' I swallowed.

'Yes, you do,' she declared, squeezing me closer.

It was an intimate way to greet someone you barely knew but, after we had taken a few steps, I told myself to unclench and found I didn't actually mind her unexpected proximity. The further we walked, the more comforting I found her unreserved friendliness and I made no attempt to untangle myself. Sophie was probably about the age Mum had been when I lost her and her maternal manner was cheering after the miserable couple of days I'd suffered.

'I can see it in your eyes,' she told me. 'But with the rain we've had, I'm hardly surprised. Almost half your holiday gone, and you've been plagued by bad weather almost since the moment you arrived.'

She was right, and I immediately found myself hoping

that Sam would let me stay on, because it was depressing to think that I'd spent the best part of the first week back in Wynmouth laying on a sofa wrapped in a blanket.

'It's not always like this here, you know?' Sophie nudged.

I did know.

'Come along with me to the café,' she insisted, 'and I'll see if I can find something to put the smile back on your pretty face.'

'All right,' I agreed, 'but only if you let me carry that basket.'

Sophie swapped it for my umbrella, which we thankfully didn't need to put up, and together we carried on towards the beach. Just as I had guessed, her business was housed in the spooky, boarded-up building I remembered from former holidays, but it looked nothing like the last time I had seen it. In fact, I soon discovered there was absolutely nothing even remotely scary about the place at all.

'Here we are,' said Sophie proudly. 'This is my little business.'

'Oh, my goodness!' I laughed, feeling overwhelmed as I took it all in. 'I was not expecting this!'

It was certainly an idyllic spot, with the cliffs rising steeply behind and curving around it and the beach in front reaching down to the shore. The backdrop of cultivated fields atop the cliffs stretched to the horizon and it all looked untouched by time. A truly pastoral British scene, that is until you spotted the vibrant café exterior (and given the explosive pop of colour, you simply couldn't fail to spot it) and were transported straight to the sunny Caribbean.

'It's amazing,' I grinned. 'And not at all what I was expecting. You've totally taken me by surprise, Sophie. I love it.'

'Well, thank you,' she smiled graciously.

She seemed pleased by my reaction, which in turn pleased me because it was wholly genuine. Even just a glimpse of Sophie's café from a distance had started to chase away my dark mood. I couldn't wait to see if it was as eye-catching on the inside as it was out.

'I'm very proud of it,' she continued. 'Although I can't help wishing it was a little busier.'

I couldn't possibly imagine why the café wouldn't be heaving but, aside from someone walking a dog in the distance, the beach was completely deserted; however, I supposed that with the recent weather that was hardly surprising. And as Sophie had pointed out on the day I arrived in the village, it hadn't been the sunniest start to the year. That was bound to have an impact.

'I'm sure things will pick up again when the sun makes a more consistent effort,' I told her robustly. 'As soon as the temperature starts to rise, folk will be flocking back to the beach, and to here. I mean, look at it. How could they resist?'

She didn't look convinced and I remembered how surprised I had been to find the village so empty and the Smuggler's so lacking in footfall. Why was no one coming to Wynmouth?

'Well, I don't know about that,' she said softly and a little sadly, 'but let's get inside before the rain starts again and I'll make you a lovely hot chocolate.'

We quickly made our way down the path and I found I couldn't stop smiling. The fence surrounding the outside eating area was painted in a rainbow of colours, as were the half a dozen wooden picnic benches arranged on the forecourt which overlooked the beach.

'The winter storms ensure the paintwork needs touching up every year,' Sophie told me, 'but I think it's worth it, don't you?'

'Definitely,' I readily agreed. 'Totally worth it.'

The interior was every bit as vibrant and matched the outside beautifully. There were no muted shades in this Norfolk beachside café. It had to be utterly unique to the area and to my mind, that should have made it even more popular.

'What's the café called?' I asked as I helped lift down the chairs from where they had been left upside down on the tables.

None of the furniture matched, but because it was all painted, everything sat harmoniously together.

'The Wynmouth Beach Café,' Sophie told me. 'That's what it's always been called so I took the name on when I signed the lease.'

It was a perfectly acceptable name for a run-of-the-mill seaside eatery, but it didn't suit Sophie's clever creation at all. There was absolutely nothing about it which even hinted at what you would find if you ventured along this side of the coast.

'That's all right, isn't it?' she asked, when I didn't say anything.

I wasn't sure how I could say no without offending her.

'Well,' I began.

'Oh,' she groaned, before starting to laugh, 'don't tell me. It doesn't match the ambience of the place; it doesn't suggest any of what's on offer.'

I didn't say anything.

'Am I right?' she said, placing her hands on her shapely hips and raising her eyebrows.

'Yes,' I squeaked, confirming what she obviously already knew, 'you are.'

'There now,' she tutted, shaking her head. 'That's exactly what my daughter is always saying. You'd get on well with her, Tess. She thinks I should have a website too.'

'Please, don't tell me you haven't?' I gasped.

'No,' she shrugged, her laughter fading in response to my reaction, 'I haven't, but I will get around to it.' She hastily added.

'And what about social media?' I quizzed. The café was pure Instagram heaven. 'Please tell me you have a Facebook page at the very least.'

'All in good time,' she said, flicking on the lights behind the counter. 'All in good time. I've managed without all that palaver so far, haven't I?'

'I'm not so sure,' I told her.

'What do you mean?' she frowned, tying on an apron which was every bit as bright as the décor.

'Well, you said a minute ago that you would like the café to be busier, didn't you?'

70

'A little busier,' she conceded. 'No one wants to compromise the tranquillity of the area. I wouldn't want to be inundated, but yes, I could do with a little more cash coming through the till.'

'Then you really do need to embrace what your daughter has already suggested and get yourself online,' I said forthrightly.

I hoped she didn't think I was speaking out of turn, but her daughter had the right idea and Sophie needed to put her suggestions in place if she wanted to see the Wynmouth Beach Café thrive. The summer season was fast approaching and some online publicity, if pitched properly, could make a big difference to the café's takings. So much for leaving my marketing brain behind, I realized as my thoughts ran away with me.

'A website, and an Instagram and Twitter account really could make all the difference to your business, Sophie,' I carried on enthusiastically. 'And, if you know where to look and how to go about it, it will cost you practically nothing.'

Sophie began to look a little more interested and I could tell that my words were adding another layer to the foundations her daughter had already laid.

'I can help you with it all, if you like,' I blurted out before I could stop myself. 'I could have you completely set up with the whole lot by the end of the day.'

'But you're on holiday, Tess,' she reminded me. 'You can't do that.'

'But I want to,' I told her, looking around again. It wouldn't *really* be like work and it would be wonderful to help the café come into its own. It had so much potential, just like the rest of Wynmouth. 'This place is spectacular, Sophie, and it should be packed, even if it is raining. It's a ray of sunshine in itself and you should be shouting about it from the virtual rooftops.'

Sophie's shoulders started to shake.

'What?'

'You,' she laughed, 'I reckon you must be quite a force to reckon with once you've got a bee in your bonnet.'

I started to laugh along with her as the bell above the door announced the first – and hopefully not the last – customers of the day.

'You've convinced me,' she said, holding up her hands in a gesture of surrender. 'I'll tell my daughter she can go ahead with all this online malarkey you youngsters are so convinced about.'

'That's fantastic,' I told her, pleased that she was on board but a little disappointed that I wasn't going to get it all up and running myself.

I would have loved to set up the Instagram account if nothing else, although without my phone, that would have been tricky.

'And I'm going to think about changing the name,' Sophie carried on. 'I rather like the ray of sunshine thing you just said. Something like, Sophie's Sunshine Café might be fun.'

'Absolutely,' I agreed, already imagining the cheery

external livery and social media headers. 'I think that would be perfect.'

With the weather only steadily improving, I ended up spending much of the day in the café. Drinking Sophie's delectable rum-laced hot chocolate was a treat and I chatted to the slow trickle of customers, even cleared the odd table and made a point of calling Sophie over to hear what a couple of people had to say.

'We searched online when we knew we were coming to Wynmouth,' the young woman explained, 'but there was no mention of this place. We would have definitely remembered it and come all the sooner had we known about it.'

'I see,' nodded Sophie, 'that's useful to know.'

She had definitely got the message now and her daughter was going to find herself inundated with work when her mum handed over the many notes we had made throughout the course of the day. Sophie had even started listing more potential new names, but we kept going back to Sophie's Sunshine Café and I reckoned that was the one she would stick with. With such a warm and charming character running the business, I felt that Sophie herself would be as much of a draw for customers as her unique fusion menu.

She told me this was the fourth year she had been running the café. It had taken her years, and one big birthday, to take the plunge and I hated the thought of her venture failing. Hopefully now she had agreed to embrace the internet it would make all the difference. I had even suggested that she could open on occasional evenings, offering slightly more formal dining. The place could be an intimate and romantic hotspot for loved-up couples. The combination of candles, the beach and Sophie's spicy curries would get pulses racing and make the perfect date place.

'Do you have a spotters' board?' an eager-looking guy with a pair of binoculars asked just as I was beginning to imagine myself sitting across a table from Sam and staring into his bewitching eyes.

'A spotters' board?' I repeated back at him, grateful for the timely interruption.

'Yes,' he said, 'you know, a board to record the local bird and wildlife that's been seen around here.'

'Oh,' I said, looking about me, 'I don't think so, but what a great idea.'

Sophie was quick to catch on.

'What have you seen?' she asked the chap. 'Anything interesting?'

'A couple of grey plovers,' he said excitedly, and Sophie gave a little gasp. 'I've never seen them here at this time of year before and, of course, the sand martins are out in full force further along the cliffs.'

'They're such lovely little things,' said Sophie fondly.

For all I knew they could have been talking a different language, but they were clearly thrilled about what the guy had seen.

'It would be great if you had somewhere to record daily

sightings,' the keen twitcher then suggested, 'then other folk could add to the list throughout the week.'

'Why not use part of the chalkboard?' I said to Sophie.

Almost half a wall was taken up with a menu board and, in truth, it looked a bit empty, with just the dish of the day written in Sophie's cursive hand. It was easy to reach and would make a great focal point.

'That's a brilliant idea,' she agreed.

'Great,' smiled the chap. 'And perhaps you could add the daily tide times, they're always handy to know.'

'And a weather symbol of two, for the morning and afternoon,' Sophie suggested.

I left the café feeling content and as if my holiday was finally underway. Helping Sophie had pulled me out of the fug I had fallen into and even though I still had lots to think about I realized I needed to strike a balance if I was going to make some real headway. Shutting myself away in the cottage with only Mum's diary for company and the temptation to turn my phone on was definitely not the way to go. Succumbing to dark thoughts and isolated misery wouldn't help me make any progress at all.

'Well now,' said George when I walked into the Smuggler's that evening, 'we'd all but given up on you, hadn't we, Sam?'

'I have to admit,' Sam confirmed, with a twinkle in his eyes, 'that I was beginning to think the weather had got the better of you and you'd left already.'

His mischievous tone was exactly what I needed to round

off the day. It might have been dangerous stepping closer to that smouldering touchpaper again, but with George acting as chaperone I was willing to risk it.

'Sorry to disappoint you, lads,' I told them both with a grin to match Sam's, 'but you're stuck with me for a bit longer yet.'

'Oh no,' George chuckled, 'now that really is bad news, isn't it, Sam?'

Sam looked at George and shook his head and I got the impression that my presence in the village might well have been the topic of conversation between the pair and I would have very much liked to know what had been said.

'So, what can I get you, Tess?' Sam asked me, ignoring George who then went to sit with another customer.

'Um,' I said, looking along the row of pumps, 'I think I'll have half a pint of Wherry please.'

'Coming right up.'

The pub was far more crowded than when I had been in earlier in the week. It was hardly heaving but the level of chatter and laughter seemed to bring the place to life and coupled with the palpable relief that it was finally Friday, it felt like a merry place to be.

'One half,' said Sam, setting the glass on the bar and taking the five-pound note I proffered.

I craned my neck to look behind him and then back over my shoulder.

'What?' He frowned, following my gaze.

'Nothing,' I shrugged.

'Okay' he shrugged back, going to get my change.

'No,' I told him, 'I don't mean there's nothing wrong. I mean there actually is nothing.'

'I don't follow.'

'When I was in before you said you had your bank holiday plans in hand,' I reminded him, 'but I can't see anything advertised. I thought you'd have a few posters up by now.'

Sam rolled his eyes.

What was it with the Wynmouth folk? First Sophie had seemed reluctant to get her café online and now Sam looked as if he'd rather do anything other than sell more beer. Was it just my marketing brain refusing to switch off, or were the local business owners I had come across so far genuinely unwilling to do a decent amount of business?

'Don't tell me,' I sighed dramatically as I picked up my glass, 'you haven't *really* got anything planned at all, have you? You just said you had before to shut me up.'

I raised my eyebrows waiting for an answer.

'Am I right,' I pushed, 'or am I right?'

'No,' Sam huffed, 'you're not.'

There didn't seem to be much conviction behind his words.

'Convince me,' I said challengingly.

'Well,' he said, 'I have had a couple of ideas, but nothing concrete.'

'Why not?'

'Because,' he said, sounding suddenly frustrated, 'I really don't have the time to organize anything properly. In case you hadn't noticed, mine and some part-time help are the only pairs of hands running this pub. It might not be that busy, but there's really no free time, Tess and I can't afford to throw money at some half-arsed attempt at entertainment. If I can't do it right, then I'd rather not do it at all.'

That rather took the wind out of my sails. When I first struck up the conversation, I had assumed he just couldn't be bothered, but now it seemed that it was a timing issue rather than not making an effort.

'That's pretty ironic, isn't it?' I said, just as he was about to walk away.

'What is?'

'Well,' I said, 'you have no time at all, and since I've arrived, I've found I've got far too much of it.'

'What do you mean?'

'Too much time twiddling my thumbs waiting for the weather to clear,' I said, taking a pull at my beer, 'it's just got to me a bit, that's all.'

'Well, you can take this on if you want,' he said. 'If you've got nothing better to do.'

'Take what on?'

'Organizing the pub's bank holiday entertainment.'

My gaze snapped back up to his.

'You're kidding, right?'

'Yes,' he said, 'I'm kidding.'

He went to move again.

'Must be a nice problem to have though,' he said pointedly, 'too much time.'

I wasn't really listening.

'I suppose I could lend a hand,' I said thoughtfully as the cogs started to whirr. On my walk back along the beach I had been mulling over the importance of not shutting myself away. If I couldn't help Sophie get the café online, then perhaps I could help Sam pull in some extra punters.

'Are you being serious?' he frowned.

'Yeah,' I smiled up at him. 'Why not? But only if you agree to me staying on in the cottage.'

Sam looked at me for a long moment. He seemed to be weighing something up. I steadily returned his scrutiny and once he'd settled on an answer, he held out his hand.

'All right,' he said as I firmly grasped it, that increasingly familiar tingle shooting up my arm as our skin touched, 'you're on. Although why anyone would want to spend their holiday helping this place out is beyond me.'

Part of the reason I had agreed to help was because I wanted to see Wynmouth thrive. The little village wasn't quite the place I had always idolized but it was still wonderful, not that I could tell Sam that. And neither was I prepared to share the more personal reasons behind my desire to keep occupied.

He squeezed my hand a little tighter, obviously expecting a response.

'Let's just say getting away and switching off hasn't quite worked out,' I began.

'Getting away from what?'

'My job. I'm a bit of a workaholic and going cold turkey hasn't gone according to plan.'

'So, in helping me out, you'd be helping yourself?'

'Exactly.'

He seemed to accept that as a good enough reason and let go of my hand.

'All right,' he said, 'you come up with some ideas and we'll compare notes.'

'Excellent,' I smiled.

'But no bloody karaoke or Abba tribute band, all right?' he laughed.

I couldn't stop myself from laughing along with him.

'I tried that a couple of Christmases ago,' he grinned, 'and it was a total flop.'

Chapter 6

I was delighted that Sam had agreed to let me come up with some ideas to entertain the fine folk of Wynmouth, even though working with him was going to play havoc with my libido, but there was one thing capable of taking the edge off my enthusiasm for the venture.

Securing a longer stay in Crow's Nest Cottage was *exactly* what I had wanted, but the thought of breaking the news to Dad I could live without. I knew I wouldn't be able to get away with another text and a quick message via Joan but I was going to go all out and try not to worry about it for the next few days. I could leave my phone undisturbed in the cottage and immerse myself in the role of joint pub event organizer, safe in the knowledge that I now had plenty of time to work my way through Mum's diary at a healthier pace.

Sam and I had started working on a list of potential ideas straightaway and by the time the shops opened on Saturday morning I had added a few more. There were some things I knew he would never give the green light for, but I figured seeing the expression on his face when he read them would be great entertainment. For me, if no one else.

Wide awake as if my usual early alarm had called me and with Sophie's welcome pack beginning to look a little depleted (which was a big surprise, given the amount it had included), I decided to walk to the shops and restock. I might have been keen to wind down and relax a bit, but my body clock was going to take considerably longer to reset.

I joined the queue in the fishmonger's, craning my neck to get a look at what was on offer and feeling right at home among the other customers with the reusable shopping bag Sophie had left in the cottage tucked under my arm. It might not have been my usual shopping experience – a last-minute, end of the day rush around the Tesco Metro – but it felt good to be giving some thought to what I wanted to eat and plan out a meal or two, rather than grabbing whatever was closest and would be ready after two minutes in the microwave and by the time I'd uncorked a bottle of wine.

'What can I get you?' asked the woman behind the counter, when it was finally my turn to be served.

I seemed to have been waiting for ages. Everyone in front of me had taken so long, what with the chatting and catching up on each other's news, but no one seemed to mind. There was no self-service aisle here and there were no impatient eye rolls or foot taps either.

'These crabs,' I said, pointing at one of the things on the

ice bed that I could definitely identify. 'Do I have to do anything with them before I eat them?'

'No, my love,' said the woman. 'They're dressed already, so they're ready to eat. Lovely in a salad.'

They were also pretty good in Sophie's curry I remembered.

'I'll have one of those then, please.'

The woman quickly wrapped it and put it on the counter and I looked at the rest of the array that was on offer. I wasn't sure I wanted anything else, for a start I wouldn't have a clue what to do with half it, but then I spotted the cockles tucked to one side.

'And some cockles, please,' I smiled, remembering how my parents used to recoil as I munched my way through them.

There was something moreish about that salty, slightly grainy texture that I had always found irresistible, especially when splashed with vinegar.

'How many?'

'Oh,' I said, 'I'm not sure.'

There were some old-fashioned pint glasses sitting next to them.

'Half a pint?' The woman suggested.

That sounded like quite a lot, but then I did like them.

'Yes, please,' I said, 'and I better have a bottle of vinegar too.' I added, having spotted the condiments on the shelf behind her.

'Wonderful,' she grinned. 'You can't beat them with a drop of vinegar.'

I fondly recalled the little polystyrene pots and wooden forks I used to spear them with and smiled back.

'Are you here on your holidays?' she asked.

'Yes,' I said, pulling out my purse. 'I'm renting Crow's Nest Cottage next to the pub.'

'It's a bit quiet around here,' she said, 'but ideal if you're looking for a peaceful sort of getaway.'

'It is,' I agreed. 'Although,' I added, throwing caution to the wind, 'according to the landlord at the Smuggler's, it might not be all that quiet next weekend.'

'Oh?'

'Apparently, there's going to be some sort of entertainment in the pub.' I elaborated but didn't go as far as to explain my involvement in it all.

The woman looked unsure.

'Oh, I doubt that,' she said.

'That's what he told me,' I said.

'Are you sure?'

'Positive,' I nodded.

'And it was Sam you spoke to?'

'That's right,' I confirmed. 'The chap who owns the pub and cottage.'

'The fella with the gorgeous green eyes?' she questioned, just to be sure.

'Oh yes,' I said, sighing without meaning to, 'that's definitely him.'

'Well, I never,' said the lad who was serving next to her. 'That's a bit of a turn-up for the books, isn't it, Mum?'

'That it is,' she frowned. 'The Smuggler's isn't known around here for offering anything much beyond a decent pint and the board game club. Sam keeps himself to himself as a rule. Always says he's got no interest in putting on anything extra.'

Given what Sam had told me, I knew the situation was more about finding the time to do things properly than guarding what little privacy his position afforded or lack of interest on his part. I wondered if everyone in the village had got the wrong end of the stick and, if so, why had he let them?

'I wonder what it's going to be?' mused the lad. 'It would great to have a night out in the village. It's a drag having to drive further afield. It always means someone can't have a drink . . .'

His excitement tailed off as his mum looked at him sharply, but she didn't say anything. He hastily turned his attention back to the queue which now almost reached the door. I got the impression that he'd said something out of turn, but I wasn't about to find out what.

'So, you think it sounds like a good idea then?' I asked them both. 'You'd go, would you?'

'Absolutely,' said the lad. 'And I wouldn't be the only one. As I said before, a night out on our home turf would be great.'

I paid for my purchases and then moved on to the grocery store next door where I stocked up on fresh salad, local fruit and large speckled eggs laid by the shop owner's very own hens. It was amazing to think that everything I had in my bag had been either caught, harvested or produced practically within walking distance from where I stood.

There were no plastic-wrapped beans or strawberries bearing the usual 'produce of Kenya' or 'imported from Spain' labels. Granted, the range of food on offer was a little limited and nowhere near as exotic as I would find in the supermarket, but it was incredibly fresh and I couldn't wait to try it all.

Even the meat in the butcher's was Norfolk born and bred.

'So, you're as keen as the chap in the fishmonger's,' I said, aiming for definite clarification as I added some sausages, bacon and chicken to my rapidly filling bag. 'You think an evening of entertainment in the pub's a good idea too?'

'Absolutely,' agreed the woman who served me. 'People around here have been crying out for something. We all support the pub of course. It's a great place to meet, but it would be even better if there was a reason to go there other than to have a drink or play Scrabble.'

I mulled over what everyone had told me as I walked back to the cottage, greedily picking at the cockles as I went. When I had broached the subject with the grocery store staff even a couple of the customers had joined in and they were all enthusiastic.

It was a shame that Sam hadn't picked up on what the locals wanted or asked for some help before making a joke out of asking me. I was certain any number of the friendly locals I had encountered would have been more than happy to lend a hand and he could have had things up and running far sooner. There was certainly enough interest to make it worth his while and this weekend, if push came to shove, I could even get behind the bar myself. I might not have pulled a pint since my days working in the union bar at university but I was certain the knack would come back soon enough.

By the time I had unpacked my shopping and had a coffee, along with another handful of cockles, the sun was shining strongly overhead and I decided to walk down to the café to see Sophie, taking my list with me. The pull of the rockpools and a trip down memory lane to the beach huts was still a draw, but with an extra four weeks now at my disposal, I was free to take my time.

I was out of the door and along the path before I realized I hadn't even thought about switching on my phone. Perhaps things were looking up, in that department at least.

'Good morning, Tess!' Sophie called when she spotted me.

She was setting up the brightly striped parasols over the picnic tables and I could see a big tub containing a stack of buckets and nets for sale just outside the door. She hadn't put those out on my first visit, probably because of the weather. They would be exactly what I needed when I decided it was the right time to explore the rockpools again.

'Morning,' I waved back, shielding my eyes from the brightness of the sun. 'It's going to be a great day.'

'And hopefully a busy one,' Sophie nodded, pointing to the beach where some families were already setting up, hammering their windbreaks in place and spreading out colourful towels to lay on.

They were clearly keen to nab what they thought were the prime spots, but truth be told, the beach on either side of the village was so beautiful, every spot was a good one. There were fewer rockpools on this side, but given what the guy with the binoculars told me the day before, there was more bird life here. It was win–win wherever you went in Wynmouth.

Sophie waited for me to reach her and we walked into the café together.

'I spoke to my daughter last night,' she told me. 'She says she'd love to meet the woman who has finally convinced her mother to get online.'

I laughed.

'You didn't take that much persuading,' I reminded her.

'Well, don't tell her that if you get the chance,' said Sophie. 'She already thinks you're some kind of wonderful, so I would go with that if I were you.'

I rather liked the sound of Sophie's daughter.

'I hope I will get to meet her,' I said. 'Is she likely to put in appearance anytime soon?'

'Oh yes,' Sophie nodded. 'Although she hasn't told me exactly when she's coming home.'

'She lives in Wynmouth too?'

'That's right. She's off on her travels at the moment, trying to fathom out ideas for her own business. She's just flown back from Jamaica.'

'Oh wow,' I said, remembering the beautiful images of the Caribbean I had looked at while trying to find my alternative holiday spot before Sam mailed to tell me I could book the cottage. 'Has she been on holiday?'

'She's been visiting family,' Sophie explained. 'Getting to know her cousins and now she's with Blossom, the aunt I mentioned with the curried crab recipe. She owns a bakery in Norwich so my girl isn't too far away now. I'm hoping she'll be home soon. I've missed her.'

'It sounds to me like you have a very entrepreneurial family, Sophie.'

'We're a resourceful bunch of women, that's for sure,' she laughed. 'And all pretty gifted in the culinary department – if it isn't too conceited to say so.'

Given how delicious my curried crab and rum-laced hot chocolate had been, I didn't think that was conceited at all. It was more a statement of fact.

'But what about you, Tess?'

'Me?'

'Yes,' she said, 'what are your family like?'

I didn't really know what to say. My current experience of family life wasn't anywhere near as comforting as hers.

'Well,' I said, dropping my gaze. 'I haven't got much. No aunts or cousins or anyone. It's just me and Dad really.'

'No Mum?'

'No,' I said, my voice catching, 'she died a while ago.'

'I'm very sorry to hear that,' said Sophie, reaching across the counter and giving my hands a squeeze.

I nodded and blinked hard.

'Please don't be nice to me, Sophie,' I said, sitting up

straighter and trying to smile. 'Otherwise you might find me crying all over you.'

During the last few months I had learned, mostly thanks to my punishing work schedule, how to keep a tight lid on my emotions, but Sophie's warmth and genuine kindness felt capable of undoing my efforts in moments. Her daughter was a very lucky woman to have such an inspirational and kind-hearted mum by her side.

'And would that matter?' Sophie whispered.

I shrugged.

'Sometimes having a good cry can be the best medicine in the world,' she said softly. 'Personally, I think a good howl is very much underrated, whether it's needed to purge you of sadness or temper, or even both.'

'But it's not necessarily good for business,' I said, nodding to the window where I could see some customers walking towards the café. 'I wouldn't want to scare anyone off.'

Sophie handed me a tissue from a packet in the large pocket on the front of her dress.

'And what about your father?' she asked, sounding tentative. 'Are you close to him?'

I had been, or at least I thought had, but given his reaction to my admittance that I was struggling at work and the subsequent discovery of Mum's diary, I now didn't feel close to him at all.

'I used to be,' I said, blowing my nose, 'but not anymore.'

Sophie nodded as the bell above the door rang out and I was grateful for the interruption.

'We work together in the family business,' I told her huskily, 'but I'm not sure we will for much longer. It's all rather complicated.'

While Sophie served the first customers of the day, I took a moment to regain my composure and look at the changes she had already made. The menu board was now completely re-designed with the 'dish of the day' taking up minimal space and the rest divided into sections where customers could list the things they had spotted on the beach, in the rockpools and in the skies as well as highlighting the weather and tide times. There was also another board hanging above the counter with a wi-fi code chalked on to it.

'It's great that you have wi-fi in here, Sophie,' I said while she was preparing drinks. 'You didn't mention it yesterday.'

'It's not always the strongest of signals, but I've had it a while,' she told me. 'It was another of my daughter's ideas. I've only put the board up because she nagged me about it on the phone last night. Personally, I wasn't keen. I want folk to come here and forget about their phones and tablets, for a little while at least.'

She had a point, but I still found myself wishing that I had my phone with me so I could have googled some extra ideas to present to Sam. As much as Sophie hated the thought, having limited or no access to the internet did make modern life pretty difficult.

'I completely understand,' I told her.

'I thought you might,' she nodded. 'I've never seen you glued to a device.'

It wasn't the time to explain why.

'But even so, Sophie, your daughter is right. It's what folk expect these days and when you get your Instagram and Twitter accounts up and running it will definitely play to your advantage.'

'How do you mean?'

'Well,' I said, 'if you have a hashtag identifying the café and you ask your customers to add it to any photos they upload, this place will be famous in no time.'

'I have no idea what a tag thingy is, or what you're talking about really,' she chuckled, 'but I'm sure Hope will be thrilled you're on board. The pair of you are going to hit it off in no time.'

'Hope?'

'Yes,' said Sophie, as she loaded the drinks on to a tray, 'that's my daughter's name.'

I worked on my list while Sophie served up snacks and drinks to a slow but steady flow of customers throughout the morning and then pushed it aside to eat the bacon and avocado toasted sandwich she set down next to me.

'Lunch,' she beamed. 'On the house, as a thank you for helping me think about all the ways I can make the café more popular.'

'You are most welcome,' I told her, 'and thank you,' I added as I took the first delectable bite.

The sandwich was divine and Sophie's freshly made, secret recipe salsa which accompanied it, gave it an extra kick which cut through the saltiness of the locally reared bacon and enlivened the avocado perfectly. She had a real talent when it came to clever flavour combinations and I was looking forward to her new marketing strategy kicking in and more people finding Sophie's Sunshine Café – which was the name she had settled on – for themselves.

'I'm wondering if I should have an aquarium in here,' she said when she came to collect my empty plate, 'full of tropical fish. This place is such a contrast to what folk expect to find on the Norfolk coast, that I'm wondering if I should just run with the theme and take it to the next level.'

I could certainly confirm that it was different.

'The next level sounds like an excellent idea to me,' I agreed. 'Especially if you keep making curried crab. That whole fusion idea is fantastic.'

Sophie's beautiful dark eyes widened at my words and I wondered what other delights she was cooking up.

'Can I have a sheet of paper from your notebook, Tess?' she asked urgently.

'Of course,' I said, tearing a page out from the back.

'What is it that *you're* working on?' she asked, once she had finished frantically scribbling. 'You've been beavering away all morning. Are you writing a book?'

'No,' I laughed, 'it's for Sam, actually.'

'Sam?'

'Yes,' I said. 'He's agreed to let me come up with some ideas for an evening of entertainment in the pub over the bank holiday weekend. We're working on it together.'

'Seriously?' Sophie gasped.

'Seriously,' I laughed.

'But won't you be gone before then?'

'Sam has said I can rent the cottage for a few extra weeks,' I told her, 'now I'm staying in Wynmouth until the end of June.'

'My goodness,' she beamed. 'That's wonderful news, but I have to say, I'm a little shocked.'

'Shocked?'

'Yes,' she nodded. 'Sam was determined the cottage was coming off the holiday market. Whatever did you say to make him change his mind?'

'Nothing really,' I told her, my cheeks starting to burn. 'I didn't say anything.'

'And now he's letting you help out at the pub too . . .'

I hoped she didn't think I'd set my sights on the friendly local landlord. George's loaded comment had already suggested that he had ideas in that direction and I didn't want Sophie joining in too.

'Anyway,' she thankfully carried on, 'what have you got on your list so far?'

'Not as much as I'd like,' I said, happily grasping the change in subject. 'To be honest, and I know you'll hate me for it, but I would have loved to do an online search to firm up some of these suggestions. Unfortunately, I haven't got my phone on me.'

'Well, I suppose I can help you there,' said Sophie, ducking down under the counter and then popping back up clasping a brightly coloured patchworked quilted bag. 'You can use my laptop if you like. It would be good for it to get an airing before Hope comes back and tells me off for not using it.'

'Goodness me, Sophie,' I laughed. 'You have a solution for everything, don't you?'

'More often than not,' she smiled warmly. 'More often than not.'

Chapter 7

Sophie very kindly said I could take the laptop back to the cottage if I wanted to and, even though the offer was both generous and thoughtful (classic Sophie traits, I was beginning to realize), I decided not to accept. I had really had to force myself to stay focused during the afternoon in the café, and I had still struggled to eschew my inbox and avoid social media. Left alone with the device overnight, I didn't think I could trust myself not to give in to temptation. My phone was proving difficult enough.

'We'll have to get our heads together and have a look at these plans of yours,' said Sam as he served my dinner on Sunday. 'Sophie tells me you've got a notebook full of ideas.'

I looked over to the bar and Sophie gave me an encouraging thumbs up. I hadn't been able to resist heading back to the pub after I'd seen the board advertising the traditional roast during my walk and I was now sitting at a table with

George and his sister, Gladys, poised to tuck into the biggest and crispiest Yorkshire puddings I'd ever seen.

'Oh, she mentioned that, did she?' I said, looking up at him and completely forgetting my former conviction to stop admiring his eyes.

'Just once or twice,' he laughed.

'And even if Sophie, hadn't,' said Gladys, reaching for the horseradish, 'he still would have known you'd taken his offer to help out seriously, wouldn't you, Sam?'

'I'll say,' Sam confirmed. 'Somehow word has got around,' he explained, 'and half the village now knows that you're the one who has talked me into doing something.'

'You said she'd nagged you into it a minute ago,' cut in George.

'Is that right?' I laughed.

'Maybe,' Sam smiled, turning a little pink. 'I take it you happened to mention something about it on your shopping trip yesterday, Tess?'

Now it was my turn to colour.

'I did,' I admitted, 'but I didn't say anything to suggest that I was involved in the organization.'

'That's village life for you,' Gladys beamed.

'I was simply trying to work out if anyone would come,' I went on.

'And?' Sam asked.

'You'll be inundated,' I told him. 'Everyone was thrilled with the idea.'

I didn't mention that they were also surprised.

'And you already know that really, don't you, Sam?' joined in George as he surreptitiously fed Skipper a morsel of beef under the table, 'because you've had folk coming in all morning asking if they need to buy tickets.'

Sam nodded.

'We'll talk later,' he said to me, 'after I've finished the lunches.'

'So,' I grinned, once the rush had died down and Sam had a couple of minutes to spare, 'that's a definite no to the selection of seaside shots party games then.'

It wasn't the first thing he had vetoed. So far, he'd managed to blackball all the things I had added purely for my own amusement.

'Absolutely,' he said firmly. 'We don't want folk to drink too much.'

That had to be the oddest thing I'd ever heard a pub landlord say.

'May I just remind you,' I said, pointing to the bar and the range of optics behind it, 'that this is a pub and people do actually come here to drink alcohol.'

'I know,' he shrugged, offering no further explanation for his strange comment.

'Okay then,' I sighed once we had worked our way through all of his ideas as well as mine. 'You really are determined that traditional is the right way to go, aren't you?'

What he had in mind sounded a bit staid to me, but then he knew the locals better than I did, even if he hadn't noticed that they were crying out for some form of entertainment.

'Yes,' he said, 'definitely. This is just the sort of thing everyone will be hoping for.'

If it was up to me, that would have been the perfect reason to give them something a bit different. I was just about to say as much when Sam leant back in his chair and gave the biggest yawn and I changed my mind. He looked absolutely exhausted.

'You know what,' I said tapping my pencil on the list, 'I think you're right. This has the potential to be a really great night.'

'Even though it's nothing like the Ibiza-style extravaganza you were hoping for?' Sam asked, leaning forward again.

'Even though it's not quite what I imagined when you first asked if I'd help,' I conceded, 'I do think you're on the right track. What we've got here will suit this place perfectly.'

'Now all the pair of you have to do,' said Sophie, as she carried over a tray of coffee, 'is organize it. Do you think you can pull it off in time?'

Sam picked up the notepad and let out a long breath.

'Of course,' I said forthrightly. 'No problem.'

'You sound very sure about that,' he said, putting the pad back down and stretching his arms above his head, treating me to a tantalizing glimpse of torso in the process.

'That's because I am,' I swallowed, my mouth had suddenly gone dry. 'We can do this standing on our heads.'

'We've literally got just five days,' Sam reminded me, holding up his right hand to further stress the point. He sounded nowhere near as confident as I hoped he would.

'And now everyone knows that something's going to be happening, we can't let them down.'

'We won't let anyone down,' I told him. 'Just you wait and see.'

As it turned out, given the nature of what Sam had agreed to, there really wasn't all that much to arrange. The difficulty for him came down to timing so, having noticed how tired he was on Sunday, I took over most of the organization and simply asked for his approval as we went along.

My body clock was still firmly fixed in work mode so getting up bright and early every day was no problem, especially as I was determined to make sure everything ran like clockwork and exceeded expectations. There might not have been all that much to do when I got down to it, but the project ensured my mind tracked back to thoughts of my phone and my father's reaction to my disappearance far less than it had when I first arrived. I was resisting the temptation of Mum's diary too. I hadn't forgotten about any of it, I was just putting it all on hold for a little while longer.

By Tuesday lunchtime everything was booked and I had even designed a poster on Sophie's laptop. I'd printed off plenty too so I could pin them up around the village.

'Does Sam know about this?' Sophie gasped, as she pointed out the name of the group listed, rather grandly, as headlining the event.

'Not yet,' I grinned, feeling well pleased with my efforts. 'He knew there were a few names in the hat because he'd approved them, but I haven't told him who I managed to get. These guys are a big deal, right?'

'Just a bit!' she exclaimed, reading the poster again.

'That's what I thought when I searched for them on your laptop.' I told her. 'I didn't want to get Sam's hopes up but they're definitely coming. I can't wait to see his face when he reads this.'

'You've certainly delivered, Tess.' Sophie said admiringly. 'I know Sam cajoled you into helping at first, but you really seem to know your stuff. Is this what you do in real life, when you're not on holiday?'

'Oh no,' I told her. 'This is purely a one-off.'

There was no denying that my marketing degree and work skills had helped, but organizing this event had been so much fun it bore absolutely no resemblance to my real job, the one that I had become so disheartened with.

'Well,' Sophie said, handing back the poster, 'perhaps you should consider a change of career, because you seem to have a knack for this.'

'Yes,' I said, 'maybe I should.'

I could imagine *exactly* what my father would have to say about that. Even though I was doing my best not to think about him he was still, annoyingly and in spite of my best efforts, popping into my head. I hoped Chris was doing a good enough job to make up for my absence from the office.

'Anyway,' I said, gathering up the posters. 'I had better get these to the pub. I can't put them up without the boss's approval, can I?'

'Absolutely not,' Sophie winked. 'But you might as well leave a couple here with me as I'm certain he'll love them.'

I slipped off my sandals and walked back to the village along the sand. Considering I had been craving the beach, I hadn't spent all that long on it. I had been taking walks every evening before bed, but I still hadn't ventured over to the beach huts or to the rockpools. Thankfully, my extended stay meant there would be plenty of time for all that after the weekend.

'The Sea Dogs!' Sam shouted, making me jump. 'You've actually managed to get *the* Sea Dogs?'

He had looked a little nervous when I first handed him the poster, but the more he had read, the wider his eyes had got and now he was looking completely astounded.

'Yep,' I nodded, 'and before you start going off on one about not being able to afford them, the event they should have been headlining was cancelled at the last minute so they're coming here for a reduced fee that easily fits your budget.'

It had taken some serious negotiating on my part, but nonetheless their final terms had been generous and, having researched them and realized just what a big deal the sea-shanty singing group were, I had wasted no time in snapping them up. I was more than confident that they would be such a draw that the evening's takings would easily balance the books.

'I can't believe it,' Sam breathed. 'I can't believe we've

organized all of this in just a few days. You've organized it, I mean.'

'Joint effort,' I shrugged, picking up another poster, 'you were the one with the best ideas and this is what you wanted, isn't it? You said traditional, so that's what you've got, along with a couple of extras.'

The weather forecast was looking good so I had also been able to plan a few things to happen in the beer garden which was just behind the pub.

'I have no idea how you've managed to get this lot at these prices.' Sam said, now looking at the handwritten fishmonger's and butcher's bills.

'Like I've already mentioned, everyone was so keen for this to happen that they were happy to shave their profits. I daresay it will be a one-off though, so you need to make the most of it.'

Even though the budget Sam had given me was tight, I had managed to make it work without too much pleading. Such was their fondness for him, the business owners had been extraordinarily generous.

'I'm going to have to find staff though,' he frowned, chewing his lip. 'If this is going to be as well attended as you're suggesting, then I'll need more hands to help out.'

'Don't worry about that either,' I told him. 'I've been inundated with offers and all on a voluntary basis.'

The butcher was going to set up his barbecue in the beer garden, which was also where a bar skittles tournament was going to be happening, and Sophie was going to make an extra-special seafood chowder in the kitchen which would need nothing more than the occasional stir to keep it warm and ready to serve.

Sam was looking a little emotional by the time I had finished explaining how everyone had been so willing to help out.

'I didn't even have to ask,' I told him, 'everyone just offered to pitch in.'

'I can't believe it,' he said huskily, for what must have been the hundredth time.

I had no idea why he was so surprised that everyone wanted to help. Not only were they in dire need of some pub fun, but they all felt a genuine affection for him and clearly wanted the event to succeed. It amazed me that Sam didn't realize just how popular he was.

'And this from George,' he went on, 'what a way to end the evening. I knew he was collecting local stories for a book he's planning to write, but to have him sit and tell them will be wonderful. A real old-school tradition.'

George had come to the cottage on Sunday evening and explained that he had spent much of his time in Wynmouth collecting home-grown tales – legends, fables, ghost stories and the like – and that if I needed something to fill in any gaps on the schedule, then he would happily tell a few to anyone who would want to listen. Personally, I couldn't think of a more atmospheric way to end the evening and had signed him up there and then.

'So,' I said, my eyes tracking back to Sam, 'you're

happy with everything? No regrets about letting the latest Wynmouth arrival boss you about?'

Sam started to laugh.

'More than happy,' he said, ducking his head. 'And I'm sorry if I came across as a bit judgemental about how you want to spend your holiday. I know myself how difficult it can be to switch off and you said yourself, you're a workaholic so it must be even harder for you.'

Then was not the moment to explain that I had come to Wynmouth with more on my mind that simply switching off from work.

'I just hope doing all this hasn't taken up too much of your time,' Sam added.

'Not at all,' I said, meaning every word. 'I've really enjoyed it and if the evening is even half the success I imagine it's going to be, then it will be a night to remember.'

Sam's eyes scanned the poster again.

'You're not wrong,' he agreed, his emotional moment now forgotten and his smile firmly back in place. 'You know, I can't believe that you've only been here a few days. It feels like so much longer to me. You seem so settled and at home.'

I felt my heart start to canter in my chest.

'Well,' I said, clearing my throat, 'it's impossible to feel anything but at home in Wynmouth, isn't it?'

Chapter 8

That Saturday morning, I held my breath as I pulled back the curtains, but I needn't have worried. The forecast had been right; the weather was looking cheerfully wonderful and I couldn't wait for the day to get started.

Practically from the moment the posters had been put up around the village, Sam had been inundated with folk telling him how much they were looking forward to the evening. In fact, it had proved itself to be so eagerly anticipated that he had decided to kick everything off even earlier than we had initially arranged and that was why I was so relieved about the weather.

Wynmouth was, surprisingly, a hotbed of young musical talent and Sam had agreed to let two star turns sing in the beer garden during the afternoon. They were both solo artists so there was no complicated setting up or acoustic arrangements to worry about and their presence would warm the atmosphere up nicely for the main event in the evening.

They were both happy to sing for nothing – aside from their supper – and said the experience and exposure would be wonderful as they were trying to get established locally.

'How's everything shaping up?' I asked Sam, as I crossed the pub threshold extra early to help set up and run through the lists we had devised to ensure nothing was forgotten.

'Very well,' said Sam, puffing out his cheeks. 'Running like clockwork so far.'

'Well, you needn't sound so surprised,' I laughed.

His tone implied he couldn't believe his luck.

'This is, for the most part, a Tess Tyler production,' I reminded him. 'Everything *will* run like clockwork.'

'Are you going to let me take the credit for anything?'

'Only if something goes wrong,' I said, with a grin. 'Which it won't, so . . . no.'

Sam stuck out his tongue and I laughed again. It might not have been what I had planned to do when I first booked my secret seaside escape, but I was thoroughly enjoying myself and having a lot of fun. Fun in my life had been rather thin on the ground of late, so it was very much appreciated, even if I was still, every now and again, having to force myself to stop thinking about family, phones and the fact that I'd run away.

'Coming through,' said a voice behind me, and I quickly moved out of the way. 'I've got the surf here,' said Toby, the lad from the fishmonger's, 'and Mike's right behind me with the turf. Where do you want it all, Sam?'

I left the menfolk organizing the eats and mulling over

the best spot in the garden for the barbecue – what was it with men, meat and fire? – and began clearing the area next to the fireplace where the Sea Dogs would be setting up. If the evening turned chilly, Sam had said he would light the fire, but I reckoned there were going to be so many bodies crammed into the place we wouldn't need to worry about providing any extra warmth. Consequently, I dotted a few extra candles in jars around the hearth and redistributed the lanterns, both of which would provide a cosy atmosphere without throwing out too much heat when the light began to fade.

'You were right about the fire,' said Sam, once the doors were open and the place began to steadily fill ahead of the early musical performances. 'If folk keep turning up at this rate, there won't even be standing room by tonight.'

'I told you this was a good idea,' I smiled back at him. 'Those extra customers you said you wouldn't mind drawing in have just been waiting for a reason, aside from your wonderfully kept beer, to come along.'

'I think you might be right,' he said, looking about him.

'Of course, I am.'

Sam rolled his eyes and, spotting the arrival of the first, slightly nervous-looking musician, rushed off to help him carry in his equipment. The poor lad looked even greener around the gills when he realized how many people were waiting to hear him, but I had a feeling he'd feel more confident once he'd sung his first few lines.

'How are things in here?' I asked Sophie when I popped

through to the kitchen to check she had everything she needed. 'It smells divine!'

For the first time ever, I thought she looked a little flustered, or at least she seemed to appear so when she spotted me.

'Tess,' she said, her eyes trained on the huge pan she was stirring, 'I didn't hear you come in.'

'Is everything all right?'

'Yes,' she said, although I wasn't sure I believed her. 'Everything's fine.'

'And you've got everything you need.'

'I think so.'

I waited for her to carry on, but she didn't and I was just about to ask her again if all was well, when Sam poked his head around the door.

'Tess, can you spare a sec?' he asked. 'I could do with a hand behind the bar.'

Now it was my turn to look flustered. Earlier in the week, I had told Sam about my stint working in the union bar at university and he had made me pull or pint or two to see if my skills were still up to scratch, just in case he ended up needing them. They hadn't been to begin with, but as with most things in life, the more I'd practised, the better I'd got and Sam had said it was good to know that I would be able to help the others keep up if the evening got as busy as he thought it might.

'What, already?' I squeaked, following him out of the kitchen.

I hadn't scheduled the extra bar support to show up until later.

'Already,' he said, pointing at the quickly forming queue.

It was all hands on deck after that. There were a couple of brief lulls while the young singers were giving a rendition of their rather accomplished repertoires, but the till rang long and loud all afternoon and the evening looked set to be an even bigger draw.

'Thank you so much for this, Sam,' said Harry, the lad who had ended the afternoon together with Delilah, the other performer, singing a moving acoustic version of an Ed Sheeran track.

I had thought there was a spark between the pair and having had the opportunity to sing together now, they looked like starstruck lovers. It was really very sweet.

'My pleasure,' said Sam, handing an envelope to each of them. 'This isn't much,' he said, 'but you've both done such a great job, and I know you said you just wanted the experience of singing in front of a crowd, but you deserve to be paid after such fantastic performances.'

They looked delighted.

'And I'd love you both to come back,' Sam carried on. 'If you'd like to?'

They nodded in perfect synchronicity, looking more dumbstruck than loved up.

'Tess and I will be having a talk about how the evening has gone at some point, so come back next week and I'll let you know what we've decided.'

'Wow,' grinned Delilah, her cat-like features lighting up. 'Thanks, Sam.'

They wandered off looking far happier than they had when they arrived and now I was the dumbstruck one.

'That is all right, isn't it?' Sam asked, turning his green gaze back on me. 'I probably shouldn't have just assumed, but it would be great if you could spare the time to talk it all through with me.'

'Of course,' I said. I'd felt rather a thrill when I heard him refer to the two of us as the decision-makers about potential future events, even though I wasn't going to be around all that long to see them happening. 'I'm more than happy to do that.'

'Great,' he said, squeezing my arm and making my heart race again as he held my gaze. 'You know, Tess . . .'

He stopped and let out a long breath. I could tell he was gearing up to say something really important, and not about the pub either.

'What?' I nudged, 'what do I know?'

'Well . . .' he began.

'Sam!'

He closed his eyes and took another breath. I was desperate to find out what he was trying to say, but he wasn't going to get the chance to enlighten me.

'Sam!'

'Yeah!' he called back, 'I'm coming now.'

The Sea Dogs were everything you could hope for from a traditional sea-shanty group. From the spotted neckerchief to the abundance of beards and big boots, they fitted my expectations to a T. They even had the obligatory scruffy terrier, wearing his own little necktie, who stalked in with an air of superiority and sent Skipper's hackles soaring. The pair took their time sizing each other up and then, thankfully, decided to ignore each other completely, assuming owner-ship of opposite ends of the room.

'Here,' said Sophie, popping up behind the bar with a tray, just before the group began to play, 'stop and have something to eat, Tess. You've been on the go for hours. I'll take over here if anyone needs serving.'

'Oh, thank you, Sophie,' I said gratefully. We had almost sold out of food and I hadn't had so much as a bite. 'I thought I was going to miss out.'

'Not a chance,' she smiled. I was pleased to see her looking and sounding more like her usual self again. 'I told Mike to save you a couple of these.'

'What exactly are these?' I asked, looking at the siz-zling shells.

'Fresh cooked scallops and chorizo,' Sophie said proudly. 'There's a little chilli too and some honey to balance out the heat.'

They looked fantastic served in the scallop shells and I hungrily dived in, dipping buttered crusty bread into the spicy sauce.

'Oh Sophie,' I groaned, after the first delectable mouthful, 'they're orgasmic.'

'Well,' she laughed. 'I don't know about that, but we thought they were pretty good.'

'What's orgasmic?' Sam asked throatily, leaning over my shoulder.

'These scallops,' I said, blushing. I hadn't realized he was behind me.

He reached around and pinched one of the shells, dithering as the heat scolded the ends of his fingers. I spun around just in time to see him pop it into his mouth.

'Hey,' I protested, as he looked down at me and raised his eyebrows, his mouth working appreciatively. 'Hands off, they're mine.'

I wasn't sure if his pupils had widened because of the food-heaven ecstasy the combination of flavours had unleashed or because of our close proximity.

'You're right, Tess,' he smiled, licking his lips, 'utterly orgasmic.'

'Sam,' said Sophie, clearing her throat, 'I think the musicians are waiting for you to introduce them.'

'On my way,' he said, his eyes never leaving my face.

Once I had cooled down a bit and finished the divine scallop dinner, I had time to relax and listen to the songs, even joining in with a chorus of one or two. The shanties were a stimulating mix, telling tales of high seas, lost loves and bewitching mermaids. They were rousing, stirring and all in perfect keeping with the pub ambience. Sam had been right to take the traditional route on his first foray into offering entertainment and George's atmospheric storytelling was the perfect wrap-up to the night.

I listened to the first couple of tall tales and then began

quietly helping with the clear-up. Sticking to the shadows, I had the chance to watch the audience as well as listen to George. The rapt expressions and the way everyone jumped in unison when he thumped his glass down on the table, proved that he had them all in the palm of his hand. George was a truly great storyteller and I hoped I would get the chance to hear him again before I had to leave the village, which then annoyingly reminded me that I would have to tell Dad about my change of plans tomorrow. A task I was definitely not looking forward to.

It took a while for everyone to leave and it was well after midnight by the time the Sea Dogs had packed their van and driven off into the night and the rest of the volunteers had drifted away to their beds.

Sam locked the door after making sure Sophie had an escort to walk her home (not that Wynmouth was a danger-ous place in any sense, but George's ghostly tales had got us all a little spooked), and leant heavily against it.

'Well now,' I said, stifling a yawn as I gave the bar one last wipe down and hung the cloth over the pumps as I'd seen being done on the television, 'I think that could be called a roaring success, wouldn't you agree, landlord?'

'It was amazing,' said Sam. 'Absolutely brilliant.'

'So,' I said, 'just remind me again, why you haven't been doing things like this before?'

'I told you,' he said, 'I just haven't had the time to organize something like this properly.'

Had he asked for help before, that wouldn't have been an

114

issue, but I didn't say as much because I was pretty certain he'd worked it out for himself now.

'And everyone's mightily impressed with you, Tess.'

'Are they?'

'Oh yes,' he smiled. 'They all know how you stepped up when I asked and Sophie has been telling them all about the suggestions you've made to improve the café too.'

I hoped I hadn't made a mistake in sticking my head above the parapet. I had been planning a quiet holiday originally, where no one took much notice of me. If Dad tried to track me down and thought Wynmouth might be a good place to look, he wouldn't have to make many enquiries before he found me, would he?

'They weren't really my suggestions,' I modestly reminded Sam, pushing thoughts of Dad to the sidelines again. 'From what Sophie said, her daughter has been suggesting most of them for far longer than I have. It's just for some reason that she decided to take them on board when I came along.'

'Well,' said Sam, coming to join me behind the bar and pulling me in for a hug I hadn't seen coming or had time to for prepare for but still very much enjoyed, 'you can't deny that tonight has been down to you, can you?'

'Of course, I can,' I said, pulling away a little so I could look up at him. 'This has been a joint effort right from the start.'

Sam looked doubtful.

'You were just like Sophie,' I insisted. 'All you needed was a little nudge in the right direction to get the ball rolling.'

Sam laughed, the sound resonating through his chest and into mine.

'And you,' he said, 'in spite of the fact that you've only been in the village for five minutes, turned out to be the girl capable of administering that little nudge.'

His sultry tone made my knees buckle a bit. It was just as well he still had his arms around me.

'I suppose I did . . .'

The words died in my throat as I realized he was going to kiss me. I moistened my lips in anticipation and took a preparatory breath. He lowered his head and was so close I could almost feel his breath caressing my mouth.

'Are you still there, Sam?' someone suddenly shouted as they hammered on the pub door, and we sprang apart. 'I think I've left my keys behind!'

I lay in bed in the early hours, imagining the kiss that hadn't quite happened, and remembering how wonderful it had felt to be held. However, even though Sam was gorgeousness personified and had got me all stirred up, with my sensible hat on, the one that wasn't fuelled by my sex drive, I knew it was probably just as well that nothing had happened. I hadn't come to Wynmouth looking for a love affair. My life was already complicated enough.

I rolled on to my side, my ears trained to the sound of the waves as they gently broke upon the beach, and I felt sleep start to take me. Even though I was relieved Sam and I had been interrupted earlier, I couldn't seem to stop my head playing out what might have happened had someone not forgotten their keys . . .

'Morning!' I cheerily shouted, announcing my arrival, as I slipped into the pub kitchen via the beer garden a few hours later. 'How's your head?'

Neither Sam or I had drunk a great deal; in fact, now I thought about it, I don't think I'd seen him with a beer in his hand all evening. In fact, I didn't think I'd ever seen him take a drink, other than the occasional fully loaded Coke, at all.

'Clear as a bell!' he called straight back. 'Not even a hint of a headache. How about you?'

'Oh, I'm all right,' I said happily, 'in fact . . .'

The words died on my lips as I walked through to the bar and found him framed in the doorway with his arms wrapped tightly around a young woman.

'Oh,' I choked, feeling a complete fool for just marching in. 'Sorry, I didn't realize. I didn't mean to interrupt.'

I turned back to the kitchen, wondering if he made a habit of going around hugging women and then reminded myself that I wasn't supposed to be bothered about things like that. The little fantasy I had indulged in as I nodded off had been just that, a fantasy. I stopped again, not sure what to do.

'I'll come back later,' I squeaked, my cheeks burning.

'No, don't go,' Sam insisted. 'You aren't interrupting. Come through. I want to introduce you to someone.'

My body temperature felt about a thousand degrees and I knew I was sweating. I must have looked a right mess.

'Tess,' Sam smiled, not noticing my discomfiture as he casually released the woman and steered her over to where I was standing, 'this is Sophie's daughter, Hope. Hope, this is Tess.'

'Oh, my god!' Hope squealed, as if I was the most exciting thing since sliced bread. 'It's so good to finally meet you!'

With her dark, heavily lashed eyes and thick curls, coupled with the way she reached out and pulled me in for a suffocating hug, she couldn't possibly have been anyone other than Sophie's daughter. I was rather taken aback to be greeted like a long-lost relative as opposed to a stranger, but I shouldn't have been surprised really.

'Mum has told me *so* much about you,' she beamed. 'I can't believe you've got her surfing the net. I've been trying forever! And now Sam tells me that last night you pulled off the most amazing evening Wynmouth has seen in years. I can't believe I missed that. Had I known I would have definitely made it back in time, but I was with my aunt Blossom in Norwich, and hadn't spoken to Mum all week—'

'Hope,' said Sam, catching her hand and giving it a squeeze, 'slow down. You're making me feel light-headed.'

'Sorry,' she laughed, taking her hand back and covering her mouth, 'I'm just so excited to be back! It feels so good to be home. I've got tonnes to tell you.'

She was off and running again and Sam looked at me over the top of her head and grinned. I was fast beginning to feel like I'd been steamrollered, but in a good way.

'Well,' said Sam, quickly butting in the next time Hope drew breath, 'you don't need to tell us *everything* you've been up to in the next three seconds, do you? We've got plenty of time to catch up, especially now Tess has extended her stay.'

I was surprised that he had included me in their party, but something told me I was going to be seeing a lot of Hope in the next few weeks.

'I'm so pleased you aren't rushing off,' she said to me. She sounded genuinely delighted. 'Now we'll really have a chance to get to know each other. I know Mum's very fond of you already.'

I was very fond of her too, but I didn't get the chance to say that.

'Shall I make us some coffee?' Sam suggested. 'We've got a couple of hours before I have to open and there's no clearing up left to do. You two could get to know each other a bit better now and we can talk about last night and what we're going to do next.'

'All right,' I accepted, even though I wasn't sure I wanted to be the third wheel or that he would have much of a chance to say anything if Hope carried on talking at the same speed. She certainly didn't need caffeine to get her fired up!

'Great,' said Sam.

He clearly didn't mind me sticking around, but I felt a little foolish. I had thought there had been this great spark between us, but I'd obviously read it all wrong. Sam definitely wouldn't have made a move on me knowing that his other half was on her way back to Wynmouth. He just wasn't the type to play the field. Was I so love-starved that I'd mistaken a simple friendly hug as a lead-in for something more? Thank goodness we had been interrupted. I could have ended up making a right fool of myself otherwise.

'What on earth's the matter with you two?' Hope frowned, sounding disappointed. 'Why are you talking about drinking coffee in here? Have you not seen the sunshine?' she added, pointing at the window.

'It is warm out,' I agreed.

'Exactly.' Hope beamed. 'Let's forget the coffee and take a breakfast picnic down to the beach instead.'

That sounded like a lovely idea to me. I had already been thinking that Sam didn't leave the pub anywhere near often enough. Relieved that I hadn't made a fool of myself with her boyfriend, I felt Hope and I had the potential to get along very well and, as I hadn't acted on my misinterpreted feelings, slipping Sam back into the friendship box shouldn't be any problem at all.

'What do you think, Tess?' Hope asked, turning her beautiful brown eyes back to me. 'Does that sound like a plan to you?'

'It sounds like a perfect plan,' I heartily agreed.

Sam groaned and shook his head.

'I'm going to be utterly outnumbered now the two of you have got your heads together, aren't I?' he moaned.

'Utterly!' Hope and I chorused in perfect synchronicity before bursting out laughing.

Chapter 9

It was a relief to discover that my concerns about taking on the role of third wheel in the presence of the recently reunited couple were completely unwarranted. There were no embarrassing quick kisses or lingering looks but, none the more for that, there had been no mistaking the intimacy behind the hug I had seen and I resolved not to take up too much of their time so they could be alone together before Sam had to open the pub.

'So,' said Hope as she handed out the croissants and cereal bars that she had commandeered from Sam's breakfast cupboard, 'tell me some more about last night. I can't believe you managed to book the Sea Dogs at such short notice.'

Between us, Sam and I filled in the details and Hope nodded along, for once quietly listening without interrupting with what I had already guessed was her own trademark brand of enthusiasm. I didn't think that she was rude when she butted in, she was just full of energy and eagerness. One of life's natural half-full types. I envied that a little.

'And I know I had my doubts about the evening turning a profit,' Sam said to me. He had aired his views quite vociferously once we had worked out the projected costs. 'But having cashed up, I've discovered I was wrong about that too.'

At this point, Hope couldn't help adding a few well-chosen words.

'Will you listen to this!' she giggled, clapping her hands together. 'You might not realize it, Tess, but getting this man to admit to being wrong about *anything* is no mean feat. Bravo my friend,' she winked mischievously at me, 'bravo.'

I couldn't help but laugh along. What fun this girl was!

'Yes,' said Sam, 'thank you, you two. As I said, the evening did turn a profit – not a huge one, as I decided to give Harry and Delilah a few quid, but it made a bit.'

'So, it didn't end up costing you, after all?' I said, firing his blunt words back at him.

'No,' he smiled. 'Well,' he added, rubbing his leg, 'nothing more than a bit of extra discomfort for having been on my feet for so long.'

I had completely forgotten about his leg. I hadn't factored in that he had spent more hours than usual standing up because I didn't realize it would make a difference.

'Foot,' Hope automatically corrected.

'What?' Sam frowned, still massaging his thigh.

'You were on your *foot* for so long,' she said. 'You haven't got feet.'

'Oh, very good,' said Sam, with a snort of laughter.

'So,' said Hope, turning her attention back to me, 'what's next?'

I reckoned the pair knew each other very well indeed to be able to talk like that.

'Next?' I frowned, tearing a croissant in half.

'Yes,' she nodded, 'don't tell me you haven't thought of anything. I bet you couldn't sleep last night for mulling over what form of entertainment to suggest next.'

I had nodded off thinking about a certain performance, but not the sort she was suggesting.

'Well,' I said, trying not to blush, 'I was wondering, what with it being the summer solstice soon, if it might be worth considering having some sort of celebration on the beach.'

Sam hadn't reckoned much to the idea of a jello-shot-fuelled beach-style party in the pub, but the celebration I had dreamt up for the solstice was a much quieter affair.

'Oh, yes,' Hope said keenly, 'I like the sound of that.'

Why was I not surprised? I think I could have suggested anything and she would have loved it.

'I thought,' I quickly carried on, in view of such a receptive audience, 'that as there would be longer to get organized, that maybe it could be a slightly bigger event, an amalgamation between the pub and the café. Perhaps with something set up here, right in the middle, to bring the two businesses together.'

'A traditional solstice beach party, with a Caribbean twist,' said Sam, looking off into the distance.

Now even he was getting into the swing of it.

'We could have cocktails,' Hope added. 'With little umbrellas on sticks.'

'And mocktails,' Sam countered.

'The curried crab your mum made last week was such a fascinating fusion, Hope,' I said. 'I bet she's got lots of other clever combo recipes tucked up her sleeve, hasn't she?'

'Absolutely,' Hope agreed.

'But what about the weather?' frowned Sam. 'That isn't guaranteed, is it?'

'Is anything in life guaranteed?' Hope laughed. 'We can't let a little thing like the weather stop us, Sam.'

'Worst-case scenario,' I said, quickly thinking of a back-up plan, 'if it rains, we'll have the first half of the party in the café and then walk to the pub via the beach, or start in the pub and walk to the café. There'll be some way around it, but it's the solstice we're talking about, remember? The sun wouldn't dare not to shine.'

'But isn't it traditional to watch the sunrise, not the sunset?' Sam frowned again. 'On the news they always show everyone at Stonehenge getting excited about the sunrise.'

'Well,' said Hope, 'folk can still come to do that, but I think Tess's right, a party in the evening as the sun is setting will be every bit as fun to celebrate, won't it?'

'Absolutely,' I agreed.

Truth be told, I didn't actually know all that much about the solstice, aside from the fact that it happened in June and that, after the bank holiday weekend, it seemed like the most logical date to pick for the next event.

'Right then,' said Hope, 'hands up who wants to have an evening summer solstice celebration on the beach?'

We all raised our hands.

'So, let's get on with organizing it then,' she announced.

Sam was quick to temper her keenness to forge ahead.

'Let me speak to the council on Monday,' he said. 'Just to make sure we won't be falling foul of any rules or regs we don't know about.'

'Oh yes,' Hope relented, sounding a little deflated. 'I suppose we should check.'

We sat quietly for a few minutes, finishing our breakfast and soaking up the sun.

'Right,' I sighed, as I stood up and brushed the sand off my legs, 'I'd better get going.'

It was time to leave the lovebirds in peace and face my fears.

'Got any plans?' Sam asked, squinting up at me.

'Just the one,' I told him. 'I need to make a quick phone call.'

At least I hoped it would be quick.

'I need to tell my boss why I won't be showing up at work for the next few weeks.'

'I had kind of assumed that you were self-employed,' said Sam, 'as you've decided to take so long off.'

'No,' I said, 'afraid not.'

'So, what is it that you do, Tess?' he asked.

'Obvious, isn't it?' Hope cut in. 'She's the ultimate party planner. She's most likely got A-listers across the globe clamouring for her attention. Am I right?'

'Ha,' I said, 'not quite.'

'Will your boss be pissed off that you aren't going back?' said Sam.

'Yes,' I breathed, 'just a bit.'

'In that case,' said Hope, 'you'd better come back to the pub later. You might need a pick-me-up.'

'Thanks,' I said. 'I'm probably going to need something.'

The dreaded call went every bit as badly as expected, helped in no small part by the fact that I had to wait so long to make it after I had turned my phone on. I had almost reached the point of thinking that it was never going to stop pinging, buzzing and announcing messages, mails and notifications, when it finally stopped and the cottage fell silent again.

I plugged in the charging cable and stared at the screen, wondering whether I should first read some of what had been sent in order to gauge the reaction I was likely to get, but then decided against it. There was precious little signal in the cottage as it was, so I wasn't going to risk losing it by trawling through Dad's many messages.

With a heavy heart, I dialled the number of the house phone. Even if Joan answered, I was going to have to ask for Dad. My feelings towards him might have changed since I'd started reading Mum's diary, but he was my boss as well as my father and therefore entitled to a first-hand explanation about my prolonged absence from work.

'Tess,' he said, sounding a little breathless when he

answered after the second ring. 'I was hoping you were going to call.'

That was something, I supposed.

'Are you back?' he asked. 'I'll come around.'

That put me on the back foot a bit. He never came to the apartment.

'No,' I said. 'No, I'm not back.'

'Still travelling, are you? Well, I need to bring you up to speed. You could call in here? That would be easier.'

'I'm afraid I can't do that,' I said, biting down hard on my lip, 'because I'm not coming back today.'

'You're coming back in the morning and going straight to the office? I suppose I could email you, but I'm not sure that's ...'

'No,' I interrupted, 'no. I'm not coming back tomorrow either.'

That seemed to knock the wind out of his sails. Bearing in mind the prestigious projects I'd got pencilled in, of which he was no doubt thinking, I wasn't surprised.

'Look,' he said, 'I know I was wrong to ignore you when you said you needed a break. Joan has made it more than clear that you were fully entitled, under the circumstances, to just take off. I get that, but I need you back, Tess.'

Good old Joan. I wondered if she had known some of what Mum had gone through. Had she fronted up to Dad because she knew what sort of husband he had been? Had she witnessed some of Mum's humiliation for herself?

'You aren't sick, are you?' Dad practically demanded when I didn't respond.

'No,' I told him, 'I'm not sick.'

'Then enough is enough. I know I'm your father, but I'm also your . . .' He hesitated and I quickly jumped back in.

'The thing is, I'm going to be away for a few more weeks—'

'A few weeks!'

'Yes,' I said firmly. 'I never should have tried to keep working after Mum died. That was a mistake and now it's all come back to bite me. I need a proper rest to get my head straight.'

I didn't specify exactly how long for, or drop the tiniest hint about the diary. I dreaded to think what I still had to discover printed on those pages. It was definitely best all round if I kept him at arm's length while I worked my way through it all.

'I see,' he said tightly when I offered no further explanation and I felt my stomach clench in response to his tone.

It was a pain I hadn't experienced since my arrival.

'And you're absolutely sure there's nothing else you want to tell me, Tess?'

'Yes,' I said, 'I'm sure.'

I wondered if he had guessed that I was having doubts about my job too. Perhaps he was coming to the conclusion that I hadn't only left because I hadn't faced up to losing Mum.

'Are you at least going to tell me where you are?'

'No,' I said, 'there's no point and besides I'm moving somewhere else today.'

I had taken the precaution of packing my passport so if

he did go looking around the apartment, he wouldn't find it and would hopefully assume I was abroad.

'You do know that if you don't come back today, I'm going to have to hand your entire portfolio over to Chris, don't you, Tess?'

'Of course.'

'He's really come into his own since you've been gone.'

'I had a feeling he might. You should have promoted him months ago.'

'Perhaps.'

He sounded tired all of a sudden and resigned, but given what I'd recently discovered I couldn't feel sorry about that.

'Look,' I said, 'I have to go. I'll ring in a few weeks, okay?'

'This is all far from okay.'

I didn't say anything. There was no point.

'If you decide to stay away beyond June, Tess, then we're seriously going to have to think about your long-term future with the firm.'

He was getting frustrated. No doubt annoyed that the Tyler work ethic in me wasn't as firmly fixed as it was in him.

'Are you going to fire me?'

'No, of course not,' he snapped. 'But I do have to think about the business, the needs of our clients and the Tyler reputation.'

The way he still prioritized the firm over family, even after my dramatic desertion, made my stomach pull even tighter.

'You know, it wouldn't hurt you to take some time off too,' I said bitingly.

'That's as maybe,' he snapped back, 'but someone has to stick around to hold the fort.'

'If you say so,' I swallowed, determined not to get upset. 'Bye, Dad.'

There was a painful lump lodged in my throat as I turned the phone off again, tossed it back into the drawer, slammed it shut and grabbed the cottage keys. Hope had been right: I was in need of a pick-me-up.

'So,' Sam asked, 'how did you get on?'

'Was it as bad as you thought it would be?' added Hope.

'Worse,' I huffed, wrinkling my nose. 'Much worse.'

The call thankfully hadn't resulted in a blazing row, but it had got me stirred up and feeling unsettled nonetheless.

Hope indicated the row of tempting optics behind her.

'What can I get you?' she asked.

'Thanks,' I said, 'but I don't think I'd better start on the hard stuff.'

I was tempted but knew I wouldn't feel any better for it.

'Coffee then?' she suggested.

'Yes, please. A really strong one.'

'You didn't get fired, did you?' Sam asked.

'No,' I told him, 'not quite, but if I stay too long, it might come to that. Not that I have any intention of leaving early.'

At least if Dad did give me the boot that would be one less decision I would have to make. I shook my head and Sam leant over the bar and squeezed my hand. I risked a look at Hope, but she didn't seem fazed by the gesture at all. My heart on the other hand, was behaving ludicrously.

'Don't worry, Tess,' Hope smiled kindly, 'whatever's wrong, Wynmouth will soon set you right.'

'Nothing's wrong,' I shrugged as Sam released my hand.

Hope raised her eyebrows.

'What?' I asked.

'Nothing,' she said. 'If that's the story you're sticking to for now, then that's fine by me. I'm sure you'll share your woes in your own good time.'

She was obviously every bit as perceptive as her mum.

'I think I might go for a walk,' I told the pair, once I had finished the extremely strong coffee and was feeling more like my old self, as well as a little jittery thanks to the extra shot (or three) that Hope must have added to my cup.

'Mind if I tag along?' she asked. 'I really should be getting to the café.'

'Not at all,' I said, 'I was planning to head that way.'

The heat had really begun to build as we walked along the seawall and there were already lots of families enjoying the beach. We stopped and watched some children dashing in and out of the sea, squealing as the icy water reached their knees.

'Everyone looks so happy to be here,' I sighed.

'Including me,' said Hope. 'As much as I enjoyed my travels, it's wonderful to be home again.'

Looking around, I could see why. Wynmouth might not have been exactly as I remembered it, but with the sea in front and the farmland, dotted with the odd wooded copse, stretching to the horizon behind, it was still a stunning little corner of Norfolk.

'It does feel like home, doesn't it?' I said huskily, the words escaping without my meaning them to. 'There's still nowhere else quite like it.'

I might have only spent my holidays here, but I had never felt the same level of comfortableness and connection anywhere else in the world. Nowhere seemed to fit me quite as well as Wynmouth.

'I thought this was your first visit,' Hope said, sounding surprised. 'You made that sound as though you've been before.'

I certainly hadn't meant to.

'No,' I faltered, 'I just meant that it's so warm and welcoming, that you can't feel anything but at home here.'

Hope linked arms and we started walking again.

'I'm really sorry your boss gave you a hard time,' she said, 'but I suppose given the amount of extra time you're taking off it probably came as a bit of a shock to them.'

'Yes,' I agreed, 'he did sound a bit surprised. And I'm pretty certain that if I was working for anyone other than my father, I most likely wouldn't have got away with it at all.'

'You work for your dad?'

'Yes,' I sighed. 'He owns the company I work for, so now I've not only upset my boss, but my father too.'

Hope was quiet for a moment.

'At least I don't have that problem,' she then shared. 'I've never known my dad.'

I thought of all the extra complications my relationship with my own father was currently facing.

'At this point in time,' I said, 'I wish I didn't know mine.'

'You wouldn't say that if you were in my shoes.'

There was no sting to her tone, but I felt uncomfortable nonetheless.

'Sorry,' I said, 'that was insensitive of me.'

Hope didn't say anything and I realized that it really was a terrible thing to have blurted out, even if I had momentarily meant it.

'Have you and your mum lived in Wynmouth long?' I asked, keen to make amends.

'Quite a while,' she nodded. 'Since I was about thirteen.'

'And you're obviously here to stay,' I said, waving to Sophie, who I could see carrying drinks out to customers.

'Definitely,' Hope agreed, the smile back on her face. 'We're going nowhere. This place is our for ever home.'

I felt a little envious to hear her sound so settled and sure.

'And you want to watch out, Tess,' she nudged, now also waving at her mother.

'What do you mean?'

'If you aren't careful,' she laughed, 'you could end up staying here for ever too!'

Chapter 10

I spent that evening alone in the cottage, but not because I was trying to avoid seeing Sam and Hope together. Yes, I might have, mistakenly as it turned out, felt attracted to Sam, but now I knew he had a girlfriend it was all forgotten. Hope was so much fun and I knew that my friendship with her, and in turn her mother, was going to far outlast any holiday fling.

My self-imposed isolation was more about delving deeper into Mum's diary. I was already in a temper with Dad so thought I might as well find out a bit more about what had happened in the run-up to Mum's untimely death. I planned to read the whole thing, but just a few pages in, I decided my stomach wasn't up to it and banished the lot back to the drawer again. According to what Mum had written, not even her friends were excluded from Dad's attention. She hadn't gone as far as naming names but there was enough detail to know that he had crossed the line on more than one occasion.

I tried to put it all out of my mind again and went up to bed, this time not thinking about Sam, but about something that had *really* happened during my last holiday in Wynmouth. After such an emotionally mixed-up day, I had decided that tomorrow I would do something cheering. I would retrace my steps to the beach huts and anchor my thoughts in my memories as opposed to the pub fantasy I had cooked up and Mum's tragically sad autobiography.

It had been behind beach hut number three that I had experienced my very first kiss, and what a kiss it was! Never to be forgotten and perfect in every conceivable way, it had never been bettered. I had kissed a fair few guys since that initial seductively sweet encounter, but no meeting of lips had ever felt so stirring, so arousing, so thrilling.

It might have been a self-indulgent trip down memory lane, and I couldn't put my finger on why it felt suddenly so important to do it, but I truly believed that going back to the place where my life had felt perfect would be a psychological boost, one that would help me untangle a few things and face my future.

'Oh shit,' I groaned as I flung back the duvet before it was even light, slammed shut the window and traipsed to the bathroom for a towel to mop up the sill.

Mother Nature clearly had other ideas about my proposed trek to retrace my steps. I snuggled back down wondering if this was a sign. Some portent sent to put me off. Even if it was, I was going to ignore it.

By mid-morning conditions had improved just about

enough for me to venture out. Bedecked in raincoat and wellies I left the cottage but soon realized I wouldn't be walking to the huts along the sand.

'You can't go on the beach in this!' bellowed a voice behind me when I took a step down the lane towards the seawall.

I turned and found the beach tractor was right behind me. The wind was such I hadn't heard it approaching.

'I know!' I shouted. 'I'm going the other way.'

'Be careful then,' said the guy as he trundled by. 'You don't want to get blown away.'

It was the first time he'd ever spoken to me and his expression, in spite of the battering it was getting from the wind, was marginally friendlier than when I first arrived. I wondered if he had been in the pub on Saturday night and was feeling more mellow after the evening's entertainment, but I couldn't tell. I wasn't sure if I would have recognized him scrubbed up and out of his oilskins.

He turned the tractor left up the lane and I followed slowly behind. The weather didn't feel quite so deadly with the seawall and the few cottages sheltering me from the brunt of it and by the time I had reached the end and was exposed to the view, the wind had dropped a little and it was hardly raining at all.

'That's more like it,' I muttered, readjusting my hood and looking at the steeply rising path ahead.

I would be fine to walk the cliff path and with any luck I would be able to look down at the beach huts from the top. It might not have been what I originally had in mind, but

I was still feeling resolute about making the pilgrimage and sometimes in life you just had to adapt.

I hadn't trundled much further, however, before it started to rain harder and the wind picked up again, but I kept my head bent low and pushed on, determined not to give in. I knew I was more or less level with the huts and took a cautious step closer to the edge. I could see the roofs and if I took just one step further, I would be able to see behind them, which was exactly where that magical first kiss had happened.

I was just wondering if it might be safer to lay on my front and peep over the edge when I felt a heavy shove in the back of my legs which made my knees buckle and I toppled forward.

In a fraction of a second, which must have been split at least a hundred ways, I saw my entire life flash before me, and then I was pulled backwards and found myself in a heap on the grass with something extremely heavy bouncing all over me.

'What the hell were you doing?' I heard someone holler from above.

'What the hell was I doing?' I shouted back, scrambling further away from the edge and trying to push away what I now saw was an extremely eager black Labrador. 'What the hell were *you* doing, letting your dog run into me like that? I nearly went over.'

'From where I was standing, it looked as if that was exactly what you were trying to do!'

'Of course, I wasn't,' I bawled back, ignoring the proffered hand and slipping about in the mud, much to the delight of the damned dog. 'I was . . .'

'What?'

Finally, on my feet, I took a moment to catch my breath. My entire body began to shake as I realized that time for me had very nearly ended, never mind just jumped back a decade or so.

'What?' came the indignant voice again.

'Never mind,' I said, pushing the hood further back on my head with a mud-encrusted hand which was far from steady.

'You're shaking,' observed the man, now sounding slightly more concerned than cross, as he tried to attach his still prancing dog to its lead. 'Look, my Land Rover's just over there. Come and sit inside for a minute.'

He didn't wait for me to answer but strode off. I followed on, feeling weak, washed out and exhausted. I had no intention of climbing into a stranger's vehicle, but I did want to distance myself from the edge of the cliff.

'Come on, you,' the man shouted at the dog, who carried on skittering around his feet, its tail wagging furiously and its face wearing what looked like a soppy grin. 'Get in, for god's sake.'

Had I not just had the biggest fright of my life I would have been amused by the farcical scene, but I was still too wound-up to laugh about anything.

'It's well behaved, isn't it?' I pointedly observed.

'It's a he,' the man said defensively. 'And he's only a baby. He belongs to my brother and his training has been a bit neglected recently.'

He wasn't wrong. The loopy thing was completely out of control.

'Oh, I give up,' said the guy, scooping the reluctant hound awkwardly into his arms and bundling him in the back. 'Now bloody stay there,' he commanded, once he had unclipped the lead and slammed the door shut.

Feeling slightly steadier on my pins, I went to make my escape, but didn't manage it.

'Let's get in,' he said, before I had a chance to move. 'I've got a flask of coffee, that'll warm you up.'

He pushed back his hood once he'd finished bossing me about and I felt my mouth fall open.

'Well . . .' I breathed, but stopped when I realized he was staring at me too.

It was hard to be sure, with the rain blurring my vision, but he seemed just as taken aback as I was. For a second, his eyes mirrored the same surprise as mine, but by the time I had blinked again he looked perfectly composed.

'Coffee,' he suggested for the second time. His voice sounded completely different now and I was much more inclined to accept. 'Yes?'

I nodded and slipped round to the passenger door self-consciously ruffling my hair. I was too numb to speak but not because of the resulting shock of my near-death experience. I could hardly believe my eyes. Not only had I finally got around to revisiting the site of my first kiss, I had also managed to conjure up the very person who had administered it. Thank goodness I had ignored Mother Nature's cyclonic portent! This was my brain's way of throwing me – quite literally – into fate's path.

I licked my lips as I remembered the soft but firm pressure of his and the tip of his tongue which had sent shocking waves of exquisite pleasure darting about my hormonally charged teenage system. I might have been much older, but I could almost feel those very same sensations as I climbed up to sit in the seat next to him.

I opened my mouth to ask if he remembered me, then closed it again. Surely if he had felt the same glimmer of recognition when his eyes had first locked on mine, he would have acknowledged it, wouldn't he? It would be mortifying if I asked if he remembered our beach hut encounter and he denied the whole thing. But then I had thought he looked surprised . . .

I pulled down the visor to check my hair and realized that his surprise, assuming I hadn't imagined it, was more likely the result of being faced with my Alice Cooper eyes, than recognition. That would teach me for not properly washing off my mascara before bed. I rubbed off what I could with the very damp sleeve of the coat.

'Here,' he said, handing me a steaming cup. 'I don't know if you take sugar, but I've added one anyway. It's supposed to be good for shock.'

'Thank you,' I said, wrapping my chilly hands around the

warm cup and thinking, given the situation, he should have added two.

'I am sorry about the dog,' he said. 'I had no idea he was going to do that.'

'It's all right,' I said, although it very nearly hadn't been.

'I just wanted to get to you as quickly as possible and didn't reckon on him knocking you for six,' he explained. 'I really thought you were going to jump.'

I supposed he could be forgiven for thinking that was what it had looked like.

'No,' I said, by way of explanation, 'I was just trying to work out where the beach huts were.'

'Far better to take a stroll along the beach to do that,' he smiled, 'and preferably not in a force nine gale.'

I wasn't sure it really was *that* windy, but I was no expert and of course, he was right. It had been a rather risky manoeuvre.

'Point taken,' I smiled back, trying not to stare.

Years might have flitted by, but it was very definitely him. I would have recognized him, and his kissable lips, anywhere. I had hoped the mention of the beach huts might jog his memory.

'You aren't acquainted with the area then?' he asked.

But apparently not. I was pleased I hadn't said anything now.

'What makes you say that?'

'Well, if you were, you would know just how unstable the cliff edges are around here.' He added seriously, 'And you certainly wouldn't have pulled off that little stunt.'

I might have been reacquainted with certain aspects of Wynmouth, but I wasn't aware of that particular change. The cliffs had all been rock solid a few years ago.

'Are you a local?' I asked, keen to turn the conversation away from my foolish behaviour.

'I used to be,' he said, staring out of the window, 'but I wouldn't go as far as to say that now.'

'I met someone when I first arrived,' I told him, 'who said that you have to have lived in the village for endless generations before you're considered a bone fide citizen.'

'That's true enough,' he smiled, pushing his damp, dark curls away from his forehead. 'And nothing much changes around here, whether you're talking about the place or the people.'

Personally, I thought that was no bad thing. Wynmouth as it was, was still perfect in my opinion, but perhaps he didn't agree. Distractingly, before I had a chance to ask, my brain fell to wondering if the feel of his lips was something else that hadn't changed. If I leant across and pressed mine against his would they still feel the same? I quickly gave myself a little shake and drained my sweetened cup.

'I'm Joe, by the way,' he said.

It didn't occur to me that we hadn't bothered with introductions because I already knew who he was. By which I meant I knew his name. I didn't know anything about him personally, besides the fact that he was a knockout kisser. Which, I suppose, was pretty personal when you thought about it.

'Pleased to meet you, Joe,' I said, trying to get a grip. 'I'm Tess.'

'Tess,' he repeated.

I thought he was going to say 'I knew a Tess once . . .' but he didn't.

'You were mad to be out in this weather, Tess,' he said instead, 'you do know that, don't you?'

'Well, you were out in it too,' I pointed out, unable to stop myself feeling a little miffed that he hadn't recognized me.

For years I had put our kiss on a pedestal, the benchmark by which all subsequent snogs were gauged and it would have been nice to have it at least remembered.

'Yes, but I have to be,' he said, 'whereas you, I would imagine are here on holiday. You could have been cosied up in some cottage somewhere, next to a warm fire with a jigsaw puzzle.'

I couldn't fail to be amused by that. Crow's Nest Cottage did have an impressive puzzle collection.

'I take it I'm right?' he said, flashing me a smile which made the lines around the sides of his deliciously dark eyes crinkle.

He had certainly aged well.

'Yes,' I conceded, 'you're right, but you know what they say, what's life without a little danger?'

'I'm not sure that's a saying I adhere to personally,' he said, leaning over to refill my cup. 'So, where are you staying?'

'Crow's Nest Cottage. It's next to the pub, the Smuggler's. Do you know it?'

'Yes,' he said. 'I know it.'

'The landlord owns both,' I said, blowing my coffee. 'Do you know him too?'

He didn't answer but climbed back out again and tried to give the dog a drink of water. The mad beast had just started to settle down but lost all common sense when he thought he was going to be let out for another run.

'You didn't say why you had to be out in this weather,' I reminded Joe when he got back in. 'Were you just exercising the dog, or was there something else?'

'I was *trying* to exercise the dog,' he said, rolling his eyes, 'but I was doing some daily checks too. My family have farmed this area forever and some of the fields run practically up to the cliff edge.'

'But not you?'

'What?'

'From what you said before, I got the impression that you don't consider yourself a local now, so I'm guessing you're not a farmer.'

'No,' he said, 'I'm not, but I do still muck in when I'm here, even if it is just a flying visit. Hence being out in this today.'

'Are you going to be visiting for long?' I asked.

'Depends,' he shrugged. 'You?'

'Depends,' I shrugged back.

Joe smiled again and I felt my face colour.

'Are you going to help with the harvest?' I asked.

I knew that happened at some point during the summer.

'I dunno,' he said. 'It's all a bit up in the air at the moment. What about you?'

'I've been here a fortnight already,' I told him, 'but I'm most likely going to stay for another month.'

'Whatever have you found to do that's so appealing that it's made you want to stay for six weeks?' he then asked. 'I know why I feel a pull to the place, but it's hardly a tourist hotspot, is it?'

'Well, I don't want a holiday hotspot,' I told him, handing back the cup. 'I'm happy with the café and beach, and the pub of course. Wynmouth has more than enough for me.'

Joe nodded, but didn't comment.

'Anyway,' I said, reaching for the door handle. 'I'd better be getting back and I daresay you've got things to be getting on with, in spite of the weather.'

'That I have,' he nodded, safely stowing the flask away, 'but I'll run you back to the cottage first. We can't have you getting blown out of Wynmouth again can we, Tess?'

Chapter 11

The weather made absolutely no attempt to pull itself together during the next couple of days and the only flames I thought that June had a chance of seeing were the ones that licked up the chimney when I lit the wood burner every afternoon. The cottage was nowhere near as chilly as it had been when I first arrived and there were some days when the fire didn't need lighting at all, but I hoped the glowing hearth might lift my descending spirits.

Confined to barracks and embarrassed that my first kiss had been forgotten, my mood had tumbled and I had fallen further into the unsavoury depths of Mum's diary. I was managing to ignore my phone, but I was constantly drawn to her words. Sad, lonely and also embarrassed summed up her emotions and there was no disputing what the line *I threw myself into doing what I now did best* meant. Dad might have moaned about Mum's colossal credit cards bills, but had he been the loyal and loving husband the world imagined him to be, she wouldn't have felt the need to compensate for his absence by continually hitting the shops.

I knew I wasn't blameless either. Had I not been so wrapped up in work, I would have noticed that something was amiss. Had I paid more attention, Mum might even still be here. I was beginning to think that the universe was conspiring against me: the rotten Wynmouth weather, my forgotten first kiss, my misplaced feelings for Sam – the evidence was adding up. Perhaps I really didn't deserve to feel any better about life. Perhaps I had made a mistake in running away. Had I stayed and faced up to things, it would all be resolved by now and I wouldn't have suffered these most recent humiliations.

'Tess!'

A loud hammering on the cottage door made me jump.

'Are you in there?'

It was gorgeous, green-eyed Sam, sent from the universe to tempt me before being cruelly snatched away again. I didn't much want to see him but dragged myself up off the sofa anyway.

'Yes,' I answered, as I tightened the belt on my dressing gown before opening the door. 'I'm here. What is it? Is everything all right?'

The rain was still lashing down and he quickly ducked inside. His bulk made the space feel much smaller than it actually was.

'As all right as it can be in weather like this,' he said, quickly closing the door behind him. 'But we've been worried about you. We've hardly seen you and now there's this blasted power cut.'

'Power cut?'

He stopped looking about the room and turned his lovely eyes to me.

'Yes, power cut. It's been off all day,' he said, now looking me up and down and taking in my nightwear and unbrushed hair. 'Haven't you noticed?'

Exactly how long had I been staring into the fire? The room was pretty dark for what I thought was still the afternoon, and a June one at that.

'Are you all right?' he frowned. 'You're not ill, are you?'

'I'm fine,' I shrugged. 'Just having a bit of a lazy day, that's all. In this weather I can't do much else. I've been reading.'

'Bit dark for that,' he commented. 'Anyway,' he carried on, 'I've just come to say that as it's looking like we won't be getting reconnected until at least tomorrow morning, I've decided to make the most of it.'

'How do you mean?'

'A cut-price dinner for everyone who turns up at the pub,' he smiled. 'Sophie and Hope are cooking up a storm on some camping stoves and George has promised an evening of spooky tale-telling for afters.'

It sounded like a great way to ride out the miserable weather.

'It was so good to see everyone supporting the pub before,' Sam grinned, shoving his hands into his cargo shorts pockets, 'and I thought this might be a nice way to carry the feeling on. You will come, won't you? Or were you planning an early night?'

Even though the evening sounded lovely, I wasn't much in the mood for socializing. I wanted to stay curled up under a blanket, eating biscuits and not reading the book I had alleged to be engrossed in.

'I'll be there,' I quickly answered, determinedly ignoring the black dog who was prowling around the edges of my mood. 'In fact, I'll get dressed and come straight round to help you set up.'

'Excellent,' he grinned. 'I was hoping you'd say that.'

Forcefully pulling myself together, I had a quick soak in the tub, then pulled on a pair of jeans and a jumper before shrugging back into the waterproof coat and running next door. It might have only been a few paces, but it was plenty far enough in the driving rain and stiff breeze.

I handed Sam the dripping coat and he set me to work. Thankfully it didn't take all that long before I started to feel like my true self again.

'Aren't you going to light the fire?' I asked, as he handed me a box of glass jars and tealights to set up along the windowsills.

'Not until later,' he explained. 'I'm expecting quite a crowd and it isn't particularly cold. If I light it too early, we'll be roasting before George has even started to scare us witless. It'll be more about creating ambience than warming us up tonight.'

Given the way my heart reacted when our fingers touched as he passed me the box, Sam was still more than capable of warming me up, but I wished he wasn't. There might have been no chance of acting on my feelings for him, but that apparently wasn't going to stop me having them. It was all very inconvenient, not to mention frustrating.

'Tess?'

'Hey, Hope.' I flushed as she popped up right on cue and looked delighted to see me.

'I thought I heard your voice,' she beamed, rushing around the bar and relieving me of the box so she could administer the hug I had come to expect every time I saw either her or Sophie.

She looked beautiful with her dark hair braided and pulled away from her face and wearing clothes so full of colour it was impossible to believe the weather outside was wall to wall grey. Had I tried to wear anything like that, I would have looked as washed out as Wynmouth currently did, but with Hope's stunning skin tone and natural vibrancy she was a reminder of the summer which was, hopefully, waiting in the wings.

'You look amazing,' I told her. 'I can't believe you can cook and still look like that.'

'Mum's doing most of it,' she said, waving my compliment away. 'I'm just her sous chef really. Come and see what she's making.'

She took my hand and led me through to the kitchen

where Sophie was rustling up another fascinating fusion using Norfolk produce and adding her own unique twist. The spiced chicken smelt delicious, as did the curried vegetables.

'There's not masses,' said Hope, as her mum continued to alternately chop and stir with her back to us. 'But there should be enough to give everyone a little taste.'

Noticing the size of the pans, there looked like there would be more than enough to go around, but I knew Sophie liked the people she was responsible for feeding to be well full. Her portion control at the café was testament to that and Hope obviously felt the same way.

'Tess,' said Sophie, turning to smile at the pair of us as we stood side by side with our arms linked, while trying not to interrupt her creative gastronomic flow. 'Sam said he was hoping that you were going to come. It's lovely to see you.'

Her eyes tracked from me to Hope and back again. There was something searching about her gaze, but it was gone in a moment. I hoped she hadn't caught on to the fact that I had a bit of a crush on her daughter's other half. That would be mortifying.

'Anything beats staring at four walls,' I told her, feeling my face colour. 'Not that they aren't lovely walls.' I gabbled. 'I didn't mean that I'm not happy with the cottage.'

'Oh Tess, don't worry,' she laughed. 'I think I know what you meant and with this weather, I can't blame you. You must have read every book in the place by now!'

'Pretty much,' I fibbed.

The only words I had devoured were the ones from Mum's diary.

'This all smells delicious, Mum,' said Hope, releasing me so she could give one of the pans a stir.

The sight of mother and daughter working in well-practised unison brought a lump to my throat. I swallowed it away and banished the tears I could feel brewing.

'Leave it now,' said Sophie, tapping Hope's hand with the back of a wooden spoon. 'That one can just sit and simmer. I haven't been able to make anything too adventurous, what with the limited facilities,' she said to me, 'but perhaps that's no bad thing.'

'Mum's saving her best recipes for the beach party,' grinned Hope, then spotting the wobbly smile on my face, quickly asked, 'are you all right, Tess?'

'Yes,' I croaked, before clearing my throat. 'I'm fine.'

I had to admit, I hadn't given the solstice celebration all that much thought, but Sam, Hope and Sophie had. We sat in the bar and they told me what they had arranged so far. The council had voiced no objection to the idea, so the three of them had forged ahead, planning the menu, drinks and a list of entertainment ideas.

'And we were wondering,' Sam said to me, 'if you would consider designing the posters, Tess, and adding the event to the online community notice board.'

'Sam said you were a dab hand with the marketing things for the pub event,' said Hope, smiling fondly at him.

'She was brilliant,' Sophie agreed, before heading back to the kitchen. 'An absolute star.'

'But we wouldn't want to eat into your holiday time,' Hope quickly added. 'We don't want you to feel obliged to get involved . . .'

'Although it would be great to have you on board,' Sam added.

It was impossible to resist the pair and, in truth, I was keen to take part. I had thought, before I arrived, that some peace, quiet and solitude would help get my life back on track, but the last few days were proof enough that I was wrong about that. What I needed was another project to sink my teeth into to help balance out the thinking time and give me some perspective. It turned out that you could have too much quiet, even if you had been craving it.

'I'd love to help,' I told them, 'as long as no one thinks I'm butting in. I'm only a holidaymaker after all and I wouldn't want to stand on any local toes.'

Sam shook his head.

'After the success of last week's event, no one's going to think that. If anything, they're all grateful to you for getting me to shake things up a bit.'

'A bit?' said Hope, raising her eyebrows.

'All right,' Sam laughed, 'a lot.'

'And now there's no stopping you,' I smiled.

'And Hope,' said Sam, giving her a nudge. 'She's got plans too.'

'All still in the early stages,' she said softly.

'What's this?' I asked.

Sam slipped away and Hope told me about her potential business venture. She explained how her recent trip to see family and her visit to Blossom's Bakery in Norwich had inspired her to come up with the idea. She was planning to develop a range of mail-order Caribbean-inspired cookies. Blossom already sold a couple and apparently they sold out almost before they'd cooled.

'Blossom has given me the recipe for her ginger and lime ones,' Hope said, 'and there's potential to develop lots more. Mum said I can trial them in the café.'

'So, you'll be able to build up a local reputation first,' I said, 'and gauge what works and what doesn't.'

That sounded like a great idea to me.

'Exactly,' she said. 'Although really, I'd like to just set up a mail-order business and go for it.'

'I think your mum . . .'

'Has the right idea,' Hope laughed. 'I know. I'm just excited to get going, that's all.'

'I'm not surprised,' I laughed back, 'they sound delicious.'

'Wait till you've tasted the coconut one I've been working on.'

'Oh my,' I drawled. 'You'll be creating a buzz in no time and once you've decided on your line, you'll be able to sell them at local food fairs.'

'That's a great idea.'

'I'd definitely focus on getting yourself a local reputation before you launch online,' I mused, my marketing head already imagining the look of the labelling and website. 'Build slowly, but strongly.'

'You're right, Tess,' Hope agreed. 'No point trying to make a splash before I've made a ripple, is there?'

'Exactly.'

'So, you think it's a good idea?' she asked. 'I know Mum does, but of course she's biased.'

'I think it's a great idea,' I told her, 'and,' I added thinking with a pang of the combined force of such a special mother and daughter, 'if you follow your mum's advice and build steadily, I think you'll be sending off your first batch of Caribbean cookies before you know it.'

Hope looked very pleased.

'Thanks, Tess,' she said, giving my hand a squeeze. 'Besides Mum and Sam, you're the first person I've talked to about it. Your reaction really means a lot.'

I felt honoured that she trusted me enough to tell me about it.

'Hope!' Sophie called, 'can you give me a hand, please?'

In the time we had been chatting, the pub had started to fill. No one looked too soaked, but it was obviously still raining and getting darker by the second. I helped Sam light the candles while everyone settled down to enjoy some fine food and, later, George's tall tales.

I had just finished my bowl of curried veg and was mopping up with a hunk of crusty bread, when my chair was almost knocked out from beneath me and my lap was full of a familiar-looking Labrador.

'Hello, you,' I said, rubbing the top of the dog's damp head before pushing him and his wet paws away.

'Bloody hell, Bruce,' said a breathless voice. 'I said you could say hello, not leap all over her.'

I twisted round to find Joe standing behind me.

'Still not dried out from Monday?' I chuckled, taking in his damp hair and the rain flecked shoulders of his jacket.

'Something like that,' he nodded. 'Have you finished eating?'

'Yes,' I said, 'are you going to have something? It's all absolutely delicious.'

'No, I ate at home,' he told me, 'but I wouldn't mind a pint of bitter. Would you like to join us in the snug? It's a bit quieter in there.'

I still wasn't sure I had forgiven him for forgetting me, but in the spirit of making an effort and banishing my low mood, I accepted his offer.

'Love to,' I smiled, as the pooch I now knew as Bruce nudged his way under the table, scouting for crumbs.

'Will you keep an eye on him while I go to the bar?' Joe asked.

I looked over and saw Sam frowning at the fuss being made because of the energetic hound. Bruce was nowhere near as calm as Skipper who generally just wandered in and made himself at home. That said, when I looked closer, I thought the expression on Sam's face was directed more at Joe than his dog.

'I'm not sure Bruce will behave for me,' I said to Joe. 'You go and find a seat and I'll get this round in.'

Joe didn't respond and when I looked up from checking I

had enough cash, I found he was staring at Hope, who was now also behind the bar. I watched as Sam closed the gap between them and bent his head to whisper something in her ear. She gave Joe a fleeting glance, her eyes wide and full of surprise, and disappeared back into the kitchen.

'Bloody hell,' Joe groaned.

'You all right?' I asked.

All of the colour had drained from his face.

'I'm okay,' he nodded.

'Do you know Hope?'

'Yeah,' he said, 'yeah, I know Hope.'

Bruce's deep-chested bark suddenly rang out and he lunged towards the bar, cutting off my next question. Joe gave chase and quickly grabbed the dog by the collar and clipped his lead back on.

'I thought it was you,' said Sam, when Joe looked up.

'Hello, Sam,' said Joe. 'Long time, no see.'

'Yeah,' said Sam, turning red. 'It's been a while.'

A few silent seconds ticked by and I realized that everyone had their eyes on the pair, their conversations were halted, drinks forgotten and breaths held.

'Is it all right having the dog in here?' Joe eventually asked.

'As long as you keep it under control,' answered Sam.

I had no idea what was going on, but you could have slashed through the tension with the bluntest knife.

'I'll get our drinks then, Joe, shall I?' I suggested brightly, trying to break the spell before the relaxed ambience we had worked so hard to create was lost for good.

'Sure,' said Joe. 'Thanks. I'll have that pint of bitter.'

He turned and made for the snug.

'Can you make that two pints, please?' I asked Sam, as the noise level began to rise again.

His gaze was trained on Joe's retreating back but eventually he nodded, grabbed two glasses and speedily filled them. He put far too much head on the first one and had to tip it out and start again. I might not have known him long, but I'd never seen him so ruffled.

'So,' he said, his voice husky and low, 'How do you know Joe Upton?'

'I don't really,' I shrugged. 'We bumped into each other a couple of days ago while I was walking along the clifftops, and his dog just made a beeline for me again.'

'And that warrants buying him a drink, does it?'

'Was that Joe Upton I just saw you with, Tess?' asked Mike the butcher before I could answer. 'You want to watch yourself with him.'

'That'll do, Mike,' Sam cut in gruffly.

'What do you mean?' I asked Mike, ignoring Sam.

'He was a right tearaway back in the day,' Mike carried on. 'Always stirring up trouble when he was a lad.'

'Well, he's not a lad anymore, is he?' said Sam, sounding cross. 'So stop bloody gossiping.'

Mike slipped away and I picked up the glasses.

'Thanks for these,' I said to Sam.

By the time I found Joe in the snug, there was no time to ask him anything other than how his week had been before George took to the floor and quickly set about thrilling and terrifying us all in equal measure. I was desperate to find out the history between Sam, Joe and Hope but, for the present, I had to be satisfied with hearing about Wynmouth's history.

My favourite tale from the evening explained why the young sailor was painted on the village sign. Apparently, the lad had been in love with a girl from the village but her father wouldn't allow the match. Heartbroken, the lad had signed up to crew on a ship heading for the Caribbean. If he couldn't marry his life's love, then he wanted to be as far away as possible.

The day before he was supposed to leave, he turned up to wish the girl goodbye but found her missing. She had left a note and her family were frantic. She had run off with the intention of stowing away on the ship so the pair could be together, but they never saw each other again.

The lad didn't make it back to port before the ship set sail and news reached him that it was wrecked just three days into its journey. His love was lost and he killed himself shortly after. It was now said that he haunted the Wynmouth shoreline, walking backwards and forwards with a lantern, calling out to sea for the girl who had perished in the waves.

'And that's why I never walk Skipper on the beach at night,' George quietly finished and I felt a shiver run down my spine.

'That's so sad,' I sighed.

'And scary,' Joe shuddered. 'I don't much like the thought of ghostly apparitions walking up and down the beach. That sailor could be practically on your doorstep, Tess.'

'I hadn't thought of that,' I squeaked.

'Don't worry,' he nudged, 'Bruce and I will walk you home.'

There was no sign of Hope or Sophie when we left and all we got out of Sam was a terse nod.

'Why do I get the feeling there's not much love lost between you and our lovely landlord?' I asked Joe, once we were outside in the refreshing but still blustery air.

'Because there isn't,' he sighed, letting Bruce's lead lengthen so he could explore the empty lane.

'And why is that?'

Joe didn't answer straightaway and I thought I'd overstepped the mark. I wanted to ask how he knew Hope too, but he clearly wasn't keen to share.

'How about I take you out for coffee on Friday,' he surprised me by suggesting, 'somewhere further afield than Wynmouth, and I'll tell you then.'

I was about to turn him down, but then I remembered my earlier determination to try and keep busy and besides, my curiosity about the situation was aroused, even if it wasn't any of my business.

'All right,' I said. 'I'd like that.'

'Great,' said Joe, taking a step closer to help me as I fumbled with the rickety garden gate. For a moment I thought he was going to kiss my cheek, but he didn't get the chance.

Bruce let out another ear-splitting bark and dragged him back up the lane, leaving me looking after him and laughing.

'See you Friday!' Joe called over his shoulder.

'Yes, Friday!' I called back.

Chapter 12

The next day dawned sunny and bright and with the electricity supply thankfully restored. The heat warmed my neck and shoulders as I walked down to the beach after breakfast and, had I not witnessed the weather of the previous few days for myself, I wouldn't have believed it had been so rough.

'Good morning, my dear,' said George, as he and Skipper fell into step next to me. 'Did you manage to get some sleep last night?'

'Surprisingly, I did,' I told him. 'Although I seem to remember my dreams featuring a ghostly apparition with a glowing lamp walking up and down the beach.'

George nodded.

'I'm not surprised,' he said. 'It's a tragic tale and not easily forgotten.'

'I daresay the two lovers passed each other on the road in their attempt to reach each other, didn't they?'

'Do you know,' he said, 'you might be right. The young girl would have no doubt been in disguise so her beau could easily have missed her and she would have shied away from folk on the path for fear of discovery. Dear me.'

'The path to true love certainly didn't run smoothly for that pair, did it?' I said.

'No,' he said, untangling Skipper's lead, 'or for the lasses of Wynmouth now either, it seems.'

'Now?'

'Yes,' he said, with a mischievous smile, 'now.'

'Whatever do you mean, George?' I frowned.

'Don't tell me you didn't notice all that posturing between the two most handsome men in the pub last night!'

'What?'

'Sam and that Joe Upton fella,' he said, before adding with a nudge, 'what a pretty pair those two make, hey?'

'George!' I laughed.

'What?' he said innocently. 'I might be getting on a bit, but I can still spot a good-looking guy when I see one. Or in this case, two. And I can certainly see when they've got their eyes set on the same beautiful young lady.'

Yes, I supposed it had been obvious that Joe had more than a friendly look in his eye when he spotted Hope, even though she was already spoken for.

'Um,' I agreed, wishing I already knew the history between the three of them.

'Must be nice to have your pick,' George added wistfully.

'Yes,' I sighed, 'I suppose it must.'

George went to say something else, but just like Bruce the night before, Skipper was in no mood to hang about, especially when he spotted someone else he recognized.

'Oh, there's Thomas,' said George, literally following his little dog's lead, 'will you excuse me, Tess? I'm sorry to rush off but I need to talk to him.'

'No worries,' I said. 'I'll see you later.'

He rushed off, brandishing his walking stick and I carried on towards the beach huts. With the weather finally looking up, I was determined to get a proper look at them.

'Morning,' said a young mum, as I skirted around the rockpools, which were almost all surrounded by fascinated underwater enthusiasts. 'Isn't it lovely to finally see the sun?'

'Morning,' I smiled back, as her daughter began to screech that she'd spotted a starfish. 'Yes, it is.'

I was almost tempted to stop and admire her five-legged find, but I carried on. I would find out for myself what surprises awaited me in the pools when I decided the time was right to explore them. They, and their intriguing inhabitants, were always such a highlight that I knew it would be worth the wait.

The beach huts were all let, and the majority were opened up, their residents enjoying tea brewed on tiny stoves and reading the morning papers on the little wooden verandas. The huts reminded me of the rainbow-patterned playhouse I had as a child. It seemed to me that, even as adults, we never really grew out of wanting to play house in miniature form.

I stopped and looked towards the back of the one where Joe and I had kissed. I didn't know what I expected to see or feel, but there was no thunderbolt or golden glow around the magical spot, just sand and a Marram grass backdrop. I wondered if the lack of sparkle was the result of having met the boy and him knocking over the pedestal I had put the cherished moment on by not remembering it at all.

'You all right, love?' asked a chap who was sitting in a deckchair just next to where I had stopped.

'Yes,' I said, giving myself a little shake. 'Sorry.'

'Don't apologize,' he said, 'you looked miles away. Are you sure you're all right?'

I had actually been years, rather than miles, away.

'Yeah,' I said again, 'I'm okay, thanks.'

I walked back to the cottage feeling a little disappointed, and found a note from Joe on the mat, written on the back of a receipt from an agricultural supplier. He said he would pick me up at one the next day and that he had booked somewhere for afternoon tea.

That sounded far more formal than going out for coffee and I hoped Joe hadn't got the wrong idea about us. We might have shared a kiss already, not that he had remembered it, but having got my fingers burnt over my feelings for Sam, I was steering clear of all love interests for the foreseeable future.

I looked at the scribbled note and scolded myself for being so presumptuous. I was new to the village and Joe was only recently back in it. Having fatefully met, surely it was only natural that we would gravitate towards one another? We were going out for cucumber sandwiches and loose-leaf tea, not an intimate candlelit dinner for two after all.

'Wow!' was the first thing Joe said when I opened the door to him that Friday. 'Tess, you look gorgeous.'

'Thank you,' I smiled, feeling my face flush. 'You look rather smart yourself.'

He bowed in response.

I had only packed two dresses, and thankfully this one was floaty, floral and ideal for an afternoon tea excursion. Teamed with smart sandals, my toenails painted the same shade of pink as my fingernails, and with a structured wicker bag over my shoulder, it was a pretty ensemble and I was pleased with the result.

'And I like your hair like that,' said Joe, rushing to open the door of the Land Rover, which I could see had had a bit of a clean. 'It suits you, as do the freckles.'

I had let my hair air dry to emphasize the curls I was usually so keen to straighten and left them loose.

'I'm not really a fan of freckles,' I said, conscious of my now speckled shoulders, neck and face, 'but they seem to like me.'

Usually in the summer, I covered them with layers of make-up but in Wynmouth I had become as detached from my make-up bag as I had from my phone. I was surprised by how confident I felt with this less polished version of myself and it was liberating to leave so many of my products and cosmetics untouched.

'They certainly do,' Joe smiled, his eyes lingering on mine as he climbed into the driving seat. 'Right, let's go,' he said, when he checked the mirror and saw Sam writing on the chalkboard outside the pub.

'No Bruce today?' I said, looking in the back at where the mutinous mutt had been confined after almost tipping me off the cliff. 'Is he not a fan of afternoon tea? He seemed to enjoy Caribbean curry crumbs the other night.'

Joe shook his head.

'The little bugger has been more Hulk than Banner today, so Charlie's dealing with him,' he said with a wry smile. 'He's his dog after all and besides, the place we're going to doesn't allow loopy labs.'

'Charlie?'

'My older brother.'

'Who runs your family farm.'

'Allegedly,' Joe muttered.

Joe drove us along the coastal route. Sitting slightly higher in the 4x4 meant that I could make the most of the view and I spent much of the journey admiring the landscape.

'I take it you're a city girl,' Joe suggested, sounding amused after I'd pointed out another picturesque view. 'Are you not used to all these wide-open spaces?'

'I'm a bit of both really,' I explained, thinking of the lovely Essex countryside, 'but, thanks to work, I haven't had much opportunity to appreciate the great outdoors recently.'

'Well, fill your boots,' Joe grinned, 'because it doesn't get much better than this. I might not have been around here much for the last few years, but Norfolk has never been far from my thoughts.'

The day we had stumbled across each other on the clifftop, he had mentioned how he still felt 'the pull of the place' and looking out of the window, I could completely understand why.

'Here we are,' he said turning off the road and on to a sweeping drive, 'we're a little early, but that doesn't matter. I don't know about you but I'm absolutely ravenous. I skipped lunch because I knew we were coming here.'

'That good, is it?'

'Hell yes,' he said seriously, 'that good.'

'Oh my,' I said, smoothing down the front of my dress and feeling mightily pleased that I had worn it as a stunning brick and flint manor house came into view, 'this place is beautiful.'

'Wait until you see the grounds,' Joe smiled.

He left word of our arrival at reception and then we took a leisurely stroll through the gardens and orchards, while the smartly uniformed staff finished setting up for the afternoon service.

I don't think I said much as we walked around the pristinely kept grounds, but that was because I was too in awe of it all. Manicured lawns, burgeoning herbaceous borders and even the odd regal peacock crossed our path, but my favourite spot was the walled garden and orchard.

'I can just imagine Mr McGregor in here,' I smiled, remembering how Dad used to read the story to me before bed when I was little.

'Who?'

'Mr McGregor,' I said again, 'from *Peter Rabbit*.'

'Oh yes,' Joe laughed, 'he wouldn't stand for any little bunnies in these neat rows, would he?'

'Absolutely not,' I sighed. 'This is my favourite part of the whole place, I think.'

'What, the veg garden?'

'Yes,' I confirmed, 'the veg garden.'

Joe's smile broadened.

'What?'

'We used to bring Mum here on her birthday every year,' he told me, his voice taking on a husky edge, 'and funnily enough, this was the spot she loved most too.'

The tea was every bit as wonderful as I knew it would be. Fresh roses adorned the tables and there were at least a dozen teas to choose from. Rather than picking a sweet or savoury menu for two, Joe insisted that we had one of each so we had the opportunity to try everything on offer. The staff carried it all to the table and made a great show of placing napkins in our laps and preparing and pouring our drinks. I felt thoroughly spoiled even before I had eaten anything.

'This is all a far cry from what I imagined when you suggested taking me out for coffee,' I said, as I selected a tiny scotch egg and thinly sliced smoked salmon sandwich.

'To be honest,' said Joe, helping himself to a caviar blini and popping it into his mouth, 'it's not originally what I had in mind either.'

He groaned with pleasure, making us both laugh and raised his hand.

'But I hope the change of plan suits,' he said, as a waiter rushed over.

'Oh yes,' I said, 'it certainly does.'

'Excellent,' he said, then turned to the waiter, 'we're going to need a few more of these,' he said, reaching for another blini, 'and two glasses of champagne, please.'

Within a short space of time, I was feeling replete, relaxed and very mellow. Joe had only drunk half of his glass of champagne because he was driving, but mine was all gone and had flowed straight to my head.

'I think I'd better stick to the tea now, thank you,' I said, picking up my cup when Joe offered to order me another glass, 'as lovely as the bubbles are.'

'All right,' he said, 'I can't very well take you back to Wynmouth tipsy, can I?'

'Not unless you want us to be the talk of the village,' I laughed.

'Been there, done that,' he shuddered, and I wondered what he was thinking of from his past. From what Mike had said in the pub, Joe clearly once had a bit of a reputation. 'Here,' he insisted, 'quick, soak some of the alcohol up with these little shrimp toasts. They're delicious.'

We both laughed as he refilled my plate to stave off the

gossips. I wasn't going to be able to manage even half of what he had given me.

'So, how's life down on the farm treating you, Joe?' I asked once I decided I couldn't manage another bite. 'Are you still enjoying mucking in?'

'Oh, the farm's all right,' he said ruminatively. 'Between you and me, it's Charlie, my brother, who's the problem. He's running the place and refuses to see reason about anything I suggest.'

'What about your parents?'

'Both dead,' he said directly. 'Mum died a while ago now and we lost Dad a few months back.'

'Oh Joe,' I said. I should have realized about his mum, when he mentioned her before in the past tense. 'I'm so sorry.'

He wasn't all that much older than me and it was dreadfully sad that he had experienced such great loss already. Having so recently said goodbye to Mum, I realized that we had more in common than a teenage kiss and being recently reacquainted with Wynmouth.

'I lost my mum not all that long ago,' I shared with him. 'She had a heart attack and was gone quicker than I could click my fingers. I still can't believe it really.'

He reached across the table and held my hand. Had he remembered me, he might have been able to recall Mum too. He might have seen her sitting on the beach in her yellow sundress. The thought brought a lump to my throat.

'That's what happened to Dad,' he said, sounding choked. 'One minute he was stacking bales, and the next . . .'

'He was gone,' I whispered, deeply regretting that I knew exactly how that felt.

'Anyway,' he sighed, squeezing my hand again before letting it go, 'Charlie's running the place now with Bruce as his willing and extremely naughty sidekick.'

I was already rather fond of Bruce but was sure I would like him even more if Joe could rein in his exuberance a bit.

He shook his head and sighed.

'I hope I don't sound bitter,' he said. 'I don't mean to. I'm just finding it all a bit frustrating at the moment. It's no mean feat trying to work with family.'

'Oh, I know all about that too,' I sighed.

This was something else we shared.

'You do?'

'Yes,' I said, 'I work for the family firm. My dad runs it and we seem to be clashing more and more these days.'

'Hence the holiday?'

'Hence the holiday,' I nodded. 'In part.'

'Seems like we have quite a lot in common, Tess, doesn't it?' He pointed out, filling my cup again.

'We certainly do,' I agreed.

'And I have to admit,' he said, taking another slice of cake even though he had only minutes before sworn that he was fit to burst, 'I was wondering how you could possibly manage to take so much time out. Six weeks is a long time, but if Dad's the boss . . .'

'He's not doing me a favour,' I shot back, feeling defensive. 'It's not nepotism, if that's what you're thinking. I work bloody hard for the company, and I haven't had a proper break in years. I'm only taking the time I'm owed.'

Joe put up his hands in surrender.

'All right,' he said, 'sorry. I didn't mean anything by it.'

'I just hate it when people assume that I've had everything handed to me on a plate,' I said bluntly, picking up my cup. 'I started out as the tea girl, just like everyone else.'

'Even the boys?'

'You know what I mean,' I said, still feeling annoyed. 'I'm just taking my holiday entitlement in one go, that's all.'

'Fair enough,' said Joe, 'I guess you're lucky to have a boss who will let you.'

'I didn't actually give him much choice,' I pointed out. 'And anyway, we're supposed to be talking about you. You promised you'd tell me what the beef is between you and Sam.'

I had reckoned it was going to be all about Hope, but when Joe suggested moving into the conservatory, where it was quieter, I wasn't so sure.

'Sam and I used to be best friends,' he began as soon as we were settled. 'We'd more or less much grown up together, having gone to the same schools, but things changed when we hit our teenage years.'

So, it was likely that Sam *had* been around when I used to holiday in Wynmouth. I wished I could have remembered him as clearly as I did Joe.

'In what way?'

Joe shrugged, his shoulders hunched.

'I suppose you could say I was a bit of a rebel,' he said ruefully. 'Got myself into a bit of trouble around the village and upset the locals, whereas Sam never put so much as a toe out of line. We were still friendly, we still talked to each other, but we had different mates.'

'But surely you can't still be holding on to all that now?' I frowned. 'That all happened years ago, didn't it?'

'Yes, but that's not the whole story.'

'Oh,' I said. 'Go on then.'

Joe ran his hands through his hair and looked me straight in the eye. I couldn't fathom his expression, but I suddenly realized I wasn't going to like what I was going to hear and I didn't think it was going to be anything about Hope after all.

'One night,' he continued, pulling in and then letting out the biggest breath, 'just after Sam had passed his driving test, Jack and I found ourselves in need of a lift.'

'And who is Jack?' I asked.

'My little brother,' Joe swallowed. 'We'd missed the last bus back to the village and we couldn't afford a taxi. I knew Dad would go spare if I called him or Charlie so I asked Sam to come and get us.'

'And did he?'

'He did,' Joe said, 'but he wasn't happy. He hadn't had much experience of night driving and wasn't keen on having to rescue me of all people.'

'What happened?' I whispered.

'The car left the road on the journey back,' Joe choked, 'and ploughed into a tree.'

'Jesus.'

'I was in the back,' he went on, closing his eyes and no doubt picturing the dreadful scene. 'Somehow I managed to smash my way through the rear window and drag myself out. Then I pulled out Jack and Sam. I got them out of the way just before the whole thing went up in flames.'

A strangled sob crept up and out before I could stop it.

'But Jack was already dead,' Joe sobbed, 'and Sam . . .'

'Lost his leg,' I whispered.

Joe nodded and sniffed, roughly brushing away his tears.

'I'm so sorry, Joe.' I said. 'I'm so, so sorry.'

As hard as I tried not to, I couldn't stop myself from picturing the horror of the scene, the grotesque sights and sounds that Joe must have witnessed.

'So that's why things felt a bit tense in the pub the other night,' he eventually said, sounding a little more in control. 'That was the first time we've seen each other in a very long time.'

'I see.'

I couldn't imagine how that moment had felt for either of the two men. Had I been in Joe's shoes there was no way I would have crossed the pub threshold, but he must have had his reasons. Maybe he thought it was time to move on. I wanted to ask but couldn't bring myself to and I didn't mention the situation with Hope either.

'The crash was the reason why I left Wynmouth,' he

carried on. 'I couldn't cope with being there and I couldn't bear to see the state Jack's death left Mum and Dad in.'

'Was Sam charged?'

'No,' said Joe, shifting in his seat. 'He was in a coma for months and I was such a wreck, I couldn't be sure . . .'

His words trailed off and he stood up.

'Sorry,' he said, striding off. 'I'll be back in a minute.'

'Of course,' I said. 'Take your time.'

There were so many questions flying around my head as Joe drove us back to Wynmouth, not least whether alcohol had been involved the night of the crash. Was that why Sam never took a drink, even though he ran the only pub in the village? But I didn't ask. Joe had shared more than enough for one day. He must have been exhausted; I know I was.

'I'm sorry the afternoon ended so sadly,' I said, as Joe pulled up outside the cottage and I noticed that the pub was shut. 'I hope you haven't felt forced into telling me.'

'Not at all,' he said. 'I wanted you to know.'

I nodded and undid my seatbelt.

'Okay,' I said, 'and thank you for the tea. It was wonderful, as was the house and gardens. I can see why your mum loved it there so much.'

'It was my pleasure.' He smiled, but it didn't quite reach his eyes.

Not surprisingly, he looked pale and a little drawn.

'It was all exactly as I remembered it,' he said softly, 'and it was a treat to see it all again.'

I went to open the passenger door.

'Here,' he said, jumping out before I had the chance to say I could manage, 'let me get that.'

'Thank you, Joe.'

'So,' he asked, offering me a hand so I could climb out without my dress riding up, 'what are your plans for tomorrow night? Saturday nights in Wynmouth aren't exactly buzzing, are they?'

I knew he was making a big effort to end the afternoon on a happier note and I played along.

'Oh, mine's going to be wild,' I said, 'there's this kitsch jigsaw featuring kittens in a basket in the cottage and it's been calling me practically since the moment I arrived.'

Joe laughed. It was good to hear.

'Sod that,' he said, handing me my bag. 'I think we should have a proper night out. Are you up for a wild night on the tiles?'

'Really?'

'Yes,' he said. 'I need to kick up my heels.'

'Kick up your heels?' I laughed. 'Who says that?'

'Me,' he said, 'apparently. So, are you up for it?'

Meeting my first kiss again, and discovering I had quite a lot in common with him, was the last thing I had been expecting when I sent off my booking confirmation, but then a lot of other things in Wynmouth I'd encountered so far hadn't turned out how I had expected them to either. My memories of the place were metamorphosing along with what I had discovered about my parents and I knew I needed to maintain some balance if I was going to stop myself from retreating to the sanctuary of the cottage and tying myself up in knots.

'Are you up for it, Tess?' Joe asked again.

'You know what,' I grinned, 'I think I am.'

Chapter 13

Before Joe left, we finalized arrangements for the next evening.

'I'll drive,' I insisted. 'My car's been standing idle since I arrived so it could do with a bit of a run.'

'But then you won't be able to drink,' Joe pointed out.

'I'm not worried about that.'

'What do you drive?'

'Why?' I frowned, not seeing how it was relevant. 'Does it matter?'

'Well,' he said, 'it does if it's anything even remotely high end, because you won't want to go bumping it down the pot-holed farm track. I'm guessing it's not an off-roader?'

'No,' I told him, grateful that he was mindful of my car's suspension, 'it isn't. It's a Mercedes C-Class.'

'Bloody hell, Tess,' he grinned. 'That's a cracking car.'

'A cabriolet,' I smiled back. 'It's okay. It gets me from A to B.'

Joe shook his head.

'Yeah, right,' he laughed. 'I'll bet it's a darn sight more than just okay.'

He was right again. The car was my pride and joy. A luxurious indulgence and a much-loved reward for a hell of a lot of hard work, which had been very well done.

'It is a beauty,' I admitted, 'and you're right. I don't fancy subjecting it to any pot-holes, but I could pick you up where the farm drive meets the road.'

'That's a good idea,' he said, reaching around me and rummaging between the Land Rover seats, looking for paper and a pen to scribble down the address.

'It's not too far for you to walk?'

'No,' he said, 'it's no distance really.'

I pulled a notebook and pen from my bag and Joe rolled his eyes.

'What?' I pouted. 'I like to be organized.'

'See you tomorrow then,' he grinned once he had finished writing. 'I promise I won't wear my muck-encrusted wellies.'

'You'd better not!' I shot back.

As arranged, Joe waited at the end of the track. Even from a distance, I could see he was smiling and gave him an indulgent flash of headlights. The sleek silver paintwork wasn't quite as shiny as it had been, but considering the recent weather that was hardly a surprise. His rapt expression suggested he was impressed nonetheless.

When he reached me, I lowered the passenger window.

His happy face bobbed down and I reminded myself that the purpose of the evening was for Joe to 'kick up his heels' for a few hours and that even though I had laid awake half the night thinking about the crash and the many questions I wanted to ask about it, this was not the time.

'Show me your shoes before you get in,' I jokingly commanded and he opened the door and lifted up one foot and then the other, presenting me with reasonably clean footwear.

'They'll do,' I nodded, 'get in.'

He slid gingerly into the seat and carefully closed the door.

'I should have got you to drive us to tea yesterday afternoon,' he said, taking in the plush interior.

'It's not that swish,' I smiled.

'Bloody is,' he shot back. 'Can you not smell the luxury?'

'Stop it,' I laughed.

'Tell me again, Tess, what was it you said you did for a living?'

'I didn't,' I grinned. 'Now, put your seatbelt on and tell me where we're going.'

I didn't have to drive all that far and I soon realized that Joe's idea of a wild night out (in Norfolk anyway), varied greatly to mine. I had thought there might be a cocktail bar or two, or a gin joint perhaps, followed by a five-course gourmet dinner and all topped off with a couple of hours dancing in an upmarket club, but I couldn't have been more wrong and, as the evening progressed, I felt very happy about that.

'What about "Don't Go Breaking My Heart"?' Joe shouted above the raucous din. 'That's a duet!'

'All right,' I nodded, wincing as the person currently on stage didn't quite make the high note Whitney had always managed so easily. 'But that's going to have to be the last one. It's way past my bedtime.'

Joe nodded and rushed off with the list clasped tightly in his hand.

We'd started the evening off at the funfair where we'd been thrown about, shook up and then very nearly thrown up and I was relieved I'd worn jeans and a fancy top, rather than the LBD which was the second dress I had packed and had been my initial choice. After that, we'd eaten fish and chips out of paper on the beach, had a quick beer in a quintessentially English seaside pub and ended up in this gaudy, noisy and absolutely packed karaoke bar.

I now understood exactly why Sam hadn't wanted this kind of entertainment for the Smuggler's, but in this vibrant bucket-and-spade resort further along the coast, it was the perfect fit and everyone, including Joe and me, was having a great time. It felt good to forget about my troubles for a while and the evening was doing me just as much good as Joe.

'We're up next,' he said as he rushed back, grabbed my hand and pulled me to the stage.

He'd had a few beers and I hoped he wasn't going to feel the worse for them on the journey home. I hadn't thought to bring a bucket.

'Do you want to be Kiki or Elton?' he asked, his eyes shining with excitement.

'Definitely Elton,' I laughed, amused that he'd thought of the switch.

I had forgotten how good it felt to abandon my inhibitions and I was pleased I had offered to drive and therefore couldn't drink. The evening was such fun, I wouldn't have wanted to lose a second of it in a drink induced haze.

The applause was rapturous as we finished, Joe wrapped in a cerise pink feather boa – which by rights should have been mine as I was Elton – and me struggling to see through scratched star-shaped sunglasses which had clearly already seen plenty of stage action.

'Always leave them wanting more,' said Joe as we handed back our props and made for the exit. 'That's the expression, isn't it?'

'Sure is,' I laughed, linking arms to stop him wandering off. 'Come on, Kiki. The car's this way.'

During the journey home Joe's mood changed.

'God, I don't want to go back yet,' he muttered, snuggling deeper into the heated seat. 'Are you sure it's home-time already?'

'Afraid so,' I told him, cutting the volume on the radio. 'Are you that unhappy at the farm?'

'It's not the farm that makes me unhappy,' he said, slightly slurring his words, 'it's Charlie. He's made such a mess of everything and I've only just found out. And that was more by chance than design. We're in deep shit financially now.'

'I'm sorry,' I said, thinking how the problem was all the worse because it was a family member who had created it. 'Did your parents used to deal with the money side of things?'

If Charlie had never had any experience of the financial running of the place then I could completely understand how it had gone wrong when the obligation fell to him, but why hadn't he asked Joe for help rather than hiding the situation from him?

'Yeah,' said Joe. 'Dad dealt with everything. He was a bit of a control freak to be honest and none of us really knew his system. He always said it was easier having just one person in charge, but of course that didn't factor in how we'd cope when he'd gone.'

'I see.'

Joe shook his head and sighed.

'I know I'm pissed with Charlie right now,' he then said. 'But I feel sorry for him too. He was the one who was pressured into following in the family footsteps.'

'Didn't he want to be a farmer?'

'No,' said Joe. 'Not really, but he was the eldest and it's what was expected. It was the same for Dad, only he had never wanted to do anything else.'

That sounded archaic to me but I didn't say so. It wasn't any of my business to question a family tradition I knew nothing about. And besides, I had followed my father into the family firm, hadn't I? It might not have been expected of me, but I supposed I had followed the pattern Dad had hoped would look the most appealing when I graduated. That said, it hadn't turned out all that well, so I could empathize with the eldest Upton brother.

'Do you know what Charlie wanted to do instead?' I asked.

'No,' he shrugged. 'I can't remember. I don't recall him going on about it because he had accepted that he wouldn't be able to do it.'

I hoped Charlie didn't still harbour regrets. Life was too short to be stuck doing a job you didn't enjoy.

'And what about you?' I asked. 'Didn't you fancy farming with him?'

'After the crash I couldn't wait to get away,' he said bluntly. 'Staying around here and having to drive along that stretch of road every day was my idea of hell . . .' He shuddered.

I was annoyed with myself for reminding him of his reason for leaving Wynmouth.

'Could you just pull over for a sec?' he asked, a sense of urgency in his tone denying me the opportunity to apologize.

'You aren't going to throw up, are you?' I frowned, checking my rear-view mirror before turning into a convenient field opening.

'No,' he said, puffing out his cheeks, 'but I really need to pee.'

The fresh air seemed to wake him up a bit and he sounded more sober when he picked up the conversation again after I'd tossed him my bottle of hand sanitizer.

'I know I should have kept more of an eye on things,' he sighed. 'But I accepted what Charlie was telling me, that everything was okay, only now it's not. It's really not.'

185

'Is it that bad?'

'Yes,' he said gravely, 'it is. And not that it'll be enough, but we're going to have to sell some land. Bloody good land too.'

'Is that the only thing you can do?'

'Yep,' he said. 'It's our only asset. Dad must be spinning in his grave. It took him years to work the farm up to the size it is now and we're already downsizing.'

'But surely it's better to let a bit of land go, than lose the place completely,' I said, trying to find a glimmer of silver lining. 'At least you aren't losing everything.'

Joe looked at me and shook his head and I wondered if there was more to the situation than he was prepared to let on.

'You know, Tess,' he said, neatly changing the subject, 'I'm really sorry my brother's dog almost pitched you off that cliff, but I'm ever so pleased we met.'

'So am I,' I agreed, laughing at how chilled he managed to make the near-death disaster sound.

'Do you believe in fate?' he sleepily yawned.

'I didn't used to,' I swallowed, 'but I'm beginning to now.'

'Well, I think it's fate that we met,' he said. 'You arriving in Wynmouth more or less the same time as me, was meant to be, I reckon.'

'Do you now?'

'Yes,' he said. 'Because you know exactly how difficult it is to try and work with family so I can talk to you, and I hope you know you can talk to me too.'

'Of course.'

'I daresay you're fully acquainted with the divided loyalty and the guilt that comes with it,' he said, yawning again.

'And the perks,' I cut in, reminding him how he had assumed I had extended my holiday on the back of being a 'Daddy's girl'.

'I'm being serious,' he said. 'I think we might be soul-mates, Tess. Maybe we met in another life?'

'Maybe we've already met in this one,' I said, throwing caution to the wind.

He didn't answer and when I looked over at him, his eyes were closed and he was breathing evenly.

'Wake up, Joe,' I said, lightly shaking his shoulder a few minutes later. 'We're here.'

Had it not been for the full moon, the countryside around Wynmouth would have been pitch-black. Joe and I leant against the wall at the end of his drive and took a moment to admire the multitude of stars shining above our heads.

'That's the milky way,' he said, competently pointing out the constellations, 'and that's the plough.'

'How appropriate,' I smiled, looking at where his finger was pointing. 'Are you sure you're going to be all right walk-ing back on your own?' The track behind us looked endless in the dark. 'I could try and get the car down. I'm happy to give it a go.'

'No,' he insisted, 'I'll be fine. My phone's got a decent torch and besides, I know it like the back of my hand. I won't go twisting my ankle, if that's what you're worried about.'

'I was actually thinking more about Black Shuck coming to get you,' I said, giving a little shiver.

George had a definite fondness for telling the tale of the hound from hell and I felt myself shy away from looking out across the fields, for fear of seeing two red eyes staring back at me.

'Oh, I shouldn't worry about that,' said Joe, moving to stand in front of me. 'He's probably down at the beach tearing backwards and forwards in search of that poor lost sailor soul.'

That was hardly a comforting thought. The beach was practically a stone's throw from the cottage's front door!

'So, he might end up coming for me then,' I said. 'I've got to walk by there after I've parked the car behind the pub.'

'I could always come back with you,' said Joe, taking me by surprise as he stepped closer. 'See you safely to your door.'

I leant further back against the wall, wondering if I was about to experience a repeat performance of that unforgettable first kiss. This wasn't the end to the evening that I had envisaged, but I wasn't going to object to the change of plan.

'But then how would you get back?' I breathed as Joe leant his body into mine and rested his hands on my waist.

His touch was gentle as was the feel of his breath against my neck as he bent to whisper in my ear.

'Maybe you could run me back in the morning.'

His lips lightly brushed my collar bone.

'But then—' I began. I didn't get the chance to finish before he covered his mouth with mine and kissed me deeply.

When he finally pulled away, I stood for a moment,

breathless and dazed. My head spinning and my heart still doing that stupid skittering thing it had recently adopted, but not because I had been swept off my feet. Don't get me wrong, it wasn't an unpleasant kiss. It was really lovely, but my physical reactions were the result of surprise rather than red hot passion.

Joe dipped his head again and I ducked away.

'I'd better be getting back,' I swallowed.

'Okay,' he said, looking a bit baffled.

'It's been a great night though. I've had a brilliant time,'

'Really?' He frowned.

'Really,' I told him. 'I haven't kicked up my heels in ages.'

'Me neither,' he laughed. 'And that kiss,' he went on. 'I didn't overstep the mark, did I, Tess?'

'Not at all,' I said, keen to reassure him.

I had completely given him the green light to go ahead and it wasn't his fault that I hadn't felt what I expected to. But then it had been a very long time since our lips first locked. Perhaps our first kiss was something else from back in the day, that I had remembered wrongly. I had always deemed the experience as sacrosanct but perhaps it had been more run-of-the-mill. It was a shock to admit that, but obviously I couldn't explain that to Joe because he hadn't remembered it in the first place.

'But you'd rather I didn't do it again,' Joe said, biting his lip.

'No,' I told him, 'but not because I didn't like it.'

'What then?'

'Well, I'm only going to be here for a few weeks, aren't I?'

I pointed out. 'And you've got all this stuff with Charlie and the farm to deal with. I don't think either of us needs another complication in our lives right now, do we?'

'It doesn't have to be complicated.'

'In theory, I agree,' I told him, 'but in practice, how often do these things stay simple?'

'That's true,' he agreed, thankfully not sounding too put out. 'So, what are you saying, Tess? That you want us to be just friends?'

I thought how I could do with a friend right now, especially since Hope was home and I didn't feel able to pop into the pub and chat with Sam whenever I felt like it.

'Given the amount we have in common,' I nodded, 'yes, I'd really value your friendship, Joe.'

I held out my hand and he shook it, before pulling me in for a platonic, but nonetheless pleasurable, hug.

'Friends it is then,' he agreed.

Chapter 14

I lay in bed the next morning while the sun crept over the horizon, filling the room with light and making the dust motes dance as I mulled everything over. Not only had I missed the signs that my parents' marriage had hit the rocks, I'd also been rating snogs out of ten on the memory of a kiss that turned out to be unworthy of the pedestal I had placed it on. I was beginning to think that nothing from my past bore any resemblance to the fantasies I had spun around them.

Visions of Dad, Mum, the diary, my job, my first kiss, Sam, Hope, Joe and me, swam in front of me, making me feel dizzy, nauseous and more unsettled than I had been when I first arrived. I needed to get out and clear my head.

'Well, don't you look a sight,' said Sophie when I walked into the café a short while later, hoisted myself up onto a stool and took off my sunglasses.

I winced as my eyes adjusted to the sharp change in light level.

'Good night, was it?' she questioned. 'I'm guessing you were out partying somewhere.'

'It's not a hangover,' I told her. 'I didn't drink because I was driving and I wasn't all that late to bed either.'

'You aren't ill, are you?' she demanded, scrutinizing me more intently, a concerned frown creasing her brow.

I shook my head, feeling touched that she cared.

'No,' I said, 'I'm not ill.'

'So, what's with the bags?' she asked, her hands planted on her hips. 'Couldn't you sleep?'

'No,' I said, putting my glasses back on. 'I hardly got a wink.'

When I had left the cottage, I hadn't planned to come down to the café. I had been heading for the pub and one of Sam's legendary sausage baguettes. I might have still been feeling a bit strange about seeing him for the first time since Joe had told me about the crash, not that I had really had any reason to, but I was in need of a hefty carb and protein packed hit. However, my cravings were destined to remain unsatisfied because the pub was shut.

'Here,' said Sophie, setting down a mug and reaching for the coffee pot. 'This isn't too strong, but it might perk you up a bit.'

'Thank you,' I said, inhaling deeply as I wrapped my hands around the mug as she poured. 'I don't suppose you've got the makings of a sausage sandwich on the premises, have you?'

'No,' she said, 'but I can manage a bacon bap.'

'That'll do,' I smiled, 'thanks, Sophie. What's happening at the pub? The board says it won't be open today or tomorrow.'

'So, I'm your second choice, am I?' she teased. 'Sam had no choice but to close,' she carried on before I could explain. 'He couldn't get anyone to cover shifts. Him and Hope have gone away ahead of the final fitting for his new leg tomorrow. They said that the head start will save them the early morning drive.'

And give them an excuse for a night away in a hotel somewhere. I was relieved the pub closure wasn't the result of bad news or anything, but I didn't much welcome the thought of the pair taking a romantic break. Perhaps I hadn't banished the feelings I had been developing for Sam quite as comprehensively as I had thought.

'I would have covered for him,' I said, making myself think kind thoughts instead of green-tinted ones, 'I could have helped, just doing drinks if nothing else. It's not as if the place is that busy.'

'But you're supposed to be here on your holidays,' Sophie reminded me, 'and besides you weren't around to ask.'

That was true enough. I'd spent the best part of the last two days at the beach, out with Joe and nowhere near the pub.

'Have you been having fun?'

'Sort of,' I said truthfully. 'But it's turning out to be the oddest holiday I've ever taken.'

The café bell rang out and Sophie was kept busy for a while preparing breakfasts, including mine, and serving customers. I ended up helping out by waiting tables as there was an influx of extra folk who had also found the pub closed.

'Word has got out about the solstice party,' Sophie told me when things died down again. 'People are beginning to ask about the details and, I know just a little while ago I reminded you that you're on holiday, but are you still happy to design the posters? We need to start advertising the event really.'

'Yes,' I said, 'absolutely. I just need to finalize some details with you and Sam and then I'll get them sorted.'

'Excellent,' said Sophie, 'and you're *really* sure you don't mind doing it?'

'I'm *really* sure,'

'You can spare the time?'

'Absolutely.'

'Because none of us want to eat into your free time you know,' said Sophie gently, 'especially now you've . . .'

'Especially now I've what?' I cut in.

I got the impression I had been talked about and I wasn't sure how I felt about that.

'Now that you've made a friend elsewhere,' she said softly.

'Are you saying that because I've made a friend somewhere else, I can't play with the ones I've already got?'

'Don't be silly,' she said. 'What I'm saying is, that the last thing any of us wants is for you to feel obliged to carry on helping when you'd rather be spending time . . . doing other things.'

'I see.'

'That said,' she carried on, 'I do think, that before you get too involved, there's a couple of things you ought to know.'

'I take it you are, in a roundabout sort of way, talking about Joe Upton,' I said, just to be sure.

'I am.'

'Well, if it's about the crash,' I said bluntly, 'I know everything already.'

'From Joe?' she asked.

'Of course, from Joe,' I told her, 'so you don't have to say any more about that particular business and I also know that he was a bit of a rebel, *and*,' I added for good measure, 'I'm also well aware that a few of the locals aren't thrilled to see him back because of his bad-boy reputation. Not that now, as a fully-grown man, he has one of course.'

'Right,' she said. 'I see.'

She was denied the opportunity to say anything further as more customers arrived, but I could tell she was bursting to.

'Look,' I said, once she had finished serving again, 'Joe's got more than enough on his plate right now without having to worry that folk are still talking about him and what happened in the past. Believe me, he isn't back in Wynmouth to cause trouble.'

'So, why is he back then?' Sophie asked. 'And why did he come to the pub? Sam's not been the same since he showed up.'

'Given that Sam was the one responsible for the crash,' I pointed out, 'that's hardly surprising, is it?'

Sophie looked hurt by my words, but her protectiveness of Sam had glossed over certain unsavoury facts. He might have lost part of a leg that night, but the Upton family had lost a son and a brother. The fact that Joe was now back in Wynmouth, or for most of the time, just on the outskirts of it, was bound to rake a few things up, but there was no way of avoiding that.

'Joe has come back,' I said trying to diffuse the fuss, 'to help Charlie. I think the farm is experiencing some difficulties and he's here to help sort them out, that's all.'

'Ah.'

'And,' I went on, not that I should have felt obliged to explain further, but I did, 'that's one of the reasons we've become close.'

'What do you mean?'

'We both work with our families and we both know how difficult that can be.'

I wasn't just explaining this for Sophie's benefit. I was hoping that she would pass the information on to Sam and that he would realize my friendship with Joe was a result of shared experiences and a similar background, rather than picking a side over an old hurt.

'Difficult?' Sophie questioned.

'Yes,' I said, my face growing hot, 'difficult. We haven't all got a perfect family dynamic like the one you and Hope enjoy. Some of us struggle to work with our nearest and dearest.'

Sophie shook her head and sighed.

'So, the farm's in trouble, is it?'

'Yes,' I said, hoping I wasn't speaking out of turn and that if she did tell Sam, then it wouldn't go any further, 'it is, and the last thing Joe needs is more local resentment. Not that I really understand why he's facing any. Things are hard enough for him right now.'

'I know you probably think we're all wrong to be looking out for Sam,' Sophie sighed, 'but there was more happened the night of that crash than any of us really knows, Tess. There must have been.'

'What do you mean?'

'Well, for a start, if it was all so cut and dried then Sam would have been arrested and charged, wouldn't he?'

'Yes,' I agreed, because I couldn't deny it, 'I suppose he would . . .'

'And he's always been such a cautious and conscientious lad.'

Another customer arrived, cutting our conversation off again, but it didn't stop me wondering if Sophie was right. Was there more to what happened than either Sam or Joe were prepared to admit? And if that was the case, would it ever be possible for either of them to truly leave the past behind and move on?

My head was starting to spin again so I took myself off for a walk along the beach before heading to the cottage. I hadn't been back all that long, when someone rapped sharply on the door.

'Sophie,' I said, surprised to see her. 'What's up?'

'Well,' she said, stepping inside as I opened the door wider to let her in. 'I was thinking over our conversation while I was closing up and I wanted to come and apologize.'

'Apologize,' I frowned. 'What for?'

'For making you feel as though you had to tell me about your friendship with Joe for a start,' she said, as we sat together on the sofa. 'It was never my intention to pry, but there's still so many loose ends to do with the crash that, whenever Joe Upton's name is even mentioned, it sets us all on edge.'

'I see.'

'Sam's grandmother was his last living relative,' she went on, 'and she died, leaving him the pub, just a few weeks after he came out of his coma. Being witness to the way he's had to cope and the extent of what he's been through, has perhaps made some of us a little too forthright in his defence.'

'He's obviously been through a lot,' I conceded, 'but then, so have the Uptons.'

'That's true.'

'Thank goodness Sam has Hope,' I said, thinking that at least he wasn't entirely alone in the world.

Sophie's face lit up.

'Yes,' she said, 'they think the world of each other.'

That was more than obvious.

'They're very lucky,' I nodded.

At least their relationship was one thing I had found in Wynmouth that was just as it appeared to be. I let out a long breath, thinking of my first kiss and wondering if I was in for any more memory-altering surprises during my stay.

'That was a long sigh,' Sophie commented. 'What's wrong?'

'What makes you think anything's wrong?' I shrugged.

'Let's call it a mother's intuition,' she said, making me tear up a little. 'Let me make us some tea and then you can tell me.'

She reached for my hand and gave it a squeeze.

'But only if you want to,' she hastily added, making me smile.

'Have you ever,' I found myself asking, once we were settled with mugs of tea and a packet of Rich Tea biscuits, 'discovered that something you wholeheartedly believed in, something you had total faith in, was a complete myth?'

'You mean it was a lie?'

'Yes,' I said, 'I suppose I do, whether that was something that someone had told you, or something you had fooled yourself into believing.'

I was thinking mostly of Mum's diary, and my parents' less-than-perfect marriage, but there were also thoughts of my first kiss with Joe and how that hadn't turned out to be picture-perfect either.

'Sort of,' said Sophie, dunking a biscuit.

'Sort of,' I frowned, 'either you have, or you haven't.'

'Let me explain.'

I waited while she gathered her thoughts.

'I once put my complete faith in a man,' she eventually said, 'who then let me down.'

I wondered if she was talking about Hope's father.

'So, you do know then,' I jumped in.

'I haven't finished yet,' she tutted.

'Sorry,' I apologized, sitting further back.

'As I said,' she carried on, 'he did let me down, but then I discovered *why* and I realized that what had happened wasn't straightforward at all. It involved him having to make a very difficult decision and, even though I was hurt, I knew his choice was the right one because it caused the least amount of heartache for everyone involved.'

'That's very magnanimous of you.'

Sophie chuckled.

'Perhaps,' she said, 'but it took me a long time to feel that way. We're talking years, Tess, but time is a great healer. It passes and gives us perspective and of course, whether we resist it or not, life does move on from such things.'

I nodded.

'So,' she said softly, 'are you going to tell me what it is in your life that you've realized isn't what you thought it was?'

I shook my head.

'Not today,' I said, 'but thank you for sharing your experience with me.'

'I haven't shared much,' she said, 'but the point is this: before you decide that you have discovered something isn't true or real, and act on it, make sure you're in full possession of all the facts and that you have them in the right order.'

Chapter 15

After our heart to heart, Sophie's words – 'make sure you're in full possession of all the facts and that you have them in the right order' – rang long and loud in my ears. I took out Mum's diary again, scouring through the pages to check that I hadn't missed anything. I certainly had 'all the facts' and, thanks to the dates typed at the top of the pages, knew they were definitely 'in the right order'.

There was no mistaking their meaning and they were the final thing I needed to help me decide that I was going to quit my job with the family firm. Long before I had run to Wynmouth I had admitted to myself that I didn't enjoy what I did anymore and now it was time to deal with Dad and put him back in the, horribly depleted, family pigeon hole. A part of me wanted to expel him from my life completely but, carrying so much guilt over one lost parent, I wasn't about to deliberately sacrifice the other.

Major decision finally made, I refused to stress about it or let it dominate my thoughts any further. I would do my best to carry on with my holiday and throw myself into doing what I could to help out with the solstice party.

'Tess,' said Sam, when I turned up at the pub Tuesday morning, 'good to see you.'

'Good to see you too,' I replied.

I looked at him for a long moment as he busied himself behind the bar but couldn't find anything different about him. I don't know what I had been expecting, but knowing now about the crash, I had thought there might be something. Some tell-tale sign perhaps, other than the obvious one, but there was nothing.

'So,' he asked, taking me completely by surprise, 'how was your upmarket afternoon tea?'

I was all set to ask him about his appointment. I'd even rehearsed it back in the cottage, but now I found I was doing my best goldfish impression and no doubt looking like a right idiot.

'I can't compete with dainty light bites, I'm afraid,' he carried on. 'It's a sausage baguette or nothing here at the Smuggler's this morning.'

I hadn't realized it was a competition.

'Well, that's just as well,' I said, sitting on a stool at the bar, 'because that's exactly what I want. And anyway, how did you know about my tea?'

'Wynmouth is a small village,' he smiled as he poured me a coffee, 'nothing stays secret around here.'

'But I didn't have tea in Wynmouth,' I pointed out.

'That makes no difference,' he told me. 'The manor isn't

that far away, is it? You have to remember that this is rural East Anglia, Tess. You aren't invisible here like you are in a city.'

'I see.'

'George's sister is friends with the grandmother of the lad who waited on your table,' he elaborated.

'Right,' I said, my brain trying to unscramble the complicated trail.

I gave up in the end, it was far too early in the day.

'So,' Sam swallowed, finally getting around to what it was that he had no doubt wanted to ask in the first place. 'Did he tell you?'

'If it's Joe that you're referring to,' I said, for some reason choosing not to make it easy for him, 'he told me a lot of things.'

'I'll bet he did,' said Sam, distractedly running a hand through his hair.

He might not have looked different when I walked in, but he did now and I felt guilty for being so awkward about answering.

'He told me a little about the crash,' I said quietly and Sam shook his head, 'but he also told me that you used to be friends. Best friends when you were growing up.'

'Before I killed his brother, you mean,' he said bluntly. 'Yes, we were.'

I winced at his words.

'He didn't put it like that . . .' I began. 'But he did say that you'd grown apart a bit. He told me that he was a bit of a tearaway, but that you—'

'Let's just leave it,' Sam snapped, 'shall we? I'll get your breakfast.'

'All right,' I said, 'whatever you want.'

I was grateful there were a fair few other customers who held his attention and that he was more like his old self when he eventually came back to me.

'How was that?' he asked, nodding at my now empty plate.

'Delicious, as always,' I said, wiping my mouth with a napkin to erase any lingering traces of brown sauce. 'I never used to bother with breakfast,' I admitted, 'but now I can't seem to manage without it.'

'Well,' he said, 'it is rumoured to be the most important meal of the day.'

'True,' I nodded.

I let a beat pass before carrying on.

'You know, I would have opened the pub while you were away,' I told him. 'I wouldn't have been able to manage the food, but I could have served behind the bar. You only had to ask.'

'Had I known where you were, I might have done.'

Damn.

'Oh look,' I said, my voice louder than I intended it to be. 'Here's Hope. I hope she's coming in because I need to speak to you both.'

Fortunately, she did come in and though it pained me (even though it shouldn't) to see her and Sam hug, I was pleased of her presence. It was just beginning to dawn on me that, given Joe and Sam's dreadful history, it wasn't going to be easy juggling the two friendships, but I didn't want to give up either of them.

Sam might have been on the scene first, but Joe needed a pal right now, someone who understood the trials of working with family and who hadn't been around during the fallout after the crash and that person was me, so Sam would just have to get used to it. Besides, he had Hope on his team, so I knew he'd be fine.

'Morning, Tess,' she beamed, once Sam had released her.

Her smile lit the place up, just like her mum's did.

'Oh, sorry,' she apologized as a massive yawn caught her out and she arched and stretched her back, 'I'm just *so* tired this morning. It's not a good way to be starting the week, is it?'

I refused to think about what she had done, or who she had done, during her weekend away which had caused her fatigue.

'A walk in the sea air will soon sort you out,' said Sam. 'Why don't you go down to the beach? It's going to be a beautiful day. I'm sure Tess wouldn't mind burning off the calories she's just wolfed down, would you?' He smiled at me.

I felt a little peeved that Hope's presence had restored his good humour so quickly when it had refused to show up for me.

'That's a great idea,' agreed Hope as she helped herself to coffee. 'Let's go for a wander before the tide comes in, shall we, Tess?'

'In a minute,' I said, 'I want to talk to you both first.'

'Oh yes,' said Sam, still smiling, 'sorry. I forgot you'd said that.'

Once he'd known Hope was in the vicinity, I don't think he'd listened to a word I'd said.

'Is it about the party?' she asked.

'Yes,' I said, trying to not to feel offended by her other half's limited attention span. 'I was talking with Sophie yesterday and promised to get the posters and flyers sorted.'

'In that case,' said Hope, 'we'd better get our heads properly together and finalize the details, hadn't we?'

'That's what I was hoping,' I told her. 'It would be good to confirm things so I can add them to the posters. I've already got a list from your mum, and I've had an idea about something else we can do.'

'Go on,' said Sam, leaning over the bar.

Now I finally had his full attention I found I didn't want it. I avoided his hypnotic gaze and focused on Hope.

'Well,' I said, thinking about my walks and how some of them had changed my perception of Wynmouth a little, 'the beach is beautiful, but there's always rubbish that washes up with the tide and there's some rope and an old metal drum wedged next to one of the groynes, which seems to be a permanent fixture, so I was wondering if we could have a beach clean ahead of the party.'

It had been on the tip of my tongue to say that the beach used to be pristine, but fortunately I bit the comment back.

'We have talked about this before,' Hope said enthusiastically, 'but nothing's ever come of it. This could be the

206

perfect opportunity to launch something regular, a monthly meet perhaps. There are specific organizations which can help with it, aren't there?'

'Yes,' I said. 'I had a quick look on your mum's laptop because there are certain things we would have to consider, such as public liability insurance and safeguarding issues.'

'It's not just rocking up with a bucket and picking stuff up then,' Sam frowned.

'No,' I said, 'not if you want to do it properly and certainly not if you want to make it a regular event in the Wynmouth calendar. Ideally, you'll need someone prepared to commit to co-ordinating and running it.'

'I'd be up for doing that,' Hope said keenly. 'I'll make a start on it today.'

'Are you sure?' asked Sam. 'It sounds like a lot of work, and what with your own venture to set up, it's important to stay focused, Hope.'

'But this is important too,' she said, sounding like she really meant business and quite a lot like her mum. 'The beach is Wynmouth's biggest attraction, and if it's contaminated and covered in debris, it won't be pulling the visitors in for much longer, will it? We need to do something positive to protect it.'

'That's true,' I agreed. 'Lots of locals, including you, Sam, have told me they love the village because it isn't like the other resorts. It isn't fit to burst with amusement arcades and rowdy entertainment.' A sudden vision of the Elton and Kiki duet Joe and I had treated the karaoke crowd to popped into my head. 'So, as Hope says,' I carried on, 'it's vital that you protect what Wynmouth is famous for; the beautiful beach and those rockpools. They're your bread and butter and they need looking after.'

In that moment I decided that as soon as I had finalized the poster design I was going to head off and explore the pools. I had been waiting for the perfect time and this was it. I had made a major life choice that morning and the pools could be my reward for finally getting on with things. I only hoped I wouldn't find anything to tarnish my memories there. It would be too much to bear if they were polluted too and I didn't just mean metaphorically.

'All right,' said Sam, holding up his hands, 'I was only worried about Hope increasing her workload, there's no need to come over all eco-warrior on me.'

'I didn't,' I pouted, but then we began to laugh. 'Well, I suppose I did a bit, but it is important.'

Hope had already got the details of one of the charities up on her phone and I knew the venture was in the best hands to make it a success.

'So,' Sam asked, 'what else?'

With Sam having to juggle customers, it was late morning by the time we had worked our way through everything. I knew there would be more additions to make, but at least we could now start officially spreading the news and making the party the best Wynmouth beach had ever seen.

'I still fancy that walk along the beach,' said Hope, giving me a nudge. 'Are you up for it?'

'All right, but I can't be too long. I'm hoping to get this poster finished today and then copied at the post office tomorrow.'

'You can print the first one out here if you like,' Sam offered.

'That would save me having to go back to the café with Sophie's laptop.'

It was kind of her to let me keep using it and I was proud that I had still resisted the urge to check my emails and log into my social media accounts. The life I was living in Wynmouth might not have been the completely idyllic one I had imagined when I booked the cottage, but the real world, the trappings of technology and having to do everything at breakneck speed, felt like a million miles away and I was very happy about that.

'I'll come back later tonight then,' I said, hopping down from the stool. 'That way we can check the details together and make sure we're all happy with it.'

Hope waited outside while I dropped my notebook and lists back at the cottage and then we ambled down to the sand and turned towards the beach huts.

'How did things go at the weekend?' I asked her. 'Sam looks as tired as you're feeling this morning.'

I hoped she realized I was asking about the appointment and not the more intimate details of their time away. Thankfully, she did.

'It went well enough,' she sighed, 'but he was in quite a lot of pain after the travelling. This new leg is going to make all the difference to him.'

'In what way?'

'It's going to be a better fit, for a start,' she said, 'and that will mean he can come and walk on the beach without worrying about how far he can get before he has to turn back.'

I hadn't thought about that before, but now I realized I'd never seen Sam all that far from the pub.

'So why is this current one so uncomfortable?' I frowned. 'Surely, they have to be carefully measured up, otherwise they wouldn't fit at all?'

'It was fine to begin with,' Hope confided, 'but now it's worn out and so he's invested in a hi-tech new model through a private company. He took some persuading though, believe me, and it's costing a fortune.'

'Yes,' I said, 'he did mention the cost before. I got the impression that he was worried about diverting funds from the pub.'

'He never puts himself first,' Hope tutted.

'But why?' I asked. 'We all need to look after ourselves and when we're talking about something as vital as a limb . . .'

'Why do you think?' Hope cut in.

'Oh,' I said, the penny dropping, 'I see. It's survivor guilt, isn't it?'

'Exactly,' she confirmed. 'As far as he's concerned, he deserves to suffer.'

'But that's . . .'

'Ridiculous,' she said. 'I know, but getting him to accept that it's ridiculous is impossible. I've been trying for years.'

I knew Sam would never forgive himself for what had happened, but he needed to move his life forward. Joe and I might not have discussed the situation at length but I could tell that he was in a very different place to his old friend and that was probably because he had moved away and carved out a life that didn't involve constant reminders of the past. Mental scars were tormenting enough, but Sam had physical ones too.

'I had hoped this new leg and being pain free might alter his mindset a bit,' Hope sighed, 'but there's no chance of that now.'

'Why not?'

'Because Joe's back, of course,' she said, sounding resigned. 'And if local gossip is to be believed, then he could be here for a while, for good even, and Sam's spirit has dropped through the floor as a result.'

'And I don't suppose I've helped, have I?' I swallowed. 'I daresay because I've been out with Joe a couple of times, Sam thinks I've picked a side.'

'No,' Hope said quickly. 'I'm sure he doesn't think that.'

I wasn't sure I believed her, but then perhaps Sam didn't think enough of me to care. After all, at the end of the day, I was just a holidaymaker renting his cottage, hardly lifelong buddy material. I wouldn't have been surprised if I had read too much into our friendship. I mean, I'd been wrong about the spark of attraction, hadn't I?

'And anyway,' Hope shrugged, 'it's no one else's business who you go out with, is it?'

'I suppose not.'

'Did you know Joe and I used to go out?' she then said, sounding almost shy. 'Did he tell you that?'

'No,' I said, 'no, he didn't.'

That said, thinking back to the night in the pub and how the colour had drained from his face when he spotted her behind the bar, I should have guessed.

'We were a couple for quite a while,' she told me. 'We were only young, but it was love at first sight and it lasted a good while. We actually used to come right here,' she smiled, pointing to the back of the beach huts, 'and snog for England.'

I bet Joe would remember those kisses, even if he'd forgotten mine.

'We were still together after the crash,' she said, the smile now banished as she sat in the shade of one of the closed huts, 'but not for long.'

'How come?' I asked, shielding my eyes from the glare of the sun as I looked down at her.

'We fell out over Sam,' she explained. 'Joe couldn't understand why I kept visiting him in the hospital. He said it was completely wrong that I still wanted to be friends with him and, in the end, we broke up over it.'

'That must have been really hard for you.'

'It was,' she swallowed. 'I was in love with Joe and of course I could understand that he was destroyed by what had happened, but Sam was my friend too. I wanted to support them both.'

I could understand that. Poor Hope had found herself in an impossible position and they had all been so young, not to mention traumatized. It was hardly the ideal time to make big relationship decisions, but then when had life ever presented perfect timing?

'And now Joe's back,' she said, 'and I can't help thinking . . .'

Her words trailed off and she stared out at the sea, her forehead furrowed in a deep frown.

'What?' I asked. 'What do you keep thinking, Hope?'

'I don't know,' she said, holding out her hand so I could pull her back up. 'I just can't seem to get him out of my head.'

'Given the history between you all,' I said, heaving her to her feet, 'that's only natural.'

'Everything's all so stirred up,' she said, brushing the sand from the back of her legs.

'It will settle again.'

'Will it?' she asked.

There was a look of desperation in her eyes and I wondered if she was referring to the memories of the crash or her feelings for Joe.

'Of course,' I nodded. 'You just need to give it time.'

'I daresay you're right,' she said, after mulling the idea over for a few seconds. 'I just need to avoid him, don't I? Joe, I mean.'

That wasn't going to be easy in somewhere the size of Wynmouth.

'Do you fancy a paddle?' she asked.

'What, now?'

'Why not?' she said, running down to the shore.

Immersion in the freezing North Sea would be one way of forgetting her worries, I supposed.

'Last one in has to buy lunch!' I shouted as I ran to catch up with her.

Chapter 16

Having finally started to get to grips with my own problems, I discovered I couldn't resist the urge to help certain other people with theirs. Having seen first-hand the impact Joe's presence was having on Sam, I became resolved to try to do something about it. Apparently, being involved in breathing new life into ailing local businesses and reinvigorating the entertainment scene was no longer enough; I was now intent on trying to mend lives and heal rifts too.

'This is the last of them,' I told Sophie when I delivered the final batch of flyers for the beach party. 'But I can arrange to get more if you run out.'

She picked one up and read it again.

'I can't imagine there's anyone left within a five-mile radius who hasn't got one or seen one now,' she chuckled. 'Or noticed the posters that have popped up everywhere.'

She was probably right; throughout the week the flyers had been disappearing as fast as I could hand them out. I had even spotted a few taped on the inside of car windows, so word was definitely spreading.

'Everyone's very excited about it, aren't they?' she said, a wide smile lighting up her face. 'It's going to be a busy night.'

Even if half those expected turned up it was going to be an *exceptionally* busy night.

'I just hope the weather doesn't let us down,' I frowned, 'and that as many people turn up to clean the beach the day before as come out to celebrate the solstice the night after.'

'I'm sure it will all be fine,' she said reassuringly. 'You worry too much, Tess.'

She was probably right, but my experience of the industry I had until recently been operating in, together with work-ing for a perfectionist like my father, meant that I always checked, checked and then re-checked every last detail, even those that I couldn't control, like the weather, so it was force of habit really.

'I'm just thinking about Hope,' I said. 'She's really thrown herself into setting up the beach clean initiative so she deserves it to be a success. If it takes off it could have a long-lasting impact on the landscape around here and even further afield.'

Sophie nodded in agreement.

'That's typical of my girl,' she said proudly, 'she always has to be doing something.'

She sounded a lot like me in that sense.

'But you were the one who came up with the idea, weren't you?' Sophie reminded me.

'Sort of,' I said, 'but it had been on Hope's mind for ages. My mention of it just got her fired up. She's the real brains behind it. She's the one who has actually made it happen. Is she around, by the way?' I asked. 'I need to run something by her.'

'She's out the back. You can go through.'

I found her in Sophie's office, surrounded by spreadsheets and notes.

'All right?' I asked. 'I can come back later if I'm disturbing you.'

'No,' she said, 'it's fine. I was about to take a quick break.'

'What are you doing?'

'Working on my business plan,' she said seriously. 'Mum and I have decided to add cookies to the dessert part of the party menu, so I'm using it as an opportunity to work out costs as well as gauge reactions. It will be a great opportunity to find out what folk think.'

'You're going to be measuring yummy noises, you mean?' I grinned.

'Hopefully,' she said, crossing her fingers.

I had no doubt her clever combinations would be a hit with everyone. I, for one, had eaten more than my fill of the coconut cookies during the last few days.

'Well, you certainly look organized,' I said, with a nod to the table.

'I don't think I've forgotten anything,' she said, biting her lip. 'Did you want to talk about the party?'

'No,' I said, 'the boys.'

'Oh, right,' she said, wrinkling her nose because she knew exactly who I meant. 'I'll make us some iced tea and we'll sit outside where no one can hear us.'

Her first words, once we were settled at a table, were proof enough of just how worried she was and I felt more determined than ever to bring the situation to a head.

'Sam's been like a bear with a sore head this week,' she told me.

'I know,' I agreed. I had heard for myself just how het up he had been. 'He practically bit poor George's head off yesterday when Skipper upset his water bowl.'

'Someone mentioned that,' Hope said, biting her lip. 'This is all Joe's fault. He should never have come back.'

'I don't think that's very fair, Hope.' I pointed out as gently as I could. 'Like I told your mum, his hand has been forced. He's had no choice but to come back because he's needed at the farm.'

'Oh, I know,' she said, stirring her tea with a paper straw. 'It's just all such a mess again and I can't stand it.'

'It is,' I agreed, 'and that's why we need to do something about it. Avoiding the situation and avoiding Joe, like you suggested before, just isn't working is it?'

'No,' she admitted.

'If anything,' I quickly added, sensing I had got her onside, 'this week feels even worse than the last.'

'I can't deny that,' she conceded, taking a sip through her straw. 'So, what do you think we should do?'

I didn't try and ease into it because there was no point.

'Get them together.'

Poor Hope spluttered loudly and started to choke.

'Are you mad?' she coughed, sounding shocked as well as short of breath.

'Probably,' I said, patting her on the back, and giving Sophie, who had rushed to the café door, a thumbs up to indicate the situation was under control, 'but they can't carry on just circling around each other like this, can they? I think we need to set a situation up which will give them the opportunity to clear the air once and for all.'

It would be risky, a make-or-break face-to-face meeting, but I couldn't think of any other way out of the deadlock.

'And how exactly are we supposed to do that?' Hope demanded, her tone suggesting that I had completely lost the plot.

'Board game club,' I said simply. 'The next session is tomorrow night.'

'Board game club,' she echoed doubtfully.

'Yes,' I said, 'I thought the four of us could play Monopoly or something. The boys could talk without having to look at each other, and . . .'

'You seriously think,' Hope cut in, sounding incredulous, 'that pitching the pair against each other in a competitive gaming environment will be the way to resolve a broken friendship which has been torn asunder for the best part of fifteen years?'

'Did you really just say torn asunder?'

'Did you really just make such a crazy suggestion?' she shot back. 'Do you seriously think this is the solution?'

'It might be,' I swallowed.

Now she'd spelt it out, the idea did sound a little off the wall.

'And it might not,' she quickly countered.

'But it can't make things any worse, can it?' I insisted, sticking with the plan. 'And we do have to do something, because I don't know about you, but I'd quite like to have the Sam who was here when I first arrived back. I miss him.'

Hope looked at me over the rim of her glass and I felt my face colour.

'All right,' she relented. 'We'll give it a go, but only if you take full responsibility. I'm holding you entirely accountable and when it all descends into chaos, I'll be pointing the finger firmly at you,' she warned me.

'I can live with that,' I shrugged, but I wasn't sure I could.

Before I left the café, I picked out a bucket and net from the selection Sophie had on display and the next afternoon, when the tide had receded, I headed down to the rockpools. The beach was quiet and it wasn't long before I was immersed in the mysterious underwater world and feeling about ten years old again.

Thankfully, my fear of finding the pools contaminated was completely unwarranted and they sparkled and shone in the sunshine, just as much as they always had. The only thing missing was Mum in her yellow sundress, occasionally looking up from her book to admire my treasured finds.

I stared in renewed wonder at a brightly coloured exotic-looking beadlet anemone as it gently swayed and then jumped when a long-spined sea scorpion darted out from under the rocks. It was so well camouflaged I hadn't spotted it before. By contrast, the progress of two starfish was uncommonly slow, but I didn't mind that. I had been biding my time for the perfect moment to explore and I was happy, having found everything as it should be, to hang around for them. My patience had been rewarded with an exceptionally packed pool and I was pleased that I had waited so long to rediscover it.

Almost too soon, it was time to tear myself away and I released the three little crabs, (two edible and one hermit), that I had carefully scooped up and deposited into the bucket for closer inspection. Checking my watch, I headed back to the cottage, intent on issuing Joe an invitation to the pub, even if it did mean having to fire up my phone to do it.

'Oh,' I smiled, as I turned up the lane and discovered I could leave my phone where it was because the man himself was here.

It took me a couple of seconds to realize who he was talking to and even though I tried not to, I couldn't help but stare. Out of view of the pub, Joe was talking to Hope. Not that it was any of my business, but I wished I was close enough to hear what they were saying. I also wished I could see the expression on Hope's face, but she turned away when Joe raised his hand to acknowledge me. They swiftly parted and he jogged down the lane to meet me.

'This is a bit of a coincidence.' I smiled, deciding not to comment on the exchange I had just seen.

'What is?'

'I was just about to message you,' I said, as I dumped the damp bucket and net on the path and unlocked the door. 'Come in.'

I filled the kettle while Joe made himself at home.

'What have you been up to this week?' I asked, further swallowing down my curiosity about his chat with Hope.

'Not staying out of your way because I embarrassed myself over a goodnight kiss,' he said, 'if that's what you're thinking?'

'Of course not,' I said, relieved to hear that he was joking. 'I haven't given it another thought.'

'I don't know if that makes me feel better or worse,' he laughed.

I didn't dwell on the fact that now he knew how I felt!

'What I mean,' I said, 'is that I've been so preoccupied with thoughts of our inimitable, never to be repeated, Elton and Kiki duet, that nothing else has really stood a chance.'

'Never to be repeated,' he said, sounding crestfallen. 'I was rather hoping that was going to become a regular thing.'

'No way,' I laughed. 'For a start, I'll be leaving before the end of the summer and you said the trick was to always leave them wanting more, didn't you?'

'Oh yeah,' he said, scratching his head. 'I do seem to remember saying something like that.'

'So,' I said, tracking back to my original question. 'How's your week been? Have you been busy?'

He didn't answer until I carried our drinks through.

'You could say that,' he said, taking a mug from the tray. 'And Charlie's still digging his heels in.'

'I'm sorry to hear that,' I said. 'I was hoping you might have found some common ground by now.'

'Me too.'

It was sad to think that between them they couldn't work it out.

'Well,' I said, trying to inject some cheer into the conversation, 'you can forget about Charlie and the farm for a while over the weekend, because I have plans for you, Joe Upton.'

I was hoping that if I kept my tone light and made it sound like a fun night out, then he might just get swept along and agree to it before he realized exactly what *it* was.

'No can do, I'm afraid,' he said, shooting me down before I'd even pitched the idea. 'I've got to go away for a bit.'

'Oh no,' I said, 'when?'

'This afternoon,' he said, nodding at the clock on the bookcase, 'almost this minute, in fact.'

'That's such a shame,' I huffed. 'I was going to enter us as a team in the board game club competition.'

The expression on his face pretty much matched the one Hope had worn when I first aired the idea to her.

'The board game club that happens at the pub?'

'Yes.'

'The club that Sam runs in the Smuggler's next door?'

'The very same.'

'You're kidding, right?'

'No,' I said, swallowing down a mouthful of the still too hot coffee. 'I thought it would be fun.'

Joe leant forward and put his mug down on the table.

'Fun,' he laughed, but he didn't sound happy. 'I think you and I have very different ideas about the meaning of the word fun, Tess. I'm the last person Sam wants to see in his pub. You saw the look on his face when I turned up the night of the power cut and when we spoke it was as awkward as arse.'

'But the pair of you can't carry on like this,' I told him. 'If you're really going to be back here for a while Joe, then you need to at least try . . .'

His jaw began to grind and I stopped talking. I had been considering throwing in a 'for Hope's sake' comment, but decided against it.

'Please don't interfere in this, Tess,' he said, sounding more upset than angry which made me feel even worse. 'Don't go getting ideas about trying to fix this because you can't, okay? It's beyond that, way beyond that.'

'It wasn't just my idea,' I said, thinking perhaps I could get away with mentioning her after all. 'Well, it was to start with, but someone else agreed to it.'

'Who?' he demanded. 'Who in their right mind would agree to something as stupid as this?'

'Hope,' I said.

'What?'

'I ran it by her too, and she thought it was about time the pair of you made your peace.'

Joe's jaw stopped grinding and his cheeks began to flush.

'Well, she would, wouldn't she?' he swallowed. 'No doubt she wants to help clear her boyfriend's conscience.'

'I'm pretty certain she wasn't only thinking of him,' I said softly. 'She told me that the two of you used to be a couple. That you were together for a long time . . .'

'What does that matter?' Joe snapped, sounding upset. 'She's with Sam now, isn't she? Just as I always knew she would be.'

'Yes,' I said, 'she is with Sam, but that doesn't mean . . .'

'Oh, Tess,' Joe butted in again, 'just leave it, all right. I daresay your heart's in the right place, but you should be grateful that I'm going away because had you got me to the pub under false pretences, then it really would not have ended well.'

He stood up and made for the door and I followed him back outside.

'I'm sorry,' I said as he struggled with the gate. I was grateful that it had stopped him rushing away. I didn't want to leave things like this. 'I just thought . . .'

'That you could make it all better,' he sighed.

'Yes,' I nodded. 'Exactly that.'

He left the gate and came back and pulled me in for a hug.

'Let's just forget it and catch up when I get back, okay?' he said, squeezing me tight. 'I'm pretty certain I'll be in need of a good moan about Charlie and the farm again by then.'

'All right,' I agreed, squeezing him back. 'We'll do that.'

'And in the meantime,' he said, letting me go so he could look down at me, 'don't get any more ideas in your head about trying to mend me, all right?'

'All right,' I smiled.

'I've got enough on my plate without adding well-meaning women with a penchant for feather boas into the mix.' He laughed as he went back to yanking at the gate.

'I think you'll find,' I called after him as he finally pulled it open and walked away, 'you were the one wearing the feather boa!'

He waved but didn't look back and it was only then I noticed Sam and Hope standing outside the pub. I had no idea what they had made of my parting shot, but Sam turned away and headed back inside with a face like thunder.

Chapter 17

I didn't even make it as far as the bar on Saturday evening before Hope appeared at my elbow and ushered me into a shady corner.

'So,' she said, her dark eyes shining, 'are we all set? I know I thought it was crazy to begin with, but Sam's moods are driving me to distraction and I'm willing to try *anything* now.'

Knowing that she was now fully on board with the idea made me feel even worse about disappointing her.

'I'm really sorry, Hope,' I whispered, keeping an eye on the bar where Sam was pulling a pint and wearing an expression that could have curdled milk, 'but it's not happening.'

'Joe's not coming?'

I shook my head.

'Damn,' she groaned, no longer bothering to keep quiet. 'Maybe you should have invited him to the cottage instead of the pub.'

'What good would that have been when we needed him here?'

'I don't know,' she shrugged, 'maybe you could have softened him up a bit at your place and encouraged him to come here after.'

I wasn't sure what her idea of 'softening him up' entailed and I didn't ask, but I was pretty sure you would have to be more than friends to do it.

'Or perhaps you could have asked him instead of me?' I suggested, thinking that would have been the easier option.

Her face was a picture, and not one I was sure I wanted to see.

'Me?' she squeaked, before throwing a cautionary glance over her shoulder. 'What difference would that have made?'

All the difference in the world if the evidence she and Joe had unwittingly presented me with so far was any sort of benchmark and I couldn't help thinking that it was.

All the colour might have drained from Joe's face the night he spotted her in the pub, but there was no denying the loving look in his eyes, or the way he had subsequently flushed when I told him that Hope had thought that the plan for tonight was a good one.

It was more than obvious to me that the pair still felt some connection and that was even without taking into account Hope's wistful tone when she told me all about her first love down at the beach huts or the cosy chat in the lane that I had witnessed.

'Well,' I said, stating the obvious because she seemed to

have missed it, 'having known Joe for so long and been in a relationship with him, you might have known how to put the idea of coming here to him in a more appealing way.'

'Hardly,' she said, now avoiding my eye. 'And besides, I knew him years ago. I have no idea who he is now.'

'Did you not get any sort of clue when you spoke to him yesterday?'

The way she shuffled from one foot to the other and focused on fiddling with a loose thread on her top, rather than answer me, confirmed what I suspected. She and Joe might have broken up after the crash and she might now be in a relationship with Sam, but there was definitely unfinished business between the pair. Hope might have said she had no idea who Joe was now, but I would have bet good money on her being willing to spend more time chatting to him to find out.

'Anyway,' I said, coming to the point because I felt bad for bringing up a moment she would clearly rather keep to herself, 'it wouldn't have made any difference, because he's had to leave. There's nothing we could have done to get him here.'

'Leave?' She said, sounding aghast as her gaze snapped back up to my face. 'You mean he's gone?'

Was it not for my concern about how, given her dramatic reaction, this particular love triangle had clear potential to develop, I would have been enthralled. By the looks of it, there was a real-life soap opera about to play out in front of my eyes, but feeling the way I did about all three members of the cast, I wished I could switch channels to something more soothing.

'Yes,' I said, 'did he not say?' She ignored the question. 'But don't panic. He's going to be back in a few days.'

'I wasn't panicking,' she said defensively. 'Good riddance.'

She wasn't very convincing, this female lead in the love triangle.

'So, you wouldn't have minded if he'd gone for good then?'

'Of course, I wouldn't,' she said, making a marginally better attempt at it. 'It would have been a relief. There's nothing I want more than to be able to get back to normal again.'

I was about to ask her to expand on that thought but didn't get the chance.

'What are you two whispering about?' Sam unexpectedly hissed.

His voice was unnervingly close to my ear and my hand flew up to my chest.

'Jesus!' I snapped. 'Where the hell did you spring from? You scared the life out of me!'

He looked somewhat taken aback by my reaction but not as surprised as I'd been by his silent approach and badly timed interruption.

'The pair of you look positively furtive hidden here in the dark,' he said accusingly, stepping around to look at us, his green eyes darting from me to Hope and back again. 'What are you up to?' he suspiciously demanded.

Fortunately, Hope was more on the ball than I was and ready with a quick answer.

'We were just working on our strategy and tactics for thrashing you at Scrabble,' she said without missing a beat.

Sam shook his head.

'If the lad who's supposed to be covering for me behind the bar doesn't turn up,' he grumbled, 'that won't be an issue because I won't get the chance to play. Not that either of you could thrash me of course.'

'Oh, is that right?' I tutted, recovering enough to join in.

Hope looked at me and winked and I knew we had got away with it, but only just.

Before long, the pub had filled up nicely and I found myself teamed at the Scrabble board with George.

'I usually play with my sister,' he told me as we picked out our first seven letters and I tried not to show my disappointment with what I had selected, 'but she's gone to the prize bingo in the next village with a friend from the WI.'

He didn't sound particularly impressed to be left high and dry by his regular gaming partner, but then given the way Sam had shouted at Skipper, I wouldn't have blamed him if he'd opted not to come to the pub at all.

'There's a big cash pot tonight apparently,' he expanded, 'and Gladys is usually pretty lucky so it'll probably be worth the trip.'

'You didn't fancy it yourself then, George?' I asked.

'I did think about it,' he said, leaning down to stroke Skipper's head, 'but Sam called round this afternoon to apologize for shouting about the water bowl incident so I thought I'd head here as usual instead.'

I was pleased that Sam wasn't so caught up in his own head at the moment that he hadn't realized that he'd upset one of his most regular and loyal customers. It said a lot about him that he had bothered to make amends.

'Well, I'm pleased you did decide to come,' I smiled at George. 'Because I didn't much fancy having to play opposite him myself.'

'That's as maybe,' George sympathetically carried on, keeping his voice low so no one else could hear, 'but we all know the real reason why he's in such a bad mood these days. Not that we'd dare to mention it in front of him, of course.'

He cast a quick glance over at the bar where Sam was putting the relief lad who had *finally* turned up through his paces. Neither of them looked particularly happy so I daresay Sam was bending the guy's ear about being so late, which I supposed was fair enough when he should have been at his post at least an hour ago.

'Obviously I wasn't a Wynmouth regular when the crash happened,' George carried on, pulling my attention back to him, 'but it doesn't take a genius to understand that something like that has a lifelong impact. And I'm not just talking about Sam's leg.'

'I know what you mean,' I said, leaning further over the table. 'His head's suffering as much as his body right now, isn't it?'

'It certainly is, my dear,' George agreed, laying down

his first tiles and scoring seventy-five speedy points with 'squeeze'.

How he'd managed to draw those letters and focus on putting them together so quickly given the conversation we were having was beyond me and, of course, his score was doubled because he'd won the chance to start the game off. I had the feeling I was in for a masterclass in the art of pulling words out a hat or, in this case, a little cotton drawstring bag.

'Oh, well done, George,' I said sportingly as I scribbled down his score.

'Thank you, my dear,' he beamed, diving back into the bag to replenish his tiles.

He looked at me again once he'd finished arranging them, no doubt in some sort of impressive order.

'I understand you and the chap responsible for our landlord's loss of humour have struck up a bit of a friendship,' he said casually.

'That's right.'

'Only natural I suppose,' he sniffed. 'Two new folk in the village being drawn to one another.'

'Joe's hardly new to Wynmouth,' I pointed out. 'His family have been here longer than most.'

'True,' nodded George. 'And they're not exactly having an easy time of it either, are they?'

'No,' I said, grateful that he sounded sympathetic. 'They're not.'

'Anyway,' he said, rubbing his hands together, 'that's

enough of your distraction tactics. You're trying to stop me from focusing by talking.'

'You're the one chatting,' I laughed.

'Well, whatever,' he smiled, nodding at my tiles, 'let's see what you've got.'

Just as I had thought, I did come in for an intellectual thrashing, but in my defence, I had a lot on my mind and with George continuing the conversation, I found it hard to concentrate. At least, that was what I kept telling myself as he relentlessly laid down one triple word score after another.

'That was a good game, Tess,' he smiled, once we had finished, 'but I can't help thinking you were a little distracted this evening. Either that, or you thought you'd let the old-timer win this one.'

'Oh, definitely the second option,' I laughed. 'I just didn't want to show you up, George.'

He laughed along with me and gave me a kiss on the cheek before picking up Skipper's lead from where it had been secured around his chair leg, just to be on the safe side, and wandering off to say his goodbyes.

'Where's Hope?' I asked Sam, who was stacking the rest of the game boxes in a pile on the bottom of the bookshelf.

I had felt a little light-headed when I stood up and realized that throughout the course of the evening, I had drunk more wine than I usually would and, because I'd had no reason to move, I hadn't noticed the impact. Perhaps that was another reason why I had struggled to stay focused on those tiles?

'She went a while ago,' Sam told me, straightening back up and wincing as he did so, 'she wasn't feeling too well.'

I watched him rub his leg, massaging the area around his knee in particular. I don't even think he knew he was doing it.

'I'll finish putting the last of these away if you like,' I offered.

'No, it's all right. I can manage,' he said, but he let me carry on nonetheless.

'I hope she isn't coming down with anything,' I said, as I tried to focus on the task I had volunteered for.

I soon found that the boxes didn't want to stack in as orderly a fashion for me as they had for Sam and I had to pull them all out and start again.

'Are you all right?' Sam asked.

'Yes,' I said, 'it's just a bit of a tight fit. Did Hope say what was wrong?'

'Just a headache,' he said. 'But a bit of a thumper and it was rowdy in here tonight so I don't think that helped.'

From what I had heard, there had been more than one heated conversation across the tables but for the most part they had been good-natured. It was good to see that the competitive spirit was alive and kicking in the usually sleepy village, but obviously not if you had a sore head.

'Sophie came to pick her up,' Sam told me. 'Are you sure you're all right, Tess? You're making a right bloody hash of that. There were only three more to stack when I was down there and now there's seven!'

I couldn't hold in the giggle which bubbled up when I looked at the mess I had made and before I knew it, I had fallen back on my heels with a bump and was sitting on the pub floor.

'Are you drunk?' Sam asked, sounding amused.

'No,' I said, scrabbling around and eventually grabbing his outstretched hand so he could pull me to my feet, 'just a tiny bit tipsy. Definitely not drunk.'

As I came to stand upright, the whole world had shifted on its axis, not just the bar, and it felt like I was on the deck of a ship. A ship that was leaning first to the left and then to the right. I closed my eyes, which I quickly gathered was not a good idea, and then gasped when I felt Sam's hands come to rest on my waist. My senses must have been heightened because I had my eyes shut and therefore the thrilling shiver which ran through me was more than justified. I slowly opened one eye and then the other.

'You aren't going to throw up, are you?' he frowned.

It was hardly a romantic question, even if he did look concerned, but the close proximity made it feel like an intimate moment. I looked up into his tanned face, taking in the dark blonde stubble, the lines around his eyes which crinkled when he smiled and the unruly sun-bleached hair which topped the vision off.

'Of course not,' I smiled goofily up at him, 'like I said, I'm just a bit tipsy.'

'Well, that's all right then,' he said, releasing me and

stepping away, 'because I have a "clear your own vom" policy here at the Smuggler's.'

Definitely not a romantic moment or a question asked in concern.

'And I've just had this carpet cleaned,' he added for good measure, leaving me in no doubt where his fears lay. He was undeniably thinking of his décor.

There were only a couple of regulars left now, they were all ensconced in the snug and didn't offer to help, so I carried on with the tidying up. That said, I was probably more of a hindrance, but Sam bore my efforts with good grace and I didn't smash anything or spill too much.

'I think that's the lot,' I said, looking around, but taking care not to turn my head too fast.

I had drunk a pint of water but I wasn't feeling much better for it. I thought I might have to break out the paracetamol before I went to sleep, just to be on the safe side.

'Thanks, Tess,' said Sam, 'I appreciate the help.'

'My pleasure,' I hiccupped. 'You know I can't resist helping out if I can.'

Given how quickly I had become involved in the goings-on in the café, pub and village in general, no one could be in any doubt of that. The thought of having to pack up and leave made me suddenly feel even more nauseous than my hangover was going to.

'Is there any chance, do you think,' I blurted out, 'that you might extend my time in the cottage even longer? If I wanted to stay on, would that be a possibility?'

'Do you think you might then?' he frowned, as well he might, given that I had already jumped from visiting for a couple of weeks to a couple of months.

'Perhaps,' I shrugged. 'I'm not sure if I could, to be honest, but right now, I don't much like the thought of having an end date to my time in Wynmouth.'

'You're enjoying being here that much, are you?'

'Yes,' I swallowed, 'yes, I am.'

'Is that because of . . .' he began, but his words tailed off and he turned away.

'Is that because of what?' I asked him.

'Never mind,' he said, sounding gruff again. 'Forget it.'

I would have bet good money that he was going to include Joe's name in whatever it was he had almost just said.

'Look,' he said, turning back again, 'I know I'm probably being paranoid, but you and Hope . . .'

'What about us?'

'You weren't scheming something earlier, were you?'

'Like what?'

'Like anything,' he said, coming to stand in front of me, much the same as he had before, although not quite as close this time. 'I don't want either of you interfering.'

'But I'm always interfering,' I reminded him with a smile. 'I interfered practically the moment I arrived and got you to lay on the bank holiday entertainment *and then* I stuck my oar in again so you'd get the beach clean going and the solstice party up and running. Interfering is what I'm known for around here. I've even put my two pennies' worth in down at Sophie's café!'

My intention in reeling everything off had been to make him laugh, or at least smile, but the frown he was wearing was going nowhere.

'That's as maybe,' he said seriously, 'but you know what I'm really talking about, don't you? And I can't cope with you, or Hope, interfering in that.'

'I see.'

'It's painful enough that it's all been stirred up again,' he said, 'so I don't want either of you making it worse because you've got it into your heads that you can somehow make it better. Whatever it is that the pair of you might be thinking you can do, I want you to forget it, okay?'

I may have had one drink too many, but I wasn't so squiffy that I couldn't see how much he was hurting. Part of me wished that Joe had been able to stay away, that everything was fine at the farm and everyone's lives could continue as before, but there was another more practical part which knew that everyone was simply pretending and that until they ripped off the band-aid and let the wound get some air, it would never properly heal.

'We just want you to be happy,' I whispered.

'And you have my best interests at heart,' he cut in, more or less word for word finishing what I was going to say.

In my head I also had Joe's name in the happiness and best interests mix and Hope's and Charlie's because they all deserved to be there, didn't they?

'Sam,' I began, as I took another step closer, 'you have to understand . . .'

I only wanted to close the gap between us a little, but my foot became caught around a chair leg and I fell forward, so that rather than simply standing a little nearer, I landed heavily in his arms and found my body pressed close to his.

'What do I have to understand?' he swallowed.

He wasn't loosening his grip and I opened my mouth to tell him, but the words just wouldn't come.

'That my head has been all over the place from the very moment ...' he began when I didn't answer. 'That my heart ...'

'Go on,' I urged.

I would have dearly loved to have heard the end of either of those sentences, but he didn't finish them and before I realized what was happening, I found my head moving closer to his, my eyes locked on his lips and my desire to kiss him blocking out all reason and all thoughts that he already had a girlfriend. A girlfriend who also happened to be a very dear friend.

'Tess.'

The sound of my name on his lips, spoken in such a sultry tone, was the most seductive thing I had ever heard.

'Yes ...'

I let out an unexpected and ungracious hiccup and thankfully came to my senses.

'I think I'd better go home,' I whispered, stepping unsteadily back. 'I don't feel very well.'

'I'll walk you back,' he said, releasing me. 'Otherwise, goodness knows where you'll end up.'

*

It was only a few steps from the pub to the cottage, but when I woke the next morning on the sofa, under a blanket and with a plastic bucket – thankfully empty – next to me, I couldn't remember taking a single one of them. Unfortunately, the embarrassing end to my time inside the pub premises couldn't be so easily blocked out and I rolled over and pulled the blanket over my head as I shamefully recalled just how close I had stupidly come to trying to kiss the man who was dating my wonderful new BFF.

When I woke again, I had a shower, attempted to eat a round of toast and swallowed down the painkillers I should have taken before I fell asleep. I pottered about for a bit trying to keep busy and inventing jobs that didn't need doing, but it was no good. By the time I found myself thinking about de-scaling the kettle, I knew the game was up and I couldn't put the inevitable off any longer.

'Hope,' I said as I stumbled over the pub threshold, but still keeping my sunglasses firmly in place. 'Are you feeling any better?'

'Much,' she beamed, 'thanks. And clearly better than you. Good night, was it?'

'Tess,' said Sam, appearing before I could answer and carrying two plates groaning under the weight of a hefty Sunday lunch. 'I wasn't excepting to see you today.'

'Let me serve these,' said Hope, quickly taking the plates from him. 'Which table are they going to?'

Once she had gone, I hopped up behind the bar and followed Sam to the kitchen.

'Look,' I said, not going fully into the room, 'about last night ...'

'What about it?' he said, picking up a carving knife and making short work of a massive joint of beef.

'You know what,' I said, feeling both too hungover and embarrassed to spell out the incident which had almost, but thankfully not quite, happened.

'Yes,' he sighed, 'I do and I'm sorry. I shouldn't have said anything.'

From what I could remember, he hadn't said anything much and I was the one who was supposed to be apologizing. I was the one who had very nearly caused us to kiss.

'No,' I said, 'I'm the one who's sorry. I don't know what came over me.'

'Neither do I,' he said, briefly looking up. 'Know what came over me, I mean.'

Although I wasn't sure why he was feeling so guilty about something I had instigated, it did make apologizing a little less mortifying.

'So,' I tentatively asked, 'can we just forget about it then?'

'No one's going to hear about it from me,' he said resolutely, 'and besides, nothing happened, did it?'

'That's right,' I agreed, standing a little taller, 'absolutely nothing happened.'

I shrugged off the thought that it so easily could have.

'Right,' he said, 'great.'

'Really great,' I nodded, 'and can I say, just for the record, that making a play for ...'

I was going to add 'someone's other half isn't my style' but I could hear Hope coming through the bar behind me and stopped. Sam looked at me, but I shook my head. I could hardly carry on now.

'Two more chicken dinners, please, Sam!' she called out, 'and they both want Yorkshire puddings with them.'

I stepped aside to let her through.

'It's busy out there,' she said, sounding glad. 'I thought you'd already gone again, Tess.'

'Not yet,' I said, 'I'm just about to.'

The smell of the roasting meat was making me feel nauseous. Not that there was anything wrong with Sam's culinary skills, but my hangover was still doing a fine job of making its presence felt.

'I don't suppose you could spare an hour to help out, could you?' Hope asked me, 'there'll be a lunch in it for you and it would save Sam from having to keep walking in and out of the bar.'

It was the very last thing I felt like doing, but given that I'd almost kissed her boyfriend the second her back was turned, I didn't feel in a position to refuse.

'If that's okay with you, Sam?' she said, turning to him.

'Of course,' he said, 'but only as long as you haven't got other plans, Tess.'

'Other than nursing this hangover,' I said trying to laugh as I eased off my sunglasses, 'I haven't got plans to do anything.'

'That's settled then,' said Hope, 'come with me and I'll run you through the menu.'

Chapter 18

I might not have been initially in the mood – physically or mentally – to be doling out platefuls of Sunday dinner, but my busy stint in the pub was the perfect way to get over what had happened the night before and by the time the rush was over, and I was tucking into the succulent roast beef I suddenly found I fancied, everything was back to normal and on an even keel.

I spent all day Monday at the café helping Sophie and Hope check the final details of the beach clean and solstice party and on Tuesday, as it was so hot, I went back to the beach for a lazy day of paddling, exploring the pools and soaking up the sun.

Not surprisingly, given where I was, my head was full of Mum in her yellow sundress, but left to its own devices, my mind skipped ahead and I saw her as the wealthy but solitary shopper who spent her days trying to make herself feel better about life by maxing out her credit cards and lunching alone.

Conversely, when I thought of Dad, first reading a newspaper in his deckchair and then years later, the only images I could conjure of him were ones where he had his head down at his desk and never on the arm of another woman or, as Mum's diary had alleged, women. For some reason, my brain was reluctant to marry up with the truth I now carried around in my heart, but I tried not to let it all dominate my day in the sun.

I had just stepped out of a refreshingly cool shower late that afternoon when someone began beating a tattoo on the cottage door and I hastily pulled on some clothes before rushing to answer it.

'Just a sec,' I shouted, fumbling with the key in the lock, 'hold on.'

I opened the door and was faced with the biggest bunch of yellow roses imaginable. In an instant I was transported back to my parents' garden and, remembering how beautifully the roses had bloomed this year, courtesy of the bunch Joan had arranged for me during my last attack of vertigo, I was completely convinced that my father was standing behind them – and I was amazed to discover that I hoped he might be.

My heart hammered hard as I tried to work out what I was going to say but I couldn't come up with anything and it didn't matter anyway, because it wasn't him.

'I'd all but given up on you,' said Joe, his face appearing over the top of the blooms as he lowered them. 'Are you going to ask me in?'

I stepped aside to let him in as my heart settled back down again.

'These are for you,' he said, handing the beautiful bunch over. 'I remembered how much you enjoyed looking at the roses when we went for our afternoon tea.'

'Hello, Joe,' I said, finally finding my words. 'They're absolutely stunning. Thank you so much. It was kind of you to remember.'

'There's not much I forget,' he grinned, evidently pleased with my reaction.

Aside from the first non-platonic kiss anyone had ever planted on my lips, of course.

'When did you get back?' I asked, brushing the thought aside.

'Not long ago,' he said, following me into the kitchen where I thought I'd seen a vase at the back of one of the cupboards. 'I haven't even been to the farm yet.'

'Are you putting the moment off by any chance?'

'In a way,' he shrugged, 'but I had a couple of things to do in the village and I wanted to see you. I've been feeling bad about how we left things last week.'

I thought back to how resolutely he had objected to my suggestion that he should go with me to the pub and how keen he had been to convince me not to try and 'mend him'.

'I hate the thought of you thinking that I don't appreciate your concern,' he said, looking at me intently.

'I know you appreciate it, Joe,' I told him, 'and I also know this isn't just any old run-of-the-mill sort of situation either.'

He nodded and ran a hand through his hair.

'That's all right then,' he smiled, 'that's settled. And you know, I have high hopes for today.'

'High hopes?'

'Yeah,' he said, 'I'm hoping we might be able to say goodbye without any confusion, mixed messages or argumentative undertones.'

I supposed that had become a bit of a habit.

'Hey now,' I said, finally locating the vase and plunging the roses into it, 'don't go mad. Let's not count our chickens until you're walking out through that door and heading back to the farm, shall we?'

I made us tea and halved the gargantuan slice of coconut coffee cake Sophie had sent me home with the day before.

'Are you sure you don't mind sharing this?' Joe asked, appreciatively eyeing the plate.

'It's imperative that I do share it,' I told him as I handed him a cake fork, 'because if I keep eating everything Sophie tries to feed me, then I'm going to be at least two dress sizes bigger before I wave goodbye to Wynmouth.'

I hated the thought of saying my farewells, whatever size I was going to be when I had to do it.

'That's not going to be happening just yet though, is it?' Joe asked.

'What, me piling on the weight, or saying goodbye?'

'Saying goodbye,' he laughed. 'I can see you've already put a bit of weight on.'

'Hey!' I objected, batting him with a cushion and almost

knocking the plate out of his hand. 'I thought you wanted to leave on friendly terms today?'

'I do,' he laughed, hiding the cushion down the side of the sofa. 'I do. You know I'm only teasing. You aren't really thinking of leaving already, are you?'

'No,' I swallowed, 'not just yet.'

There was a part of me that was beginning to think about it though, in spite of my tipsy request to stay on. Not that I wanted to go, of course, but now, having decided that I was quitting my job, I needed to tell Dad and I also needed to clarify a few things that I had discovered in Mum's diary because I just couldn't get some of them to add up.

'Well, that's a relief,' said Joe, bypassing the fork and taking a massive bite straight from the slice. 'Oh, my god,' he groaned, after chewing for a few seconds. 'Oh. My. God.'

'Oh my god, stop,' I sniggered, before taking a bite myself, 'if anyone walks by, they'll be wondering what the hell's happening in here.'

'You have tasted this, right?' he asked, clearly offended that I thought his reaction was over the top.

'Oh. My. God,' I mimicked as I swallowed the sweet, moist mouthful down.

'Exactly,' he grinned. 'Thank you.'

'It's so good,' I laughed.

'So good,' he agreed.

We sat in silence for a few seconds, chewing, smiling and swallowing until all that were left were a few tiny crumbs that even Bruce would have been hard pushed to sniff out.

'You know,' said Joe, picking up his tea, 'over the years, I've been trying to convince myself that Sophie's cooking and baking wasn't really as good as I remembered it, but . . .'

'It is?'

'It's better,' he sighed. 'If anything, even better than I remembered!'

'I'm guessing you used to eat at Hope's place a lot when you were together?'

'Yeah,' he replied, 'all the time and Hope used to come to the farm too, whenever she could get a lift out of the village.'

It was really sad to think that him, Hope and Sam, who had once shared so much, couldn't now be a part of each other's lives because of what had happened the night of the crash and because Hope was now in love with Sam. Don't get me wrong, I did understand how difficult it all was and that it wasn't a situation you could tie up with a neat bow and hand back fixed, but it was still sad, especially now they were all living in such close proximity again.

'You know,' Joe ruefully smiled, 'the taste of that cake makes me want to go back to the café.'

'You should go,' I told him. 'There's no reason why you shouldn't.'

'No way,' he said, shaking his head, 'it's not worth the hassle. I wouldn't want Sam to think I was talking to Hope or even trying to see her behind his back.'

'She's not in the café half the time,' I said, 'because she's in the pub and, even if she was, I'm sure Sam wouldn't think that.'

That said, given that I had seen Joe and Hope talking pretty furtively in the lane, he might be justified in jumping to that very conclusion if he also saw them with their heads together like that.

'No,' Joe shrugged. 'I couldn't do it. I know how it feels to have a mate muscle in on your other half and I wouldn't want him thinking I was doing anything like that. Even if he has already done it to me.'

I didn't point out that, if what I knew of the situation and the timings were correct, then Sam had still been in a coma when he and Hope split up and consequently capable of doing very little.

'That's something you might want to think about, Tess,' he then floored me by adding.

'What?'

'It's not nice when a so-called pal makes a play for your other half.'

'What on earth are you talking about?'

'You and Sam after hours in the pub Saturday night . . .'

'What about me and Sam in the pub after hours Saturday night?'

'You kissed, didn't you?'

'No,' I snapped, 'we didn't, of course we didn't.'

'You've gone a bit pink,' he said, raising his eyebrows.

'Well, so would you, if I'd just accused you of doing something you hadn't done. I'm angry, that's why I've gone red!'

I couldn't believe the turn the conversation had taken. Here we were eating cake, drinking tea, bathed in the scent from the beautiful and fragrant roses and he was accusing me of pinching someone else's man!

'I haven't brought this up to make you angry, Tess.'

'Then why have you brought it up and, more to the point, who told you about this non-event in the first place?'

'I heard it in the pub,' he further shocked me by saying. 'I called here after I'd done in the village, but as you weren't in, I risked a coffee in the Smuggler's and that's when I heard about it.'

'I see,' I said.

I was surprised that he had gone in unaccompanied.

'And I'm mentioning it because as much as I hate to see Sam and Hope together, I don't want her to get hurt. If you've started anything up with Sam, then please put a stop to it, Tess.'

I couldn't believe what I was hearing.

'I haven't started anything up,' I said, louder now, 'with anyone. I have no idea who was gossiping but it's all bullshit.'

'Fair enough,' he said, sounding unconvinced. 'I suppose this is my cue to go.'

'Yes,' I said, jumping to my feet and thinking that we were parting on less than ideal terms again, 'I suppose it is.'

I slammed the door behind him and paced about the cottage wondering why the hell Sam had been talking about, and embellishing, what had happened when there was every chance that Hope might find out. It really didn't make sense, but as the only person who knew about it, Joe couldn't possibly have got his 'first-hand' information from anyone else, could he?

I grabbed my keys, slid my feet into my sandals and made a beeline for the pub, determined to get to the bottom of it all.

'What can I get you?' asked the lad behind the bar who was helping out on a regular basis now business had picked up.

'Nothing,' I said, pointing along the bar to where Sam was tipping ice into a glass, 'I don't want a drink, thanks. I just want him.'

'Oh landlord,' laughed the two guys next to me, 'there's a woman here who wants you.'

'He's still as in demand as ever,' teased another, sitting at a table. 'I reckon I need to get me one of those bionic legs. That must be the thing that attracts the ladies, coz it can't be his rugged good looks!'

Sam smiled and shook his head.

'And there was me thinking it was my lived-in, careworn features and my unrivalled wit,' he laughed.

I hadn't realized that my voice had been raised enough to draw that much attention but I was too annoyed to care. Perhaps, I thought, it wouldn't hurt to call Sam out in front of a few people. Maybe that would make him think about keeping his silly words to himself in the future.

He finished serving and then came to me.

'Is everything all right?' he asked, finally spotting my scowl and lighting the blue touchpaper by pointing it out, 'You don't look very happy.'

'No,' I said, banging my keys down on the bar, 'everything is not all bloody right and I look like this because I'm not happy.'

There was a cheer from somewhere behind me and then everyone fell silent. You could have heard a pin drop.

'Why did you tell Joe Upton that we kissed on Saturday night?' I demanded, all thoughts of keeping it from Hope shoved aside as the red mist descended.

'What?'

'Why did you tell Joe Upton that we had an after-hours snog?'

I fixed him with my best death-stare, ignoring the confusion I could see clouding his usually bright green eyes.

'You know as well as I do, that nothing happened,' I said, lowering my voice a little, but not enough to make it too difficult for everyone else to hear, 'so why lie?'

Sam sighed and looked over the top of my head to where everyone was still holding their breath, waiting for his explanation and, hopefully, heartfelt apology.

'I haven't seen Joe Upton,' he said.

His volume matched mine, but he sounded angry and not, as I had hoped, at all contrite.

'The last I heard he'd left again,' he hissed.

'So,' I said, feeling more indignant than ever, 'how do you explain the fact that he's just turned up at the cottage and told me that he called in here earlier and heard straight from the horse's mouth all about what happened Saturday night.'

There was a low-level murmuring breaking out behind me, but I didn't take my eyes off Sam.

'I have absolutely no idea,' he said, looking right back at

me, 'because I've been at the cash-and-carry all afternoon. I only got back about ten minutes ago.'

That rather took the wind out of my sails and I could hear a titter as well as muttering coming from the rapt crowd of listeners.

'What?'

'I haven't been here since lunchtime,' Sam said. 'Not that I need to explain my movements to you as you seem to think you know them already. I haven't seen Joe, I haven't heard Joe and quite frankly, I can't believe that you would think that I'd tell anyone about what happened Saturday night, especially as it was something and nothing.'

I swallowed, my eyes stinging with tears.

'Perhaps you should ask Patrick over there if he knows any-thing about it,' he said, pointing. 'He's one of Joe's farmhands and he was hanging on in here until I turfed him out Saturday night. Maybe he saw something and had a word with his boss.'

I slowly turned to find a guy with scruffy shoulder-length hair, nursing a pint and looking sheepish.

'Well?' I demanded.

'I was having a smoke out front earlier when I saw the boss,' he explained, 'and I might have mentioned that I had seen you and Sam having a bit of a moment.'

I felt my misplaced anger oozing away and puddling around my feet.

'I'd had a pint or two that night,' he admitted, 'so I might not have quite got all the details right, but the pair of you were definitely in some sort of clinch.'

Sam shook his head in disbelief and let out a guttural growl.

'She'd had a pint or two as well, you prat,' he growled at Patrick, as he pointed at me. 'She fell over and I caught her.'

It had been wine rather than beer, but that was a minor detail and not worth mentioning.

'Oh,' said Patrick.

'It was a reflex action,' Sam went on, 'nothing more. And besides, I could hardly risk her bloody suing me if she took a knock on the way down, could I?'

I didn't think it would be helpful either to mention that when I had ended up in his arms, he had started to say something very interesting to me about his head and his heart, but it was all clear as a bell in my head now.

'I suppose not,' Patrick muttered.

Sam turned his attention back to me and shook his head.

'The show's over, folks,' he announced, trying to draw a line under the completely unnecessary scene I had just instigated.

It took a few seconds, but eventually everyone went back to their drinks and their own conversations, which were no doubt about me and my big mouth, and I bet a few of them were keener to still believe the fiction rather than the facts.

'Well,' said Sam, 'that was unpleasant, wasn't it?'

'I'm so sorry,' I said, feeling every bit as bad as I deserved to. 'Joe said—'

'I don't care what he said,' Sam interrupted. 'I'm more upset that you thought I would break the promise I'd made.'

'I'm sorry,' I said again.

'Words spread like wildfire around here,' he reminded me. 'This will be all over Wynmouth by closing time tonight.'

'But what about Patrick,' I reminded him. 'I daresay he'd already told everyone anyway.'

'No, he hadn't,' said Sam. 'You only had to see the look on everyone's faces. This was completely fresh news. The only person Patrick told was his boss and that was because he no doubt wanted to curry favour.'

The implications of what I had just done were beginning to hit home and I rather wished I'd ordered a stiff one when asked.

'And it won't matter that nothing happened and I've told everyone that nothing happened,' Sam went on, 'not when the alternative is so much more appealing.'

'What do you mean?'

'Well, which version of this do you reckon will have the most mileage?' he asked. 'The landlord catches a drunk punter as she stumbles, or, the landlord who happens to be renting his cottage to an attractive holidaymaker is caught in a steamy embrace with her after hours.'

'The one with the most sex in it,' grinned the lad serving as he reached behind Sam for a bottle of tonic mixer.

'Oh god,' I said, snatching up my keys and ignoring how flattered I'd felt that Sam had said I was attractive. 'I need to speak to Hope.'

I dashed out of the pub before he could stop me and ran down to the café, hoping to catch her before she closed up for the day.

'Hope!' I called, spotting her as she was just about to leave.

'Hey, Tess,' she smiled.

'Hey,' I puffed, as I bent to nurse the stitch in my side and catch my breath.

'What's going on?'

'I need to talk to you,' I panted. 'Have you got a minute?'

I was more than mildly confused by Hope's reaction when I described what had happened between Sam and I. Obviously, I didn't share that he had made mention of his head and heart, or the fact that I had really wanted to kiss him and have him kiss me back. Neither did I mention the role Joe had played in the whole debacle, nor the total arse I had just made of myself in the pub having taken his words at face value.

I stuck to the simple facts, i.e. that there was now a rumour going around that Sam and I had kissed, but we absolutely hadn't. It was all a silly misunderstanding and the person who had thought he'd seen us in an embrace had actually seen me fall and Sam catch me.

'Okay,' Hope shrugged.

She seemed completely unconcerned.

'You do believe me, don't you?'

'Of course, I do,' she laughed. 'Why wouldn't I? Stop looking so worried,' she insisted. 'Folk are always happiest when they're gossiping, Tess, and this will only run until the next thing comes along. Honestly, just let it go.'

'All right.'

'I need to head home,' she said walking over to her car.

'I told Mum I was on my way ages ago. I'll see you tomorrow, okay?'

'Okay,' I said. 'I'll see you tomorrow.'

It wasn't until she had gone that it dawned on me she had got the wrong end of the stick. It seemed she thought I was worried about what people would think of me, rather than what she would think. But in spite of the misunderstanding, I was pleased to have reached her before the rumour mill did, and I had to be satisfied with that.

Having tried to make amends with Sam in the pub and given the low-down to Hope before she heard the enhanced part deux version, the only other person I needed to talk to was Joe. I could understand that he felt protective towards Hope because he was clearly still smitten with her, but why let me assume that the person who had gone blabbing about our non-kiss was Sam?

I can't deny that as I drove out to the farm, I was beginning to feel scared that he was purposefully trying to stir up trouble for his old friend. After all, the guy was responsible for his little brother's death and he had also won Hope's heart but, surely, Joe understood that moving back and making everyone's lives a misery was not going to give him any satisfaction or peace in the long run.

'Hey!' I called as I swung my car off the road, on to the farm drive and came bumper to bumper with a tractor. 'I need to talk to you.'

'What the hell are you doing?' Joe shouted, opening the

door and jumping out with Bruce hot on his heels. 'I could have hit you, swinging in here at that speed.'

I quickly climbed out before Bruce's jumping up and sharp claws left their mark on the paintwork.

'Never mind my driving,' I insensitively bit back. 'I want to know why you told me that it was Sam who told you what had happened between us in the pub.'

'I thought you said nothing had happened.'

'You know what I mean.'

He made a grab for Bruce's collar and made the dog sit at his feet.

'I never said it was Sam,' he frowned, keeping a tight hold on Bruce, who had started to whine and looked like a coiled spring, his tail thumping on the dusty drive.

'Yes, you did,' I shot back.

'No,' said Joe, 'I did not.'

It seemed we had reached an impasse and I mentally trawled back over everything he had said in the cottage, just to be sure.

'Well,' I flushed, when I recalled he hadn't actually mentioned Sam by name, 'you told me you'd been to the pub and had been given a first-hand account.'

'So?'

'So, you let me *think* that it came from Sam, didn't you? As far as I knew, he was the only person in the pub that late at night. I thought everyone else had left while we were clearing up. I had no idea that this Patrick guy, who works for you, was still there.'

'But that's not my fault,' Joe pointed out, sounding annoyed. 'I can't be held responsible for what you thought I'd said, as opposed to what I'd actually said, can I?'

I didn't answer. I suppose it did make more sense that he would stay and have a coffee in the pub once he'd realized Sam wasn't there.

'You were the one who jumped to conclusions, Tess,' Joe carried on. 'I only mentioned it because I was looking out for Hope.'

'Right,' I said, 'I see.'

'So, are we good?'

'Yes,' I said. 'We're good.'

I was embarrassed but also relieved that I had read the situation wrong. Joe hadn't been trying to stir up trouble after all. I had just imagined he had.

'I'm sorry,' I told him, 'and you needn't worry about Hope because I'm not interested in Sam that way.'

'You're not?'

'No,' I lied, 'and even if I was, I'd hardly do anything about it, would I? I've struck up a great friendship with Hope and I'd never go behind her back.'

'Of course, you wouldn't,' he said, shaking his head, 'and I'm sorry for inferring that you would.'

'Okay.'

'So, can we just forget about this then?' he asked.

'Well,' I said, 'we can try, but given that I went to the pub after you left and accused Sam of spreading gossip in front of a packed bar, that might be easier said than done.'

'Oh no,' said Joe, 'you didn't?'

'I did,' I said, wincing at the memory. 'You know, things would be a whole lot easier around here if you two could leave the past in the past and at least try to get along. That way there wouldn't be anything to misinterpret or get muddled up.'

I wasn't trying to shift the blame for what I had done on to either him or Sam, but if they could just rub along, it would be a help to everyone.

'You make it sound so easy,' said Joe, biting his lip.

'It could be,' I began.

'No,' he stepped in, cutting me off, 'it couldn't and I'm sorry, Tess, but I really need to get on.'

I watched as he climbed back into the cab and tried to settle Bruce. He looked like he had the weight of the world on his shoulders and I wished I knew what I could do to make it all melt away.

Chapter 19

More than aware that my assumptions had led me to making a mess of things, I decided to stay out of everyone's way and lay low for a couple of the days. I had upset, angered and disappointed both Sam and Joe, and let Hope down to boot, so the best thing I could do was bide my time and let the dust settle. It didn't feel good to have cocked up so badly and I didn't like myself very much. I had steamed in like a bull in a china shop and had consequently scuppered my chance to act as intermediary between the two men I had become friends with. That is, assuming they still wanted to be friends with me.

I constantly thought back to what Sophie had said just a few days before – *'before you decide that you have discovered something isn't true or real, and act on it, make sure you're in full possession of all the facts and that you have them in the right order.'* I had been in no doubt that Joe had heard some gossip in the pub, but I certainly hadn't gathered 'all the facts' about it or checked their order before reacting to them.

Mulling all this over led me back to Mum's diary again. For a while I had been utterly convinced that I had interpreted everything correctly, but now, having made such a silly mistake and upset my friends in the process, I was doubting the evidence typed out in front of me.

There was nothing specific to keep nudging my belief in what Mum had written into disbelief, but there was something niggling away nonetheless and this involved my last living relative so I really couldn't afford to get it wrong. If I unjustifiably acted on the information and confronted Dad with it, then the implications could last for the rest of my life.

I daresay some people would have said that what went on in my parents' marriage was nothing to do with me and, now that Mum had gone, I should let it all lie, but there was more to it than that. What Mum had written about Dad's behaviour made a mockery of everything he claimed to believe in. If what Mum had recorded was true then he was the biggest hypocrite and his whole ethos about life, as well as business, was a sham and, as I was still (for the moment) his most senior employee, that made it a lot to do with me. These weighty accusations had the potential to be about more than just my parents' marriage, they were calling Dad's whole character into question.

Having opted to keep a low profile, I left it until the last minute to head out and quietly mingle with the gathering crowd at the beach huts, just as the tide was on the turn mid-morning on the Friday of Hope's meticulously planned 'Big Beach Clean'.

I knew she had been a bit concerned about how many people would turn out as it was a weekday and not yet the holidays, but there were more than enough of us to make an impact. She had arranged that in subsequent months the event would happen over a weekend, but with the solstice falling on a Saturday this year, she had thought it best not to have both things on the same day, which made perfect sense to me. There was going to be plenty to do ahead of the party tomorrow without having to worry about keeping an eye on everyone's safety and disposing of the waste we had all gathered to collect.

I tried to stay out of his way, but Sam purposefully came to stand next to me, before giving Hope an encouraging thumbs up as she climbed on to the seawall and clapped her hands together to gain everyone's attention.

'Good morning!' she shouted, once they had quietened down. 'And welcome to this, the first Wynmouth beach clean event. I'm hoping many more will follow, but that in the future we won't have anywhere near as much rubbish to clear as today.'

Everyone clapped and cheered in response.

'Before we get started,' she quickly told them before they started chatting again, 'there are a few things I need to bring to your attention.'

Having listened to her health and safety, safeguarding and

'what to do with the rubbish you collect' speech at least a dozen times already, I found myself zoning out.

'Did you ever find out if any of the huts were available to rent?' Sam asked me, nodding towards the prettily painted row.

I was relieved he wasn't going to ignore me, but I couldn't help thinking that it was a rather out of the blue thing to ask, but then he was probably looking for a convenient conversational opener that didn't involve me accusing him of anything.

'No,' I whispered back, my eyes still focused on Hope. 'I didn't bother. To be honest, I didn't think I'd use one enough to warrant it.'

Sam nodded.

'Probably for the best,' he said. 'From what I can make out, they're still a popular courting spot in the evenings so perhaps not the most relaxing place to be.'

'Unless of course you're courting,' I pointed out.

My heart began to leap as I grasped that what I really should have said was that I didn't know the huts were a popular courting spot. The last thing I needed now was to accidently reveal that this wasn't my first time in Wynmouth and that I knew all about the huts and their romantic – for want of a better word – history.

'I suppose that's true,' he agreed.

'And what do you mean, *still* a popular place?' I asked, trying to throw him off the scent he might not have even picked up. 'Have they always been the place for romantic assignations?'

'Well, I don't know about romantic,' he smiled. 'But the local kids and teens on their holidays have always come down here to get out of sight of their parents.'

'Including you?' I blurted out.

'Me?'

'Yes,' I swallowed, risking a speedy glance at him and finding he was looking at Hope, 'you.'

'I may have had a memorable moment down here,' he admitted, his cheeks colouring a little, but probably nowhere near as much as mine.

'Just the one?'

With his good looks and alleged popularity with the local female population I'd bet it was a whole lot more than just one.

'Yes,' he confirmed with real conviction, 'just the one.'

There was no doubting that he was telling the truth. I wondered if that was because, like me, the moment had been so sweetly perfect that it couldn't possibly be bettered or if because the crash and his lengthy recuperation from it had put a stop to him coming back.

'So, why . . .' I began, turning to face him as I grappled for the right words to frame the question, 'when . . .'

He turned at the same time to look at me, his eyebrows raised in expectation as my words trailed off and I suddenly found myself back in the room, or in this case back on the beach, with the distinct impression that I'd missed something.

'Well, go on then,' he said, pointing at Hope, who was now beckoning to me. 'You're up.'

266

'What?'

'Look alive,' he said, 'you're supposed to helping, aren't you?'

'Oh my god, yes,' I muttered, 'yes, I am.'

I quickly made my way through the crowd to the front.

'Sorry,' I said to Hope as she jumped down to join me on the sand, 'I was distracted.'

'You could hear me though, couldn't you?' She frowned. 'I probably should have borrowed a megaphone or something.'

'No, you were fine,' I reassured her. 'Clear as a bell. It was all perfect and you were brilliant.' I smiled, certain that in spite of my inability to listen to her and Sam at the same time that she had been. 'Now pass me the gloves and buckets and I'll start dishing them out.'

The plan was to work from the beach huts to the rockpool area, then to the café – where Sophie was providing free refreshments for everyone who was taking part – and finally, if there was still time, further along the stretch under the cliff to the third groyne. As the time progressed, and because the tide was still rushing out, more and more beach was exposed and everyone was shocked by the amount and variety of rubbish they picked up.

As expected, there were plenty of things made from plastic such as straws, bottle tops and bottles, but wet wipes, food wrappers and cigarette butts made up an alarming amount too.

'Would you just look at all this,' said Sophie in dismay.

Everyone had convened at the café to drop off what they

had collected next to her bins and stock up on her fortifying snacks.

'The most depressing thing is that lots of these things haven't even been washed up,' she said crossly. 'It's all rubbish that folk have been too lazy to take away with them.'

'I can't believe how many cigarette butts we've found,' said one young woman who was with the local parent and toddler group. 'They were the last thing I was expecting to find.'

'Especially in these numbers,' said another, shaking her head as she peered into her half-filled bucket.

'It's really disappointing,' said Hope.

'And all these plastic water bottles,' said Sophie, 'there's really no need for them to be a one-use wonder. I'm going to get on to the water company next week and find out how I can register to become a water-filling station.'

'Won't that put your bill up though, Mum?' asked Hope. 'If everyone who visits the beach decides to ask you for a refill, you're bound to see an increased cost in your water bill.'

'I'll find out,' said Sophie. 'I'll ask how it works because the world can't carry on like this.'

It was a truly sad state of affairs but we consoled ourselves with the fact that all the rubbish we'd collected was no longer littering the beautiful stretch of beach and Hope already had a list as long as her arm of people who were promising to come back on a regular basis now the scheme was finally off the ground.

'I should have done this months ago,' she admonished herself.

'At least you're doing it now,' said Sam, giving her hand a squeeze from where he was sitting at one of the tables.

'Are you all right?' Hope asked him, noticing how tired he looked.

'Just about,' he said, stretching his legs out in front of him, 'but it might take me a while to get back.'

'I'll run you up in the car,' Sophie offered.

'No need for that,' he said, looking even more uncomfortable. 'I'll manage.'

The area of beach the other side of the café was in an equally bad way. Most people had gone by this point, but a hardcore few pushed on, mindful that the tide would soon be turning. Sam had stayed at the café, ostensibly to help Sophie, but really because it was too difficult for him to carry on.

'Walking on sand is bloody hard work,' he had told me, as he thumped the bottom of his prosthetic leg in frustration. 'But it'll be easier when I get my new one fitted.'

'You'll outrun us all then,' I told him.

It didn't even cross my mind that I would most likely be long gone before he had it.

'Well, I don't know about that,' he smiled, 'but it will be nice to be able to keep up.'

There was a storage shed next to the bins behind the café and we lugged all the rubbish in there, sorting it as best we could, ready for it be collected the next week. The local councillor Hope had been in touch with hadn't been able to make the inaugural clean, but she had pledged to post the photographs Hope had taken on the council website and social media accounts to raise awareness, as well as promising everything would be correctly disposed of. She had also said she would come along to the next event and bring a local journalist with her.

'Not bad for one day's work,' said Hope, standing back to look at the unsavoury array of what had been gathered. 'I'm hoping it won't take anywhere near as long next time.'

'And I'm hoping there won't be anywhere near as much stuff,' Sophie tutted.

I looked back along the beach towards the rockpools.

'Oh damn,' I said.

'What?' Sam asked.

'No one got that barrel out, did they?'

It was the biggest piece of litter I'd seen anywhere along the stretch of beach, and because I knew I couldn't deal with it on my own, I'd completely forgotten about it.

'Too late now,' said Hope, looking at her watch. 'Maybe we could have a go at it tomorrow.'

'Yes,' I agreed, 'it's probably going to need digging out.'

'Oh, come on,' said Sam, rallying himself as well as us. 'Let's give it a go now. There's still time if we hurry.'

Hope drove us back along the seawall as far as the groyne where the barrel was wedged and then carried on to the pub to say Sam would be back soon to take over from the lad who had been holding the fort. Sam had tried to call, but there wasn't a strong enough mobile signal so he opted to let Hope rush back so he could stay and help me.

'I really don't think we'll be able to do anything if it's just the two of us,' I told him.

'Oh, ye of little faith,' he muttered, walking down to where we could see the barrel sticking out of the sand. 'We might as well at least give it a try.'

But as loath as he was to admit it, within a minute, it was obvious that I had been right. Even with our hands encased in thick gloves, we couldn't get enough purchase on it to move it even an inch and I could see the sea was making a rather rapid approach.

'We'll have to come back tomorrow after all, won't we?' he said, sounding frustrated.

'Or perhaps not,' I said pointing to where I could see the beach tractor used by the fisherman to haul the little boats in and out heading in our direction. 'Looks like reinforcements are on the way.'

I could hardly believe my eyes when Joe jumped off the back and ran over to join us.

'We passed Hope up the road,' he said, his face flushing, 'and Charlie said he'd come and lend a hand.'

I watched the driver climb off the tractor and amble over. He was taller than Joe, thick set and after decades spent bearing the brunt of the brutal coastal winds, decidedly weather-beaten. Close to, he looked like the beefed-up hardcore version of his brother and not really someone you'd want to pick an argument with. Not that I intended to, of course.

'*This* is Charlie, your brother,' I said to Joe. 'I've seen the tractor about, but I had no idea who was driving it.'

'Yeah,' said Joe, quickly glancing at Sam, who hadn't said a word, 'he's been helping out a mate who's had a stroke. Charlie's more farmer than fisherman, but when a friend is in trouble . . .'

His words trailed off and Charlie stepped forward.

'Good to meet you, Tess,' he said, the surprisingly soft lilt of his voice not quite matching his powerful physique, 'I've heard a lot about you.'

Thankfully there wasn't time to wonder what it was that he'd heard.

'Come on then,' he said, quickly cutting through the silence between Joe and Sam and striding over to the so far immovable barrel, 'let's have a go at getting this bloody thing shifted.'

Within minutes we'd secured a chain from the back of the tractor around the barrel and Charlie had revved the engine, slowly moved off and heaved it out. The hefty machine made it look easy, but it had evidently been stuck fast and would have been impossible to dig out by hand, no matter how many of us had committed to the cause.

'That's been there a while,' said Charlie, shaking his head as he secured it to the back of the tractor to take away. 'It's falling apart, look.'

The edges which had been buried were rusted and brittle and I wondered if it had been sealed and full when it was first washed up. If the contents matched what was written on the side had leached out into the sand, then I sincerely hoped not.

'I think we'd better make a move,' said Sam, as the sea inched ever closer.

I noticed his limp was even more pronounced and his mouth was set in a grim line.

'Thanks for coming to help,' he said, addressing Charlie and giving a nod in Joe's direction. 'We certainly couldn't have shifted it on our own.'

'No problem,' said Joe, looking at the sand, 'I'm glad we could help.'

'Shit,' I said, jumping out of the way as a freezing wave covered my feet.

I had been so distracted by the guys' awkward exchange, that I hadn't noticed just how quickly the tide was now chasing us, but at least I had been on the spot to witness the monumental moment. I wished Hope had been there too, but for some reason she hadn't come back.

'Why don't you hop on the back of the tractor,' Joe suggested to Sam, 'and I'll walk back up with Tess.'

'Good idea,' said Charlie, before Sam had a chance to object.

'You must be needed back at the pub by now,' said Joe, looking at his watch, 'and Charlie can have you there in no time on this thing.'

It was thoughtful of him to give Sam a reason for taking up his offer that meant it didn't look like he was having to give in because he couldn't manage the walk and I was relieved to see Sam step up to where Charlie directed, telling him to hang on as he turned the engine over again.

'I'll have a pint ready for you when you get back,' Sam said to Joe.

'Thanks,' Joe replied. 'But can you make it a half? I'm off the beer a bit these days.'

They exchanged the briefest of looks and then Charlie was away, leaving the smell of fuel in the tractor's wake as he headed for the slipway which would get him back on to the path.

'Thank you for coming,' I said to Joe as the noise of the engine faded away.

'And thank you,' he said, as we hastily left the beach to the incoming tide.

'For what?' I asked. 'Accusing you of something you hadn't done?'

'Sort of,' he smiled wryly. 'You might have got it all wrong, Tess, but I didn't exactly go out of my way to make sure you hadn't.'

That was true.

'I'm going to make sure that doesn't happen again,' he told me. 'I don't want there to be any more drama in Wynmouth involving the Upton family. There's been more than enough of that in recent years and it's time things settled down.'

His words were music to my ears.

That evening in the Smuggler's was one of the best I'd spent since I arrived back in the village. Sam and Joe were ignoring the furtive glances which were being thrown in their direction and if not completely comfortable in each other's presence they were doing a mighty fine job of making the best of it.

Their conversation was still a bit stilted, but that was a vast improvement on non-existent. I wondered if some of the way Charlie didn't seem to have a problem being around Sam had rubbed off on Joe, and if Joe hadn't left Wynmouth in the first place whether they might have been at this point years ago. Not that I could blame Joe for wanting to get away because I myself had made a dash for it when life and work had got too much – and I didn't have the added complication of seeing the person I was in love with going out with the person I was trying to avoid.

'Did you, by any chance,' Hope asked me, when Sam was serving at the other end of the bar, 'have anything to do with this pair finally finding they could rub along?'

'No,' I said, 'not really. I might have got Joe to have a think about a few things, but to be honest, after my last faux pas, I'd decided I was going to stay out of it all.'

Hope couldn't stop smiling.

'Well,' she said. 'Whatever the reason behind this positive shift in their relationship, I'm truly grateful for it.'

'It was a clever move on your part to ask Charlie and Joe to help with that barrel,' I pointed out.

Hope shrugged, but looked pleased that it had all turned out all right. I wondered if she would be as happy if she knew Joe was still carrying a torch for her.

'I didn't think a bit of male bonding over a practical task would be any bad thing,' she smiled.

I knew that it was going to take a whole lot more than a bit of male bonding to make things properly right, but fingers crossed what we were witnessing was a healthy and long-lasting move in the right direction for Joe and Sam's relationship, even if Joe was going to struggle to get used to seeing Hope on the arm of his former best friend.

'Right,' Joe said to me, just a little while later, 'I'm going to head home.'

'What, already?' I frowned, unable to keep the disappointment out of my voice.

The evening was only just in full swing and even though I knew there was going to be plenty to be getting on with ahead of the party tomorrow night, I was keen to keep the guys together and talking for as long as possible.

'Yeah,' he said, looking about him, 'I need to go.'

I could see Sam and Hope talking cosily together and wondered if that was the reason behind Joe's desire to get away. I could hardly come right out and ask him in the packed bar, but I wished I could.

'Are you sure you can't stay just a little bit longer?' I asked, pulling him out of earshot of everyone else. 'You and Sam seem to have really turned a corner tonight.'

'We have,' he told me. 'We really have, but you have to understand Tess, that no matter how easy you want this to be, it just isn't.'

'Okay,' I relented, not wanting to push him if he really had reached saturation point. 'You do know though,' I carried on nonetheless, trying to make him aware that if he wanted to open up to me about his feelings for Hope then he could, 'that if there's anything you want to talk about, Joe . . .'

'Well, now, good evening you two,' said George, neatly stepping between us. 'How are you, Joe?'

'Good,' Joe smiled, still looking at me, 'I'm good, thanks, George.'

'That's lovely to hear,' George smiled back. 'Now, Tess,' he said, turning his attention to me, 'I wonder if I might borrow you for a moment, my dear? I seem to have mislaid my glasses.'

Joe took the moment to slip away and it turned out that George had his glasses all along.

'Why do I get the impression that you did that on purpose, George?' I asked as he pulled the case out of his pocket with a flourish and a not altogether convincing look of surprise.

'Because,' he said wisely, 'some things in life simply aren't meant to be rushed. You have to let them run their own course and allow them to happen in their own time.'

'Even if that's taking literally years to happen?' I asked.

'Even then,' he sagely replied, and I knew that he was right, 'especially then in fact.'

First Sophie and now George. I seemed to be surrounded by people in Wynmouth who were keen to impart words of wisdom at opportune moments!

Chapter 20

That night, I mulled over what George had said. I might have wanted to hurry things along between Sam and Joe now they were finally moving in the right direction, but I knew he was right. It had taken years for the pair to achieve what they had just managed to do, and there was nothing to be gained from trying to force the situation further. As far as repairing their relationship was concerned, and in spite of whatever it was that was still troubling Joe, it would be playing the long game that scored the final victory.

There were just a handful of us gathered on the beach before five the next morning to watch the solstice sun come up. Most people were clearly more interested in turning out for the party and watching it set under the merry influence of Sophie's legendary rum punch, but I was pleased I had set the bedside alarm and made the effort. As I watched the day dawn and the sun slowly climb over the horizon, I wondered how many more Wynmouth sunrises and sunsets I was going to be privy to.

'Penny for them,' asked Sam, who had also turned out and was standing between me and Hope.

'I was just thinking what a relief it was that the sun has decided to turn up for his own party,' I told him, the fib tripping easily off my tongue as my gaze flicked up to his.

'That's funny,' he smiled down at me with a knowing look in his green eyes. 'I was thinking exactly the same thing.'

'What do you think are the chances of everyone who said they were coming, turning up tonight?' I asked Hope as we worked through the checklist of things we were going to set up on the beach.

'I'm not sure, to be honest,' she said, then added, 'but I do know someone who definitely won't be with us.'

'Oh, who?'

'Joe.'

'How do you know that?' I questioned, feeling marginally more awake all of a sudden.

'He sent me a text when he got back to the farm last night,' she explained. 'He said he was sorry, but he wouldn't be able to make it after all.'

'He messaged you?'

To be honest, I was more surprised that he knew her mobile number than I was about him not coming to the party.

'Yes,' she said, stacking the compostable cups in neat rows to count them. 'He said that something had come up and that he wouldn't be able to get away. I'm not sure I believed him though.'

I wondered if his decision had been prompted by the sight of seeing her and Sam standing cosily together behind the bar. It hadn't made me feel all that great.

'What do you think?' she asked me.

'I don't think Joe would just make something like that up,' I answered, still deliberating the fact that the pair of them were privately in touch.

I wondered how Sam would react if he knew his girlfriend was exchanging late-night texts with her ex, especially given who the ex was.

'I guess not,' she sighed. 'You aren't too disappointed, are you?'

'Me?' I frowned.

'Yes,' Hope carried on. 'He said he would have let you know if he could, but as you've refused to so much as even turn your mobile on since you arrived in the village, he had no way of contacting you. What's that all about, Tess?'

Clearly, she and Joe had talked and messaged about a whole lot more than just his decision not to come to the party. Perhaps their conversation in the lane wasn't the only time they'd got together for a bit of a catch-up.

'Have you really abandoned your phone?'

'Pretty much,' I told her, knowing there was no point in denying it because if I was still a slave to my screen then I would have had it with me, and it was nowhere in sight.

'But why?' she asked.

'Lots of reasons really,' I began, 'but mostly because I felt I needed a proper break from it,' I carried on. 'I decided the day I arrived here in Wynmouth that I would be eschewing all technology for the duration of my stay. No emails, no texts and no social media.'

She narrowed her eyes and chewed thoughtfully on the end of her pen. It was an annoying habit and I knew someone else who did it, but for the moment I couldn't think who it was.

'Everyone thinks that their lives have to revolve around their phones,' I carried on when she didn't say anything, 'and to a certain extent I suppose they do these days, but I've found the ban truly liberating. It's done me the power of good not to be constantly checking and updating.'

I didn't point out that I had needed to borrow her mother's laptop on more than one occasion since my arrival because that had never been for private use. Logging on courtesy of Sophie had happened purely so I could help her, Sam and the village.

'Oh well, that's all right then,' Hope smiled as she released the pen long enough to speak. 'To be honest, I'm relieved we were wrong.'

'Wrong?' I frowned again, 'about what?'

'Well,' she confided, fixing me with her pretty dark eyes, 'we were beginning to think that the reason you weren't using your phone and were hiding out here in Wynmouth was because you'd run away from something.'

I wondered who the 'we' was that she was referring to – her and Sam or her and Joe, or her and the pair of them or perhaps even the entire village.

'That's ridiculous,' I bluffed, 'I'm hardly in hiding, am I? I've spent more time out of the cottage than I have in it and there can't be many people left in Wynmouth who don't know who I am. I'm just here for a holiday.'

'A really long one.'

'Well, yes, I suppose it is a bit longer than average, but it's what I needed.'

'Along with the tech break.'

'Along with the tech break,' I swallowed.

'Fair enough,' she shrugged.

She seemed to accept what I had said, but having run through it all, I wouldn't have blamed her if she didn't.

'I can't help thinking there is someone around here who's on the run though,' she said, sucking the pen again.

'Oh,' I said, happy that her thoughts had moved on from me, 'who would that be then?'

'Joe, of course,' she said, as if I should have known. 'He's definitely someone who's on the run.'

I was inclined to agree with her, but thinking back to what George had said, I knew it was important not to interfere.

'How can he be on the run when he's come back?' I pointed out.

'You know what I mean.'

'I think he's most likely just finding it hard to settle back in,' I said, offering her my take on the situation. 'What with the trouble at the farm and everything, it's bound to take him a while.'

'That's as maybe,' she said, 'but I still think there's more to it than that.'

'You do?'

I was fast beginning to feel that I was fighting a losing battle. She might not have intended to do it, but her words were wearing down my non-interfering resolve.

'Yes,' she carried on, sounding more convinced than ever, 'and you've spent a lot of time with him, don't you feel it too?'

'I haven't spent that long . . .'

'And I'm getting exactly the same vibe from Sam.'

'How so?'

'Well, whenever we talk about how he feels about Joe being back, he starts off all right and then he just clams up. I don't think it's just Joe who is holding something back, I reckon Sam is too.'

'Maybe it's the same thing,' I suggested, before remembering my conviction to keep out of it, 'but whatever it is, there's nothing we can do. We can't force them to talk about it and I don't think we should try.'

'Do you not?'

'No,' I said firmly, 'absolutely not.'

'But if they don't properly get their heads together soon,' she pointed out, 'they might carry on like this into their forties.'

'Oh,' I said, eager to scotch her fear, 'I don't think it will come to that. I mean, look at how they worked together at the beach clean yesterday. That was amazing progress, wasn't it?'

'I guess,' she said, 'but I still think a little extra encouragement wouldn't do any harm.'

I really thought it might, but once Hope had a bee in her bonnet, I knew it was impossible to flush it out until she was ready to let it go.

'What are you thinking?' I tentatively asked.

'I'm not sure,' she said, biting her lip, 'but you'll help, won't you?'

I didn't know what to say. On the one hand I wanted to follow George's sage advice and let the situation carve out its own course, but on the other, I wouldn't have minded hurrying things on a bit. And, I reasoned with myself, it probably wouldn't hurt to keep an eye out, just from the sidelines, to make sure Hope didn't do anything too obvious or OTT. Given what was at stake, I didn't want to see any of my friends getting hurt further, especially as they'd now started to find their way back to each other.

'Oh god, Tess,' she said, noisily dropping her clipboard and making me jump before I had even tried to form an answer. 'I'm so sorry.'

'Why?'

'Because I shouldn't even be asking you,' she said, slapping her forehead in frustration. 'I keep forgetting that you're here on holiday.'

'Sometimes so do I,' I told her.

That was totally true, because the more time I spent in Wynmouth, the harder it was to believe that I had another life somewhere else. A life that I was going to have to face up to at some point in the not too distant future, whether I wanted to or not.

'It's because you feel so much like one of us,' Hope smiled.

'I do?'

'Yes,' she laughed, 'you do. These days, you feel like more of a local, than some of the locals!'

'Sometimes,' I admitted, getting carried away and thinking how wonderful it would be to live in Wynmouth forever, 'I wish I was.'

'You just fit in so well,' she told me, her smile then disappearing as quickly as it had arrived. 'I wish you didn't have to go.'

I swallowed hard and blinked away the tears her kind words had prompted.

'Same,' I whispered.

She came over and grasped my hand and I could almost hear the cogs whirring as she chewed her lip and frowned, deep in concentration. I was a little afraid of what she was going to say next.

'Stay longer then!' she wildly suggested. 'Ask Sam to let you stay in the cottage for the whole of the summer.'

I suddenly remembered that I had already asked him if he would consider lengthening our agreement, but given what happened after, the subject hadn't been broached again.

'But he wants to take the cottage off the rental market,' I reminded Hope, squeezing her hand before she let mine go.

'Only so he can try and sell it while the sun's out,' she told me. 'He wants cash in the bank now he's depleted his savings by buying his new leg.'

I wasn't sure she should be divulging Sam's plans and

financial position, but that was Hope all over. Her enthusiasm often ran away with her and this latest lapse was a timely
reminder that it might be a good idea for me to stick around,
if Sam was willing, so I could, if necessary, temper her passion to get things between him and Joe settled.

'But as you're in already,' she rushed on, 'I'm sure he
wouldn't turf you out.'

'Well . . .'

'But could you take more time?' she asked, her eyes wide,
as she flitted from one thought to another faster than a fairy
could fly. 'You must have a job you need to get back to?
We've never talked about that, have we?'

'No,' I said, 'we haven't.'

I had already decided that I was leaving the firm but, with
savings in the bank, affordability wasn't currently an issue. It
was a nice position to be in, but I didn't know how to explain
it for fear of coming across as big-headed.

'And I do have a job,' I told her, 'but I could probably
wrangle a little more time away from it.' She began to squeal
even before I had finished the sentence. 'But only if Sam
agrees to me staying on, of course.'

'I'll talk him round,' she grinned, clapping her hands
together, 'but I know he won't say no.'

She sounded very sure about that. Perhaps they were so in
love that he would give her anything she asked for.

'And now we have a bit more time to play with,' she said
as if it was all a fait accompli, as her eyes darted back to her
clipboard, 'we needn't worry about how we're going to sort

the guys out just yet. We can come up with devising the perfect plan after tonight.'

The fact that 'we' were now sorting them out as opposed to Hope flying solo wasn't lost on me and I hoped George wouldn't find out about my involvement and, in light of their former requests for me to steer clear, I hoped Sam and Joe wouldn't suss it all out too soon either.

'Let's just focus on the party for now,' said Hope, sounding much more business-like. 'And finding someone to help us hang this bunting.'

With the bunting eventually untangled and hung, everyone agreed that it looked so good it could stay in situ until the autumn, and we set about arranging the finishing touches which we hoped would make the evening one to remember.

A few people had asked if there would be fireworks to see out the end of the longest day, but Hope explained that as you never knew where the spent waste was going to end up, they weren't the best idea for an area which had just undergone its first volunteer-led beach clean. As an alternative, I had suggested sparklers which could be plunged into buckets of damp sand for collection and efficient disposal.

'They're not exactly eco-friendly,' I said, thinking of the cocktail of chemicals which went into them, 'but they've got to have less impact than fireworks.'

Hope hadn't been sure about the idea, but when someone suggested sky lanterns, she hastily relented.

'I think I'm going to give a little talk about the dangers of some of the things that get washed up before I start each of the beach-cleaning sessions,' she said seriously. 'Those lanterns might look pretty but they're an absolute hazard and I'm amazed that so many people still don't know that they're banned around here.'

'That's a good idea,' I said, thinking back to a story in a local paper which had covered a minor celebrity's birthday celebration on one page and on the next, the fire which had been caused by the thirty lanterns which had been released to celebrate the three-decade milestone. 'You'll have a captive audience.'

'I don't want to come across as all preachy though,' she frowned.

'It's not preachy if you're raising awareness,' I told her.

'That's all right then,' she nodded, 'and with any luck, the lanterns will be banned nationwide before long. Joe told me that Charlie had found a barn owl completely tangled up in one the other day. It had been dead for a while.'

'That's awful,' I shuddered, thinking of the beautiful bird before wondering when this conversation had taken place.

'Charlie was devastated,' she said sadly.

The sparklers were stored in a box under one of the three trestle tables which had been lined up and covered in a vibrant patterned oilcloth borrowed from Sophie. She had closed the café early to ensure she had enough time to transport all the food she had made, along with Hope's cookies and a vast amount of secret-ingredient rum punch, down to the beach.

'I'm so pleased that the sun has decided to put in an appearance,' she said, puffing out her cheeks as she handed over a heavy box to one of the many people who had turned up to help. 'When I watched the forecast at the beginning of the week, I thought we were going to be celebrating the longest day under a blanket of cloud!'

'Oh blankets,' tutted Hope, scouring her list. 'I knew there was something.'

A few of the hardier souls were planning to sleep out under the stars and Hope had collected a big box of blankets and sleeping bags for anyone who forgot to bring one.

'They're all still at the pub,' she tutted, sucking the end of her pen again.

'I'll go,' I said. 'You stay here and hold the fort.'

'Thanks, Tess,' she said, taking out her phone and waving it about. 'I would text Sam and tell him but there's absolutely no signal down here.'

It was only a short walk back from the stretch of beach where we'd decided to set up to the Smuggler's but, given the problems Sam had been having with his leg, he was going to drive his car down as far he could. Not only was he saved some uncomfortable steps but he was also ferrying a few things he had been keeping at the pub. The box of blankets could go in with those.

Having decided that as everyone was going to be at the beach anyway there was no point in staying open, he was just locking up as I arrived.

'All right?' he frowned, when he spotted me.

'Yes,' I said, 'everything's running like clockwork, but Hope remembered she hadn't got the box of blankets so I said I'd come and get them.'

'I've just loaded them into the back of the car,' he said, wincing as he picked up the chalkboard from the path.

'Here,' I said, 'let me take that.'

'No,' he snapped, pulling it away. 'I can manage. I'm not completely useless.'

I took a step back, my face burning with embarrassment. I realized I had made a mistake, but there was no need to bite my head off about it.

'I'll go back then,' I said quietly.

'You might as well come in the car with me now you're here.'

After his uncharacteristic flash of temper, I wasn't sure I much wanted to.

'Just go around the back to the car park,' he said, before I could object. 'It's unlocked. I won't be a minute.'

I did as instructed, but he took so long I was beginning to think something must have happened. I was just about to go and look for him when he bumped through the beer garden carrying a guitar case. I could see he was struggling to manoeuvre it but knew better now than to interfere.

'You might have helped,' he muttered, climbing behind the wheel once he had managed to balance it on top of everything else stacked on the backseat.

'Why would I do that?' I shrugged. 'You could manage. I mean, it's not as if you're completely useless, is it?'

He looked at me and I was relieved to see him crack a smile.

'Sorry,' he said, shaking his head.

'No worries,' I smiled back, accepting his apology. 'Do you play?' I asked, nodding at the case and feeling relieved that the moody moment had passed.

'Nah,' he said, securing his seatbelt, 'I thought I'd just bring it with me so we would have something else to sit on.'

I leant across and lightly punched him on the arm.

'Has no one ever told you that sarcasm is the lowest form of wit,' I tutted.

'Funnily enough,' he said, locking his gaze on to mine as he turned the key and started the engine, 'they have.'

I felt my heart rate quicken and the inside of the car seemed to shrink around me. Finding myself in such close and confined proximity to him was making my temperature rise. It didn't seem to matter how hard I tried, I just couldn't shrug off my feelings for him.

'Do you mind if open the window?' I murmured, looking away and trying to locate the right switch. 'It's a bit warm in here.'

'It's this one,' he said, his hand reaching for it, just a millisecond after my fingers found it.

We pressed it down together and then his hand closed around mine. What was he doing?

'Tess,' he said, making me feel even hotter.

I couldn't look at him.

'There's something you should know . . .' he began.

'Are you two now going to the beach?' asked George, his

291

head shoved so far through my window he was practically in the car.

'Yes,' I told him, pulling my hand free and thinking that he really did have the most amazing timing, 'yes, we are.'

'I would offer you a lift, George,' said Sam, 'but I'm out of space.'

'It's all right,' I said, quickly hopping out. 'You get in George. I don't mind walking back.'

'Well as long as you're sure,' he said as Skipper hopped nimbly into the footwell. 'I know it's not far, but I've got this cool-bag of snacks from my sister and it's heavier than I thought.'

With the bag balanced on his lap, he buckled himself in and Sam pulled away.

'See you in a minute!' George shouted out of the window.

'Yes,' I called after him, as I looked down at my hand and realized that those inconvenient feelings I still harboured for my new best friend's boyfriend just might be reciprocated, 'I'll see you there.'

Chapter 21

In my defence, I did what I could that evening to keep extra busy and out of Sam's way. To begin with, it wasn't too difficult because seemingly everyone who lived within and around the village had turned out to celebrate and I was easily lost among the throng.

However, after the cheering, chanting and drum-banging which accompanied the setting sun as it left behind a sky beautifully streaked with gold and rose-coloured clouds, most of the crowd began to dwindle away. Everyone was full of the delicious food Sophie had provided and Hope's cookies, which had gone down a storm, along with a measure or two of the far from innocuous punch, and staying out of sight became considerably harder.

'Tess, would you mind helping me hand out the sparklers?' Hope asked as it began to get dark. 'I don't want to leave lighting them too much longer because I think Mum's punch is a bit stronger than usual.'

No one was falling-down drunk, but I could understand her concern about offering around mini explosives to revellers who weren't quite in full control of their faculties. I was beginning to feel a little light-headed myself.

'I think you're right,' I said. 'I've only had one cup and I'm already feeling it.'

Hope, taking in my chilled-out aura, rolled her eyes and smiled.

'Come on then,' she said, handing me a few of the packets. 'Let's see if we can find any takers.'

It turned out that everyone wanted to light a sparkler and make a wish and there weren't quite enough to go around. I was willing to forgo the pleasure of burning one, but Sam wouldn't hear of it.

'Here you go, Tess,' he called, when he noticed I wasn't joining in. 'They were your idea, so you can't miss out. Come and share mine.'

'But what about Hope?' I said. 'She hasn't got one either.'

Sam pointed to where Hope was laughing with a guy I hadn't seen before. He was standing behind her, a little too close for comfort, I couldn't help thinking, and together they were making shapes in the air with the sparkler she had given him.

'She's all set by the looks of it,' said Sam.

He didn't seem at all bothered by the sight of his other half wrapped up with a random reveller.

'All right,' I relented, thinking it would be rude to refuse, 'we'll share. Thank you.'

Rather than go for the cosy set up Hope and her friend had opted for, I held the sparkler until it had burned halfway down and then, fumblingly, handed it to Sam. When our fingers touched this time, I didn't go quite as hot as when he held my hand in the car, but it was a close-run thing.

'What did you wish for?' he huskily asked, ramping up the heat again in spite of my best efforts to keep it at bay and making my insides fizz as dramatically as the cheery display which was still going on around us.

'If I tell you that,' I swallowed, 'it won't come true.'

The truth was, I hadn't made a wish. I'd been so preoccupied with keeping my temperature in check, that I hadn't had time.

'That was fun,' said a girl next to me as she pushed her extinguished sparkler into the bucket of sand. 'Are there any more?'

'Afraid not,' I said.

'We'll have to buy more next year,' remarked Sam, as he breathed in the evocative but not unpleasant acrid tang the sparklers had left behind.

I liked the thought of Wynmouth celebrating the solstice again next year, even though I wouldn't be there to join in with the fun.

'Smells like autumn,' said Hope, as she wandered over, with a big grin on her face. 'Don't you think?'

'It does,' I agreed, 'we'll all be wanting toffee apples for breakfast at this rate.'

'I have a spicy baked alternative to those,' said Sophie as she began refilling everyone's cups with yet more punch. 'Remind me to give you the recipe, Tess.'

'I will,' I said, throwing caution to the wind and holding out my cup for a refill. 'Thank you.'

'Are you going to play?' Hope asked Sam with a nod to where his guitar case was propped against a deckchair.

'I'm not sure,' he said, 'perhaps later when everyone is too tipsy to take much notice of my mistakes. It's been a while. One thing I am sure of though, is that we need to move the party further up the beach before the tide catches us.'

By the time we had moved everything and were settled on to the sand in front of the café where I'd never seen the sea reach, there weren't many of us left. Multiple stars were beginning to shine and someone had lit a small fire in a brazier in celebration of the season. I helped pass around the blankets and sleeping bags to the hardy last few which would help stave off the developing chill.

We all found a comfy spot and Sam began to quietly strum a melody on his guitar and sing a few words. I didn't hear any bum notes as I closed my eyes, thinking that I probably shouldn't let Sophie top my drink up again. I couldn't remember if I'd three or four cups now, or possibly even five. I breathed slowly and deeply, thinking that there was something very hypnotic about the lapping waves, the crackle of the fire and Sam's surprisingly soulful voice.

I sat and listened as he softly worked his way through Ed

Sheeran's 'Perfect'. I remembered how much I had loved the video which had accompanied the release and how I had wondered whether I would ever find someone who would feel like that about me.

I had once thought I could have felt like that about the person who had given me my first kiss and I had certainly still believed it might be possible the day he dramatically pulled me away from the cliff edge, or rather rescued me from his dog who was intent on tipping me over it, but my memories were a fantasy. That kiss hadn't been what I remembered at all, just like lots of other things in my life, including my parents' far-less-than-perfect marriage. It seemed I had skipped merrily through life either wearing rose-tinted specs or a blindfold.

Before I had a chance to check them, I felt warm tears running down my face. I quickly wiped them away with the back of my hand, stood up, turned my back on the party and walked down the beach back to the shoreline. I wasn't quite as steady on my feet as I would have liked, but I needed to compose myself away from the group. Sophie's punch was clearly having an impact I hadn't expected. It was releasing my pent-up emotions as well as relaxing my body – a truly heady combination as it turned out.

'Tess!'

I closed my eyes and ignored the voice behind me because it was the last one in the world I wanted to hear.

'Hey!' it called again. 'Wait up.'

'I just need a minute,' I croaked, still not looking back and taking a few further steps.

My voice was filled with so much emotion, I knew he wouldn't leave me alone, but I wished he would. Perhaps that was what I should have wished for when we burned the sparklers: to free myself of the stupid feelings I had for a man I couldn't have.

'Are you all right?' Sam asked, eventually catching up with me and sounding out of breath. In my haste to get away from him I'd forgotten that he found walking on the sand so difficult. 'My singing wasn't that bad, was it?'

He was trying to coax a smile, but he had no chance of achieving that.

'No,' I said, 'of course not.'

I shook my head and took another step. There'd been music the night I went out with Joe, but it had been loud, brash, raucous and fun. What Sam had just delivered was completely different. Stirring, sensitive, and expressive, he had moved me in a way I hadn't been touched in a very long time. Probably forever. It had felt like far too intimate a moment to share with someone who was supposed to be just a friend, and a friend who was attached to another friend at that. I couldn't let him see the impact his impromptu performance had had on me.

'It was wonderful,' I sniffed, pulling my sleeves down over my hands and staring out to sea.

I really didn't want to carry on crying, but I just couldn't seem to stop now that I'd started.

'I just needed a minute to myself,' I sobbed, my breath catching in my throat as I tried not to sound as if my heart was breaking and roughly brushed the relentless tears away with my cuffs.

'Hey,' said Sam, quickly closing the gap between us again as my sobs grew louder and before I had a chance to move away, 'come here.'

He wrapped his arms around me and instinctively I clung to him. His embrace felt warm, safe and strong and I let myself melt into it even though I knew that I shouldn't, even though I knew that it was wrong, even though it felt like I was betraying Hope. In spite of my guilt-ridden awareness of each and every one of those things, I also knew that there was no magnet in the world strong enough to pull me out of his arms. It was where I needed to be. Exactly where I had wanted to be from the moment I had caught sight of him for the very first time.

He pulled away a little so he could wipe away my tears with his thumb before gently tucking my hair behind my ears. I couldn't be sure if it was the feel of his fingers on my skin or the act of kindness itself, but something stirred within me. As he bent his head and lowered his lips to mine there was an electrifying certainty coursing through my system that I was about to feel something familiar, even though it was years and years since I had first felt it, and only then for a minute or two.

The touch of him and the taste of him was exactly as I remembered it. Sam had been the boy at the beach hut who had delivered my first unforgettable and never since matched kiss, not Joe. Sam had made my legs shake then and he was doing it again, only now with double the intensity. So, I hadn't embellished this memory or woven it into an improbable fantasy, I had simply kissed the wrong man before and that was what made me think that I had, but now I had found the right one.

Lost in the moment, soft, slow, sweet and tender kisses rained down, before gathering in passion and purpose. This latest development was a brand-new addition and goodness only knows what we would have ended up doing were we not on the beach, at the party, just a stone's throw from where other people were sitting, including Hope . . .

I was the one who stopped, and quite suddenly once the thought of Hope spotting us had popped into my head. I looked over to the group but no one was taking any notice of us and thankfully I couldn't see my friend among them.

'Tess,' Sam murmured seductively, his voice thick as he dipped his head to kiss me again.

As much as my body yearned to reciprocate, as tempted as I was, I couldn't let the magical moment carry on and I turned my head slightly away, but that didn't help at all because he then began to caress and kiss my collarbone. Tiny kisses which blazed a trail and lit up every erogenous zone in my body, some of which, until that moment, I had no idea even existed.

We had decided not to have fireworks at the party but my libido was experiencing the biggest display. The rockets launching in my loins far outshone those which lit up the midnight sky over the Thames every New Year's Eve.

'Sam,' I managed to gasp, 'stop. Please stop.'

He pulled back and looked down at me, pinning me to the spot with those green eyes that I had always found so intoxicating. His pupils were massively dilated and I realized now it was little wonder that I had felt that magnetic pull towards him from the very first second I had seen him.

I might not have been aware of it, but the universe had known he was the answer to a question which hadn't even existed when I first arrived in Wynmouth. I didn't know how it had happened, why Sam and Joe had switched down at the huts, or why I couldn't remember Sam at all, but it had. For some reason they had swapped places; Sam had delivered that all-consuming first kiss and I had just been treated to a toe-tingling, mind-blowing second performance. Only now the boy was a man and he was the boyfriend of someone I had come to consider a very great friend.

It pained me to think that I could never kiss him again, but at least now I knew that there was one thing about Wynmouth that hadn't changed. That kiss had been every bit as amazing as I had remembered and that had to be worth celebrating.

'I'm going to get another drink,' I said, tearing my eyes away from Sam's handsome face and looking back to where the fire was burning like a bright beacon of hope. 'Do you want one?'

I broke away from him and the chilly air which pushed

its way between us made me shiver. Locked together we had generated enough heat to rival the log burner in the cottage, but now it was gone.

'No,' said Sam, shaking his head as his eyes followed my progress back up the beach, 'not for me, thanks. I've had enough.'

I hadn't. In fact, by the time I had taken the short walk back to the revellers I felt ready to indulge in at least another half a dozen measures of the stuff. I took a clean cup from the stack.

'Any chance of some more rum?' I asked the guy currently in charge of the ladle.

What happened after that soon became hazy. I was fairly certain another cup full followed it, and there might have been another after that. I was pretty certain there had been music and then dancing because everyone got a second wind as the moon appeared, bright, theatrical and full, above the horizon.

I know I looked for Sam and Hope among the happy throng who were partying with abandon, but finding neither, I carried on without them. Some time after midnight, I was struggling to remember what it was that we had all come down to the beach to celebrate and when I eventually settled on the sand under a blanket that wasn't quite thick enough and gazed up at the stars, I found the sky was spinning, and when I closed my eyes, it whirled all the faster.

*

When I woke again, just a few short hours later, it was already beginning to get light and I could feel the blanket I had fallen asleep wrapped up in had left a haphazard imprint down the left side of my face. I was freezing cold and my body ached almost as badly as my head. Although not quite. My head seemed to be the real problem, or so I thought until I sat up and felt my stomach churn.

Gingerly, and as quietly as I could, I shakily stood, carefully stepping over the half a dozen or so other partygoers who had also opted to sleep under the stars and were still out for the count. From the little I could remember, we hadn't ended up identifying the constellations, as had been the original plan, but we had had fun nonetheless. I also thought I had, at some point, been intent on celebrating something, but whether that was the solstice or something else entirely, I had no idea.

I steadily walked back along the beach and up the lane to the cottage. I trod lightly, feeling like I was taking the walk of shame, turning up on the doorstep in last night's party gear, but I'd done nothing to be ashamed of, had I? After the classic painkiller, caffeine and dry toast combo, I took myself off to bed, barely registering when the letterbox rattled as my head hit the pillow and only coming back to life much later.

The letterbox had rattled courtesy of a note shoved through it from Joe. He said that he hoped everyone had enjoyed the party, that he was sorry to have missed it, that maybe he would be able to manage it next year if he was invited and then issued me with an invitation of my own.

With harvest waiting in the wings, I'm going to be around even less, so I was wondering if you would like to come to the farm for a tour of the place and then stay and have a meal with me, Charlie and Bruce after?

My curiosity about the farm had been piqued for ages, so I was keen to accept and, if I played my cards right, I might even be able to use my visit to work out how I could, discreetly of course, help Hope get Joe and Sam back on even friendlier terms. I didn't know why, but I had the strangest feeling that I owed Hope a massive favour.

Later that day, when the world had stopped spinning and I had managed to cram enough carbs to stop my legs shaking, I walked slowly up to the pub.

'Hey,' I said, slowly raising my hand in greeting when I spotted Hope and Sam together behind the bar.

'Aren't you a sight for sore eyes?' Hope grinned, taking in my ashen complexion and Jackie O shades.

'Don't,' I said, not daring to shake my head.

'Feeling rough?'

'Just a smidge,' I told her, 'and I've come to apologize.'

'Oh,' Hope giggled. 'What for exactly?'

Sam was staring at me with the strangest expression on his face.

'Yes, Tess,' he said. 'What for?'

Now he was looking at me like that, I wasn't sure exactly

what I was apologizing for, but I knew I needed to say sorry for not helping with the morning-after mess.

'Well,' I began, slowly removing my sunglasses now I was safely inside the pub which was always a little on the dark side. 'Not helping with the tidy-up, for starters. As part of the party task force, I should have been around to help out, but instead I've been cowering under the duvet with the world's worst hangover.'

Hope laughed but Sam didn't look too impressed.

'I had a feeling that's where you were,' she said. 'I did knock on your door earlier, but when you didn't answer I guessed you were still sleeping Mum's punch off. And don't worry,' she kindly added, 'there was hardly anything to tidy away. It was all sorted before the tide turned.'

She certainly sounded more forgiving than Sam looked. He had barely uttered a word and his frown was far from sympathetic.

'Please don't mention the word punch,' I said to Hope. 'It's going to be a long time before I can drink another drop of that stuff. I think I had more than three, although . . . crikey, I can barely remember a thing . . .'

'So, you don't know if you got lucky then?' Hope teased.

'Hardly,' I said, biting my lip and thinking it was no way for a grown woman to behave. 'But perhaps . . . oh, I don't know, but I woke alone this morning so not that lucky.'

The tiniest flicker of a sensuous sensation stirred, but focusing on it, while listening to Hope laugh, made my head pound and, as I was pretty certain it was my imagination playing tricks on me, rather than an actual memory from the night, I dismissed it.

'I need to change a barrel,' Sam muttered grumpily and walked off.

'What's with him?' I asked. 'Didn't he enjoy himself?'

Hope's eyes followed his back as he disappeared down the hatch to the cellar.

'I'm not sure, to be honest,' she sighed, but didn't elaborate on why.

'He's probably still suffering from the after-effects of the p-u-n-c-h too,' I suggested, spelling the word out to stop my stomach rolling over again.

Chapter 22

The week after the party, I threw myself back into the role of holidaymaker. I did all the things I had always loved to do in Wynmouth – I visited the rockpools, swam in the still freezing sea, topped up my tan and explored the dunes. On the outside, I no doubt looked like someone making the most of her time in the fleeting British sun, but I was very much on the inside and I knew that wasn't the case at all.

As enjoyable as it all might have looked to anyone else, my days spent on the beach were really my way of coping with the internal turmoil that descended whenever I set my mind to sorting out what I had run to the village to work my way through.

Rather than helping me come to terms with the shell that I had discovered my parents' marriage really was, reading Mum's diary had created more questions than answers and, even though I had decided I wouldn't be going back to work with Dad, I still hadn't done anything to match my actions to the decision.

I was even beginning to wonder if my involvement in village events and my desire to keep an eye on Hope and stop her making relations between Sam and Joe worse rather than better, were a way of putting off the inevitable.

Was the role I was playing in Wynmouth *really* essential to the fabric of local life, or was I simply using it as yet another excuse for not moving on with my own issues? I had made a few inroads into getting on with things but, considering the amount of time I'd now been away, I hadn't travelled anywhere near far enough and I knew I was running out of diversionary events on the Wynmouth calendar to throw myself into.

I absolutely couldn't carry on in the same vein, hiding out and treating my weeks away as just a jolly when they had always been destined to be so much more, but maybe just one more afternoon soaking up the sun on the beach wouldn't hurt . . .

'He said yes!' I heard Hope shout from further along the beach as I generously applied another layer of sun cream to my freckle-speckled shoulders and arms.

'Who said yes to what?' I responded, laughing as she tripped in her haste to reach me.

'Sam said yes to you staying on,' she puffed, flopping down on the sand next to me and covering my already sticky arms in a gritty layer. 'Turn over,' she offered, grabbing the factor 30, 'and I'll do your back.'

Her explanation, along with her efforts to convince Sam to let me stay in the cottage even longer, did nothing to encourage my conviction to get on with things, but I was grateful that I could stay on. I had become so used to the confined space, quirky stairs and gate that stuck, that I almost considered my residency a permanent one now. If Sam had said no, then this would have been my last week in Wynmouth. Perish the thought.

'And how exactly did you manage to get him to agree to that?' I asked, rolling over as requested. 'He's been in a right grump all week.'

His continued post-party bad mood had been the reason she hadn't rushed into making the request and I felt my face redden in case she was about to reveal that some kinky or athletic bedroom behaviour had been the key to putting him in more malleable frame of mind.

'I asked and he said yes,' she said, squirting a liberal amount of the chilly cream on to my back.

I can't deny I was relieved.

'As simple as that?' I asked.

'As simple as that,' she confirmed. 'I reckon he's got a soft spot for you, Tess.'

I was pretty certain the soft spot was all the other way, but obviously I wasn't going to correct her. If only I could remember what had happened in the run-up to and during the solstice party, then I could say with complete certainty that she was wrong, but there were great chunks of it that were still hazy and some parts were completely non-existent.

'Well, I don't know about that,' I told her, knowing I couldn't magic back my memories even though I wanted to, 'but I do know that I wouldn't mind another lend of your Mum's laptop.'

'I thought you were eschewing all tech,' she reminded me. 'Mum said you were in the café yesterday using the phone as well. Are you beginning to crack, Tess?'

'No,' I told her, 'of course not. I needed to use the phone to confirm my visit to Home Farm, that's all.'

'Of course,' she said. 'I'd forgotten you were doing that. I wonder if Joe will make any startling revelations while you're there?'

'Who knows?' I said, wondering if I'd done the right thing in agreeing to get involved in the whole Sam and Joe scenario. 'But,' I carried on, 'I did give Joe my email address in case he needed to alter the arrangements, so I need to log in to check it's all still on.'

Hope looked slightly sceptical that he would change plans once they were confirmed.

'You know he has a tendency to come and go,' I reminded her, 'and I'd rather check my email account than risk getting sucked into messaging him via social media because that really could be a slippery slope.'

I didn't of course add that, if Sophie didn't mind me logging back on, then I was about to write something that had the potential to change the course of my life forever.

'Why don't you go and sit at one of the tables,' Sophie said kindly, as she handed her laptop over, 'you'll be more comfortable than at the counter. I'll bring you over a drink in a minute.'

'Thanks, Sophie,' I smiled.

My legs were a little shaky as I slid into the last free booth, and my mind was already working through the many and varied sentences I could call on to compose the life-altering email.

'Here you go,' said Sophie, just as I was about to start, 'this'll cool you down.' It was a lovely tall glass of iced tea. 'You look a bit flushed. I hope you're using sunblock when you're soaking up the sun, my love.'

I was feeling hot, but it had nothing to do with the weather.

'I am,' I told her.

'I'll leave you to it then.'

In the end, I stuck to efficient and formal. Tendering my resignation from Tyler PR had to be dealt with profession-ally. Emotion-laden accusations and explanations addressing the contents of Mum's diary could come later. Business first had always been Dad's mantra and, on this occasion, I was willing to stick to it. Once I'd got this out of the way we could revert to being father and daughter again. Perhaps that's what we would have been better off as all along.

'Therefore,' I muttered under my breath, as I read through the mail again before hitting send and setting the wheels in motion, 'I am resigning from my position in Tyler PR with immediate effect and in the hope that, if you haven't already, you will promote Chris, enabling him to officially take over my role within the company.'

I hadn't gone into the whys and wherefores, the details of how I had become increasingly disillusioned with my role and unwilling to babysit and spoon-feed adults who were old enough to know how to behave and conduct themselves. I was certain my resignation would be a big enough shock for Dad to deal with and, even though I was still appalled by how he had treated Mum and their marriage, I felt there was nothing to be gained from rubbing salt into the wound by revealing my distaste for the firm he had spent the best part of his working life growing.

To close the mail, I veered a little on the side of personal, stating that I was in perfect health and happy, although I omitted to mention where I actually was. I knew I was pushing my luck in 'resigning with immediate effect' but as it was my Dad who owned the firm, I hoped he wouldn't use the weight of the law to make me honour a period of notice. That perhaps wasn't particularly professional of me, but there had to be one perk I could use in my favour after all my years of dedicated service.

'All done?' Sophie asked, as I returned the laptop to her yet again.

'Yes,' I said, swallowing hard, 'all done.'

I had thought that having finally acted on my decision I would be feeling footloose and fancy-free, but as I later prepared for my visit to Joe's family farm, I discovered that wasn't the case at all. I couldn't pin down the reason why, but the lump I had felt forming in my throat in the café was very firmly fixed and if I turned around, or stood up too quickly, there was a definite feeling of dizziness waiting in the wings to catch me out.

I knew my physical reactions weren't the result of worrying about the financial implications of what I had done because I had already made some rough calculations of my assets and knew I would be okay. If I sold my beloved car and the impersonal apartment, in which I had a sizeable chunk of equity, I would be able to afford a move, possibly even to the Norfolk coast, and still have a little money left over.

There wouldn't be much, and it would be one heck of a lifestyle downsize, but I would be all right. For someone my age, I was in an enviable position, so my body's responses to the more practical parts of the situation were in no way justified and I decided the best thing I could do was ignore them.

'All set?' Joe asked, when he turned up to collect me.

'Just about,' I said, checking I'd locked the back door.

He had insisted that he would taxi me to and from the farm, for the sake of my beautiful car's suspension and, given that I wanted to get every penny that I could for it in resale value, I was grateful about that.

'You're looking good, Tess,' he smiled, 'very freckly.'

'Thanks,' I smiled back. 'I've spent most of the week chilling on the beach. It's been a total indulgence and I'm feeling pretty relaxed right now.'

As I had decided to ignore the moments of light-headedness, I didn't mention them.

'Oh dear,' Joe winced.

'What?'

'Well, that's all about to change, I'm afraid,' he warned me. 'Say goodbye to blissed out, Tess.'

'Why?'

'Because I've had to bring Bruce,' he said apologetically. 'So, you'd better brace yourself for impact, and an assault on your eardrums, because I've got a feeling that he's going to bark like mad when he spots you.'

And he did. It had been a while since I had seen the loopy mutt and I was pleased that he was secure in the back of the Land Rover and that we were separated by a metal grille *and* the back seats.

'Hopefully he'll have settled down by the time we get to the farm,' I said to Joe, shouting above the din. 'Perhaps he won't be bothered by the time we get out.'

'Yeah right,' Joe laughed. 'Do you want to bet on that?'

Fortunately for my bank balance I didn't, because even though Charlie was in the yard to meet us and clipped a lead on Bruce before letting him out, the dog still launched into a frenzy of tail thumping, whining and jumping up when he saw me close to.

'The training's going well then,' I laughed.

'You must be joking,' said Joe. 'I reckon he's beyond help.'

'He just needs taking in hand,' I said, eventually managing to pat Bruce's head as he finally quietened and sat panting at my feet.

'That's a job you fancy, is it, Tess?' asked Charlie.

'No chance,' I told him. 'It's good to see you again, Charlie.'

'And you,' he nodded, then turned to his brother. 'It's going to get hot before it breaks, Joe,' he added, 'so I'll keep Bruce with me if you want to show Tess around sooner rather than later.'

I was grateful that I wasn't going to have to share a tractor cab with the dopey dog and hoped it was air-conditioned because Charlie was right, it was getting hot.

'Good idea,' agreed Joe, 'but don't worry about this storm. I've had a look at the radar and I don't reckon it's going to clip us after all.'

'Yeah, well,' said Charlie, leading Bruce away, 'we'll see about that, won't we?'

Joe nudged me and we wandered over to the tractor.

'Climb in,' he said, opening the door. 'It's going to be a bit bumpy, but you'll be able to see more in here than if we take the Land Rover.'

He wasn't wrong. From the elevated cab, which was thankfully blissfully cool, I was able to see the whole of the farm and the fields, as well as some of the coast, in all its glory.

'This is amazing,' I said to Joe as he took us right to the very edge of one field which had the most stunning sea views. 'You can see for miles.'

Joe nodded in agreement.

'This is my favourite spot on the whole farm,' he said, 'and it was Dad's too.'

'I can see why,' I smiled, then I remembered the reason

why he had returned to Wynmouth. 'I'm really sorry the farm is in so much trouble, Joe.'

'Me too,' he sighed sadly, before stopping the tractor again and climbing out.

We ate a simple picnic lunch of sandwiches, fruit and lemonade and then walked around the field margins which were awash with wildflowers and separated from the land on either side by dense, high hedgerows.

'Can you hear that?' said Joe, cocking his head. 'It's too hot now for the birds to be singing, but the insects are out in full force.'

I listened to the thrum of intense buzzing, the lazy drone of a plump bumblebee and watched the progress of a pair of butterflies as they fluttered elegantly by.

'Amazing,' I said again, hoping there weren't too many of the stinging varieties close by. 'It sounds like a very busy spot.'

'There are places like this all over the farm,' Joe said proudly. 'Dad was very keen on keeping the hedges when everyone else was ripping them out. He always had a respect for the land, and I'll be the first to admit that that did sometimes mean compromising yields and profits, but he knew it was going to be worth it for the sake of diversity. We've even got a large pond taking up the middle of one of the fields further inland. Charlie was all for draining it and filling it in, but Dad dug his heels in about that too.'

I wondered if Charlie would forge ahead regardless

now. Probably not if Joe had anything to do with it. He was clearly passionate about all that his father had achieved and even though I was no expert in farm management I could appreciate that it couldn't have been an easy decision to sacrifice money in the bank for the benefit of flora and fauna.

'Your dad sounds like a great man.'

'He really was,' said Joe, sounding a little choked, 'and Mum was a wonderful woman.'

He had obviously been close to his parents and loved them very much. That, combined with his love of the landscape and former admittance that he still 'felt the pull of the place', made me wonder why he had never pushed to be more involved with it all.

He had told me that it fell to Charlie as eldest to take over and that he had wanted to get away after the crash, but surely if he'd stuck around, he would have eventually come to terms with driving by the crash site?

But then, that was easy for me to say, wasn't it? Because I hadn't been subjected to the horrors that he had seen that night or lost the love of my life to the person who had been the cause of it.

'Joe . . .'

'Sorry, Tess,' he said, cutting me off, 'but I think we should get back. I don't much like the look of that horizon.'

I followed his line of sight, but everything looked fine to me.

*

317

Clearly, Joe had a far more experienced weather eye than I did, because within an hour the weather had changed completely. Where there had been blue sky, there were now rolling dark clouds which threatened rain, thunder and hail, and they had been quickly blown in by a roaring wind.

'Do you think we should at least try to get the dog out from under here?' Joe asked Charlie as he set the table in the kitchen for what I considered a very early dinner. When I mentioned it, the brothers had responded that it wasn't all that early when you'd been on the go since dawn.

The farmhouse was absolutely beautiful, although a little run down, and the kitchen was an interesting mix of magazine-style country touches combined with practical functionality. The large scrubbed pine table looked as though it had been in situ for as long as the house had stood and it was that which Bruce was cowering under with his tail between his legs and his muzzle between his front paws.

'No,' said Charlie as a flash lit up the room and what sounded like a handful of gravel was dashed against the window. 'He's fine where he is.'

Joe didn't look impressed, so I slipped off the sofa on to the floor where I was level with the dog. He might have been a pain in the backside, but I hated seeing him so cowed. Spotting me, he slid out on his belly and thrust his nose in my lap. The poor thing was shaking like a leaf.

'I'll keep him over here if you like,' I said, trying to

dissipate the tension I could feel building and which wouldn't help Bruce's nerves at all.

Neither brother answered and I wondered if the pair bickered a lot. I know Joe wasn't happy that Charlie wouldn't take on board any of his suggestions for the farm and I wondered if the elder brother resented what he might consider interference from the sibling who was rarely around.

By the time dinner was served Bruce was practically sitting on my lap and when I took my seat at the table and accepted the glass of red Joe offered, he somehow squeezed himself under my seat and rested his heavy head on my feet.

'I did wonder,' said Joe as he lifted a gargantuan pie out of the Aga, 'if it was going to be too hot for this today.'

'So did I, to be honest,' said Charlie, as he deposited three large tureens of vegetables down the middle of the table.

He sounded far happier now he was faced with a plate the size of a platter.

'Did you make this?' I asked Joe, eyeing the crisply baked pie which was decorated with golden pastry leaves.

'I did,' he said proudly, then added with a frown, 'oh god, you aren't vegan or vegetarian, are you?'

'No,' I laughed, 'I'm not. I thought you'd remember that from the afternoon tea we shared *and* the fish and chips we ate at the seaside.'

'Oh yeah, of course,' he said, sounding relieved. 'This isn't really as fancy as it looks.' He added, with a self-deprecating nod to the table.

'It looks pretty fancy to me,' I told him.

'You haven't tasted it yet,' said Charlie with a wry smile as he dug in.

Joe ignored him.

'It's one of Mum's recipes,' he said to me instead. 'The filling is cooked in the slow cooker all day and then it's a quick assembly job with a packet of shop-bought puff pastry, before finishing off in the oven.'

My stomach grumbled loudly in response and we all laughed, except for Bruce, who was still shaking under the table.

The meal tasted every bit as delicious as it looked and accompanied with the fruity, warm wine I was left feeling replete, relaxed and a little sleepy, in spite of the storm outside raging louder than ever.

'You stay where you are,' Joe insisted, as I made a move to gather the empty plates. 'Charlie and I are used to clearing up.'

'We'll get washed up and then I'll go back out to check the yard,' said Charlie.

I didn't much like the thought of him going out into the storm and I wasn't much looking forward to the journey back to Wynmouth either. That said, if I couldn't prise Bruce off me, I wouldn't be going anywhere anyway.

'I'm not sure ...' Joe started to say but stopped as a crack of thunder seemed to suck in the walls of the room before releasing them and taking the electricity away with it. 'Bugger.'

Clearly, the boys were prepared for such eventualities and

within minutes the room was bathed in candlelight and Joe was cranking the handle on a wind-up radio while Charlie ran the water to wash up.

'I was going to say, Tess,' said Joe, setting the radio down on the table and picking up a tea towel, 'that if this carries on, I might not be able to get you home tonight.'

'Are you thinking of those two oaks before the bend?' Charlie asked.

'I am,' Joe confirmed.

'They should have been felled long before now,' Charlie tutted.

'If this wind keeps up,' said Joe, 'that might not be an issue.'

'If either of those are down, you won't be able to get through at all,' Charlie pointed out.

'I don't mind staying,' I told them, thinking I didn't much fancy heading out with the threat of falling oak trees hampering our journey back to Wynmouth. 'As long as you've got a bed and a spare toothbrush I can borrow.'

'I can manage the toothbrush,' said Joe, 'but there's no bed, I'm afraid. No one sleeps in Mum and Dad's room.'

'And Jack's room is still like a bloody shrine,' Charlie tutted.

His tone was disapproving and, even by candlelight, I could see how red Joe had turned.

'Sofa then,' I said quickly, 'makes no difference to me. Besides, if this racket keeps up, we won't any of us be getting much sleep anyway, will we?'

That turned out to be not strictly true. Once the kitchen

was set to rights, Joe, Bruce and I moved through to the sitting room, taking the candles and the radio with us, and Charlie said he'd changed his mind about going out and was going to have a bath and turn in. He hadn't been gone all that long before we heard him snoring somewhere above us.

'He had an early start,' Joe grinned, reaching to turn the radio up a bit. 'And he's not used to relaxing in the tub. He's a two-minute shower type of guy as a rule.'

I smiled back.

'I wonder if it had bubbles,' I giggled.

'Or a bath bomb,' Joe suggested.

I was about to throw essential oils into the mix but was pulled up short by the radio.

'Whatever is it?' said Joe, reaching for my arm which was resting along the back of the sofa. 'You've gone as white as anything and you look like you've seen a ghost.'

'This song,' I stammered, feeling a little dizzy again.

Joe listened for a moment.

'It's "Perfect", by Ed Sheeran,' he said, 'it has the loveliest video. Not that I'm much of a fan of romantic rolls in the snow. It's too cold for a start.'

It wasn't the official video that I was concerned with, it was the far more intimate showreel running through my head. As I listened to the lyrics about a hundred things rushed into my formerly befuddled brain and none of them made much sense.

'What is it, Tess?' Joe asked again.

If my memory served, I had kissed Sam on the beach, under the stars and behind Hope's back. And, worse than that, I'd absolutely loved doing it, so much so that it felt as good as my first time. In fact, I now knew with the utmost certainty that Sam *had* been my first time.

'Tess,' said Joe, now squeezing my hand and sounding even more concerned. 'Talk to me, for god's sake.'

What could I tell him? Certainly, none of what I had just remembered. He hadn't been my first fabulous kiss – Sam had – but what had happened down at the beach huts all those years ago to prompt them to swap places? And, more to the point, why hadn't I understood this after the kiss at the party? Or maybe I had?

It must have been the effect of all that rum which made me forget again. I had no doubt been punch-drunk, literally, all week. Perhaps I had realized the truth before I drank myself into oblivion and had felt so felt guilt-ridden for going behind Hope's back and so deeply shocked that I had let my cup be topped up in order to forget again.

Then my thoughts flicked to Sam. He'd been the archetypal bear with a sore head all week but surely he should have been on cloud nine. My memory loss had ensured I had been oblivious to what had gone on and consequently I hadn't breathed a word to his girlfriend. We might have kissed, but I certainly hadn't told and that should have put him in a half-decent mood at least. Unless he had been too busy worrying that I would remember and then drop him in it? And what about that first time? Never mind Joe simply remembering me, did he remember what he and Sam had done from way back then?

'Tess!' said Joe again, much louder this time.

'Oh god, sorry,' I said. 'I'm sorry. I was miles away.'

'No shit,' he frowned. 'Whatever is it?'

I shook my head, freeing it of the dizziness, but still not knowing what to say.

'It's not my cooking, is it?' Joe demanded. 'You don't feel ill, do you?'

'No,' I said, 'of course not.'

'That's all right then,' he said, sounding relieved as he released my arm.

'Although I do think that wine was pretty strong.'

'You're right, it was,' he said, 'and we drank the lot once we'd decided you were staying over.'

'No wonder I'm whacked,' I yawned, 'I feel as though I could sleep for a week.'

'It's all this fresh, country air,' he smiled, accepting my explanation. 'Do you want to turn in? I can get you a sleeping bag and that toothbrush, if you like?'

'Would you mind?' I asked.

'Of course not,' he said. 'Come on, Bruce,' he added, nudging the dog off the sofa. 'You best sleep in my room tonight, my lad.'

'You can leave him here with me, if you like,' I said, looking at Bruce's martyred expression and thinking that I wouldn't mind the company. 'There's just about enough room for two.'

'No, best not,' Joe laughed. 'Once this storm blows itself out later, he'll be back to his bouncy and mischievous self in no time, and he'll be up and about long before you'll want to be. I can guarantee it!'

It turned out he was spot on about that.

Chapter 23

Just as Joe had predicted, Bruce was up early the next morning. However, I had heard someone, presumably Charlie given where the snores had emanated from the night before, moving about overheard even earlier and then slamming the outside door. Turning over, I'd disregarded the rumpus because it still felt like the middle of the night but when Bruce came bounding in a little later it was considerably lighter and his exuberance was impossible to ignore.

'For pity's sake, Bruce,' I groaned, trying to push him away, which wasn't easy because I was bound up in the sleeping bag. 'Get off.'

The action of giving him a shove only served to further excite him and it wasn't many seconds before the inevitable happened and his tail brushed the coffee table completely free of the piles of paperwork, folded-up newspapers and remote controls which had been quite happily settled there, completely minding their own business.

'You,' I said, as I struggled to sit up, 'are a total pain in the butt.'

He cocked his head to one side, as if weighing the accusation up, then rushed out of the room again, his claws scrabbling on the tiled floor, before he reappeared with a tea towel which he dropped on my lap.

Clearly, it was time to face the day, but first I had to corral the mess on the floor into a heap so I could put it back on the table – although how long it would stay there with Bruce's rapidly rotating rudder still in the vicinity was anyone's guess.

'Why don't you go and wag somewhere else?' I asked him, adding the last of the papers to the pile as the sound of Joe's voice drifted through from the kitchen.

He didn't sound particularly happy.

'So, what you're telling me,' I heard him say, 'is that it could be another week before this is sorted?'

He was quiet for a second and as I didn't hear an answer, I guessed he was on the phone rather than chatting to an early visitor.

'Two,' he almost shouted, 'you're kidding?'

I didn't mean to pry, but my eyes caught the words 'land sale' at the top of one of the sheets of paper and I picked it up. I remembered how Joe had mentioned that saving the farm meant selling off some of the land. Having been given the grand tour yesterday, I very much hoped the proposed sale didn't include the field we had picnicked in. It would be a shame if they lost that magnificent sea view as well as the acreage.

'Sunny Shores,' I whispered, spotting the company name.

'But Sunny Shores were saying last week,' came Joe's voice again, his words echoing those printed in front of me, 'that they wanted to finalize before that.'

Unfortunately, I knew all about Sunny Shores and not because I had had 'the holiday of a lifetime' at one of their mammoth developments, as their advertising tagline promised, but because Dad had set up a campaign for them.

They were one of the largest holiday village companies in the country now and Dad's clever strategy had quelled some of the controversy which followed them taking over an area of land which local residents had hoped would be sold to the Woodland Trust. The campaign had been a success, but it hadn't completely drowned out the local element. I remembered I had secretly felt rather pleased about that, although it didn't make any difference to the outcome.

'Remind me again why I'm paying you such an exorbitant amount?' Joe demanded. 'I want it all wrapped up in half that time.'

My eyes quickly scanned the rest of the page. I had always assumed the plan was to sell a field or two to a near neighbour, but I couldn't have been more wrong. If my understanding of the land mass mentioned was right, then Sunny Shores would be taking over a whole lot more than that. Practically the whole farm looked earmarked to be swallowed up by a brand-new holiday village, complete with its own avenue of shops, Sun Splash pool complex and at least three restaurants to cater for all appetites and tastes.

How was it possible that this had all got so far and no one in the village knew about it? Surely there should have been some sort of public consultation by now? Hope and I might have figured out that Joe and Sam were holding something back, but it obviously wasn't the same thing after all and to think I'd been sucked in by Joe's suggestions that he still felt a connection to Home Farm, when in reality he wanted to be free of it. No wonder Charlie was so against his ideas and shut his suggestions down! Clearly the youngest Upton brother was still a rebel, and now he'd found himself a very lucrative cause.

'Do you want tea, Tess?' he called from the kitchen, making my heart leap into my mouth.

I had been so absorbed in the paperwork I hadn't heard him end the call.

'Yes, please,' I swallowed, hastily rearranging the pile with a magazine on top, 'that would be great.'

Now I was harbouring two bits of bad news for Hope. Not only had I kissed her boyfriend, but her ex was set to change the face of the landscape that she, and everyone else living in Wynmouth, loved so much. Joe might have told me that his being back in the area was difficult, and that driving by the crash site was painful, but obliterating it all – because having seen Sunny Shores handiwork I knew that's what would happen – was extreme. Was he really that desperate?

'How'd you sleep?' he asked as he appeared in the door-way with mussed-up hair and a tray holding mugs of tea and slightly overdone toast.

'Badly,' I said, sitting back down again. 'But given how long the storm raged and how early Charlie got up, that was only to be expected.'

I felt a whole jumbled-up mix of emotions as I watched him arrange the tray. I was still frustrated that he couldn't remember me from former holidays and desperate to find out why he and Sam had swapped places when it came to my first kiss, but I couldn't ask because then they'd know I had lied about visiting before. And now, as if that wasn't enough to contend with, my head was full of the farm situation too.

I knew the finances needed fixing, but to go to such lengths, for Joe to turn up and set about selling off everything his father had worked to create, especially when he had presented it to me so proudly yesterday, just didn't make sense.

'It hung around for a while, didn't it?' he said. 'You often find that here. Bad weather can hug the coast for hours.'

I wondered if the Sunny Shores team had factored that into their plans.

'Well,' I said, 'at least it's moved off now and the power's back on,' I added, holding up my steaming mug of hot tea. 'No harm done.'

'If only,' he said, shaking his head. 'I dread to think how many acres of crops have been flattened and right before we're due to gather them in. It couldn't have been worse timing as far as the harvest's concerned.'

I hadn't thought of that. Farming was certainly a

precarious business. A whole year's profits at the mercy of Mother Nature.

'Is that why Charlie went out so early?' I asked.

'Yes,' said Joe, offering me a slice of toast, 'he wanted to assess the damage.'

'Do you think it will be that bad?'

'It might be,' he explained. 'Low yields and high drying costs can have a huge impact on the bank balance and if the quality isn't there this year and it all has to go for feed, well . . .' he said, swallowing hard, 'it doesn't bear thinking about. This is exactly why I want to diversify a bit more.'

Sunny Shores didn't seem like your everyday farm diversification project to me, but I was beginning to understand the temptation of it when faced with odds you had absolutely no way of tipping in your favour.

We both jumped as the back door flew open and then banged shut.

'Joe!' Charlie roared and Bruce scuttled out of the kitchen and back to the sofa.

'I'll just go and see what he has to say,' said Joe.

'You can leave Bruce with me if you like,' I suggested.

'Thanks,' Joe nodded, 'that might not be a bad idea.'

The two men were in the kitchen for quite some time. I could hear their voices through the closed door, but I couldn't make out what they were saying. There didn't seem to be any escalation in volume, so I didn't think they were arguing. The stack of papers was just beginning to tempt me when Joe came back in.

'How's it looking?' I asked.

'Not great,' he said.

'It's a bloody disaster,' Charlie shouted in response.

Joe shook his head.

'I'm guessing you're going to have your work cut out this morning,' I said, 'and I've really enjoyed my visit, but if you want to run me back now, I don't mind.'

'Are you sure?' Joe asked.

'Absolutely.'

Truth be told, I was looking forward to shutting myself away in the cottage and having a think about things.

'All right,' said Joe, 'just give me a minute and we'll go.'

'Home sweet home,' Joe smiled when we finally arrived at Crow's Nest Cottage.

It had taken longer than expected to get back as one of the roads was blocked by a fallen branch. The limb wasn't from one of the trees the brothers had mentioned the night before, but the whole area looked to be littered with debris courtesy of the storm.

'Yes,' I said, looking fondly at the little place, which didn't look any the worse for wear given what had happened. 'Here we are. You know, my time in Wynmouth seems to have been punctuated with one storm or another,' I commented, thinking of the evening Joe had turned up at the Smuggler's.

'It's certainly been a tempestuous summer so far,' he nodded.

I had a feeling that neither of us were referring only to the weather.

'I don't suppose I'll see much of you for a while now, will I?' I said, thinking of the impending harvest.

'I'll still be about a bit,' he smiled, 'and I'll keep in touch, although,' he added, 'that would be a damn sight easier to do if you turned your phone on.'

'No chance,' I said.

There were probably dozens of extra messages clogging it up now. Dad was bound to have had a reaction to my resignation email and not necessarily a good one.

'If you're so determined not to switch on the one you've got,' Joe suggested, 'then why don't you go somewhere and buy a cheap pay-as-you-go to tide you over. That is, assuming you aren't leaving just yet?'

'That's a great idea,' I said, 'why didn't I think of that?'

Joe shook his head.

'I'll ask Sophie if I can borrow her laptop again and I'll order one.'

'That'll make my life easier than having to drive here and shove notes through your door.'

'You could always leave a message at the pub?' I suggested. 'Or send word with Hope.'

'I'm sure Sam would love that,' he tutted.

'Which bit?'

He didn't answer.

'Well,' I said, unclipping my seatbelt, 'thank you for inviting me to the farm. I loved the tour and the dinner.'

'You are most welcome,' he smiled.

'You're very lucky to have such a beautiful place to live,' I told him. 'It's truly stunning.'

'I couldn't agree more,' he nodded, confusing me even more. 'Take care, Tess.'

I waved him off and let myself into the cottage. It felt deliciously cool compared to the heat outside which had started to build again. Had I not lived through the storm I might never have believed that it had even happened.

I took a long shower then slipped on my dressing gown because I didn't feel like getting dressed again. I was just contemplating the idea of taking a nap when someone began beating on the door.

'Oh,' said Sam, who I found on the doorstep, looking absolutely livid. 'That's all right then. You are alive. I won't keep you. I just wanted to make sure.'

He turned around and was already at the gate by the time I grabbed his sleeve.

'What on earth's the matter?' I asked, all thoughts of my cosy nap forgotten.

He spun around, his face flushed and his lips set in a thin tight line. The memory of my mouth pressed against his suddenly jumped into sharp focus and I looked up at his eyes instead. Faced with his fury, it was hardly the moment to wonder, but why hadn't he mentioned our kiss after the party? There was no way that he had, like me, forgotten it, because he hadn't been drinking. Was his recent bad mood a result of guilt, or did he consider himself blameless and think it was all my fault? Was that what this fiery outburst was all about?

'I've just been worried sick, that's all,' he said, roughly tugging his sleeve out of my grasp. 'We all have, I mean,' he added, turning red.

An elderly couple on the other side of the lane looked at us curiously and given the show we were putting on I could hardly blame them.

'Look,' I said to Sam, 'come inside for pity's sake. Before we're the talk of the village.'

'Thanks to you,' he said, reminding me of my outburst in the pub, 'we already are. Folk are still gossiping about that you know.'

'Well, let's not make the situation worse then,' I said, walking back inside.

He reluctantly followed, slamming the door behind him.

'Is that why you're so angry?' I asked. 'Because we're still the hot goss?'

'Of course not,' he snapped. 'I'm angry because you buggered off yesterday without a by your leave and no one knew where you were. In case you hadn't noticed, there was one hell of a storm raging last night and for all we knew, you were out in it.'

'Well, in that case,' I told him, 'I'm sorry, but Hope knew where I was. She knew days ago where I was going to be yesterday. Why didn't you ask her?'

He shifted from one foot to the other.

'Because we aren't talking at the moment.'

'But she still would have told you,' I insisted. 'She wouldn't have let you worry unnecessarily.'

I hoped the pair of them hadn't fallen out because Hope had somehow found out about The Kiss.

'Well, whatever,' he said, running a hand through his hair. 'At least I've found you now. Why you don't buy another bloody phone to use while you're here is beyond me. Hope told me ages ago that you aren't using your usual one right now, so why not just get a cheap temporary thing so folk can get hold of you.'

'Funnily enough,' I said, 'someone else suggested the very same thing less than an hour ago.'

We were quiet for a second. Sam focused on the view beyond the window and I re-tied the belt on my dressing gown which had come a little adrift.

'Do you want a coffee?' I offered. 'I was just about to make one.'

I didn't much feel like taking a nap now and I was keen to find out, as we were alone and out of earshot of everyone else, if he might broach the topic of our moment on the beach.

'Just a quick one then,' he said, checking his watch. 'I'll need to be back in time for the lunch rush.'

I was surprised but pleased that he accepted my offer and that there was a lunch service to rush back for. It was a stark contrast to when I had first arrived and there had been empty tables as far as the eye could see.

'Where were you then?' he asked, as I filled the kettle and arranged mugs and he made himself comfortable on the sofa. 'Not that it's any of my business,' he carried on, 'but as your car hadn't moved, we were worried that you'd gone somewhere on foot.'

On this evidence, I couldn't deny that his and everyone else's concerns were justified. I was touched that they had noticed and that they cared.

'I was at Home Farm,' I told him, thinking nothing would be gained from lying, especially when he and Hope were bound to kiss and make up and she would probably tell him anyway. 'Joe invited me to take a tour of the place yesterday and then to stay for dinner. When the storm blew in, we decided it would be too risky to try and drive back.'

I was just about to add that I'd dossed down on the sofa, but a noise from the other room caught my attention and I looked through to find Sam standing back up again.

'On second thoughts,' he said, as he reached the door in two quick strides and offered me a smile that didn't reach as far as his eyes. 'Don't worry about that coffee, Tess. I've just remembered I've got a delivery booked. I'd better head back after all.'

Chapter 24

I went up to bed after Sam left, but I couldn't sleep and found myself reaching for Mum's diary again. It was hardly a soothing bedside read, but it was a distraction and with the memory of *that* kiss coupled with conflicting thoughts about Joe's deal with Sunny Shores running through my mind, I certainly needed one. And talking of the one . . .

The last line Mum had typed, '*she's the one,*' really broke my heart. The first few entries had suggested the early affairs Dad indulged in were frivolous interludes, but the later ones came across differently and towards the end, Mum was aware that there was one person in particular who meant more to her husband than she did. I was deeply saddened by that and found myself wishing that the pair had parted and moved on with their lives instead of sticking it out in a loveless marriage and, in Mum's case, never discovering what was possible beyond it.

I kept a low profile for the next couple of days, trying to

decide what I should do with the overwhelming amount of information my head was stuffed with. Should I cut and run, go back and face my father? Should I announce to everyone what Joe had in store for their lovely landscape or should I keep quiet and let the Upton family move on and free themselves from the fear of the unpredictable farming cycle? Should I ask Sam why he had been my first kiss? Should I confess my disloyalty to Hope and ask why she and her beloved weren't talking? Or, should I pretend that I knew nothing about any of it, and just carry on enjoying my holiday?

I was still no closer to coming to a decision when I wandered down to the café on Tuesday. The weather was warm, but I couldn't see the sun because it was blocked by a thick blanket of cloud and I couldn't help thinking that it felt like the perfect metaphor for my life.

'Tess,' beamed Sophie when I walked in. 'Where have you been hiding yourself? It feels like ages since I last saw you!'

'I've been around and about,' I told her, wishing I could lift my mood high enough to match hers.

Sophie had a mother's knack for spotting melancholy a mile off and I didn't want her delving too deeply into my current muddled mindset.

'Well,' she said, 'grab a seat and I'll bring you something delicious to eat.'

'I'm not really hungry,' I told her. 'I only came—'

'To borrow my laptop?' she interrupted, raising her eyebrows.

I nodded, feeling a little guilty.

'That's all right,' she said, bustling back behind the counter, 'you can surf and snack at the same time, can't you?'

'Yes,' I said, sliding into the last empty booth, 'that I can do.'

It didn't take many minutes to find and order a phone and I opted for express delivery, wishing I had thought to do it weeks ago and thinking that at least I had made one decision. If I was investing in a mobile, even just a cheap one, then I wasn't planning to leave Wynmouth any time soon, was I?

'Find what you wanted?' Sophie asked, taking the seat opposite mine when there was finally a lull in customers.

'Yes,' I said, sliding her laptop back across the table, 'thanks, Sophie. I didn't expect you to be this busy today, what with the downturn in the weather.'

'Actually,' she said, looking out of the window to see what the sky was up to, 'I think that's what has encouraged folk in. This mixed summer weather we've experienced so far has been perfect for the café.'

'I bet Sam would say the same about the pub,' I said, thinking of his former mention of the lunchtime rush, 'that's been busy too.'

'But not *too* busy,' Sophie smiled. 'Word on the village high street is that Wynmouth has finally found the right balance. Everyone's telling me they're busier, but not overrun. Somehow we've managed to enjoy increased footfall without becoming completely overwhelmed.'

'Uh huh,' I nodded, my stomach churning as I thought

how that balance could so easily be upset by the influx of Sunny Shores visitors.

'We all seem to be turning a healthy profit,' Sophie said happily, 'but not losing the tranquillity, and thanks to the beach clean and the party there's an emerging sense of community pride and spirit that the place has been lacking in recent years. It's all perfect in every possible way.'

'That's great,' I swallowed. 'Really great.'

'Are you all right, Tess? Sophie asked. 'You look a little pale.'

'Too many churros,' I told her. 'You know I can't resist.'

'And too much sauce!' she laughed, peering into the empty pot. 'Here's Hope,' she added, waving at her daughter who was about to come in. 'I'll get you both some lemonade. That'll cut through the sweetness.'

Sophie took her laptop back to the kitchen and Hope, after hugging her warmly, slid into the seat she had just vacated.

'I'd all but given up on you,' she told me. 'I've just been to the cottage to find you, and the beach. Where have you been hiding yourself?'

'I haven't been hiding.'

She waited while Sophie deposited our lemonade before picking up the questioning pace.

'So,' she said, her dark eyes shining, 'what happened at the farm? Did you make any inroads into finding out what's bothering Joe?'

I was beginning to wish, given that the pair were still in touch, that she'd made more of an effort to find out for herself rather than rope me in but, given her friendly tone, she obviously still hadn't found out that Sam and I had kissed at the party, so that was something to be thankful for.

'Before we talk about that,' I said, 'can I ask what's going on with you and Sam? I saw him the other day and he said you weren't talking.'

'Oh,' she said, waving the question away and making her many silver and gold bangles jangle, 'it's nothing. Just a silly disagreement. I'd made up my mind to do something and he said I shouldn't. It's all forgotten now,' she went on, 'although of course, it's meant that I haven't had a chance to find out what's going on with him and Joe, so I hope you've come up with something.'

I sucked at the paper straw in my lemonade and swirled the ice around.

'Oh well done,' she said, sounding excited, 'you can't have gone that colour for nothing. Spill the beans, Tess!'

At the point when Sophie had sat down and told me how brilliantly her business, and everyone else's in Wynmouth, had been faring this summer, I had pretty much made up my mind to keep quiet about Joe's impending deal. After all, it was nothing to do with me, but Sophie's words had made me doubt my decision and as Joe clearly still had feelings for Hope and they were still friends, I reasoned that she was the one person I could tell.

'I have found something out,' I confessed. 'Let's go down to the beach and I'll tell you.'

Hope had thought my cloak-and-dagger suggestion was

excessive, but as I explained what I had seen and overheard, her steps faltered and her eyes grew wider and wider.

'And you're absolutely sure?' she asked, as we sat on the sand out of earshot of the few visitors to the beach.

'Yes,' I nodded. 'One hundred per cent.'

'The paperwork was definitely current?'

'Yes,' I reiterated, 'dated this summer, and there was no doubting the phone call. He was standing practically right next to me, so I didn't mishear any of that.'

We looked behind us to where the land in question sat atop the cliffs, currently undisturbed. I tried to imagine how the view would change when it was covered in rows and rows of caravans and the local roads were choked with cars trying to get to them.

'But this could ruin everything,' said Hope, sounding tearful.

'I know it's not ideal,' I said, trying to help her see it from Joe's point of view, 'but having listened to Joe talk about falling yields and failing crops, especially after that storm, I can understand why he's doing it.'

Sophie looked at me as if I'd gone mad and I began to think I'd made a mistake in telling her.

'And at least now we know his secret has nothing to do with the crash,' I pointed out, trying to paint a silver lining. 'Getting him and Sam back on proper speaking terms might be easier to achieve than we first thought.'

'You've got to be kidding?' Hope laughed. 'Can you not imagine how Sam's going to react when I tell him about this?'

'Do you have to tell him?' I asked. I could feel my face beginning to burn in spite of the fact that the sun was still hidden. 'I only told you because—'

'Of course, I have to tell him,' she interrupted. 'I do understand why you are sympathetic to Joe's cause, Tess, because he's talked to me about how difficult it all is, so to a certain extent I get it too, but the implications of what he's proposing are going to be felt a whole lot further than the Upton farm boundary.'

'Why don't you talk to Joe before you tell Sam?' I suggested.

'What and drop you in it?' She frowned. 'If I talk to him, then he'll know you were snooping.'

'I wasn't exactly snooping,' I reminded her. 'It was all right there.'

'Even so.'

'All right,' I said, changing track. 'How about I talk to him? I'll explain about Bruce knocking off the papers and how I heard his side of the phone call and maybe he'll tell me the rest.'

Hope didn't look convinced.

'It might not be as bad as we think it is,' I pleaded.

Having seen the marked-out boundaries on the map, I knew that it was, but I had to try and do something to stop the flood I had just unleashed. Even if I could plug the dam long enough to give Joe a heads up, that would be something.

'Please,' I said, 'before you tell Sam, or anyone else, let me talk to Joe.'

*

Hope headed back to the café, having reluctantly agreed not to say anything to Sam, and I went back to the cottage. I knew that time was of the essence and wanted to get to Home Farm and talk to the Upton brothers before she had a change of heart. Hope was the sort of woman who wore her heart on her sleeve and I knew it wouldn't take much prompting if someone picked up on her preoccupied mood for her to tell all.

It hadn't entered my head before but having always worked the farm I now considered that Charlie might not be in favour of selling it and, if Joe's deal hadn't progressed too far, then we might be able to persuade him to change his mind. Surely, while Charlie was the manager, Joe couldn't just sell it all out from under him?

Unfortunately, my plan fell at the first hurdle, as I discovered a note from Joe on the cottage doormat, explaining that he was leaving again. Only temporarily, but most likely long enough to unsettle Hope and have her telling everyone what he had in the pipeline. I supposed I could drive out and talk to Charlie on his own, but it wasn't an ideal compromise.

I sat on the sofa, with my head in my hands, wishing I'd stuck to sorting out my own dramas rather than getting drawn into everyone else's and wondering what on earth I was going to do. Why hadn't I stuck to being a holidaymaker, someone keen to unwind and de-stress, rather than turning into someone intent on becoming embroiled in the minutiae of local Wynmouth life?

Just as I was set to sink even deeper into the murky depths

of the 'one is fun' pity party of my own making, a heavy knock at the door pulled me back into the cottage.

'This was delivered to the pub earlier,' said Sam gruffly, handing over a package and walking in. 'You weren't in and it had to be signed for.'

'Come in, why don't you?' I frowned, wondering what on earth it could be. Certainly not the phone I had ordered because that would have been super-fast, even for express delivery. 'Thanks.'

'But never mind that,' he said, pulling it out of my hands and dumping it on the sofa.

'Hey,' I objected.

'You can look at it later,' he said dismissively, 'right now I'm more concerned about what you saw and heard at Home Farm.'

'What?'

Surely Hope couldn't have cracked already.

'I've had Hope in tears at the pub.'

Or perhaps she had.

'I thought the two of you weren't talking,' I tersely reminded him.

'We weren't,' he said. 'We are now.'

As loath as I was to offload, I couldn't help thinking that if I didn't fill Sam in then he was likely to go out to Home Farm and tackle Charlie himself and that was the last thing I wanted.

'Thanks for that,' he said, once I had finished explaining what I had discovered.

His expression was unfathomable, but I had the feeling that Joe's Sunny Shores project wasn't going to be under wraps for much longer.

'I'll see myself out,' said Sam.

I didn't dare ask what he intended to do with the information I had supplied him with and, as the door shut behind him, I turned my attention back to the package. I could hardly believe my eyes and took a moment to let my galloping heart settle before looking at it again. My eyes weren't deceiving me, the label was definitely written in my father's hand.

My initial reaction to the missive had been to throw it in the wood burner – had it been lit – but then I was seized with a desire to open it and find out my fate. Was it a heartfelt plea for my return to the fold, or a court summons demanding I appeared and explained the reasons behind my desertion from the family firm?

Befuddled and dazed, I didn't know what to do with it so, unopened, I set it aside. I had no idea how my father had tracked me down, but I knew I couldn't stay in Wynmouth now. I felt truly sorry to be leaving so many loose ends in my wake, but the shocking sight of Dad's handwriting was enough to tell me that I still wasn't ready to face up to everything and therefore I had to go. If he'd put a package in the post, he could just as easily turn up on the doorstep and that was the last thing I wanted.

'Could I have a quiet word, in private please?' I asked Sam in the pub later that evening.

'Come through,' he said, lifting the bar hatch so I could follow him into the back.

'Thanks,' I swallowed.

'You haven't gone blabbing to Upton, have you?'

For someone who had the ability to make my temperature soar his tone left me cold.

'Of course, I haven't,' I tutted.

If only I'd kept my mouth shut, we wouldn't be destined to part on such unsatisfactory terms. It broke my heart to think that I would be leaving Wynmouth feeling that I would never be welcome to come back.

'What is it then?'

'I've just come to say that I'm going to be leaving tomorrow.'

'Oh,' he faltered, looking completely taken aback.

'I'm going in the morning, but of course I'll pay for the extra time you said I could stay.'

'There's no need for that,' he frowned.

'It's the least I can do,' I swallowed. 'What shall I do with the key?'

He looked at me and chewed his lip and I made a point of looking anywhere but into his spellbinding green eyes. I wasn't sure how I had been expecting him to react to my announcement, but the fact that he wasn't reacting at all was horrible. He could have at least asked what had prompted my decision or whether I might change my mind. Not that I would have known what to say in response.

'You can leave it where you found it.'

'Under the pot on the doorstep,' I said for confirmation and he nodded. 'Okay,' I said, walking back into the bar. 'That's where I'll leave it.'

'You know, Tess,' he suddenly said, closing the hatch between us again, 'you really aren't the person I thought you were when you first arrived.'

'Oh?'

'Yeah,' he carried on, not caring to lower his voice. 'For a while, I had you down as someone who had fallen in love with Wynmouth. I thought you got the place and really wanted to see it thrive, but now I know it was all a sham. I daresay you actually wanted everything you suggested to fail, didn't you?'

'What?'

'We all thought you were the sort of person who could make a difference,' he said bitterly, 'and you did have us fooled for a while, but you're not the girl I thought you were, Tess Tyler.'

I had no idea what he was talking about and it was on the tip of my tongue for me to blurt out that he hadn't been the boy I'd thought he was either, but I'd learnt my lesson when it came to making rash announcements in packed bars so instead I turned away and walked out.

Chapter 25

I didn't pack properly before I went to bed, thinking that a good night's sleep would be of more benefit than time spent sorting and tidying. And besides, that would be a welcome distraction to busy myself with when I got up and was waiting for the courier to deliver the phone I no longer needed. Needless to say, I didn't sleep, but lay awake scrutinizing Sam's words and wishing that I'd never set foot in Wynmouth again.

I wasn't in the best of tempers by the time I realized sleep was never going to come and my mood slumped even further as I trundled down the stairs only to be disturbed by a far earlier than expected knock on the door.

'This isn't the slot I booked,' I snapped. 'What's the point in me paying for timed delivery when you don't stick to the schedule?'

I wrenched the door open, my best scowl in place as I made ready to take my annoyance out on the driver, but it wasn't the courier.

It was my father.

The words died in my throat as I stopped dead on the threshold, staring at him, but not really believing what or who I was seeing. This had to be some trick, some joke my brain was playing, the result of not having slept and all the recent emotional turmoil.

'I told myself I wouldn't come,' he said huskily as his eyes met mine, 'but when you didn't respond to my letter, I just couldn't stay away any longer.'

Now, not only did the vision look like my father, it sounded like him too, so I had no choice but to accept that it was him, standing on the doorstep of Crow's Nest Cottage at some ungodly hour of the morning on the day I had finally decided to leave.

He looked careworn and almost as tired as I did, and just for a second, before the memory of Mum's diary tapped me on the shoulder and I checked myself, I very nearly gave in to instinct, threw my arms around him and told him that I loved him.

'I haven't read your letter,' I replied, my voice every bit as husky as his. 'The package only arrived yesterday and I haven't opened it,' I added, a little louder. 'I didn't even know there was a letter inside.'

'I did wonder if I should give you more time,' he said, a frown pulling his brows together, 'but I was scared that you would move on once you knew that I knew where you were and I couldn't risk that. I couldn't risk losing you again, Tess.'

I didn't know what to say. Dad hadn't been an emotionally demonstrative father for a very long time and confessing that he was scared, of anything, was something I didn't think I had ever heard him admit before.

'I suppose you'd better come in,' I said, opening the door wider.

I was mindful that George would soon be walking Skipper and didn't want to add more fuel to my holiday story which was weaving its way among the great, good and downright grumpy of Wynmouth.

'Although you won't be able to leave your car parked there.'

If Charlie came bowling along on the beach tractor, he wouldn't be able to get through the gap and that would cause even more talk than if George spotted me in conversation with an unknown man on the cottage doorstep.

'It's all right,' Dad said, still standing in the same spot. 'I don't want to come in. I was rather hoping that you would come with me.'

I looked at him and raised my eyebrows. I knew it was a work day, and a miracle that he was so far from his desk, but if he had plans to get me to the office and clocked in for nine, then he was in for a rude awakening.

'I'll only keep you for a few minutes,' he said, 'and I promise I'll bring you back.'

No plan to charge back to Essex just yet then.

'All right,' I agreed, thinking that now he was here, I really had no choice, 'wait there.'

I padded back upstairs, pulled on some clothes and tamed my hair into a ponytail.

'You're looking really well,' Dad smiled when, just a couple of minutes later, I locked the cottage door and climbed into the car. 'That tan looks more West Indies than Wynmouth and it's been years since I've seen you with so many freckles.'

That was most likely because it was years since he'd seen me without make-up.

'And I'd forgotten how much your hair curls,' he carried on. 'It looks just like your mother's used to before she started to straighten it.'

I wasn't much in the mood to listen to him harking back to the good old days, especially when his reminiscing included Mum.

'So, where are we going?' I asked, shrugging off his seemingly light-hearted chat.

His small talk was rather unnerving. As a rule, Dad's feet were firmly planted in the 'if you haven't got anything constructive to say, then don't say anything,' camp, but that morning for some reason he'd switched sides and the only reason for defecting that I could come up with, was because he was working his way up to saying something he wasn't sure about. The chattiness was completely out of character and I didn't like it, not one little bit.

'There's a café right on the beach I rather like the look of,' he said, turning up the lane which led back to The Green. 'I daresay you know it already.'

I did of course, but I didn't ask how he did. The route into the village would hardly have taken him along the seafront and past Sophie's door.

'It won't be open yet,' I said instead, checking the time. 'It won't be open for at least another hour.'

But, unexpectedly, it was.

'Good morning,' said Sophie, when we entered.

Dad had ignored the 'closed' sign and walked straight in, holding the door open for me to follow him.

'Morning,' he said back.

'What can I get you both?' Sophie asked.

She didn't appear to be quite her usual sunny self, but then it was still early. Not that I really thought the time would influence Sophie's mood. She always had a ready smile and was full of cheer.

'Just a coffee for me, please,' said Dad.

'And I'll have the same,' I said, 'thanks.'

Dad and I sat opposite one another, in the booth I always tried to nab because it had the best view of the sea. Now Dad was quiet and neither of us said anything as we stared out at the view while Sophie prepared our drinks. The sun shone, the sea sparkled and there wasn't a cloud in the sky. To all intents and purposes, it looked like the beginning of the perfect day, but I had the feeling that it was going to turn out to be anything but.

'I have things to do in the kitchen,' said Sophie, as she carried over our drinks, spilling a little of mine as she served it, 'but call me if you need anything.'

'I can't be long,' I told Dad as he slowly stirred milk into his cup. 'I'm expecting a parcel and I have to be there to sign for it.'

'Of course,' he nodded, carefully putting down the spoon. 'I don't want to interfere in your plans.'

'Then why are you here?' I asked.

Surely, he must have realized that his unexpected arrival was going to interfere with my schedule, because he wasn't a part of it. Had he been just a couple of hours later, I would have ticked the first thing off the plan for the day and been miles away.

'The week you left,' he finally began, 'all I wanted was to track you down and make you come back.'

'But Joan said I deserved a break,' I cut in, trying to hurry him along. 'You told me that when I called. You told me that she had said I was entitled to some time off.'

Dad nodded.

'That's correct,' he agreed, 'and having looked over your work records, I couldn't deny that she was right.'

'Crikey,' I blurted out, sounding more sarcastic than I meant to.

'In fact, Joan has told me quite a few home truths recently,' Dad added, with a wry smile.

'And you've listened?' I asked, wondering how on earth she'd managed to pull that off.

Usually Dad would have given the impression that he was listening, he was the master of it, but then he would have carried on with whatever it was that he'd set his heart on anyway.

355

'Believe it or not,' he said, clearly in tune with the wavelength my thoughts were travelling along, 'I have. As it turns out, she's a very wise woman, my housekeeper. She makes a lot of sense.'

'I could have told you that years ago,' I said bluntly, 'not that you would have listened. However,' I charitably added, 'I'm pleased that you've finally sussed it out for yourself.'

'It's quite something, coming from your old dad, who thinks he always knows best, isn't it?' Dad smiled.

I looked up at him, equally as surprised to see the amusement in his eyes as I was to hear him admit that he was even remotely aware of what he was like to live – and work – with.

'It's nothing short of a miracle,' I told him. 'However, it doesn't alter the fact that you're here now, does it? You clearly didn't heed her words about leaving me alone for long.'

'On the contrary,' he swallowed. 'She's part of the reason that I'm here.'

'Oh?'

'When you called to say that you were staying away for even longer,' he explained, 'Joan told me she was surprised you'd done that and we both began to worry that you would never come back.'

'I see.'

I don't suppose I'd really thought about how my decision would impact on anyone else. I had simply done what felt right for me at the time.

'I couldn't bear the thought of losing my girl for good,' Dad then said, his voice suddenly choked with emotion and, when I looked at him, I could see it in his eyes too, 'and as there was no further word from you, I went . . .' He stopped and bit his lip.

'You went where?' I asked, urging him on.

'I went to your apartment,' he said, letting out a long breath, 'to see if I could find some clue that might help me track you down and,' he added, shaking his head, 'I found the trunk. Your mother's trunk.'

He pulled a piece of paper out of his pocket and smoothed it out on the table. It was a page from Mum's diary. A sheet I must have somehow missed in my haste to get away.

'So, you know then,' I said, looking from the paper and back to him. 'You know what it was that finally tipped me over the edge and made me run away.'

No longer the self-assured boss who never let his confident façade falter, he looked far more human now and vulnerable. As he appeared to be finally facing up to what he had done, admitting that he had been an unfaithful and disloyal husband, I supposed that was only to be expected.

He nodded.

'You know why I couldn't bear the sight of you a moment longer . . .' I choked, the bitter words catching in my throat as my eyes filled with tears.

The last thing I wanted to do was cry in front of him, but now we were here, with the awful evidence on the table between us, I couldn't stop the sudden influx of emotions.

'Me?' Dad asked, the shocked tone of his voice making me look up again.

'Yes,' I said, 'you. You were the one who used to moan about the sort of woman Mum had turned into. You were the one who resented the amount of money she spent on clothes and the fact that she was so obsessed with always looking her best, but,' I added, jabbing a finger at the printed page, 'did you ever stop to think about why she did all that?'

I didn't give him a chance to answer.

'She did it,' I charged on, 'because she was trying to put a brave face on things. She didn't want the rest of the world knowing that she was crumbling inside because of your endless affairs, so she made the outside of herself as beautiful and groomed as she possibly could. She invested in all those designer outfits,' I raged, 'because—'

'Because,' Dad interrupted, reaching for my hand before I could move it out of his reach, 'the woman who owned her favourite boutique was your mother's lover, and your mum used her shopping habit as an excuse to spend time with her.'

The silence which descended was so complete, so deep, I was sure I could hear waves lapping the shore, even though the tide was out. Or was the rushing sound just in my head? It seemed to fill the spaces in and around me and was accompanied by a sudden light-headedness which before had heralded the arrival of a vertigo attack.

'What?' I croaked.

'I'm sorry to just blurt it out like that, Tess,' Dad said as he squeezed my hand harder and everything began to look fuzzy around the edges, 'but it wasn't pages from your mum's diary that you found. They were from mine.'

I closed my eyes, but that didn't help stave off the spinning sensation and I slowly, very slowly, opened them again.

'You've been reading my reaction to your mother's affairs,' he said, 'not her reaction to mine.'

The expression in his eyes and the set of his mouth suggested he was telling the truth, but surely that couldn't be right.

'But Mum wasn't a lesbian,' I finally whispered, 'she was married to you. She had me ... and the way the diary was worded ...'

'She was,' he whispered back. 'I know it's hard to get your head around Tess, but your mum was gay. Throughout the early years of our marriage, she did everything she could to make herself believe that she wasn't, but she was and, in the end, she gave up trying to pretend otherwise.'

'But the diary,' I stammered.

'I had to be careful how I wrote it,' he explained, 'I wanted, needed, to get my feelings out of my head but knew a book could be found and a computer could be hacked, so in the end I settled for trying to make it read as if ...'

'A woman had written it,' I interrupted, 'you messed around with the pronouns and that's what made me think that Mum had written it.'

'Yes,' he nodded.

He'd almost succeeded too, but now I realized that was why a few things hadn't quite added up, no matter how many times I read them. That was why the words hadn't always scanned quite as seamlessly as they should.

'I see,' I whispered, even though I was struggling to. Dad then explained that it was Mum who had been the adulterous one in their marriage, not him. She had had numerous affairs over the years and they had all been with women.

'But the final one,' he said, sighing deeply. 'That was different.'

'You wrote that she was "the one", didn't you?' I interrupted.

'Yes,' he nodded, 'I did and she was.'

'What do you mean?'

'She was the love of your mother's life.'

'How do you know that?'

'I've talked to her,' Dad said, looking uncomfortable. 'I now know that your mother was planning to leave me for her. Once she had discovered the diary, she realized the emotional damage she had caused and knew it had to stop. She was planning to make a clean break of it and let us both move on with our lives.'

That was something, I supposed.

'So, you knew Mum had found the diary?'

'Not until I discovered this page in her trunk,' he said, looking at the sheet, 'and then I spoke to the other woman, Vanessa, before realizing that you most likely had the rest of it and had assumed that . . .'

It was a relief that he couldn't finish the sentence. I didn't want to hear him say out loud that I had jumped to the one conclusion that couldn't have been any further from the truth.

'But why didn't you leave her first, Dad?' I stole myself to ask. 'Why didn't you divorce her when you first discovered what was going on? From what you've written, the affairs had been happening for a really long time.'

He squeezed my hand again and shrugged, 'I couldn't leave her,' he said, 'because there was a part of me that still loved her.'

It broke my heart to hear him say that and I suddenly understood that trying to ignore what had been happening in Mum's life was the real reason behind why he had thrown himself into the business. He had wanted something which would occupy as much of his time as Mum's lovers did hers.

'And it was why I pulled you into the business, Tess,' he went on. 'I thought if I could give you something to focus on, you wouldn't have time to worry over or question your parents' failing marriage. It was why I worked you harder than everyone else,' he added. 'I wanted to keep your eye trained anywhere other than on the home front.'

My head felt lighter than ever and my stomach rolled in response. Not only was I having to reassess everything I thought I knew about my mum, I was also reeling from how my own life had been moulded as a result of Dad's misguided attempt to protect me.

'Why didn't you just tell me?' I whispered. 'You could have told me.'

I don't know how I would have reacted but I hated that he had lived with this for so long and not confided in anyone other than his laptop.

He let go of my hand and sat back.

'I didn't feel that it was my place to,' he said. 'I didn't want to be the person who set the ball rolling. I couldn't risk either you or your mum resenting me for forcing her hand.'

'So, you just put up with it.'

'I tried to,' he said, 'but it wasn't easy.'

Easy or not, it wasn't something I could have done.

'But you did it.'

'As I said,' he sighed, 'I tried. I didn't always manage particularly well, but I did my best.'

'Oh Dad,' I said, shaking my head again before thinking better of it.

'It's okay,' Dad smiled.

I wanted to believe it was, but I couldn't. He had sacrificed so much of himself, so many years and I hated the fact that I had been so ready to accept that he was the one in the wrong.

'I really don't know what to say,' I sighed as I tried to make some sort of sense of it all.

No wonder he had struggled to show his grief. I could see now that Mum had left him long before she died and his reaction to sorting through her clothes wasn't because he didn't care, it was because he knew the real reason behind why there were so many wardrobes full of them.

'Why didn't you tell me after Mum had gone?' I asked him. 'Surely, it would have been easier then.'

'I was going to,' he said, 'the day we started sorting through everything in the dressing room. That was the day I had decided that I would explain.'

'So, why didn't you?'

Dad smiled.

'It was your mention of the yellow sundress that she used to wear when we holidayed here,' he told me. 'The way you described her reminded me that you still had the perfect image of her in your head. You might have grown apart as you got older, but that was still the Mum that she was to you, Tess. I wasn't going to destroy that.'

'Oh, Dad.'

I watched as he leant over and added another spoon of sugar to my coffee. It was going to take a lot more than that for me to get over the shock.

'Hey,' said Hope, who suddenly burst in and set the café bell jangling. 'What's going on? I just had a text from Mum saying she needed me to come down. Is everything all right?'

Sophie came out of the kitchen, untied her apron and took the seat next to Dad, before telling Hope to squeeze in next to me.

'What's up with you?' Hope said to me. 'You look as though you've seen a ghost.'

'I'm all right,' I croaked, wondering why on earth the four of us were sitting together when Dad and I clearly still needed more time to talk and I needed some space to think through everything he had just told me.

'Well, you don't look it,' Hope said again.

'I'm fine,' I sniffed, 'really.'

She didn't push me further, but turned her attention to Dad.

'Sorry,' she said, 'I don't think we've met.'

Now it was my turn to apologize.

'Sorry,' I said, finally remembering my manners. 'This is my dad. Dad, this is my friend, Hope.'

'Pleased to meet you,' said Hope, looking between the two of us. 'I didn't know you were expecting a visitor,' she said to me, obviously trying to gauge my reaction to Dad's unexpected appearance.

Thankfully, I didn't have the opportunity to try and work out how to answer her.

'Are you sure you're all right, Tess?' Sophie asked, noticing my pallor now Hope had pointed it out.

I nodded.

'I'm okay.'

Sophie looked at Dad.

'I don't think . . .' she began, but Dad stopped her.

'It's time,' he said. 'And I really don't want to have to stop, not now that I've started.'

Hope and I looked at each other again, both of us now sporting deep frowns. The morning had already held enough shocks for me, but clearly there were more to come.

'As I said a minute ago, Tess,' Dad said, looking directly at me, 'I did try my best to be a good husband.'

'Of course,' I nodded.

'But no one's perfect,' he swallowed, biting his lower lip to stop it from trembling.

'Please,' said Sophie, looking first at me and then to Dad, 'let me explain.'

Dad nodded and dropped his gaze to the table.

'Your father,' she said, her own voice now thick with emotion, 'only had one lapse in his marriage, Tess, and it was many, many years ago. One moment of weakness after he discovered something about your mum.'

I was relieved that she didn't elaborate on what that was.

'Hope,' Sophie carried on, now looking at her daughter as she drew in the deepest breath and her eyes filled with tears.

It was a shock to see. I'd never seen her face do anything other than smile.

'What?' Hope asked, sounding as unsure as Sophie looked.

Dad lifted his eyes from the table again.

'You know I told you that your father was a holidaymaker from here in Wynmouth?'

'Yes,' said Hope, her eyes now tracking from my dad to her mum and back again, as were mine.

'You can't be serious?' I whispered.

'Are you telling me . . .' Hope joined in.

'Yes,' Sophie cut in, her voice barely louder than a whisper, 'Hope, this is your dad.'

Stunned silence descended and I came to the conclusion that this was all a dream. I would wake up in a minute and find myself back in Crow's Nest Cottage, sweating and with the sheet wrapped tightly around me.

'Say something,' Sophie begged her daughter. 'Please.'

'I remember you,' Hope slowly said, pointing at Dad and dashing all thoughts that I was in a dream-state and not really sitting next to her in the café. 'You spoke to me, didn't you? And I went running to Mum because I thought you were some weirdo.'

Dad nodded, clearly remembering the same thing.

'I thought I'd worked out who you were,' Dad said, 'and ended up getting carried away and asking too many questions.'

'Was that the year you cut our holiday short?' I asked. 'It was our last holiday in Wynmouth, wasn't it? You said we had to leave because of work, but that wasn't why, was it?'

'Yes, it was that year,' said Dad, 'and no, we didn't really have to go because of work. I was convinced that Hope was my daughter and thought it best if we left.'

I couldn't believe it.

'So, you've been here before?' Hope asked, twisting around to look at me. 'This isn't your first time in Wynmouth?'

'We used to come here every year for our summer holidays,' I told her. 'I know the place like the back of my hand.'

'Oh my god,' she gasped, not sounding like herself at all.

'Your father wrote to me after you left that summer,' said Sophie, filling in more of the cracks which had opened up in my understanding of that time. 'He said he was sorry for leaving. That discovering Hope had been one of the biggest shocks of his life. He also said that he would support us financially, that he would have been doing it since you were born, Hope, had he known about you. He also said that his marriage was a sham, but he couldn't bring himself to end it, Tess. He said he couldn't do anything that would risk your happiness and that he still loved your mum.'

I looked at Dad and, finding tears in his eyes, let mine flow unchecked. All the time I had assumed he loved work more than me and Mum, he was in fact using it as a sanity saver and to help keep two families financially afloat. He wasn't the selfish, work–driven guy I had him down as at all and he never had been.

'I had no idea,' I sniffed.

This time I reached for his hand while Sophie reached for Hope's. Dad slipped his other hand into Sophie's and Hope grabbed mine.

I've no idea how long we sat there, each of us lost in our own thoughts, but I was the one who eventually spoke first.

'So,' I asked, 'have you and Sophie been in touch all this time?'

'Yes,' he said. 'Ever since that summer.'

'And you hadn't been here long before I worked out who you were, Tess,' Sophie admitted. 'I didn't say anything to your dad to begin with, but he was so worried when you told him you were staying away for longer, that I had to tell him you were here and safe in Wynmouth.'

'So, all the time I thought I was free,' I said aloud, 'you were keeping tabs on me, Sophie.'

'Sort of,' she acknowledged. 'But had you gone home when you originally planned, I would have kept your secret. I'm sorry for dobbing you in, Tess.'

'But what else could you do?' I said, feeling slightly rattled but at the same time knowing that she had been in a difficult position. 'It's fine.'

It was strange, and if I was being truthful, a little annoying to think that there had been a spy in the camp from the moment I had arrived, but not as strange as realizing that she had been living with the knowledge that—

'Oh my god,' I said, turning to Hope. 'We're . . .'

'Sisters!' Hope gasped back. 'Bloody hell, Tess, we're sisters!'

I was still well and truly reeling from the revelations the beginning of my day had brought about, but thankfully I wasn't treading the unexpected path alone. Hope was journeying along it with me and it was a comfort to have her by my side.

'You know,' she told me, shaking her head in wonder as we walked back into the village together. 'I've always wondered if I had brothers and sisters somewhere in the world.'

'Have you?'

I had cited my phone parcel as an excuse to leave the café, but really, I needed a bit of fresh air and some space in which to pull my thoughts together. Hope's quick offer to accompany me told me that she was feeling much the same way.

'Yes,' she said. 'I have and,' she added with a nudge, 'here you are.'

I nudged her back, still struggling to find the words.

'Yes,' I managed to whisper, 'here I am.'

We carried on a few steps in silence again.

'Do you think they're going to get together now?' she then shocked me by asking.

'Who?'

'Our parents,' she said, 'Do you think they're going to become a couple?'

'Crikey,' I said, 'I don't know.'

'I reckon they're still into each other,' she said, as she linked her arm through mine. 'You can just tell, can't you?'

'I don't know,' I swallowed, 'it was all such a shock I can't say that I had time to notice details like that.'

'Well, I did,' she said.

I pressed the tips of my fingers into my temples.

'Are you all right?'

'I think so,' I said breathing slowly in and out. 'It's just such a lot to take in.'

'It's epic though, right?' she said, stopping to look at me, her head cocked to one side.

I could sense her concern. She needed some reassurance from me.

'Totally,' I agreed, 'and I honestly couldn't wish for a better sister, it's just . . .'

'Too much for a mid-summer morning?' she suggested.

'Way too much,' I agreed.

Hope might have just discovered who her dad was but I was still recovering from the revelation that my mum wasn't who I thought she was and she never had been. It was a miracle I was still on my feet.

'Would you mind if we kept this to ourselves for now?' I asked, when we reached the cottage.

'I was just about to ask you the same thing,' she smiled. 'I want to get it all fathomed out first before we go making any big announcements.'

'Same,' I smiled back, relieved that she agreed with me, but surprised nonetheless.

For Hope to hold back on anything it must have been a really big deal, not that I was in any doubt just how life-changing this all was, but it was yet another shock, to have her agreeing to hang fire when it came to telling everyone.

'I won't tell a soul,' she said, 'not even Sam, but let's not take too long working it all out. After all, we've got almost three decades of sisterhood to make up for.'

After hugging at the gate, I slipped into the cottage, banishing the thought of how difficult it was going to be making up for all that lost time with my half-sister when her partner and I had kissed and he had subsequently taken against me, and thought instead that I should probably open Dad's letter. However, as seemed to be the way of it these days, the universe had other ideas.

I had barely had time to fill the kettle when I was stopped in my tracks.

'Tess!'

'Joe,' I smiled, turning to find his face peeping around the door I hadn't thought to lock behind me. 'This is a surprise.'

'A good one, I hope?'

I knew my smile was strained, but it was the best I could offer him.

'I thought I might pop down to the pub for a bite of breakfast,' he said. 'Will you come with me?'

My head might have been caught up in an emotional maelstrom, but I still had enough about me to know that there was no way I could let him go to the Smuggler's.

'I'm not really in the mood.' I said. 'Let's have something here instead. I've got bacon from the butcher's so I could make us sandwiches.'

'No,' he said, holding the door further open. 'Come on. Let's go to the pub. That way Sam gets to deal with the washing up.'

Sam was the last person I wanted to see, but I couldn't let Joe face him alone so, with a heavy heart I followed him up the lane, forgetting all about my expected phone delivery, and quickly ushered him into the snug before he was spotted.

'I'll order,' I said, making for the bar, 'you stay here. It can be my treat.'

'Tess,' Sam frowned as I approached. 'I thought you'd be long gone by now.'

'Yes,' I said, 'about that . . .'

'I think I'll have a sausage bap, instead of a bacon roll,' said Joe's voice, unexpectedly close behind me, 'if you haven't already ordered, Tess?'

Sam looked from me to Joe and back again, his expression darkening with every beat of my heart.

'Are you actually serious?' Sam said to me.

'What's going on?' Joe retaliated, instantly ruffled by Sam's belligerent tone.

'Nothing,' I said, turning around and trying to push him away. 'It's nothing. Come on, let's go.'

'How dare the pair of you even think about coming in here together?' Sam hissed. 'I always knew you had some front, Joe, but this is too much.'

Joe suddenly looked every bit as pale and peaky as I had earlier.

'What's that supposed to mean?' he demanded, pulling himself out of my grasp. 'What are you talking about?'

Sam scowled at him and ground his jaw and I looked between the two of them. For a moment I thought Hope really had been right, that there was some complication between the pair that was still to be unearthed.

'I'm talking about the land sale,' said Sam, 'what else?'

'The land sale?' Joe frowned, and although he sounded confused, there was also an edge of relief.

'When were you going to tell us, Joe?' Sam glowered. 'When were you going to warn us that the village was about to be changed forever. Don't you need some sort of public consultation before you go ahead with something like that?'

'How do you know about any of that?' Joe demanded, now looking at me.

'Had you come to us and explained,' Sam went on, 'we might have been able to help, you might have even drummed up a bit of support, but this is a whitewash, and if you think,' he went on, now including me in his argument, 'that just because you've hired her and the fancy bloody PR company that her family owns, that you're going to convince us otherwise, then you're a bigger fool than I thought you were.'

'How do you know about Tyler PR?' I stuttered.

'I told you yesterday,' Sam said to me, 'that you weren't the person I thought you were, didn't I? Turning up here and helping pull the community back together, what a joke.' He laughed. 'I saw the franking mark on that letter, Tess Tyler. I know who you work for and how Joe has planted you here to soften us all up and convince us that a few more visitors to the area will be a good thing.'

'No,' I said. 'That's not it . . .'

'Your boss even turned up here this morning looking for you,' he cut in, 'so you can hardly deny it, can you?'

'Tess,' Joe frowned. 'How did *you* know about the land sale?'

'I heard you on the phone and I saw the paperwork when I stayed at the farm,' I admitted. 'Bruce knocked it off the table and I spotted it when I picked it up.'

'And you told everyone?'

He sounded absolutely wretched.

'Yes,' said Sam, 'she did. Although I'm still trying to work out her motive for doing that. How she thought that telling us what was going on was going to create some good PR for the cause, god only knows!'

That was the last straw. I couldn't cope with any more. I was going to pack up the last of my things, turn my phone back on and let Dad know that I was getting the hell out of Wynmouth for good.

Chapter 26

It didn't take long for me to fling the rest of my things into the bags I had just a few weeks ago so carefully packed in anticipation of my seaside escape, but I found myself lingering in the cottage and reluctant to turn the key in the lock for the last time. I sat on the sofa, with my head in my hands thinking how impossible it was to comprehend that I had arrived in the village with so much mental baggage and now I was about to leave with even more.

Not only was I trying to get my head around the truth behind what had really been happening in my parents' marriage and having to rethink everything I knew about the woman who had taken pride in her simple sundress, I was also assimilating the knowledge that I had a sister. The fact that I loved her as a friend, hated myself for having betrayed her and was already having to leave her behind, was too much. It was all too much!

And that was even before I factored in the complications

surrounding the Sam and Joe scenario. In my attempt to help Hope find a way to push the pair back together, I had ended up pulling them even further apart. And now Sam hated me, just as I was daring to admit, if only to myself, that I had fallen in love with him.

I knew that his being in love with Hope made my being around him unbearable, but now he'd got some skewed idea about me being Joe's spy and there really was no chance of my ever returning to Wynmouth. The long-lost family get-togethers which Sophie was doubtless already arranging were always going to be missing one family member.

I glanced up at the kitchen clock, amazed that so much of the day had already disappeared and knowing that I couldn't drag my departure out any longer. I took my mobile out of the drawer where it had lived, for the most part, undisturbed since my arrival and thought how I was going to block my confused thoughts out until I had put at least a hundred miles between me and the village. I was just about to turn the phone on and message Dad to ask where he was and let him know that I was leaving, when Joe came bursting through the cottage door, only this time, with Charlie in tow.

'What the hell?' I shouted, jumping back in surprise.

'Come on you,' said Joe, pulling the phone out of my hand and tossing it onto the sofa. 'You need to come with me.'

'Don't be so ridiculous,' I snapped back. 'I'm not going anywhere with you.'

Joe shook his head.

'In fact,' I pushed on, 'I'm beginning to wish that I'd never set eyes on either one of you.'

'You don't mean that,' said Joe.

'Yes,' I resolutely carried on, 'I do, because my life has been nothing but a disaster from the moment you walked back into it.'

He didn't catch my faux pas and I bit my lip to stop myself adding another revelation to the drama the day had become. All I had wanted when I came back from the café earlier was to sit and quietly think about all the things Dad and Sophie had told me, but now this post-pub argument was going to be the cause of even more stress. I could feel something was coming and cursed myself for lingering in the cottage when I could have been long gone.

'Please, Tess,' said Charlie, sounding far more reasonable than his sibling. 'It would really help if you could just give us a minute.'

The words were sincerely spoken and, as I was the person responsible for letting the cat out of the bag about the farm sale, I supposed I did owe them something. I looked at Charlie's forlorn face and felt my resolve to refuse Joe's demands crumble a little.

'Please,' Charlie said again.

I let out a long breath.

'Where exactly is it that we're going?' I asked, as I reached for the cottage keys.

This wasn't going to be the last time I locked the place up after all then.

'To the Smuggler's,' said Joe, peering through the window as a van pulled up.

'You've got to be kidding me,' I gasped, taking a step back again. 'After what happened earlier?'

'A hell of a lot has happened since earlier,' he said mysteriously. 'Trust me.'

Given his track record, I wasn't sure I wanted to.

'Are you expecting a parcel?' Charlie asked.

I took delivery of the phone I now didn't need and the three of us walked back up the lane to the pub. The brothers were far keener to cross the threshold than I was, and I felt my heart kick in my chest as I discovered the place was even more packed than the evening I had arranged for the Sea Dogs to entertain us.

'Is this everyone?' I heard Joe ask Sam.

'It's as many as I could rally at such short notice,' Sam told him.

'Okay,' said Joe, puffing out his cheeks, 'thanks.'

Sam nodded, looked at me for the briefest moment and then turned back to the till. The pair sounded almost civil and that was the last thing I had been expecting. When Joe had said back at the cottage that a lot had happened since earlier, he clearly wasn't wrong. Exactly how long had it taken me to pack my bags? Long enough for the pair of them to come to some sort of tolerance agreement, by the looks of it. At least I could rest easier knowing I hadn't been dragged in to witness a barroom brawl.

'Do you know what's going on?' I mouthed to Hope as Joe pulled me further inside.

She shrugged in response, looking as clueless as I was and then came over.

'No idea,' she said in a low voice. 'Joe sent me a text a few minutes ago, asking me to come and wait in here and it was already packed like this when I arrived.' She turned to Joe. 'Are you sure you're all right?' she asked him, laying her hand lightly on his arm.

It was the tiniest gesture, but it spoke volumes.

'I will be in a minute or two,' he smiled at her.

My guess was that he had gathered everyone together, somehow with Sam's help, to confess about the Sunny Shores deal, but what I was thrown by was the fact that he was looking so calm about it. He took Hope's hand and squeezed it before following Charlie further into the room.

'Have you seen . . .' I began to ask Hope but then hesitated, not quite sure how to frame the question. I supposed there was only one way really. 'Have you seen your mum and dad?' I swallowed.

It would have been too much of a mouthful to say 'your mum and my dad' and besides, it wouldn't have been accurate either because as it turned out, the man who was my dad, was every bit as much hers.

Hope looked at me and bit her lip.

'God, that sounds strange,' she whispered, and I was pleased I wasn't alone in thinking it. 'Don't you think?'

'Just a bit,' I agreed, 'but I daresay we'll soon get used to it.'

That made us both smile.

'I haven't seen either of them,' she then told me. 'I tried

the café phone earlier, but Mum didn't pick up and she's not answering her mobile.'

'Perhaps they've gone somewhere together then,' I suggested. When I thought about it, I rather liked the idea of the two of them being together. Dad deserved to have some fun and happiness in his life and I was certain Sophie could supply both in abundance. 'They've got plenty to talk about, after all.'

Hope nodded in agreement but didn't have time to comment further as Joe clapped his hands and the room instantly fell silent.

'I think you'd better come and stand up here,' Sam said to Joe, 'both of you,' he added. 'That way everyone will be able to see and hear you.'

I felt my mouth fall open in shock. First, the pair had been civil to one another, in spite of their earlier argument, and now Sam was inviting both Upton brothers up behind the bar. Hope and I exchanged a look, both of us clearly as amazed as the other.

'Thanks,' said Joe, weaving his way across the room with Charlie close behind him. 'That's a good idea.'

'I've had a few in my time,' said Sam, lifting the bar hatch to let them through.

I couldn't help wondering if this was damage limitation on Sam's part. If Joe was going to talk about selling the farm and changing the face of Wynmouth forever then the crowd might take against him, but at least with the width of the bar between them, Sam could quickly usher the pair out through the kitchen if it looked like a fight was about to break out.

'What's this all about?' someone shouted from the back of the room.

'Yeah,' joined in another. 'Get on with it, Upton. I've shut up shop to come and listen to you.'

Sam rang the bar bell to quieten everyone again as a low muttering broke out and then stepped aside.

'Thanks, Sam,' Joe swallowed, before looking around, 'and thank you all for coming at such short notice. I know not everyone could make it, but I daresay those of you who are here will be able to fill the others in so, here goes ...'

'What have you done now, Joe?' the voice from the back shouted again. 'You always were bloody bad news and I'm guessing nothing's changed just because you're a few years older.'

Charlie shook his head and stepped forward before Sam had time to make the bell clang again.

'No,' he said, his voice booming out and commanding everyone's attention, even the person intent on stirring up trouble at the back, 'this has nothing to do with Joe.'

I was as quiet, and confused, as everyone else now. Joe and Charlie exchanged a look and then Joe stepped back so Charlie could carry on.

'I know,' he began, 'that a few of you have found out that Home Farm and much of its prime land has been—'

'Sold!' someone couldn't resist calling out. 'To Sunny bloody Shores!'

Charlie then had to wait while everyone digested the

news that I had started to spread. I stared at my feet wishing the floor would open up and swallow me and, given the way Hope shuffled from one foot to the other beside me, I would have bet good money that she was wishing she could disappear too.

'I knew the farm was struggling,' said George, his voice only just rising above the others, 'but I had no idea it had come to this. Why didn't you tell us, Charlie?'

Charlie shrugged and shook his head.

'We might have been able to help, lad,' said another voice.

'We might have been able to find a way,' added a third.

I was pleased to hear sympathetic voices rising above the angry few.

'This is all your doing, is it, Joe?' shouted someone else. 'You thought it the best chance you had of getting rid of the place for good!'

'No,' said Charlie, his voice rising above the rest. 'No,' he said again, quieter this time.

'What do you mean, *no*?'

'Joe has had nothing to do with it,' he carried on, sounding choked. 'I'm the one responsible. I'm the one who put the deal together. Joe had no idea about any of it.'

That didn't tally with the side of the telephone conversation I had heard, but I knew better than to interrupt. I had already had one lesson that day in what could happen when you jumped to conclusions, and I wasn't about to do it again.

Everyone was quiet now, waiting for Charlie to explain properly.

'I'm not going to lie,' he said, turning red, 'I was sick of the place and I was sick of hearing about Joe's great life away from Wynmouth and how he didn't have to worry about crop yields and prices and long-range weather forecasts and on top of all that, I was bloody lonely too. When I was growing up at Home Farm, there had been three brothers and two parents and now there's just me, and my stupid dog and . . . well, it's all got too much for me . . .'

His words trailed off and Joe stepped up again. He placed a hand on his brother's shoulder and gave it a squeeze.

'The only thing I'm really guilty of,' he said, picking up the thread, his voice wracked with emotion, 'is that I didn't know any of this. I had no idea that Charlie was at his wits' end and worn out running the farm that I was, if I'm honest, jealous had fallen to him. I didn't know he was lonely or how he had planned to rid himself of the place, before he did something even more drastic.'

There was a sharp intake of breath as everyone realized what Joe was suggesting might have happened.

'So,' he carried on, 'when I came back to Wynmouth and discovered what was in the offing, I felt every bit as shocked as you lot. Not only because we were going to lose Home Farm, but also because I had been so divorced from the place, that I hadn't seen the toll it was taking on my big brother.'

'So, what are you going to do?' Hope asked.

Her voice was soft and kind and Joe's eyes gratefully sought out hers from the crowd, safe in the knowledge that there were people listening to him who were prepared to wait and hopefully understand before shouting the odds and causing more unnecessary concern.

'Well,' Joe carried on, 'I've been working tirelessly for the last few weeks, sometimes from the farm itself and sometimes further away, to untangle the deal and see if we can unravel the contract.'

'Is that where you've been going?' Hope asked.

'Yes,' he said. 'I daresay some of you thought I was still running away from Wynmouth, but I can assure you that wasn't the case.'

At this point he looked at Sam and the pair shared, not quite a smile, but something close to it. Hope nudged me and I shook my head to indicate that I didn't know what that was about either.

'He was sorting out the mess I'd made of things,' Charlie said, his cheeks flushed red again.

'And has he managed to do it?' Sam asked, his eyes still on Joe.

I got the impression that he already knew the answer.

Joe nodded and smiled and clapped his brother on the back. Charlie wrapped his arms around him and almost lifted him off his feet. I don't think I'd ever seen Joe look so elated, not even after our roof-raising duet in the karaoke bar.

'Yes,' he sobbed. 'Yes, I have. The contract hadn't got so far that the farm couldn't be saved and I can tell you all for certain that none of the Home Farm land or property is going to fall into Sunny Shores' hands now.'

A collective cheer went up and Joe looked at me and smiled

and I blinked back a tear. I felt incredibly guilty to have been the one who had gone public on this whole debacle, but at least there was a happy ending. The irony wasn't lost on me, however, that just like the diary scenario, had I tackled the situation head on, there wouldn't have been the subsequent misunderstandings, heartache and wasted time. It was a valuable life lesson and one that I wasn't going to forget.

'Everything has been unravelled,' Joe added for the benefit of those close enough to hear, 'and while Charlie goes off to travel for a while and live the life he has been dreaming about, I'm going to take over the running of the farm. There'll be some changes to what we grow and how things are managed, but there won't be a holiday complex springing up out of the hedgerows!'

Everyone cheered even louder, happy that the brothers had found a way to keep the farm and find a compromise which ensured they both got what they wanted. I guessed that Charlie had been reluctant to take on any of Joe's ideas and suggestions because he just wanted to be rid of the responsibility.

'I had been hoping,' Joe continued, coming out from behind the bar once everyone had settled down a bit, 'that Charlie and I would be able to keep this business to ourselves.'

'I'm so sorry,' I said, feeling the tears well back up again as I imagined how the atmosphere could have turned if he'd had to tell everyone that he hadn't been able to pull out of the deal.

'But there was someone among us who genuinely had

Wynmouth's best interests at heart,' he said, coming to stand right next to me, 'and Charlie and I both know that she only did what she did because she thought it was best for the village.'

I risked a glance at Sam and found he was now as red as Charlie had been before.

'So, when I heard her being accused of colluding with me,' Joe went on. 'I knew I was going to have to say something. Tess Tyler might have said more than she should, but she did it with the best of intentions and the fact that her family owns a famous PR firm is a complete coincidence.'

Everyone was focused now on Joe, Sam and me.

'I'm so sorry, Tess,' Sam said huskily. 'When I saw that letter with the firm name stamped on it, I just assumed, well, the worst I suppose.'

I nodded, disappointed that he could have thought so little of me, but I could hardly protest. Twice recently I had jumped to conclusions and got things wrong myself so it would have been hypocritical of me to complain.

'It's okay,' I told him. 'Had I been in your position, I probably would have thought the same thing.'

'And while we're on a roll,' said Joe, looking at Sam, and keeping me close, 'and getting a few things sorted, there's something else we need to discuss, isn't there, Sam?'

'There is,' Sam confirmed. 'But in private.'

Hope looked at me and frowned and I wondered if my kiss with her other half was about to be revealed. I might have been all for clearing the air, but that was one confession that I thought would do more harm than good if it was set free, especially in view of our earlier half-sibling revelation.

'So,' Sam shouted, above the rapidly rising din, 'I'm going to ask everyone if they wouldn't mind drinking up because I need to lock up for a little while, but I'll be open as usual this evening.'

'Don't look so worried,' Joe said to me, 'everything's going to be fine.'

'What's going on?' Hope asked.

'All in good time,' he told her, another broad smile lighting up his face and making her blush.

If Sam hadn't sussed out that she and Joe were still mad about each other, then he was even more short-sighted than I had been recently.

'Well,' said Charlie, once most people had gone. 'That wasn't too bad, was it?'

'No,' Joe agreed, 'not bad at all.'

'Although,' Charlie admitted, 'I can't help wishing I'd talked things through with folk a bit before I made that call to Sunny Shores.'

Joe rolled his eyes.

'That might not have been a bad idea, mate. You should have talked to me, if no one else.'

'I just wanted shot of it all, Joe,' Charlie went on, 'and I had no idea you were genuinely interested in taking it on. I just assumed . . .'

There was that word again.

'That you were happy where you were.'

Heidi Swain

'And you also assumed that folk wouldn't pitch in and help,' Joe rather unnecessarily pointed out.

'I know,' Charlie tutted. 'I did everyone a huge disservice in thinking that, but I'd got so low, I couldn't see beyond my own problems.'

'We've all been there, mate,' said Sam. 'There's been many a time that I've wanted to lock up and never do another shift behind this bar myself.'

It was kind of him to say that and the expression on Charlie's face confirmed that he appreciated the show of solidarity.

'We need to keep talking, don't we?' he said. 'A problem shared and all that.'

'Exactly,' said Sam, 'although us blokes are a bit crap at it sometimes.'

'Which is why you need to keep opening the pub,' said Joe. 'There's nothing we can't sort out over a pint.'

'You're probably right,' Sam smiled.

Hope and I exchanged another quick look. From what I could work out, talking things through had made all the difference to Sam and Joe. There had been no need for my sis and me to pry or push at all and I was now feeling rather pleased that I hadn't rushed out of Wynmouth when I had the chance.

'Right,' said Charlie. 'I suppose I'd better get back. There's no telling what that dog's been up to while we've been gone. I'll come and pick you up in a bit, Joe.'

'All right,' said Joe. 'I'll see you later.'

'I'm going to check flight prices this afternoon,' Charlie

said keenly, 'because after the harvest is in, you won't see me for dust. Not for a while anyway.'

That made Joe smile all the more and once Charlie had gone, Sam locked the door behind him and led the remaining four of us into the snug.

'So,' said Hope, eager as ever as she took the chair next to Sam, who had quickly made us all a drink, 'what's going on?'

'Joe still has more to say,' said Sam, handing out mugs of tea, 'but none of it is for public consumption.'

Joe didn't say anything.

'Don't you?' Sam prompted, staring hard at Joe who was opposite him.

'Okay,' said Joe, rubbing his hands together and taking a deep breath, 'Okay.'

Sam sat back in his chair and shook his head.

'I'm doing it,' Joe told him, 'I'm doing it. Just give me a minute, all right.'

'Don't let him bully you, Joe,' said Hope, giving Sam a sharp nudge. 'I don't know what's gone on between you two today, but—'

'Just shush for a minute will you,' Sam cut in. 'Let the man speak.'

'Okay,' Joe said for the third time. 'The thing is—'

'Just spit it out man,' Sam cajoled. 'Don't worry about how you say it, just bloody get it out!'

Joe closed his eyes and when he opened them, he was looking at Hope.

'I'm still in love with you, Hope,' he blurted out. 'I always have been and I always will be. I didn't know how I would feel when I came back to Wynmouth, but the second I caught sight of you again, I knew I was still as smitten as I always had been.'

Well, if Sam hadn't worked it out before, the look on Hope's face was proof enough that Joe's feelings were well and truly reciprocated. That said, it was Sam who had just encouraged Joe to make this declaration and, given the look on his face, I got the distinct impression that a whole lot more had been talked about than just the Sunny Shores deal after I had rushed back to the sanctuary of the cottage.

'Oh Joe ...' Hope whispered, cutting off my train of thought.

'And I know I said always way too many times just then,' Joe blushed, 'but Sam hardly gave me time to rehearse it, did he? And anyway, it is the right word. It's always been you, Hope. Always.'

'Joe,' Hope said again, this time with tears in her eyes.

'I should never have let you go,' Joe carried on. 'I should never have been so jealous of you wanting to look out for Sam after the crash and if I hadn't let my stupid imagination get the better of me, I would have known you were nothing more than friends.'

Sam nodded and my thoughts rolled on, only I wasn't sure I believed them. Was Joe suggesting that Hope and Sam had *always* been just friends?

'And I need to apologize to you too, Tess,' Joe then said, making me jump.

'Do you?' I asked.

Sam shifted in his seat.

'Joe,' he said.

'No,' said Joe, looking at him, 'we need to get this sorted.'

'What are you talking about?' I frowned.

'I recognized you, Tess,' Joe stunned me by saying, 'the very second I stopped you tumbling over the top of the cliff.'

'What?' I squeaked.

'I knew you were the girl who used to holiday here with your parents all those years ago, because you'd hardly changed at all.'

'Joe,' Sam said again.

'You were the very one I'd promised to kiss behind the beach huts,' Joe went on, 'but the thing was, Hope had arrived back in town just after I'd made that promise and as it was love at first sight, I found I didn't want to kiss anyone else.'

'So, what did you do?' Hope asked, going straight for the heart of the matter, rather than trying to fill in the details.

'Well,' Joe smiled. 'Sam here had the biggest crush on Tess back then, but he was beyond shy and couldn't even bring himself to talk to her. He used to disappear whenever she turned up on the beach.'

Poor Sam was puce. I'd had absolutely no idea, but then if he'd always ducked out of the way, it was hardly surprising that I hadn't remembered him.

'Jesus, Joe,' he cursed, pushing his hands into his hair and dropping his gaze to the table.

'So,' Joe carried on in spite of Sam's discomfiture, 'we swapped places.'

'You did what?' Hope gasped.

I didn't need to ask the question, because courtesy of the solstice snog, I'd already worked out that Sam was my first blistering kiss, but at least now, I knew *why* they'd traded.

'It was late,' Sam said, huskily, still staring at the table, 'and it was dark, so Tess didn't realize and I can't begin to tell you how guilty I've always felt about doing it. It was a disgraceful thing to do, inexcusable, but it was also—'

'The best kiss of your life,' I cut in, unable to stop the words. 'The one kiss you've never been able to forget.'

'Yes,' Sam said, finally looking up, 'the very best kiss of my life and certainly one I've never been able to forget.'

'Well,' said Hope, 'it was the best one until the night of the party on the beach.'

My eyes snapped back to her.

'You know about that?'

'Of course,' she grinned, 'Sam's not stopped going on about it.'

Oh my god! There was no way Sam would have mentioned it if he and Hope were a couple. I had got it wrong! They were just friends.

'Hope,' Sam squirmed, and Joe began to laugh.

'Apparently,' Hope added with relish, 'it was even better than the first one.'

'So, you recognized me too?' I asked Sam as multiple cogs

in my head began to shift and settle my memories of the last few weeks into a brand-new pattern.

'Of course I did,' he said, 'as soon as you walked in here, but as you didn't seem to know me, I thought I'd save myself the embarrassment and awkward explanation and not say anything. I had no idea why you wanted to keep it a secret that you'd visited Wynmouth before but when that letter turned up, I thought I'd worked it out. It hasn't stopped me fancying you though. Where you're concerned, Tess, I just can't seem to help myself.'

He turned an even brighter shade of red and I started doing a very passable goldfish impression. His admittance that he fancied me had me floating on cloud nine, but I was still in shock that another assumption I'd made had been so wide of the mark.

'And you fancy him too, don't you?' Hope beamed.

I couldn't believe she was going to out me like that.

'Yes,' I swallowed, 'I do actually, but I had kind of assumed . . .'

'What?' asked Sam.

'Well . . . I assumed that you and Hope were a couple,' I said sheepishly.

'If it makes you feel any better, until this afternoon, so did I,' Joe admitted.

'But we're not,' said Hope, looking shocked. 'We never have been.'

'But the day you came back from your travels,' I said to Hope. 'You and Sam were—'

'Hugging,' she cut in. 'Because we hadn't seen each other for ages.'

'Oh,' said Sam, clicking his fingers before pointing at me, 'now I get it. At last, it all makes sense.'

'What do you get?' I asked, my thoughts freefalling.

'You changed,' he said, biting his lip, 'when Hope got back, you were different, Tess.'

'Was I?'

'Yes,' he said, 'to start with, when she wasn't here, I thought you might fancy me and I was beginning to think that I could finally act on that crush I had all those years ago, but then when Hope came back you became more distant. Was that because you thought we were together?'

'Yes,' I admitted. 'Yes.'

'And you thought I'd snogged you behind Hope's back at the party?' Sam tutted. 'And that's why you never acknowledged our second kiss, even though it was so phenomenal?'

'Yes,' I swallowed. 'And I've been feeling as guilty as hell about it.'

'I can't believe you thought that of me, Tess,' Sam said, shaking his head.

'And I can't believe that you thought I was here to smooth the way for Joe telling everyone that he'd sold up to Sunny Shores,' I pointed out, eager to remind him that I wasn't the only one in Wynmouth who had got the maths wrong when I'd put two and two together.

'Touché,' he grinned, making my stomach flip.

'So, that's it, then right?' Joe announced. 'We're sorted,

yes? All the romantic muddles have been unravelled. I love Hope, Hope loves me and you pair fancy the pants off each other?'

'Sounds about right to me,' Sam laughed.

'Great,' Joe said, leaping up and dashing around the table before lifting Hope off her feet, wrapping her in his arms and kissing her deeply.

'This has been like a Shakespearean comedy,' said Sam, reaching across the table for my hand.

'You're not wrong,' said Joe, when he finally came up for air.

'But this is it, right?' I said, lacing my fingers through Sam's and revelling in the sensations that his warm skin touching mine kicked off. 'There really are no more muddles?'

'No more muddles,' everyone chorused but it didn't escape my notice that it was Sam and Joe who were looking at one another when really, they should only have had eyes for me and Hope.

Chapter 27

I don't think that Hope, who was experiencing that heady rush of love all over again, picked up on the fact that the guys hadn't been as resolute in our 'no more muddles' announcement as we had. Unfortunately, there was neither the opportunity to point it out to her, nor the time to spend catching up on the kisses I had missed out on during the last few weeks because the wheels of everyday life were still turning and the minutiae had to be attended to.

No sooner had we got everything settled than our intimate moment was interrupted by Sam's delivery from a local brewery and Joe announcing that he'd had a text from Charlie who was about to leave the farm to collect him.

'Let's all meet tonight then,' suggested Sam. 'After closing time, down at the beach by the rockpools.'

We all agreed that was a wonderful idea and having

spotted Joe and Hope saying a very tender goodbye, Sam pulled me close to him and rested his hands low on my waist. The action literally made my knees weaken and I had barely a moment to become ensnared in his emerald eyes before he was closing them and lowering his lips to mine.

His kiss was purposeful and full of promise and when I felt the tip of his tongue caress mine, I thought I was going to pass out. I let out a lust-filled gasp, so quiet that only he could hear it, and in consequence his hands held me tighter and he kissed me harder.

My light-headed feeling from earlier had only just settled back down and I knew that if he carried on like this for the duration of my remaining time in Wynmouth, I would be a physical wreck by the time I had to leave.

Instinctively, my hands then reached for his hips and I pulled him right in to me, his breath catching as the gap between us closed.

'Bloody hell, Tess,' he murmured, pressing himself close enough to leave me in no doubt that he was enjoying the moment too.

Had we been alone, I'm not sure where we would have ended up, but the sound of Joe clearing his throat restored our decorum and we slowed the moment down.

'I see you've learnt a few new tricks since our assignation behind the huts,' I whispered.

Our first kiss had been perfect and I was pretty certain the second one had been too, although the influence of

Sophie's rum punch had ensured certain details weren't quite as focused as I would have liked, but there was no doubting the quality of the third one.

'Shall I let you into a secret,' he said, punctuating each word with another kiss, 'that night down at the beach huts all those years ago, was my first kiss too.'

'Really?' I smiled.

'Scout's honour,' he smiled back.

'Hey guys,' I heard Joe say. 'I'm sorry to break things up, but you've got barrels to sign for, Sam.'

Although disappointed to feel his hands move away, I knew we were going to have plenty of opportunities, and more private ones than this, to carry on where we'd left off.

'I'll see you tonight,' Sam whispered. 'And we'll do more of this very soon.'

'Lots more,' I agreed, 'lots, lots more and very, very soon.'

'And don't you even think about leaving Wynmouth,' he commanded. 'You go back to the cottage and unpack right now. Do you hear me? You need to stay put in Wynmouth for at least a few more weeks.'

I very much liked the sound of that and I didn't need telling twice. Hope and I walked back to the cottage together, still giggling about the mistake I had made in assuming she and Sam were a couple, and when she left, I hastily unpacked again and switched my phone back on. I didn't bother even looking at the older messages but focused on the last text which had landed from Dad.

Darling Tess, I know that me turning up here
earlier and telling you everything must have
been a shock. Please let me know how you
are feeling as soon as you get this. Please
also know that it was never my intention to
hurt you, or make you think any less of your
mother, I just couldn't live with the secret
any longer and felt you deserved to know the
truth. I hope, in time, that you will come to
understand.

It was a relief to be able to message him straight back and
say with complete honesty that I was feeling surprisingly fine,
even though I knew that the revelations about Mum would
take some assimilating. It was incredibly sad to think that
she had lived a lie for much of her life and I wished things
could have been different, for all our sakes. Had she not died
so young – and given what Vanessa had told Dad – then it
might have been, but that was something I couldn't dwell
on. Nothing would be gained from wasting time grieving
over the unknown.

What I could say with complete certainty, however, was
that it wouldn't take me long to get used to the idea that
Hope was my sister. The fact that I knew her and Sophie
so well was obviously a huge help and I already loved them
both dearly.

I ended my text back to Dad with words that I hoped
would settle his head as well as his heart:

> Coming back to Wynmouth and getting to
> know Hope and Sophie has made me realize
> the true value of female friendship and I'm
> looking forward to a future which includes
> these wonderful women in our little family.

Dad's message also said that he would see me soon and requested that I didn't open his letter. Thanks to our earlier exchange, I already had an idea of what the missive said and was happy to leave it. Guessing that he had headed back to work, I returned my attention to thoughts of my three friends and the fun we were going to have as a result of finally getting our relationships on the right tracks.

Thankfully, it was a warm, dry night and the tide had been on its way out for some time when we met down by the rockpools. Hope came carrying leftover snacks from the café, Sam had bottles of beer and Coke in an ice bag and Joe and I had blankets and candles. We lay in a row, quiet for a while, staring up at the stars and revelling in the fact that Wynmouth had almost zero per cent light pollution.

'This is nice,' said Hope, who was lying next to me with our respective fellas either side.

'It is,' I agreed, giving her hand a squeeze.

'All finally feels right with the world,' she sighed, turning her head to look at me, a very content smile lighting up her pretty face.

'It certainly does,' I smiled back, feeling amused to have

earlier worked out that she had inherited Dad's awful pen-sucking habit.

I wondered what other Tyler traits we had in common. We were in complete agreement that we wouldn't share our news about being half-sisters for a few days at least, and only then if Sophie and Dad were happy for us to go ahead, but I knew that when the time came the boys would understand that we had needed to get used to the change in family dynamics first. That said, I was very much looking forward to seeing the expressions on their faces when they did find out.

'Do you agree with that, Joe?' Sam asked, pulling himself into a sitting position and unzipping the bag with the drinks in. 'Do you feel as though everything's right with the world?'

Joe sat up too and Hope and I then followed suit, passing on the bottles Sam handed out.

'Of course, he does,' said Hope. 'Don't you, Joe?'

He didn't answer straightaway and we all twisted around to look at him.

'Almost,' he eventually said, 'it's definitely better than yesterday anyway.'

Hope looked concerned and I guessed that my hunch in the pub earlier had been right. There was still something between him and Sam.

'Do you think we should tell them?' Joe then asked, leaning forward so he could see Sam.

'That's entirely up to you,' Sam answered. 'It's your call, mate.'

Joe took a long swig from his bottle and then stuck it in the sand.

'What is it, Joe?' Hope asked. 'Is it something to do with the crash?'

I had a feeling she was on the right path and when Sam's eyes met mine and he nodded, I felt sure.

'Yes,' Joe said heavily, 'it's everything to do with the crash. Sam and I talked about it earlier and we were going to just keep it between ourselves, but now we're a foursome, and I get the feeling that we always will be, I want to tell you and Tess too.'

I would have loved to have been a fly on the wall during this earlier meeting between the two men. They hadn't had all that long to talk, but it was obvious they hadn't wasted a single second and I was glad about that. They should have had the conversation years ago of course but I did understand that what was often obvious for someone to see and easy to say from the outside, could be hidden on the inside.

'I always wanted to believe that Sam's memories of that night were hazy,' Joe began. 'I told myself that the length of time he was in a coma and the trauma of the surgery and the fact that he never said anything, meant certain things were never quite as clear in his mind as they were in mine. But,' he added, his lip trembling, 'I did sometimes wonder if he suspected . . .'

'Suspected what?' I asked, looking between the two of them.

'That he wasn't the person driving,' Joe said quietly. 'If he knew that it had been Jack.'

My hand flew up to my chest and Hope looked like she might faint.

'Are you sure it was him?' she whispered. 'Are you sure it was Jack behind the wheel?'

'Yes,' Joe continued, 'completely sure and it was all my fault.'

'Why?' Hope and I asked together.

'Because I was the idiot who took him out drinking,' he said, shaking his head. 'Even though he was ridiculously underage. I thought it would be a laugh. I thought it would be fun to have my little brother bending the rules I was always so determined to break, but it all backfired because I was also the one who couldn't stop him jumping into the driving seat when Sam came to pick us up.'

Hope and I looked at each other. The expression in her eyes told me that she had no former idea about any of what Joe was saying. She was as shocked as I was, more so because she had been a part of Wynmouth when the crash happened.

'By the time I had come out of the trance the shock of the crash had plummeted me into,' Joe continued, 'everyone was running with the assumption that it was Sam who had been driving because it was his car.'

'But you were never charged?' I said, turning to Sam. 'You weren't arrested, were you?'

'No,' he said, 'I wasn't. Joe always maintained he couldn't remember which seats he'd pulled me and his brother out of and so there was insufficient evidence to arrest me.'

'But I did know,' Joe elaborated with a sob rising in his chest. 'I knew it was Jack, but seeing my parents so bereft and so broken by the loss of their boy, I just couldn't bring myself to admit it. No matter how hard I tried, I couldn't tell them that, or confess my part in it. I was the biggest coward.'

'No,' Sam said, 'like I told you earlier, you weren't a coward, Joe.'

'And, I never wanted to leave Wynmouth either,' Joe carried on, refusing to acknowledge Sam's kindness and sniffing hard as his tears flowed, 'or the farm, but I couldn't stay here and live with the guilt. I might have saved my parents from further heartbreak, Sam, but there hasn't been a single day since that horrific night when I haven't hated myself for letting you shoulder the blame.'

'Did you know?' Hope asked, turning to Sam. 'Did you know it was Jack?'

There was a beat of time before he answered.

'Yes,' he nodded. 'I always knew. I had got out to open the back door, because the car was old and it stuck, and that was when Jack jumped in.'

'But why didn't you ever say anything?' Hope asked, her tone was incredulous. 'I barely left your side in that hospital and you never said a word.'

'Because to begin with I wasn't sure whether or not Joe could remember,' Sam explained, 'and by the time I had worked out that he did, I knew I wasn't going to be charged and that calling him out would have been too much for his poor parents to bear.'

'So, you let everyone think it was you,' Hope whispered, and Sam nodded.

I had heard the occasional muttering from various Wynmouth locals about things from that night not adding up and I was fairly certain that no one was entirely convinced that Sam had been responsible, but having no proof, and no denial from the man himself, they had let it lie. That said, I could now see Sam's reaction to Joe's return for what it really was and understand why, given his track record, people had assumed the farm sale was Joe's doing. Hopefully now things were settled, and the friendship between Sam and Joe was re-formed, they would see that he wasn't the same person he had been back then.

'I didn't have it confirmed that Sam knew the truth about that night, that he wasn't the cause of the crash, until earlier today,' Joe told us.

'The farm sale wasn't the only thing we talked about earlier,' said Sam. 'And when Joe said he had something to tell me about the crash, I shocked the hell out of him by telling him that I already knew.'

'I can't believe you've carried it all these years, Sam,' Joe said huskily.

Sam shrugged.

'I would never have told anyone,' he said, 'but I did always hope that you would come and talk to me about it, and today you have.'

In that moment, I fell even deeper in love. Not only was Sam the best kisser on the planet, he was also the most compassionate and generous person. He had been prepared to sacrifice his reputation to save a friend's family from further hurt. There couldn't be many people willing to go to such extraordinary lengths to deliver an act of such unprecedented and unselfish kindness.

'I would have said sooner,' Joe began.

'But you wanted to get the farm situation sorted first,' Sam finished for him and Joe nodded.

'I can't tell you what a relief it's been to get it all off my chest,' he sighed, drying his eyes and letting out the longest breath.

'Oh,' Sam smiled, 'I've got a pretty good idea.'

Hope leant over and kissed his cheek.

'And,' he added, 'I want to keep this between the four of us. There's no need to rock the boat by announcing any of it to the great and good of Wynmouth. It won't change anything. Some would argue that Joe should have spoken up at the time, but I understand why he didn't. I'm just grateful that he has now and I want this to be the end of it.'

We clinked our bottles together to seal the deal and quietly finished our picnic. After all the weeks of wondering what was really going on between the two men, it felt like a massive weight had been lifted.

When I thought back to the day Joe told me about the crash, I was certain that he'd never said that Sam had been the one driving. At the time it didn't register because given that it was Sam's car, I thought it was obvious, but now I knew the truth. Joe hadn't pointed the finger of blame at Sam because he wasn't the one responsible.

'What a day,' I sighed, as I thought back over everything that had happened with Dad and Sophie too.

Hope smiled and nodded in agreement. The guys didn't know the half of it. It was little wonder I felt so exhausted.

'I don't know about you lot,' Hope yawned, 'but I'm all in. I think I'm going to call it a night.'

She stood up, stretched out her back and then offered a hand to pull me to my feet. She was clearly intent on giving the guys some 'alone time' and I didn't think that was a bad idea at all.

'I'm with you on that one,' I said, quickly kissing Sam before she pulled me up. 'I'll walk back with you, Hope.'

Once off the sand, we linked arms and when out of earshot began quietly discussing our day.

'Sisters,' said Hope, squeezing me into her side. 'Can you believe it?'

'I couldn't to begin with,' I admitted, 'but I'm quickly getting used to the idea.'

'Well, that's because I'm so brilliant,' giggled Hope, with a hip-swaying swagger. 'Who wouldn't want me as a cool younger sister?'

'Exactly,' I laughed. 'Brilliant *and* modest. Two very admirable Tyler qualities.'

'You know,' she said confidentially, lowering her voice even though there was no one else around, 'this was what Sam and I argued about.'

'What?'

'I wanted to start searching for my dad,' she told me, 'but

Sam said I shouldn't. I think he was worried that it might upset Mum, but then lo and behold Dad turns up anyway and it turns out the pair of them have been in touch for years!'

'And how do you feel about that?' I asked her.

'I was a bit miffed to begin with,' she admitted.

I could understand that.

'But it wasn't as if I'd ever really wanted to know who he was before. I had always been more than happy that it was just me and Mum.'

'So, what changed your mind?'

'Going to visit family,' she said without any hesitation. 'Having seen everyone together, even if they didn't live together, was the thing that did it. Everyone's lives seemed so complete – not necessarily perfect, but full – and I was pretty certain by the time I came back that I was going to try and track my dad down. I was a bit nervous, but as it turned out, I didn't have to worry about how he might react if I turned up on his doorstep, because he turned up on mine!'

I tried and failed to imagine what I would have said, had I opened the door at Dad's house and found Hope standing there. I was just about to say as much when two other midnight strollers appeared out of the darkness and Hope and I practically jumped out of our skins.

'Dad!' I gasped.

'Mum,' Hope gulped.

'What are you doing here?' we all said at once and then burst out laughing.

'Tess and I have been on the beach,' said Hope.

'And we've spent the day talking,' said Sophie, looking fondly up at Dad, 'so we thought we'd come out and get a breath of air.'

From the colour I could just about make out that Dad had turned, I wasn't sure they had been talking all day. Hope looked at me and raised her eyebrows, but neither of us commented.

'I thought you'd gone home,' I said to Dad, then teasingly added, 'you are aware, that's it's the middle of the week and there's no Tyler to keep on top of things in the office?'

Dad laughed again.

'I have to hand it to you,' I said to Sophie, 'you really must be one very special lady if you can keep Dad away from work on a Wednesday.'

'Why, thank you,' she smiled, 'but it's not all down to me.'

'No?'

'No,' said Dad, 'you've all played a part in dragging me away from my desk. Starting with you, Tess.'

'Me?'

'Yes,' he said, 'you. Your sudden departure got me thinking about a lot of things.'

'Like what?'

'Well,' he said, 'for a start, how terrible I felt when I realized that I'd been completely oblivious to how difficult you were finding things at work.'

'I see,' I nodded, thankful that he had finally noticed, even if Joan had had to help him get there.

'And then,' he carried on, 'once I'd grasped how little of

a decent work–life balance you had, I began to realize that I wasn't faring any better myself.'

'But when I called you . . .' I began.

'That was the conversation that really got me thinking,' Dad cut in. 'You said that I should take some time off, and I know,' he carried on before I had a chance to remind him how scathing he had been about the suggestion, 'that I was dismissive, but you were right.'

That wasn't the first time he'd owned up to being wrong about something since he'd arrived and I looked at him with fresh eyes. He appeared different, standing next to Sophie. There was no tension in his shoulders and his brows weren't pulled tight in a frown. It was refreshing to see him looking so relaxed.

'It was your resignation that was the clincher, Tess,' Sophie then joined in.

Clearly, she had been aware of the transformative awakening Dad had been going through during the previous few weeks.

'You had decided to leave for good,' Dad said to me. 'And that was so brave and I recognized that I needed to be brave too. Work had been my refuge when your mother was alive but now . . .'

'She's gone,' I said for him.

'Yes,' Dad nodded, 'now she's gone and I don't need it anymore. Now, I have the chance of a whole new life. I can finally get to know my other beautiful daughter and spend time with her equally beautiful mother.'

He turned to Sophie and kissed her softly on the lips.

'Does this mean that you two are together?' Hope asked, wide-eyed.

Sophie looked at her and nodded and I could tell she was close to tears.

'Yes, my love,' Dad said to Hope as he kissed Sophie again. 'We are and I'm going to be spending a lot more time here in Wynmouth.'

'That's wonderful,' said Hope breathlessly.

She sounded absolutely thrilled and I wanted to match her excitement, but . . .

'But it's way too far to commute,' I pointed out, 'even if you only make the journey three days a week it will be too much.'

If he thought shuttling backwards and forwards was going to be an option then it wouldn't be long before he was running himself even further into the ground and I was certain that was the last thing any of us wanted to happen. It sounded to me as though he had made great strides mentally when it came to thinking through his work-life balance, but that wasn't going to transfer into reality if he spent all his time in the car.

'I'm not,' he shrugged.

'Not what?'

'Going to commute,' he said, 'that's what I had written in your letter, Tess, but then I asked you not to open it because I decided it would be better to tell you in person.'

'Tell me what exactly?' I asked, my voice catching in my throat.

Dad grinned and I couldn't recall a time I'd ever seen him look so happy.

'This isn't quite where or how I had planned to tell you,' he said, looking about him.

'Just tell me,' I urged.

'I'm selling the business,' he said. 'I'm selling up and relocating permanently to Wynmouth. And what's more, Tess,' he laughed, seeing the look on my face, 'I think you should do the same.'

Chapter 28

By the August bank holiday weekend, just eight weeks later, my life had changed beyond all recognition, and I wasn't the only person now living in Wynmouth who could say as much. We had been planning another beach party to celebrate the changes, but the good old British summer weather had other ideas and the event had been relocated to the Smuggler's, not that anyone really minded.

Later, there would be musical entertainment from Harry and Delilah and storytelling from George – in much the same manner as there had been on the last bank holiday I had helped to organize – but the place was packed early today as everyone had turned out to see Charlie off on his travels. The Home Farm harvest was well on its way to being gathered, with friends drafted in to help with the rest and it was time for the eldest Upton brother to finally make the mark he wanted on the wider world.

'So, tell me again,' I said above the din, 'where are you starting from?'

'London,' Charlie grinned, checking the straps on his gargantuan backpack for the umpteenth time.

'She knows that,' said Joe, rolling his eyes. 'She means after that bit, you fool.'

'All right,' Charlie conceded, 'Paris then. I'll be staying in Paris for a couple of days and then spending the next three months travelling around Europe in a sort of clockwise direction before arriving back here for Christmas.'

'And you're going to be keeping us all updated via the blog?'

'As long as I can get a signal,' nodded Charlie, 'then yes. I'm going to keep it as up-to-date as I can.'

There had been a lot in the news and on social media recently about the loneliness farmers in rural communities were facing and Charlie had joined a group called 'The Farmer Wants a Life'. The group was made up of a dozen or so farmers up and down the country who were tackling the problem in unique ways and encouraging others to do the same by sharing their experiences via an online community. There had even been rumours about a possible TV series and Dad and I had been hard pushed not to step in and offer Charlie some advice. Old habits, as it turned out, died hard.

'Taxi's here!' someone shouted from the door and we all spilled on to the road to wave our wanderer off.

'You okay?' Hope asked Joe, coming to stand next

to where Sam and I stood with him and slipping her hand into his.

Joe nodded and cleared his throat as his brother gave one last wave before slamming the car door shut.

'Yeah,' he said, trying to sound more in control than he probably felt. 'I'm okay, just a bit overwhelmed by the thought of being solely responsible for Bruce, that's all.'

'Don't you worry about that,' said Hope stoically. 'I'll have him to heel in no time.'

Hope had now moved permanently to Home Farm and I knew the pair were looking forward to having the place to themselves, aside from Bruce of course. The mad mutt hadn't completely switched allegiance from me to Hope, but I was happy to leave her in charge.

'I don't doubt it,' Joe laughed, kissing her on the lips. 'You've already worked wonders.'

Hope was loving life on the farm and had wasted no time at all in helping convince Charlie that Joe's potential diversification project ideas were all good ones. Joe was keen to carry on the environmental work his father had started and he had also offered Hope the use of the currently empty stable block which she could convert for her business if she wanted to.

I knew she was extremely excited about the idea, but didn't want to rush too far ahead. Her re-kindled relationship with Joe was still getting off the ground and she didn't want to put it under any pressure.

'Did we miss him?' said a breathless voice behind us.

It was Sophie and Dad. They were both clearly out of puff

and I didn't want to consider why. The look on Hope's face told me she was thinking the same thing.

'Just gone,' said Sam. 'You two look a bit flushed, did you jog here?'

Sophie looked embarrassed but the smile on Dad's face was reminder enough that the pair were extremely happy together. Dad was currently living at Sophie's now Hope had moved out and was thoroughly loving life by the sea. He'd even been spotted waiting tables in the café, which was something I would have to witness with my own eyes before I believed it.

'I've had a call from the estate agent,' he said to me, opting not to answer Sam's question. 'It's good news.'

Both my apartment and the family home were up for sale and attracting a fair amount of attention. Joan and her husband were looking after both properties and Dad was insisting that the house was sold with them in situ. I wasn't sure if that was going to be possible, but I knew he would still do right by them should they have to leave.

I had been negotiating the apartment sale myself, but as I couldn't always get a phone signal, I had instructed the agent to talk to Dad as well.

'They've had a full asking price offer on your place, Tess, and the house has had one come in at ten thousand under.'

'That's fantastic,' I gasped, 'and so fast. Are you going to haggle over the house?'

'No,' said Dad, 'because the woman who wants to buy it

also wants Joan and Jim. I didn't think we'd get lucky on that front, so I've cut my losses and accepted already.'

'That's great news,' said Sam, putting his arm around my waist. 'So Wynmouth has gained not one, not two, but three Tylers this summer.'

Sam and Joe's expressions had been even more memorable than I had expected them to be the day Hope and I told them we were sisters. In fact, they had looked so hilarious, I rather regretted not having my phone to hand to record the moment.

'It certainly has,' I said, kissing his stubbly cheek, 'and now we can push ahead with our plan too.'

Sam had agreed to let me buy Crow's Nest Cottage and although I still hadn't decided what I was going to do about work, I did have the cosiest abode in the village to live in as I made up my mind. The sale of my car was going to free up enough funds to live on for a while and, because my life in Wynmouth was far less expensive than in Essex, downsizing felt like no hardship at all.

'Let's get back in,' said Joe, 'it's starting to rain again.'

It was already dark in the pub and I helped Hope light some candles while Sam went back to serving behind the bar. If it stayed overcast, we might even consider lighting the fire later.

'So, how are things with you and Sam?' Hope quietly asked me.

'So good,' I told her, trying not to sound smug or let thoughts of our cosy nights in make me blush too much.

'He's like a new man,' my sister grinned, which made me colour up anyway.

'I'm not sure if that's down to me or his bionic new leg, to be honest,' I told her.

Hope rolled her eyes.

'You, of course!' she laughed. 'Although it's so good to see he's not in pain anymore.'

It certainly was. There was a new light in Sam's beautiful green eyes and he spent a whole lot more of his time smiling now. In the end, Joe had decided to also tell Charlie that Sam hadn't been responsible for the crash and I knew it was a weight off both of their minds. Sam had been hailed a hero by the eldest Upton brother and although unwilling to accept the moniker, he really was a changed man.

I left Hope lighting the last of the candles with Joe and stepped behind the bar myself. I had been helping out a bit and had fallen in love with my change of lifestyle every bit as much as I had fallen for the man who had given me my first kiss.

When I had planned my secret escape to the Wynmouth seaside, I'd had no idea that I wouldn't be leaving again, or that Dad would be joining me, but I was delighted with how everything had turned out.

'All right?' Sam asked, walking to the end of the bar and pulling me into the shadows.

I wrapped my arms around his waist and laid my head against his broad chest.

'Perfectly all right,' I said, breathing in the comforting combined scent of him and his aftershave.

Being held by him felt like coming home and I relaxed into his embrace before looking up so he could kiss me on the lips. Every time we touched it felt every bit as stirring as it had that first time behind the beach huts all those years ago.

'Everything is very perfect indeed,' I sighed contentedly. 'I always knew it would be if I made my way back to Wynmouth.'

Acknowledgements

It's not the first time that I've written this (and I'm certain it won't be the last), but there are many, many people to thank for helping this book along its journey from conception to completion.

Regular readers may recall that, when my sixth book, *Sunshine and Sweet Peas in Nightingale Square* was published in 2018, I admitted that it was the scariest release by far because I was taking you away from beloved Wynbridge and setting you down in a brand-new setting. My wonderful team told me not to worry, and they were right because you embraced the changes and fell in love with the Grow-Well gang (as they were called in *Poppy's Recipe for Life*). This time around, I've got all of my fingers and toes crossed that you will feel the same way about the wonderful village of Wynmouth and the folk who live there. I'm even hoping that we might head back there again at some point in the future.

Just like Tess, my love for one particular seaside place on the Norfolk coast was the result of a memorable childhood trip and when I started writing, I knew that one day there would be a character waiting to journey back to see if the present lived up to her past. I hope I have done her story justice.

Fittingly then, my first round of hugs and thanks is reserved for my wonderful readers who buy, borrow and love the books, along with the loyal band of bloggers who unfailingly respond to the call to champion my work. I'm eternally grateful to my merry #swainette crew! I'm including libraries and the hard-working staff and volunteers who run them here too. During the last year, my books have been borrowed thousands of times and I've had some truly memorable events talking in libraries, both in Norfolk and further afield, so thank you all.

My ideas wouldn't make the leap from laptop to bookshelves, e-readers and audio if it wasn't for the skill of my publishing team so, as always, huge and heartfelt thanks to Rebecca Farrell, Harriett Collins, Amy Fulwood, Pip Watkins, SJ Virtue and the entire Books and the City team.

Thanks, and much love to my agent and dear friend Amanda Preston, who has gone above and beyond this year, and what a memorable few months we've had so far! It's only spring and already there's been gin, cake and many, many laughs. Long may it continue!

Hugs are also reserved for my family and the cat – whether

they submit to them or not – and my wonderful author chums, Jenni Keer, Clare Marchant and Rosie Hendry, I don't know what I'd do without you all!

Thanks also to the support of the RNA in this its 60th anniversary year. The romance author tribe is large, loveable, supportive and kind and I feel truly blessed to be a part of it.

Wishing you all a fabulous start to the new decade and may your bookshelves – be they virtual or real – always be filled with fabulous fiction.

H x

Don't miss Heidi Swain's brand new Christmas novel . . .

The Winter Garden

Freya Fuller is living her childhood dream, working as a live-in gardener on a beautiful Suffolk estate. But when the owner dies suddenly, Freya finds herself forced out of her job and her home with nowhere to go. However, with luck on her side, she's soon moving to Nightingale Square and helping to create a beautiful winter garden that will be open to the public in time for Christmas.

There's a warm welcome from all in Nightingale Square, except from local artist Finn. No matter how hard the pair try, they just can't get along, and working together to bring the winter garden to life quickly becomes a struggle for them both.

Will Freya and Finn be able to put their differences aside in time for Christmas? Or will the arrival of a face from Freya's past send them all spiralling?

COMING OCTOBER 2020.

AVAILABLE NOW TO PRE-ORDER.

**SIMON &
SCHUSTER**